Metamorphosis

Metamorphosis

Selected Stories

PENELOPE LIVELY

FIG TREE
an imprint of
PENGUIN BOOKS

FIG TREE

UK | USA | Canada | Ireland | Australia
India | New Zealand | South Africa

Fig Tree is part of the Penguin Random House group of companies
whose addresses can be found at global.penguinrandomhouse.com.

Penguin
Random House
UK

First published 2021
001

This collection first published by Fig Tree 2021

'In Olden Times' was previously published in *Good Housekeeping*,
'The Clarinetist and the Bride's Aunt' and 'The First Wife' in *Living*, and
'Marriage Lines' and 'The Butterfly and the Tin of Paint' in the *Daily Telegraph*

Illustrations copyright © Vasilisa Romanenko

Set in 12/14.75 pt Dante MT Std
Typeset by Jouve (UK), Milton Keynes
Printed and bound in Great Britain by Clays Ltd, Elcograf S.p.A.

The authorized representative in the EEA is Penguin Random House Ireland,
Morrison Chambers, 32 Nassau Street, Dublin D02 YH68

A CIP catalogue record for this book is available from the British Library

ISBN: 978–0–241–51476–4

www.greenpenguin.co.uk

Contents

Contents

Introduction

This selection ranges from two extra-long stories written in 2019, at the end of my writing life, to several written back in the nineteen seventies, when I was first trying to write fiction. A span of forty writing years, and, making this selection, I have found that the stories themselves tell a story – one about writing development, about my own preoccupations, about the issues of the times.

The two long, late stories bookend the rest, all of which appeared in three earlier story collections. There were sixty-three stories in all; this selection could only find room for twenty-six. So . . . much to be discarded, some to be favoured and all with the dispassionate eye of an editor, as though someone else wrote them. Definitely not this, no way include that . . . Here's a possibility, this may be worth having.

I remember being asked, many years ago, to lead a creative writing group on short-story writing. The group comprised fifteen or so, and I suggested that we start by talking a bit about the short story, about what it can do, about stories that we had enjoyed and admired. There was a silence. Then a spokesperson said crisply that no, they didn't want that sort of thing – they knew all they needed to know about the short story, what they wanted from me was advice on presentation and marketing. Startled, I asked what it was that they knew about the short story. 'The short story,' said the spokesperson irritably 'is three thousand words long. Possibly three thousand five hundred.'

The short story is of course as long as a piece of string. It is as long as it takes. Alice Munro writes stories the length of novellas; Raymond Carver could produce a masterpiece in a few pages. The long story invites you into a climate, a setting, the unfurling of a situation. The short short story achieves its effect with concision, accuracy, saying most by saying least. Two different styles, two different effects – equally to be relished, in the right hands. I have relished both, from hands like William Trevor, Jane Gardam, Muriel Spark, Elizabeth Bowen, Katherine Mansfield, many others. I have enjoyed, and learned, starting to wonder, way back in about 1975, if maybe I could have a go myself.

Looking at this selection, with detachment and with the wisdoms of forty years and more, I can see a progression, a move from one approach to another. Earlier stories are longer, roomier, more expansive – *A Clean Death, The Crimean Hotel*. Later, there is brevity, concision – *Old as the Hills, Licence to Kill*. But then at the very end, in 2019, there come these two bookends, *Metamorphosis* and *Songs of Praise*, the longest stories I have ever written, teetering towards novella length. What is going on? And I have to say that I have no idea. These two pieces of fiction somehow arrived, as they do, and they required to be written like this – they took as long as it takes. All of which sounds unconsidered, unprofessional, but that is how story writing works, for me. There is the idea, the lightning strike, the glimpse of what can be made, and then comes the realization, the translation, the expansion of a thought into characters, setting, narrative.

And where do these ideas come from, these glimpses? Well, very much from life as lived, for me. I am a novelist quite as much as a story writer, and for me the novel is a matter of hacking at the rock face, for months, for years. There is a concept, some notion of what this novel is going to be about, and then there is the process of hacking away to find the people and what is going to happen to them.

The short story is a different matter entirely. It arrives from something seen, something overheard, something that happens, and then the task is to turn that into a story that has nothing to do with me, or how I have lived. Two women talking at a bus stop; one says 'And there were kittens from one end of the village to the other.' From that arose the story *The Emasculation of Ted Roper.*

In 1984 I was one of a party of six British writers who went to the Soviet Union, as it then was, to have talks with members of the Soviet Writers Union. When, after the talks, we were despatched to a Crimean resort for rest and recreation, we were approached, when on a walk along the promenade, by an agreeable but somewhat mysterious English-speaking Russian seaman who had served on a container vessel plying the Baltic to Hull. Some time later, I wrote the story *The Crimean Hotel*, prompted by that encounter but about much else.

There is only one story here that is unashamedly autobiographical, and in this case it was a matter of recognizing, decades later, the significance of an event in my own life. When I was fourteen, mired in adolescence, not long arrived in this country from Egypt, where I was born and spent my childhood, and bleakly unfamiliar with England and its ways, I spent Christmas with an aunt and her family at their country home. There were small children, there were animals that were doted on – cats, dogs, a pony, chickens. I struck up an acquaintance with a boy my own age from a neighbouring cottage – a farm labourer's son. He invited me to go rabbit shooting with him early one morning. When I arrived back in time for breakfast and confessed where I had been, I was met with displeasure, frosty looks. I was consumed with guilt for the rest of my stay. The issue, I assumed, was cruelty to animals – shooting rabbits. It took thirty years to understand that my transgression had been the boy, not the rabbits – not a fit associate, according to the rigid class structures of the day. Out of that came *A Clean Death*, a story about social assumptions, and the definitive social changes of the late twentieth century, along with other stories set in that period.

So that is how they arrive, for me, stories. They are served up by life as lived, but in disguise – something happens, and there is the sudden recognition that this is a potential story, that I can consider this and recreate it as something entirely different that is in no way concerned with me, but is owed to something in my life. A decorator knocks over a tin of paint on our bedroom carpet, and this becomes a story about chaos theory – *The Butterfly and the Tin of Paint*.

Novels too can have an autobiographical element. My own don't, on the whole, but you do, of course, write out of your own experience, your observation, your perception. The novel owes its truth, if it has any, its accuracy, to your understanding of how people behave, how they are likely to behave. But this is very different from the lightning strike of the short story prompt; it is back to hacking at the rock face, the slow extraction of shape and form.

And that is what has made stories a special, and specially valued, form of fiction for me. A story often arises from personal experience, but you then work to transcend that experience. And it is this wonderfully flexible form – long or short, diffuse or terse, you can make what you will of it.

July 2020

Metamorphosis

Metamorphosis, or the Elephant's Foot (2021)

Metamorphosis, or the Elephant's Foot

The Elephant's Foot

The story begins with the elephant's foot. Except that it is no longer a viable foot but an umbrella stand in a house in London's Harley Street in 1915. The elephant in question perished many years before, but this is still an unappealing metamorphosis, which is what Connie Mayfield thought for a moment as she snatched up her parasol, in a state of irritation because this visit has not gone well.

'Hurry up,' she snaps. 'Put your hat on, Harriet.'

The long-dead elephant had its foot – all four feet – in the nineteenth century and in the heart of Africa. It is – was – a long way away in every sense, but also relentlessly here, in early-twentieth-century London, doing duty as a receptacle for umbrellas. The elephant had been brought down by a white hunter. This is a euphemism; brought down means shot. Shot and then dismembered. The white hunter had posed for a photo, leaning nonchalantly against the carcass, rifle in hand, and had then left, leaving the dismembering and disposal of useful bits to be done by an African entourage. The tusks are of course the prime resource. Ivory. Essential material for billiard balls, piano keys, false teeth, chess pieces, dominoes and much else. Thank goodness for elephants. And there is more. Hair from the tail is twisted up by African craftsmen into bracelets, considered attractively exotic things. Some entrepreneurs are also finding that the skin can be made into jewellery pieces. And the feet – well, we know how useful the feet can be.

Connie Mayfield and her seven-year-old daughter are now out in the street, the elephant's foot forgotten. Harriet had not even noticed it.

'And you weren't at all nice to Great Granny,' says Connie. 'You didn't answer when she asked about your dancing class. You never even looked at her when she was talking to you,'

'I don't really like Great Granny,' says Harriet. Casual.

'Why ever not, for goodness' sake?'

'She's old,' says Harriet. 'I don't like old.'

Connie stops. She pulls Harriet to a halt. She looks down at her. 'Harriet,' she says 'one day you will be old, like Great Granny.'

Harriet laughs. 'No, I won't.'

Connie is exasperated, as she is rather often, with Harriet. 'And how would you feel, if a little girl was rude to you and didn't like you?'

'You're just being silly,' says Harriet 'how can I be old? I'm me.'

'And you don't call me silly. That's enough, Harriet.' Connie now whisks her daughter ahead. She can't wait to get home and hand her over to Nanny. Tonight, she and her husband are dining with the Laycocks. She will wear her new purple silk with the matching pumps.

A hundred years later, a child like Harriet would be described as feisty. Upfront. A child with attitude. In her own time, she is perceived as pert, cheeky, too big for her boots. She asks too many questions and is uncompliant. She trots along now beside her mother, not particularly dismayed and keen also to get home and out of her best frilled muslin dress which is itchy around the neck, while her waist is uncomfortably clamped within a wide satin sash. She has been made to wear a straw boater on top of her long hair, which is styled in ringlets. The ringlets are achieved by way of a fiendish procedure involving long strips of rag which drives both Nanny and Harriet mad, but Mrs Mayfield insists. So pretty, ringlets. A bit old-fashioned now, but all the more charming for that. Harriet is an only child and Connie means to make the most of a little girl while she has one.

Harriet is dimly aware that she will one day be a grown-up but that day is so unlikely, so unimaginable, that the thought does not bother her. Her mother sometimes reads to her from *Alice In Wonderland*; Harriet is disturbed by the accounts of Alice changing size, getting larger, and averts her eyes from the illustrations of a distorted Alice.

Could that happen? Well, no – this is just a story book. But she herself has just grown out of the boots she wore last year, which is worrying. She does not like Nanny to measure her height against the nursery door.

The Mayfields live in a large house in Wimbledon. John Mayfield is a solicitor; Connie Mayfield is a mother. John is a father, of course, but in his case that is the secondary role. If things proceed in the normal and expected way, Harriet will in time also become a mother, having married sensibly, or expediently. There will be a problem with that, though, because the intervention of a world war will mean that the best part of a generation of young men of around Harriet's age have been killed off, which leads to an unseemly scramble to secure one of the survivors. Or be condemned to spinsterhood, which means that a woman has failed in both the essential ways: she has failed to attract, she will not become a mother. The Mayfields have in a sense been spared the war; at forty-one when it began, John was too old for conscription.

All this lies ahead for Harriet, as she grows up in the Wimbledon house, goes to school at the Academy for Young Ladies nearby, where she learns some history, some geography, reads the occasional Shakespeare play. Attention is paid to her handwriting, and also to her sewing skills. There is instruction on how to manage servants, and on household economy – how to spend your husband's money adroitly. She has piano lessons. Harriet should emerge from this nicely equipped for marriage and motherhood.

In fact, Harriet quite enjoys school. She is exceptionally good at everything except sewing, and has the teachers running for cover because she never stops asking questions. When she is nine she wants to know why it gets dark at night, which is not relevant to the principal rivers of Europe – that is Science, and the Academy does not do Science. When she is twelve she wants to know how babies are made, which has nothing to do with the six wives of Henry the Eighth. At least not on the face of it, and her intervention means that she must write out the names of the six wives thirty times, in best writing. Despite these frustrations, Harriet manages to keep herself quite agreeably occupied, reading everything she can lay hands on and relishing the panic-stricken look in a teacher's eye when she puts her hand up in class. One way and another, she is so immersed over these years, and the shape-shifting process so gradual, that she hardly notices that she has left child Harriet behind and emerged as a fully fledged adult of eighteen, with her hair up and her skirts down.

The society in which she lives has mutated also. The war has come and gone, with all that that implies. Connie Mayfield is finding it fearfully difficult to get a good cook these days. She has the vote now, though of course she will always consult her husband on what to do with it. In earlier years, in the Mayfield household, John Mayfield had forbidden the name of that Pankhurst woman to be mentioned again. It was Harriet, of course, who had done the mentioning after she had picked up newspapers and seen intriguing pictures of ladies being hauled off by policemen, had read the accompanying text and cottoned on to what all this was about. How interesting. The more so since it apparently annoyed her father.

So, the world has moved on, and in the clear blue air of 1926 – the somewhat clearer blue air – Harriet told her parents that she thought she would like to go to university. That she was going to go to university.

Connie was aghast. 'Darling, I don't really think . . . We've been wondering about a nice finishing school.'

Harriet said she thought she would be finished better at a university.

John Mayfield said he was aware that some girls went to university nowadays. A certain type of girl.

'Exactly,' said Connie. 'And that's why it really wouldn't be the thing for you.' Harriet was so pretty, she was thinking – she was bound to get married quite quickly, despite – well, despite the wretched war and everything. There were still some men, the ones who had been too young.

There was an argument. Connie dropped out early on, sensing defeat. Harriet and her father were at it for about a week, after which Harriet was enrolled at Royal Holloway College and, shortly after, became seriously grown up. The status of an early-twentieth-century student was very different from that of one a hundred, or even fifty years later. The pioneering woman student was applied, and purposeful. She did not get drunk. She did not have sex (well, there may have been the few who lapsed). Harriet had chosen to study history because even the abundantly deficient syllabus of the Academy for Young Ladies (wives of Henry the Eighth, Queen Boadicea, the Battle of Trafalgar) had made her aware that history seems to be about change, and she thought that she would like to have a look at this.

Harriet studied with great efficiency, of course, and sailed out of Royal Holloway with a first class degree, a few friends, and not much idea of what to do next. Connie had networked frantically with other Wimbledon mothers so as to make sure that Harriet met young men, was invited to dances. The young men were initially rather taken with Harriet, who was indeed pretty – a deceptive English rose face with pink cheeks and wide eyes, framed no longer by ringlets but by fashionably cropped hair. They soon found that she was alarmingly combative, had opinions about everything, didn't play tennis or like dogs. Most fell by the wayside and headed for less challenging Wimbledon pickings. A more discerning few were intrigued. Wondering if perhaps a different kind of girl wasn't rather amusing.

Determined to get away from Wimbledon, Harriet realized that work of some kind was the only option. A couple of her Royal Holloway friends were training as teachers, but the prospect of a life in the schoolroom did not appeal to Harriet at all. She considered, then had an idea, visited Bumpus, the prestigious bookshop in Oxford Street, where she had chosen Christmas presents for herself over the years, and landed the offer of a job.

Connie Mayfield calmed down eventually, reflecting that a bookshop is the very highest class of shop and Harriet therefore the very highest class of shopgirl, though it was still hard to take. Her husband said little, having got the measure of Harriet by now. Harriet moved out into a flat that she shared with the Royal Holloway friends, and set about a most enjoyable period of arranging books, selling books, reading books and talking to Bumpus customers about books, many of whom were charmed to be served by a fetching young woman. On one occasion she sold a copy of *A Passage to India* to Clive Bell, of the Bloomsbury set, who spent rather longer than was appropriate chatting to the attractive Bumpus assistant. Harriet had never heard of any Bloomsbury set, but knew Virginia Woolf's name – one dropped by an aspirational reading colleague. Harriet herself was doing a lot of reading, eclectic rather than aspirational, and much liked to get into conversation with customers.

It was this that was to lead to the next step in her life. Howard Granger was often in Bumpus; he was ten years older than Harriet and making something of a name for himself as a travel writer. Invariably, he sought Harriet out for conversation and advice, and Harriet was only too happy to oblige. Here was a man with a dramatic lifestyle – always just back from Macedonia or just off to Corfu, vigorous, good looking, as far from Wimbledon as possible and evidently rather taken with Harriet.

Indeed. They were married within six months, a hasty register office affair, with Connie Mayfield mourning the lovely church event she had dreamed of, with Harriet radiant in white. Harriet gave in her notice at Bumpus and went to live with Howard in his cottage in the Chilterns, which was rather lacking in modern conveniences. Outside privy and oil lamps. Travel writing was not yet proving very lucrative.

But that was fine where Harriet was concerned. For now, anyway. She was entranced with her new liberated condition, released from Wimbledon, inhabitant of another world, it seemed. As indeed it was, this world of 1933. Occasionally Harriet looked back, incredulous, at her own childhood persona, which seemed to be in another age: the pinafores, the buttoned boots, the hats, the gloves. The century was powering ahead, taking her with it, and things were good in the Chiltern cottage, where books were read, matters of the day discussed, Howard was writing his book on Armenia and wondering about an extended trip to the Lebanon for his next project, and Harriet was quite happy to attend to domestic matters, which were more like some form of indoor camping than the elaborate procedures of her Wimbledon home and therefore not to be despised but seen as an invitation to be ingenious and adaptable.

The only cloud was that she kept feeling sick in the mornings, and couldn't work out why until enlightened at a consultation with the local doctor.

Oh.

The elephant's foot, with which the story began, was still in the hall of the house in Harley Street. Great Granny had died some while ago, and in any case the house was not hers but that of her son, a surgeon with whom she had been living. The foot's days were numbered, though. The surgeon retired in 1952 and sold the house in order to move to Henley. Dispersal and sale of the contents took quite a while, and the last scouring of stuff that nobody wanted was left to a house clearance operator, who stared for a moment at the umbrella stand, realized what it was, and chucked the nasty thing into a skip. Which was foolish of him because if he had hung onto it for sixty years or so he could have got two hundred and fifty pounds for it on eBay. Tastes can change, too.

The Pearl Button

The pearl button lies on Harriet's knee, waiting to be sewn as a fastener to the neck of the baby dress that she is making. She sets down her needle, reaches for the button, and at that moment the baby – which is still inside Harriet – jounces about, making her heave herself up in the chair. The pearl button shoots off her knee and down between a crack in the floorboards of the Chiltern cottage, where it will lie for the next sixty-two years.

The button was once a part of the inner layer of a pearl oyster, resting on the bed of a tropical sea until ripped from its home by a fisherman and flung into the hold of a boat, at the start of a long metamorphosis from living creature to small objects of utility. Until plastics come along, the western world depends upon the pearl oyster, the abalone, the great green turban snail, for the attachment of its clothing.

Harriet was not particularly bothered about the loss of the button. She had others. She was extremely bothered about the baby. She is still reeling from the realization that she is no longer one person, but two. She is invaded by this being within. She had not bargained for this, for this form of fission. She had not realized that this was how it would be. That she would no longer be simply herself, but a person who was generating another person, which would change things for ever. Change her.

Harriet had of course been perfectly well aware that what she and Howard were doing regularly and with much enjoyment was likely to lead to this, but she had not given the matter much thought. She had a vague notion that you had to go on doing it for ages, and anyway she was busy with the novelties of life in the cottage, and life with Howard, and then this had happened, after a matter of a few weeks. And now, after a further eight months, here she was in this state of gross enhancement, violated, twice her normal size. Sitting in the cottage *sewing*, if you please, because it had emerged that they were really rather hard up, and bought baby clothes are expensive.

'You make them, my dear,' explained the farm labourer's wife who lived in the neighbouring cottage. Sewing had been the only item at which Harriet had not excelled, on the curriculum of the Academy for Young Ladies. Now, she struggled, even with the kindly help of the neighbour, and the loan of a Singer sewing machine. She stabbed her fingers with the needles, cut things out all wrong, dropped buttons.

Furthermore, she had had to learn how to knit.

The baby was born, a process so painful and undignified that Harriet knew she wouldn't be doing that again, if she could possibly avoid it. A boy; Robert. Howard had managed to get back from a trip to Andalusia in time but left again fairly soon in fulfilment of a commission from a Sunday newspaper to write extensively about Corfu. And so it would go; Howard came and went, while Harriet and her son got to know each other in the Chiltern cottage.

That lasted for a couple of years, by which time the charms of the cottage had worn off entirely, Harriet no longer felt quite the same about Howard, in fact she no longer much cared for him at all, and Robert was rampant in a way that she would not have thought it possible for a small child to be.

There was only one thing to do. A return to Wimbledon was humiliating in the extreme, but the only way out, for now. Connie Mayfield had visited the cottage just once, and had left after an hour or so, shattered. Harriet was welcomed home, and the problem of Robert solved by bringing Harriet's old nanny back into service. Harriet heaved a sigh of relief, on that front, and set about a consideration of what was to be done next. Howard was being petulant about her departure, and saying that he didn't see how he could do much for the boy if he wasn't going to be living under the same roof. He was also talking of going to live in Italy. Howard would have to be written off, Harriet decided, both as husband, father, and means of support. The support had been flimsy in any case, she now saw.

The birth of Robert meant that she was now a different person. Pre-Robert, she had been just herself; now, she was herself with an extension. It had not even occurred to her to leave him with Howard, patently even less well equipped to cope with a child than she was. She was now not just Harriet, but Harriet plus Robert. He was an encumbrance, an obligation, and a frequent delight, though child-minding was decidedly a mixed pleasure; thank heaven for Nanny. No, Robert was best left largely to Nanny, Harriet's mother, and, rather surprisingly, her father, who had been denied a son and now took to this late substitute with enthusiasm.

Harriet went job-hunting, in an age when most young women of her class and qualifications – or lack thereof – did not. She reasoned that the only thing she knew anything about was books, since she had spent two years selling them, and had always read a great deal.

She had been with Howard to his publisher a couple of times, and had noticed that there was a well-spoken girl working in the office there. This, then, would seem to be the industry in which there might be an opening for someone like her. She made a list, went into central London day after day, and put herself about.

Within a few weeks she was successful. Of course. Sooner or later there was bound to be some harassed editor unable to resist a charmingly persuasive Harriet, out to convince him that she was everything he had been needing by way of amanuensis, general fac-totum, office dogsbody, anything he preferred. She was taken on by Peabody and Gulch, a small publishing house whose list favoured biography, popular history, literary fiction. After a year or so Harriet had made herself indispensable, a shrewd reader of manuscripts, deft manager of difficult writers, burgeoning thief of prized authors from other publishers. She could edit, it turned out; not for nothing had she cast a critical eye over some of Howard's work in progress, and found it wanting.

The second escape from Wimbledon came when John Mayfield agreed to fund the purchase of a small house in Chelsea for Harriet and Robert. Nanny, who was getting on a bit, was sufficiently devoted to Robert by now to put off retirement for a while and come along too. Harriet was now nicely set up with a home of her own and a salary that just about met her needs, and Nanny paid for by John Mayfield, who had decided to cover his grandson's expenses, given the poor boy's unfortunate paternity. Harriet had in any case set about divorce proceedings, a matter of great distress to her mother – divorce was absolutely not done, something you associ-ated with people who got themselves into the newspapers. The divorce eventually went through, not without difficulty since How-ard had indeed gone off to Italy in a permanent sort of way, and seldom answered letters. Once divorced, Harriet more or less lost touch with him; he had been an aberration, she now realized, some-one she had welcomed because he was unlike any man who had ever shown an interest in her before. His erratic lifestyle had been a novelty to begin with, but in time became merely tiresome; when around, he never stopped talking, or disappeared to the village pub and came back squiffy. He was an early mistake of hers, Harriet decided, though a significant one because he had given rise to Robert, and Howard effectively drops out of the story at this stage. In fact, he was to perish in Turkmenistan at a relatively early age, victim of virulent food poisoning, leaving behind a young Italian widow and several more children.

The next few years were a satisfactory time for Harriet. She was an essential figure in the Peabody and Gulch office, and enjoyed herself bustling around the world of books; in the little Chelsea house, she entertained her expanding cohort of friends, and found Robert increasingly more manageable, thanks to his upbringing by Nanny. When he was eight he was despatched to his grandfather's old prep school, for further training.

Times were changing, and Harriet was ahead of them, if anything. None of her old contemporaries at the Academy for Young Ladies were divorcees with a job. From Wimbledon and beyond, they eyed Harriet with misgivings. And anyway Harriet had no time for people like these; her world was rather different. She knew writers of one kind and another – those who wrote books, those who wrote for the newspapers – theatre people, colleagues in the publishing world. From time to time she took a lover; with circumspection and extreme caution – there were to be no more Howards and definitely no Roberts. A dalliance with a highly regarded poet lasted for a year or so, until Harriet decided that he was a bit too keen to settle into the Chelsea house; and poets are no better as bread winners than travel writers. Harriet was by now up to speed with the economics of publishing, and the rather more straightforward matter of what it costs to live in the way you need and prefer to live. She was managing her own life nicely, and had no intention of managing anyone else's. The poet was dumped, and for a while Harriet was mistress to a married colleague, who was financially self-sufficient, and too worried about discovery to be demanding.

All in all, her late twenties went well, for Harriet. It was the century's thirties, with things not going quite so well on that front.

Dark clouds are gathering, and in just a few years the lamps will be going out all over Europe. Harriet was attentive; she had been to Berlin once, on a trip with friends, had seen Hitler's stormtroopers, and Nazi flags. After Munich, she was one of those who said that 'peace for our time' would prove to be a fallacy.

On 3 September 1939, Harriet and Robert were in the Wimbledon house. John Mayfield was unwell, had been in and out of hospital. He had cancer, which was never named back then, but simply referred to as 'a long illness' when people died of it. Harriet was visiting, to give sympathy and prop her mother up; Connie was getting very overwrought. They listened together to Chamberlain's broadcast: '. . . this country is at war with Germany.' Connie moaned: '. . . just the *last* thing we need.' John Mayfield sighed. Robert, who was eleven, wanted to know if this war would go on long enough for him to be a soldier. Harriet began to consider her options.

One was not going to hang about in a publishers while there was a war going on, that was for certain. Oh, no. Harriet would be part of the action, in one way or another. For the next few months she investigated possibilities. You could be in the ATS, or you could be a WAAF or a WREN, none of which appealed to her: uniforms, and being bossed around. There must be something else. She had acquired secretarial skills at Peabody and Gulch; her shorthand wasn't brilliant but would pass, her typing was excellent. Harriet was now thirty-one and would consider a secretarial role beneath her. She had never been that at Peabody and Gulch, but those skills were necessary adjuncts for the position of personal assistant. That was the thing to go for: personal assistant to someone really important who was heavily involved in the war and with whom one would get about. Harriet liked to travel – she had holidayed much in France and Italy – and as 1939 became 1940 it was clear that this war was going places. Harriet decided she was going there too.

It was a question of surveying her now pretty wide acquaintance and seeing who was doing what. She needed some high-up in the army, who would be in need of staff. This seemed at first to be out of her range entirely, but eventually, after much thought and enquiry, she remembered a girl she had been friendly with at one time whose older brother she had once met at a house party – army, he had been, a brigadier. She managed to track down the girl, who was surprised to find Harriet desperate to renew the friendship, to pin her down to a lunch, to ask purposefully after her brother.

Harriet had been hoping merely for some introductions, but it turned out far better than that. Once in touch with Brigadier Gladwell, it emerged that he was about to be posted to the Middle East, to take charge of the Army Headquarters in Jerusalem. Harriet pounced.

Brian Gladwell found himself subjected to much the same assault as that experienced by the editor at Peabody and Gulch, some years ago. After half an hour or so he was persuaded that, well, yes, this seemed a very go-ahead, competent young woman – secretarial skills, office experience. GHQ in Jerusalem could indeed use someone like this. There would be a shortage of English-speaking staff out there.

And so it was that in April 1940 Harriet crossed the Mediterranean in a troopship, accompanying the Brigadier and his staff, which she rapidly infiltrated. By the time the ship docked at Ismailia in Egypt, Harriet was generally accepted as Gladwell's personal assistant, the twenty-one-year-old who had previously managed his diary, paperwork and signals shunted down to secretarial status. Other members of the staff were young officers, who found Harriet both entertaining and attractive.

From Ismailia they were driven across the Sinai desert into Palestine and eventually to Jerusalem. Harriet posted cards, to Robert and to her parents. She was in high spirits by now, aware that she was living in interesting times. She had had no compunction about leaving Robert, tucked up at his prep school, from which he would soon move to his grandfather's old public school; there was Wimbledon for the school holidays, where he would be good company for his grandparents. The house in Chelsea was let to an acquaintance, a useful bit of extra income. She was footloose, and up for anything that might come along.

In Jerusalem, GHQ was based within the King David Hotel, in offices that were constricted but nicely convenient for a vibrant social life, since the King David was the cosmopolitan social centre of the city. The streets were equally cosmopolitan and polyglot, almost like a fancy dress parade to Harriet, who had never stepped beyond the more staid countries of Europe. There were orthodox Jewish men in black with their long hair, Arab men in robes and their women in the burqa, Greek and Abyssinian priests, not to mention the diverse wartime dress codes of the western world – British troops and officers, Free French, Americans. She found it all enthralling, and quickly became informed about the political turmoil of the time and the place; should one sympathize with the Arabs or the Jews, what should the British position be?

On the boat, Harriet had done a crash course in mastering the ciphers for the signals that would be coming in all the time to the Brigadier, and now took pride in making these her concern, delegating the more mundane correspondence to secretary Dora. This was a lot more fun than reading manuscripts from the slush pile, or sweet talking difficult authors; one had signed the Official Secrets Act, one was in the thick of things. And the war itself was not far away at all; the Italian forces had moved from Libya over the Egyptian border, there were rumours that German reinforcements would be sent.

And, as 1940 gave way to 1941, it became clear that they were indeed at the heart of this particular theatre of war, the term now used that seemed an odd distortion, given the realities of what was going on. Deciphering signals, listening to the wireless, Harriet was well aware of what was happening not far away, in the Libyan desert. But that too was sanitized; men taken prisoner were 'in the bag', those killed had 'bought it'. In the King David Hotel, of an evening, and in the Jerusalem bars and restaurants, the atmosphere was febrile. If men were on leave they were out to have a good time; it was up to girls like Harriet to see that they did. There were other girls who had fetched up here like herself, working for the various organizations clustered in the city; she made friends with twenty-five-year-old

Kitty, on the High Commissioner's staff, and they found a flat to share. Many years later, Harriet would look back at that time and be astonished by how young everyone had been; she herself was often older than the men with whom she wined and dined in the evenings. A man in his forties was either a general or a civilian.

Everyone told her that she must get herself to Cairo at some point: 'That's where it's really happening.' So on the rare occasions when she had a few days' leave she either cadged a lift or got on the train to Cairo. And found that the frenetic activity there made Jerusalem seem almost a quiet backwater. Polo and racing at Gezira Sporting Club, drinks and dancing at Shepheards Hotel; so long as you had a few contacts – and Harriet's diary bristled with contacts by now – you could have the time of your life.

While others lost their lives. It was not until much later, looking back, that Harriet would recognize the stark contrast between the surface gaiety and excitement that she had known and the truth of the war that raged in the desert, so near: the tank crews who had been burned alive in tanks that 'brewed up', the thousand upon thousand of deaths, the men who 'stopped one'. Just as the language of the day evaded reality, so she and those she consorted with in Jerusalem and Cairo had focused upon this unexpected, stimulating, exotic experience that had been handed to them.

She fell in love. Of course. Twice. The first was a New Zealand officer on leave in Jerusalem, met in the King David on a Saturday, her lover by Tuesday, gone for ever on Friday. 'I'll be back,' he had said. She had waited. Much later, she had learned that he had been killed in one of the early battles of the Libyan campaign.

She told herself not to be so stupidly susceptible, next time. To no avail. He was based at GHQ in Cairo, first encountered from her office, exchanging signals, when the Brigadier was about to visit Cairo, and that had somehow led to a meeting next time she had some leave and made it to Cairo. David Lennox; not out in the desert, desk job in Cairo, would probably survive the war. He shared her interests – they talked about what both were reading, had read, went sight-seeing, amazed by the complex past of this country, by its roots in distant time. 'Rather puts us in perspective,' he said, as they stared at wall paintings thousands of years old, buried under the desert. 'As transient as they were. Just briefly here.' He came to Jerusalem; she wangled trips to Cairo. In the Libyan desert, the battle front moved back and forth. Then Rommel was within seventy miles of Cairo; there was Alamein, a victory, and the tide turned. 'That's it,' he said. 'There'll be an end, out here.' They seldom talked of a future. He had been a school teacher before the war, was unsure that he would go back to that. 'And you?' he said, as they lay in bed early one morning, in his flat in Zamalek. 'Any plans? Will I be seeing you?' It was the nearest he – they – had come to any discussion about how things stood. Both had said 'I love you.' Many people were saying that, at that time. It was perhaps too easily said.

What had she replied? She would not remember, much later, just that both of them had seemed to hold back from commitment, as though it were tempting providence to sign up to a pre-determined future. The war had to end; everyone would have to move from this artificial existence to some kind of normal life.

And, in the event, they had somehow drifted apart well before that time. He was posted away from Cairo, first to Tripoli, then to Algiers. It was hard to meet. At first she felt bereft; gradually, the need for him became less pressing, she thought of him not every hour, then not every day, and eventually just sometimes. In due course, he sank away in her mind and became a part of the whole eventful backdrop of those years, to which she would return often, not so much with nostalgia as with amazement that there could have been so much packed in, so much seen and heard, so many people, so very many.

Late in 1944 the Brigadier too was posted elsewhere. There was no further role for Harriet in Jerusalem and her employment was terminated, with a passage home to England, and a memorable farewell party at the King David.

She arrived back in time for a cold, grey English winter, she who had known only sunshine for the last four years. The end of the war was in sight. Harriet found her son, who was no longer a child but a gawky adolescent she did not know, and her mother, who was older and given to complaint, perhaps with some reason. The Wimbledon house was too big, too cold, and her husband had died the year before, succumbing at last to the never-mentioned cancer.

Harriet set about getting to know her son again, and finding them somewhere to live. The Chelsea house seemed poky, and she was even thinking of moving out of London. Prospecting, she found herself one day in the Chilterns and, on an impulse, drove past that cottage. It looked exactly as it had in her own day – distinctly run down and out of date, one foot in another century.

She had long forgotten the pearl button, which still lay under the floorboards. It would stay there until, in 1992, the cottage was eventually hauled into modernity as someone's weekend retreat, tricked out with an Aga, halogen lighting, en suite bathroom, granite worktop and all appropriate appliances. The builder who was installing the underfloor heating came upon the pearl button, glinting up at him. He picked it up, did for an instant think of that person who must have dropped it, and pushed it into his pocket. Someone at home might have a use for a button.

The Parasol

Harriet did not move out of London to the Chilterns or anywhere else. Her removal plans were facilitated by Connie Mayfield's sudden decision to sell the Wimbledon house in favour of somewhere smaller and easier to run, which meant that there was some surplus money that Connie declared Harriet should have: 'Daddy would have wanted that, for you and Robert.' This enabled Harriet to consider more expensive properties, and in time she and Robert were settled into a nicely roomy house off Kensington High Street; a study for her, whole attic floor for him, guest suite, and so forth. In return, Harriet had spent a good deal of time helping her mother with clearing out the Wimbledon house, and it had been in the course of this that she came across the parasol.

It was in a box in the junk room; old clothes of Connie's, and this

Edwardian or Victorian parasol. Cream silk, with a fringe, ebony handle.

'I remember this, Mother,' said Harriet. 'Goodness, proper antique – but I can remember you using it.'

Connie said that the parasol had been her mother's. 'French, I think – expensive.'

Harriet examined the parasol. The fabric had rotted and it was torn in a few places, revealing the struts – thin, creamy white. She considered these: some sort of nylon? But they didn't have that. Not wood. So – what?

'Whalebone,' said Connie. 'I remember that's what they made them from, the best ones. Lighter than metal, you see.'

She was right. The ribs of the parasol were baleen and were once a part of a humpback whale's mouth, the wall of thin strips that act as a filter for the whale, straining from the water the krill on which it feeds. An element of Connie's parasol once cruised the dark waters of the Arctic.

Harriet was intrigued. She was intrigued by this piece of information, and also because of this image she has of her mother carrying the parasol when she was a child – opening it, putting it into an umbrella stand – has made her sharply conscious of the chasm between that time and this. Nearly forty years, that's all, but another age, it was. How she was, and how I am, at around the same age. Rather different. Very different. We assume differently, perceive differently.

Harriet was thirty-eight.

When she came back from Jerusalem, she knew that she was far from the same as the young woman who had gone there in 1940. Not just older, more experienced, but somehow also with new expectations, a need to look around and make assessments, consider what was now possible, what she might do. And she had found a country, a homeland, that had also changed. It was as though after the five years of war it had shaken itself violently and become somewhere different. A Labour government arrived. 'So wretchedly ungrateful to Churchill,' said Connie Mayfield. 'After all he's done for us.' It was no longer merely difficult to get a cook, or any other kind of menial, but nearly impossible; valiantly, Connie took a cookery course, but it was the washing-up that broke her spirit.

Harriet was for some reason rather taken with the parasol. 'Do you want it, Mother? Or could I have it?'

'Goodness, darling,' said Connie. 'Have anything. We're clearing out, aren't we? There's only room for a few of the nicest things in the new house. I'm going to be living like a pauper.'

Not quite true. The new house was a pretty little mews cottage near Harrods. Connie would be living very comfortably, but without the infrastructure of service to which she was accustomed.

Harriet, at that time, was working again at Peabody and Gulch, where she had been received back with enthusiasm. Publishing had been in the doldrums during the war. Now was the time for initiative, expansion; bright and relatively young people like Harriet were needed. Old Mr Peabody was overdue for retirement; Gulch had departed long since. For Harriet, though, there was something stale about this return. Yes, she had always enjoyed her job; yes, there were various interesting projects in the pipeline, and this was indeed the moment for some creative publishing. But the thought of carrying on like this for ever was no longer satisfying. She was wondering about alternatives when her mother's old parasol arrived as the prompt, the inspiration.

Interested in its evocative construction – this strange link to distant ocean creatures – she found that she wanted to know something about the whaling industry, and repaired to the London Library, where she had long been a member. She wanted a book that would tell her about the origins of whale hunting, about the many uses of whale material, about the history and topography of the industry, and about its wider context: about the metaphorical significance of the whale – Moby Dick, the story of Jonah. She wanted to know about whale diversity, and why they are so compelling.

There did not seem to be such a book. Not on that scale, not that comprehensive. And this set her thinking. One of her authors from before the war was a man who had done quite well with amiable books on a particular topic: the expansion of the railway system, the botanical pioneers – the plant hunters. Maybe she should suggest this to him as a new venture.

Or, in fact, maybe not. She thought of this writer, and of his books, for which amiable was in some way the right word, but this idea deserved . . . Well, deserved something more pungent, more imaginative.

Harriet will not be the first editor to have cast a critical eye upon an author's work and think: I could do better myself. She considered, and the more she considered the more she knew what she was going to do.

She negotiated a new role at Peabody and Gulch whereby she would work as an editor for three days a week. The rest of the time would be her own, in which she would research and write this book. It was a gamble, would mean a reduced income, but she was now set on it.

The next three years were to prove a fascinating new departure. Harriet found that research was a pleasure. She liked libraries, and she liked even more taking to the road for essential research trips. She went to Hull, she went to Orkney, to see for herself the places in this country from which men had set off for cold northern waters on their bloody missions. Harriet was of course entirely on the side of the whales, and there was some satisfaction in reading that loss of life was not merely on the side of the whales; plenty of ships sunk, men drowned. Though, she had to remind herself – and that would of course go into the book – the men had to make a living, women were left widowed in Hull and Orkney, children fatherless.

One summer she crossed the Atlantic, taking Robert with her. Nantucket was an essential destination, hub of the American whaling industry. Robert was now nineteen, a young man, adolescence over and done with, thanks be; Harriet enjoyed his company, Robert was appreciative of a mother outside the common run. Not every mother is writing a book, whisks you off on a trip to America. They spent a couple of weeks in Nantucket; Harriet amassed information, Robert swam and went fishing. When they came back to England, Robert went to university and Harriet began to write.

She was up to the eyes in whale knowledge. She lived with whales, she dreamed whales. She knew how to flense a whale on the deck of a ship, and then use cauldrons to render the blubber into oil. She knew the best stance for hurling a harpoon from a whaleboat. She knew, of course, what whaling was all about; never mind the oil, and the meat, for those with a taste for it, there was all that essential baleen for corset stays, collar stiffeners, crinolines, those parasols, there was that curious stuff called ambergris, valued in the manufacture of perfumes. Amazingly useful creatures, whales; as good as elephants, if not better. Harriet followed the decline of the whaling industry, as dispassionately as possible. She learned about the whales themselves, from the great blue whale to the lovely little white beluga and the narwhal with its unicorn horn. She steeped herself in whale mythology; every country has a mythic whale, from China through Iceland to Alaska, New Zealand. Nineteenth-century America threw up its own great myth; Harriet's exegesis of *Moby Dick* would be one of the most admired chapters.

The book was well received. Extremely well received, indeed. Critics remarked on the writing, both elegant and robust: 'a gripping story, told with scholarly panache.' They admired the book's range and eclecticism, its absorbing pursuit of detail, the evident depth of research. Harriet's name was noted – an interesting newcomer. Peabody and Gulch had had to come to terms with Harriet's frequent absences; now, the firm could feel compensated, at least she was something of a minor celebrity in the publishing world.

The nineteen fifties arrived. For a while Harriet sat tight, looking about her, considering a new venture. As ever, she was nicely attuned to the zeitgeist. And, thus, the idea came to her. Of course, what else should one be writing about now!

She hit the jackpot with her study of world cuisines. The nation was now aspirational, where cooking was concerned. Middle-class England was reading Elizabeth David and yearned for ratatouille, cassoulet, moussaka, daube de boeuf, even if no greengrocer had heard of aubergines, peppers, or garlic, and olive oil could only be found at the chemist, for medicinal purposes. Never mind that it was pretty well impossible to do Elizabeth David in your own kitchen, the nation had got interested in food, had realized that there is more to life than cottage pie, bubble and squeak, rice pudding, toad in the hole. Harriet's book was not a cookery book – oh, no. What she set about was a comprehensive survey of world cuisine, an examination of how people cook and have cooked at other times and in other places. It was ambitious – a history of cookery as well as a forensic study of the extraordinary diversity of cookery. Everything from Inuit processing of the Little Auk to the creations of Escoffier. From the Neolithic hearth to the Aga. It was superbly produced, lavishly illustrated, and everybody gave it to everybody else for Christmas in 1956.

Peabody and Gulch had a runaway success. No one said a word any more if Harriet failed to show up on the days when she was still supposed to do a bit of editing. She was now known; you heard her on the radio, read her in the papers. Harriet Mayfield, the writer (Harriet had jettisoned her married name soon after she acquired it). Now, it was a question of what she would turn to next.

There was a while to wait. Indeed, knowing that this one would be yet more comprehensive, and would startle, Harriet kept silent about the subject matter for as long as she could. Yet again, the zeitgeist had struck. She had looked, and listened, and realized that while people had been interested in cookery, what they were extremely interested in now was sex.

The Kinsey Reports on sexual behaviour in the human male and human female had come out in 1948 and 1953. There had been time for people to digest their shocking contents, for critics to contest the methods used, but most of all for people to understand that what was under discussion was what everybody had always been doing but you didn't really talk about it. Sex was no longer taboo; not only was it fine to talk about it but the thinking person really ought to do so. And then came the Wolfenden Report, in 1957. Fifteen respected men and women said that homosexual behaviour between consenting adults should no longer be a criminal offence. Whew! By this time Harriet was well into writing her book, nicely anticipating Wolfenden and with Kinsey as her launch pad.

Once again, she ranged over time and space. Sexuality then, sexuality over there. Sexuality in classical Greece, sexuality in contemporary

Samoa. She considered attitudes: the frankness of the eighteenth century, the prudery of the Victorians. She looked at birth control, and lack of any, at childbirth. She drew heavily on literature, on how novelists have presented the sexual lives of their characters, or refrained from doing so. She devoted much attention to the love that dare not speak its name, but could now do so openly and indeed rather fashionably. This was a time of seismic social change, though that would perhaps not become apparent until later. The nation had once again shaken itself, and changed; you could talk differently, things that had previously been unacceptable were now fine. And Harriet's book was perfectly timed. Once again, people were giving it for Christmas, though rather more selectively.

The sex book, as it would always be called by her friends, established Harriet as a cultural commentator. She was by now in her fifties, while the century was moving into its sixties. Harriet found middle age hard to take, but fought back. She had been working hard on her books all the time that it had begun to bare its teeth, to manipulate her weight, to interfere with her looks. She had determined to face it down, not with stupid stuff like cosmetic surgery, but simply by acknowledging that this happens and one is not going to be held up by it.

There were men in her life, during those years. In it, and then, usually, out of it. Her mother had kept hinting at a fresh marriage: 'Never too late, darling, and I do feel . . . the right man . . .' Connie Mayfield retained absolute faith in marriage as a woman's goal and sanctuary. However, in 1958 she died, and Harriet, who had never shared her mother's views, was no longer obliged to make vaguely acquiescent noises and to ensure that some of her visits to Connie's mews flat were in the company of some compliant male friend – just to keep Connie quiet, show that Harriet was testing the waters.

Harriet had no great desire to re-marry; once had been quite enough. But she liked men – particular men; she liked to have a lover from time to time. Companionship could be welcome; Robert, in his twenties, had moved away from home, naturally enough, into a flat of his own. He had graduated from Cambridge and, after an apprenticeship on a local paper, was working as a young journalist on *The Times*.

Harriet liked him, an odd term perhaps for maternal feeling, but it was the case, quite aside from love, which she also felt. She saw something of herself in him – he was applied, resourceful – and nothing, mercifully, of his father, whose very name she could forget. Robert was of course Robert Granger, but the rest . . . ? Oh yes, Howard, that was it. She never even wondered what had happened to Howard Granger; there had been a Christmas present for Robert for a few years, and then silence. Robert, tactfully perhaps, showed no interest in him.

Rather neatly, there was a temporary lover for each book. The whaling book had brought Harriet together with an archivist at the British Museum Library. James Redwood had been recently widowed, was adrift and more than somewhat smitten with Harriet; he would have liked a permanent arrangement, but Harriet was not sufficiently committed. While researching Indian cookery and its effects on our own by way of the British Raj, she had met the author of the then most comprehensive work on that period. Paul Finchley was married, but unhappily so. Eventually he became too keen to make Harriet his reason for ending the marriage, which would not do at all so far as she was concerned, so she had to dump him, an expression not yet in use, but the procedure the same.

So, by the time the sex book came out, Harriet was without any significant other, and not especially concerned about this. She was enjoying the extra clout its publication had given her – attention from the media, a general attitude at Peabody and Gulch that Harriet must be allowed to do exactly what she liked, in the interests of her next project. She herself had no idea what that project might be, and was not bothered about that either. It would arrive. Or not. On the whole, this mid-life period was feeling rather good, despite her thickened waistline, and a face that seemed out of kilter, not what she was used to. I was seen as quite good-looking, she would think. Not any more?

Actually, yes. At least that was the view of the man seated opposite her in a BBC studio, where both, and three others, were contributing to *The Critics*, the weekly discussion programme on arts topics. All contributors were expected to have views on all topics, though it was usual for most to have a speciality. Charles

Newcombe was there as a cultural journalist with a special interest in film; Harriet was, generally speaking, the books person. He had been observing her across the table, the way her face lit up when animated – an interesting face, those large brown eyes, a mobile mouth – or became intense, concentrated, when listening. Something rather compelling about her . . . late forties . . . (he was wrong there, Harriet was fifty-four). He knew her name, had heard of the sex book, the food one too. He found himself gratified when she agreed with some of his criticisms of the film *Lawrence of Arabia* – Peter O'Toole miscast, various anachronisms – and was amused at her own ambivalent position on Doris Lessing's *The Golden Notebook*, with which she was clearly not entirely in sympathy, but not prepared to tolerate the destructive attitude of a couple of the other critics. Feminism was not yet a word much flung around, but was lurking in the wings.

As they left the studio he said, 'The BBC coffee was appalling. Would you care to join me for something better? There's a nice place just near.'

And so it all began.

Harriet was startled by her own feelings. At first, she had assumed this would be . . . well, another of those passing relationships. Enjoyable, refreshing – and transient. But as the weeks went by, and their meetings became more frequent, the phone calls daily, she understood that this was different. She did not want this to be transient, she was immersed, she was in this for the long haul, she was . . . she was in love, of all things. At fifty-four, middle-aged, for heaven's sake, she was clobbered by that most youthful of experiences. She was in love with Charles Newcombe.

He was a couple of years older than she was, so old enough too to know better, but he seemed equally affected, in a brisk, no nonsense sort of way. He had been married – a marriage that broke down some while ago. A grown-up daughter. He was a critic, commentator, had written film scripts – a literary jack of all trades, he called himself. And, for Harriet, he was the person she most wanted to talk to, be with, now, and quite possibly for ever.

The first time they went to bed together she said, undressing: 'I am not what I was.'

'I wouldn't expect you to be,' he said amiably. 'Same here, as it happens.'

They talked about this age thing.

'We are now. Here and now,' she said. 'Like this. But we've both got a long back story. Hidden history. And we can't know about each other's. That kind of bothers me.'

He observed that that is always the case. It would have been the same if they were younger.

'Not quite. It's being – goodness, being half a century old.'

'Well, true. I know what you mean. Something a bit climactic about that. We shall have to fill in these back stories. Shall I start with my primary school?'

He could tease her, and that was fine. He could tell her about things of which she knew nothing – the shenanigans of the film industry – and she would be enthralled. He could make her laugh, he could sit with her in friendly silence, both reading, he could sleep beside her and she would lie amazed at what had happened.

She liked his friends, she liked his daughter; after six months it was as if she had always known him. They went to Ireland for a few days' holiday, because neither had ever been there and when they got back he moved out of his Bayswater flat into Harriet's house.

'Does this mean I'm a kept man?' he wondered.

'No, because you'll be putting out the dustbins.'

She had never known this kind of cohabitation – well, not since the Chiltern cottage, and that she barely remembered. This was domestic life, as lived by most people, but not, so far, by Harriet. And she found that she relished it. Breakfast, daily, with a man who buried himself in *The Times*, in considerate silence, unless she wished to talk; evenings of eating – she and Charles both liked to cook – talking, music, reading. Nights when a shared bed was the norm, and all that went with that. Someone to complain to, argue with, go to a film with, walk in the park with.

They were married in a register office, with his daughter Marian and Harriet's Robert as witnesses.

'It's so good they don't mind,' said Harriet. 'Either of them.'

'They're glad to get us off their hands.'

'If only my mother could have lived to see me now. Respectably married. Redeemed. At least for the last part of life. That sounds awful, doesn't it? The last part.'

'Would you like to have the first part all over again?'

'Dear me, no. Far too much *Sturm und Drang*. Would you?'

Charles considered. 'An hour or two, here and there. Otherwise, I rather agree. Best just to soldier on into the unknown. Much more interesting, the unknown.'

Charles was a pragmatic man. That is not to say that he was without ideals or principles, just that he tended to take life as it came and deal with it as appropriate. Harriet had soon learned this, and indeed the tendency chimed rather with her own outlook, acquired in apposition to her mother. Connie Mayfield had spent much of her time concerned about conformity – how to behave in a way that would be approved by those whose approval she needed, how to respond to any circumstance in compliance with received wisdoms. It was a relief for Harriet to be, now, entirely in the company of someone whose outlook was as flexible as her own.

He was also genial, considerate, and hard working: 'You have to be, in my trade, self-employed means get out there and make yourself a living.' Harriet decided to make changes to the house. The top floor – Robert's old territory – had become a sort of junk room. This could be a study for Charles. She set about clearing it out, with enthusiasm.

The cupboard that had once held Robert's clothes now held clothes of Harriet's that should have been thrown out long ago – not worn for years. She set about a cull of these – cotton dresses from her Jerusalem days, for heaven's sake, that purple coat acquired in some lapse of sanity, the miniskirt set aside when she came to her senses – it is not wise to wear a miniskirt when you have hit fifty – sweaters that had long been host to moths, various size fourteen

garments which Harriet no longer was, shoes that didn't fit either . . .
Why has one kept all this?

This was said aloud, as Charles arrived, to see what she was up to.

'Optimism? Nostalgia?' she went on. 'There seems to be both in here.'
She stared at a red bathing costume, stuffed it into the rubbish sack.

'Or simply that you have the space,' he suggested. 'So why not?'

'Pity one can't do this with the inside of the head. Weed out
what's not wanted. Useless information. Bad memories.'

'Your cupboard rather reflects that – random storage. You can't
control what may pop up – memory metaphor. What's this about?'
He had delved into the back of the cupboard and was brandishing a
hat that erupted with blue tulle and feathers.

'Oh, heavens – that. I went to a wedding. Now . . . all this is going.' –
she waved at the rubbish sacks – 'And the cupboard too, and what I'm
thinking is – you have a desk under the window, here, and we have
bookshelves built all along that wall. You'll need a filing cabinet.'

Charles was still intent on the cupboard. 'And this? I hadn't realized you went that far back, fashion-wise.'

The parasol. Charles was holding the parasol. He opened it. 'Seen
better days, I fear.' The silk had rotted further, ribs were exposed.

'Oh,' Harriet took it from him, closed it, turned it over, ran her
finger along a rib. 'My mother's. Actually, her mother's, I think. And
that does strike a chord. It inspired the whale book – the ribs, you
see. Baleen. This I need to keep. Goodness knows where.'

'We start a new junk cupboard,' said Charles.

The Tortoiseshell Mirror

The mirror lives on Harriet's dressing table, centre stage – she uses
it every day. Charles gave it to her once for Christmas – found it in
an antique shop. The back of the mirror is a disc of warm golden-
brown tortoiseshell, framed in silver, with a silver handle.

It has never had anything to do with a tortoise; it was once part of
a hawksbill sea turtle, and roamed some tropical coral reef, perhaps

in the Caribbean, or maybe the Philippines, or the Red Sea, or the Malay Archipelago we can't now know where, suffice it that, wherever, it was a long way from Harriet's London bedroom. Once upon a time, there were plenty of hawksbill sea turtles. Now, there are not. They are critically endangered, because too many people were keen to make them into mirrors, or combs, or spectacle frames, or furniture inlays. That will not happen any more – should not happen any more – and the remnant left will swim the coral reefs unmolested. Their ancestors continue to haunt antique shops and museums.

Mirror-side, today, is Harriet's face, as seen by Harriet now, in 1990. She studies this, one morning, with detachment. What exactly has gone wrong with this face, so that it in no way resembles another Harriet face, in the photo on the dressing table – Harriet aged around seven, with her mother and father, muslin frock, wide sash, ringlets (oh, those ringlets)?

Well . . . Large pouch under each eye, above the eyes the skin sags, obliterating the top eyelids, minimal eyebrows, jawline sags at each side (where has all this extra skin come from?), beneath the chin, a further hefty pouch – two chins, effectively. This seems to be a face in meltdown. Somewhere beneath it she thinks that she can still detect the ghost of a face that she remembers, the face that confronted her for decades. But there has been this invasive change, sneaking in, and now the mirror reports this other face.

So it goes, she tells herself. You are eighty-two, what else would you expect? You are in the departure lounge. Check-in was a very long time ago.

Time went into overdrive, it seems. The years have raced. And here she is at this point to which she had never given much thought. You don't. Old age is an ambush. She looks back, rather than forward, now.

The century has hurtled ahead, too, laying waste as it went, springing surprises, confounding expectations. Back in 1961, Harriet and Charles sat through the Cuba crisis together, day by chilling day.

'Is this it, do you think?' she said. 'End of the world as we know it.'

'Reason may prevail. May. Just may.'

It did. The world could draw breath, and then later, much

later – what is this? The Berlin Wall is gone. The Cold War is over. Who could have predicted that? It is as though, this time, the planet has shaken itself and come out different.

Those were indeed interesting times. With the sex book now somewhat in the past, Harriet was puzzling about what to do next. What were people focused on now, as the sixties rolled into the seventies? Well, clearly, feminism was the topic of the day, that was what people were concerned about, whether they were in favour or not. Harriet considered this as a subject and decided, sensibly, that it was already being addressed more than adequately by others. She doubted she could match up to Germaine Greer, Kate Millett, Elaine Showalter.

There was still Peabody and Gulch, of course. She was spending more time there, with no book in progress, was the senior editor and in fact now the presiding figure at the firm, largely responsible for its reputation as leading publisher of serious and innovative non-fiction. The sort of book Harriet had been writing herself, in other words. If you had a smart idea and were in search of a commission, you tried to see Harriet Mayfield at Peabody, as it was usually known.

Harriet rather enjoyed this. 'It's not exactly a rags to riches story,' she said to Charles. 'But I joined the firm as a junior dogsbody and now – well, I call the shots, on the whole. Nicely in tune with the times, is how I see it. When I joined there wasn't one woman editor there. Old Mr Gulch must be spinning in his grave.'

'Oh, well, plenty of people are doing that, I dare say. The times they are a changin' – Dylan was spot on.'

'And the thing is,' Harriet continued. 'That you have to be old enough to realize what's happening – like you and me. The young think it was always like this.'

Harriet was a grandmother, which was of course an enrichment, but she also felt slightly affronted. What, me? Has it come to that? Robert and his wife Milly had two boys. Robert was an established journalist, a political commentator; Milly was a BBC radio producer. The boys went to their local primary school, and, no, said Robert, they would certainly not be going to his old public school: 'They'll be better off in the real world, and anyway we couldn't afford it. It'll be the comprehensive, for them.' Harriet had continued to like her son, aside from any deeper feelings. He seemed to her to have his head screwed on right, as Charles liked to put it: level-headed, broad-minded, hardworking.

So, a grandmother . . . What had happened to youth, to late youth, even, to her high-kicking thirties, the Jerusalem years? Gone, all gone, packed away with that set of random slides we call memory.

'And that is acceptable, I suppose,' she told Charles. 'But the trouble with this last leg of life is that one doesn't know what to do with it.' Harriet was into her sixties; young turks at Peabody were eyeing her, wondering about retirement.

'Well, let them,' said Charles. 'Take your time.'

'I shall. It's still a question of what next.'

'Take up gardening? We could move to the country.'

She laughed. 'Can you honestly see me . . . *gardening?*'

'Maybe not. Start a ceramics collection? Martial arts? Meditation? Macramé?'

'Come on, take this seriously. What do I do for the next ten, twenty, years? You too, for that matter. Till old age has us by the throat.'

'I suppose,' he said, 'that it's a question of resources. What do we have that could be used – exploited?'

A pause – looking at each other.

'Actually,' said Harriet. 'Experience. That's it. A whole bank of experience.'

'And experience is versatile stuff. Comes in all shapes and sizes. Personal. Collective. Well, then?'

'I shall think of something,' she said briskly. 'I've got a prompt now. The thing is, until the recent past, most people were dead before their sixties. You didn't live to see sixty. We have bonus time. It should be used.'

A few weeks later, she had it worked out.

'You,' she told Charles, 'are going to write a book. Enough reviews and articles. A book.'

'Oh. Am I?'

'You know an inordinate amount about film. Film is the crucial new art form of this century. You are going to write a book on twentieth-century movies, and the cultural impact and influence of film in our times.'

He raised an eyebrow. Both eyebrows. 'Well . . . Put like that, it sounds . . . a possibility. And what about you?'

'A book, too. At last – the idea. I'm going to write about the century. I'm one of those who have lived their lives parallel with the century, and I'm going to write about what that has meant – how public events have skewed private life. How we think we make choices but many have been made for us.'

'Trust you,' said Charles. 'To go for broke.'

Harriet retired from Peabody and Gulch and was given an elaborate send off, with champagne and eulogies. The young turks competed in the eulogies, feeling in fact a touch apprehensive and with thoughts about a hard act to follow running through their heads.

At sixty-six, Harriet could have passed for late fifties. The century that had nannied most people out of smoking and served up improved medical care had done well by Harriet's generation. She had given up her (moderate) smoking when the dire warnings began; antibiotics had seen her through several episodes that in earlier times could have had disastrous consequences. All of this would be material for her book – the benign hand of fate as well as the malign.

So, Harriet was still vigorous, fresh-faced, her hair in a flattering cut – no greys visible, stouter than she would have wished, but still within hailing distance of younger versions of herself. Charles too was in good nick, but what neither could know was what none of us can know, the hidden nemesis.

Released from Peabody, Harriet flung herself enthusiastically into the new project. As, indeed, did Charles with his, admitting that in fact he had less work now anyway: 'Sidelined, somewhat. Seen as an old hack, I dare say. My James Bond chapter is going swimmingly, by the way.'

'Old hack you are not,' said Harriet. 'Ageism. I shall be having a few things to say about that. This has been the century of isms. Ageism, sexism, racism.'

'Surely they were around earlier?'

'Oh, yes. But differently so. Not recognized, just entrenched.'

He wrote. She wrote. The days passed easily, in the Kensington house; they would meet up at lunch-time, compare notes, consider a walk in the park if it was a nice day. In the evenings, they sometimes went to a theatre, or a film ('Got to keep up to date,' said Charles), entertained friends.

It was the best of times, Harriet thought. But she had thought that before, on occasion: when working at Bumpus, aged twenty-three, escaped from Wimbledon, in Jerusalem in 1942, while the Middle East seethed around her. And this was different; it was a time that had a tranquillity about it, an acceptance of things, an absence of anticipation.

'We are people who have completed,' she told Charles. 'At this point in life. We are who we are – the outcome of various other incarnations.'

'Really? I've been feeling fully mature for years now.'

She laughed. 'Well, yes. But this is a plateau, sort of. A levelling off. We shan't change much now.'

'Glad to hear that. What about my dodgy knee?'

'Oh, physical decline. That's another matter.'

Indeed. Charles died in 1982. So then it was the worst of times. In the weeks, the months, that followed his death, Harriet would reflect that if you have been fortunate enough to know what it is to love someone, then you should also know what it is to grieve. To know that grief is all consuming, like love.

But that, once again, you arrive at a kind of plateau. A condition of stasis. And, thus, there came that day when Harriet considered herself as displayed by the tortoiseshell mirror, seeing a woman who was in some way alien but also, now, familiar. She had learned to live with this form of reincarnation, and could think that pragmatic acceptance is perhaps the only way to deal with change.

Though others might not agree: the elephant, the pearl oyster, the whale, the hawksbill sea turtle.

Pack of Cards (1978–1986)

The Emasculation of Ted Roper

Jeanie Banks, rigid with emotion, her cardigan on inside-out, muttering rehearsed words, deaf and blind to the bright morning, made her way down the village street. Past the post office, the one, two, three, four cottages, past the pub, Mrs Halliday's, the garage, the one, two, three new bungalows, the Lathams', Cardwell's yard. She stopped outside Roper's, simmering, reached out to open the gate, lost her nerve, plunged on down to the lamppost where the village ended, yanked up her resolution again, turned, aimed back, fumbled furious with the latch on Roper's gate.

The front garden a disgrace, as always, strewn with empty oil cans, plastic sacks, rusting iron objects, the excretions of Roper's hand-to-mouth odd-jobbing dealing-in-this-and-that existence. Furtive, unreliable, transacting in dirty pound notes, dodging his taxes without a doubt, down the pub every evening. Dirty beggar, cocky as a robin, sixty if he was a day.

Feeling swelled to a crescendo, and courage with it; she hammered on the door. Then again. And again. No answer. He'd be there all right, he'd be there, nine-thirty in the morning, since when did Roper go out and do a decent day's work? She shoved at the side gate.

He was round the back, fiddling about with a great pile of timber, good timber at that, planks all sizes and shapes and how did he come by it one would like to know? A whole lot of tyres stacked up in one corner, stuff spilling out of the shed, filth everywhere.

'Hello, Jeanie.'

She halted, breathless now. Words fail you, they do really. They leave you huffing and puffing, at a disadvantage, seeing suddenly the run in your tights, seeing yourself reflected in the eyes of others – angry, dumpy, middle-aged widow, just Jeanie Banks. In the beady spicy nasty eyes of Ted Roper, stood there in the middle of his junk like a little farmyard cock. A randy strutting bantam cock.

'What can I do for you, Jeanie?'

She said, 'It's not what you can do it's what's been done, that's what's the trouble.'

'Trouble?' He took out tobacco, a grubby roll of cigarette papers. 'Trouble?' His dirty fingers, rolling, tapping, his tongue flickering over the paper.

'My Elsa's expecting.'

'Expecting?' he said. 'Oh – expecting.' A thin smile now, a thin complacent smile. Grinning away at it, the old bastard, pleased as punch. As if it were something to be proud of, as if it did him credit even, stood there with his thumbs stuck in his trouser pockets like those boys in western films. Some boy – Ted Roper. Boy my foot, sixty if he's anything.

'That's what I said. Expecting.'

He put the cigarette in his mouth; thin smoke fumed into the village sunshine. Not trousers, she saw now. Jeans – jeans just like young men wear, slumped down on his thin hips, the zip sliding a bit, a fullness you couldn't miss below, stuck out too the way he stood, legs apart, thumbs in pockets.

'Well,' he said, 'I s'pose that'd be in the nature of things. She's getting a big girl now.'

Grinning away there, wiry and perky and as blatant as you like. She felt her outrage surge.

'It's rape,' she said. 'That's what it damn well is. A little creature like that, a little young thing. Bloody rape!' The colour rushed to her cheeks; she didn't use language like that, not she, never.

'Now, now, Jeanie. Who's to know who gave who the come on.'

She exploded. She shouted, 'You take that blasted cat to the vet, Ted Roper, and get it seen to, the rest of us have just about had enough, there's kittens from one end of the village to the other and my Elsa was nothing but a kitten herself.' She swung round and stormed to the gate. When she looked back he was still standing there, the cigarette laid on his lower lip, his jeans fraying at the crotch, the grin still on his face. 'Or you'll find it done for you one of these days!'

All the way back to the cottage her heart thumped. It didn't do you any good, getting yourself into a state like that, it took it out of you, she'd be jumpy all day now. Back home in the kitchen, she made herself a cup of tea. The old cat, the mother, was sprawled in the patch of sun on the mat and Elsa was in the armchair. When Jeanie came in she jumped down and shimmied across the floor: pretty, graceful, kittenish and distinctly lumpy, no doubt about it, that unmistakable pear-shape forming at the end of her. And Jeanie, subsiding into the chair, drinking her tea, eyed her and eyed the old cat, not so old come to that, five or was it six, and as she did so a whole further implication leaped into the mind – why hadn't she thought of it before, how disgusting, if it were people you could have them slapped in prison for that.

'Fact is,' said her sister Pauline, that afternoon, 'there's probably hardly a one in the village isn't his. Being the only tom round about, bar him on Lay's farm and he's beyond it if you ask me. So you let Ted Roper have it? Good on you, Jeanie.'

Jeanie, cooler now, calmer, righteous and ever so slightly heroic, went over it all again, word for word: I said, he said, so I said, and him as cocky as you like.

'He's a cocky little so-and-so,' said Pauline. 'Always was. I bet he got the wind up a bit though, Jeanie, with you bawling him out, you're bigger than he is.' She chuckled. 'Hey – d'you remember the time they got him in the girls' playground and Marge ripped the belt

off his trousers so he had to hold 'em up all afternoon? God –
laugh . . . ! Donkey's years ago.'

'Funny, isn't it,' Pauline went on, 'there's four of us in the village
still as were at school with Ted. You, me, Nellie Baker, Marge. Randy
he was, too. Remember?'

'Funny he's never married,' said Jeanie.

Pauline snorted. 'Out for what he can get, that one. Not that he'd
get it that often, is my guess.'

'Can't stand the man. Never could. 'Nother cup? Anyway, what I
say is, he ought to be made to have something done about that cat.
It's shocking. Shocking.'

In the basket chair the old cat raucously purred; Elsa, in a patch
of sunlight, lay flirting with a length of string.

'Sick of drowning kittens, I am,' said Jeanie. 'I'll have to get her
seen to after, like I did the old cat. Shame.'

'Shame.'

The two women contemplated the cats.

'I mean, we wouldn't care for it, if it were you or me.'

'Too right.'

'Not,' said Pauline, 'at that time of life. That's a young creature,
that is, she's got a right to, well, a right to things.'

'Hysterectomy's the nearest, if it were a person.'

'That's it, Jeanie. And you'd not hear of that if it were a girl.
Another matter if it's in middle life.'

'That cat of Roper's,' said Jeanie, 'must be going on twelve or
thirteen.' Later, as she walked to the shop, Roper's pick-up passed
her, loaded with slabs of timber, belting too fast down the village
street, Roper at the wheel, one arm on the sill, a young lad beside
him, one of the several who hung around him. She saw Roper see
her, turn to the boy, say something, the two of them roar grinning
across the cross-roads. She stood still, seething.

'Cardwell's boy, weren't that?' said Marge Tranter, stopping also.
'With Roper.'

'I daresay. What they see in that old devil.'

'Men's talk. Dirty stories, that stuff. Norman says he doesn't half go on in the pub, Roper. He's not a one for that kind of thing, Norman isn't. He says Roper holds out hours on end sometimes, sat there in the corner with his mates. Showing off, you know.'

'Fat lot he's got to show off about,' said Jeanie. 'A little runt, he is. Always was. I was saying to Pauline, remember the time you . . .'

'Pulled his trousers down, wasn't it? Don't remind me of that, Jeanie, I'll die . . .'

'Not pulled them down, it wasn't. Took his belt. Anyway, Marge, I gave him an earful this morning, I'll tell you that. That cat of his has been at my Elsa. I went straight down there and I said look here, Ted Roper . . .' A quarter of a mile away Ted Roper's pick-up, timber dancing in the back, dodged in and out of the traffic on the A34, overtaking at sixty, cutting in, proving itself. Cardwell's boy and Roper, blank-faced, bejeaned, the cowboys of the shires, rode the Oxfordshire landscape.

In the village and beyond, Roper's cat – thin, rangy, one-eyed and fray-eared – went about his business.

And, according to the scheme of things, the ripe apples dropped from the trees, the *jeunesse dorée* of the area switched their allegiance from the Unicorn to the Hand and Shears taking with them the chattering din of un-muffled exhausts and the reek of high-octane fuel, the road flooded at the railway bridge and Jeanie's Elsa swelled soft and sagging like the bag of a vacuum cleaner.

'Several at least,' said Jeanie. 'Half a dozen, if you ask me. Poor little thing, it's diabolical.'

'There's a side to men,' said Pauline, 'that's to my mind just not like us and that's the only way you can put it. And I don't mean sex, nothing wrong with that when the time and the place are right. I mean . . .'

'It's a kind of men rather, I'd say. Harry's not that way, nor was my Jim. I mean, there's men that are normal men in the proper way but don't go on about it.'

'In Italy,' said Pauline, 'all the men are the other kind. All of them. From the word go. Young boys and all. They wear bathing costumes cut deliberately so you can see everything they've got.'

'Which is something you can take as read, in a normal man. It doesn't need shouting about.'

'Exactly. If I were you, Jeanie, I'd give that cat a drop of cod liver oil in her milk. She's going to need all her strength.'

Perhaps also according to the scheme of things, Ted Roper's pick-up, a while later, was involved in circumstances never clarified in a crash with Nellie Baker's Escort at the village cross-roads. No blood was shed and the pick-up, already so battle-scarred as to be impervious, lived to fight again, but the Escort was crippled and Nellie Baker too shaken and confused to be able to sort out exactly what had happened except for a strong conviction that aggression had been involved. At the Women's Institute committee meeting she held forth.

'He came out of nowhere and was into me before I knew what was happening. I was either stopped or the next best thing, that I'll swear.'

'What does he say?'

'Whatever he's saying's being said to the police. He took off, without a word hardly. It was Mr Latham ran me home and got the garage for me. I've told them my side of it, at the police station. It's up to them now.'

'The police,' said Jeanie Banks, 'have been down at Ted Roper's more than once. Asking about this and that. They could do some asking just now, the stuff he's got there and one wonders where it all comes from.'

'The police,' said Pauline, 'are men. Remember Ted Roper at school, Nellie? Jeanie and I were talking about that only the other day – how we used to take him down a peg or two.'

And, according to a scheme of things or not, no case was brought against Ted Roper for careless driving or dangerous driving or aggression or anything at all. Those who failed to see how that pick-up could have passed its MOT continued to speculate; Ted Roper's insurance company ignored letters from Nellie Baker's insurance company.

Jeanie's Elsa had five kittens, two of them stillborn.

Ted Roper, wiry and self-assured as his cat, continued to cruise the local roads, to make his corner of the pub an area of masculine assertion as impenetrable and complacent as the Athenaeum. From it came gusts of hoarse laughter and anecdotes which were not quite audible, bar certain key words.

It may have been the stillborn kittens that did it, as much as anything, those damp limp little rags of flesh. Or the sight of the emptied Elsa, restored to a former litheness but subtly altered, wise beyond her years. Or months.

Jeanie, tight-lipped, visited Marge to borrow her cat basket.

'You'll take her to be done, then?'

'Have to, won't I? Or it'll be the same thing over again.'

'Shame.'

'Just what Pauline said.'

Marge, lining the cat basket with a piece of old blanket, paused. 'It's like with people. Always taken for granted it must be the woman. Pills, messing about with your insides . . .' She swung the door of the basket shut and tested the catch. 'There's an alternative, Jeanie. Thought of that?'

'What do you think I was down Ted Roper's for, that time?'

'And much joy you got out of it. No, what I'm thinking of is we see to it ourselves.'

The two women stared at each other over the cat basket. Marge, slowly, even rather terribly, smiled. 'I wouldn't mind, I wouldn't half mind, giving Ted Roper his comeuppance.'

In a village, people come and go all day. Women, in particular – to and from the school, the shop, the bus stop, each other's houses. The little group of Jeanie, Pauline, Marge and Nellie Baker, moving in a leisurely but somehow intent way around the place that afternoon, glancing over garden walls and up the sides of cottages, was in no way exceptional. Nor, unless the observer were of a peculiarly enquiring turn of mind, was the fact that they carried, between them, a cat basket, a pair of thick leather gardening gloves, and a half a pound of cod wrapped in newspaper.

Presently, the cat basket now evidently heavy and bouncing a little from side to side, they emerged somewhat breathless from the field behind the pub and made their way rather hurriedly to the garage of Nellie Baker's house, where an old Morris replaced

47

the deceased Escort. The Morris drove away in the direction of Chipping Norton passing, incidentally, the very school playground where once, donkey's years ago, four outraged and contemptuous schoolgirls had a go at the arrogance of masculine elitism.

In a village, also, change is more quickly observed than you might think. Even change so apparently insignificant as the girth of a cat. In this case, it was habits as much as girth. A cat that has previously roamed and made the night hideous, and which takes instead to roosting, eyes closed and paws folded, in the sun on the tops of walls, idling away the time, will be noticed.

And the more so when the change eerily extends to the cat's owner. At first it was just the paunch jutting below the sagging belt of Ted Roper's jeans. Then, balancing the paunch, came a fullness to the face, a thickening of the stubbly cheeks, a definite double chin. 'Put on a bit, haven't you, Ted?' people said. 'Have to cut down on the beer, eh?' And Ted would wryly grin, without the perky come-back that might have been expected. With physical expansion went a curious decline of those charismatic qualities: the entourage of youths dropped off. Some nights, Ted sat alone in the pub, staring into his glass with the ruminative and comfortably washed-up look of his seniors. A series of mishaps befell the pick-up: punctures stranding Ted on remote roads, a catastrophic fuel leak, a shattered windscreen. It was driven, presently, in a more sedate way; it no longer rode or cruised but rattled and pottered.

It was as though the old assertive stringy cocky Ted were devoured and enveloped, week after week, by this flabby amiable lethargic newcomer. The jeans gave way to a pair of baggy brown cords. He began to leave his corner of the public bar and join the central group around the fireplace; there, the talk was of onions, the ills of the nation, weather and fuel prices. And, in the village or outside his own gate, meeting Nellie Baker, say, or Marge or Pauline or Jeanie Banks, he would pass the time of day, initiate a bit of chat, offer small gifts by way of surplus timber, useful lino offcuts, the odd serviceable tyre.

'Poor old so-and-so,' said Pauline. 'They're easily taken down, aren't they? That's what comes of depending on the one thing. You can almost feel sorry for them.'

A Clean Death

The train windows were still painted midnight blue for the black-out. Here and there, people had scraped at the paint, making channels and circles of bare glass behind which fled the darkening landscape. They had left King's Cross at four, in twilight, would be home, Aunt Frances said, by seven at the latest. Do, she had announced at the ticket office, assembling her welter of Christmas shopping – parcels and boxes from Harrods, Fortnum's, Marshall and Snelgrove – do call me Frances, just, I don't really like aunt, and Clive would like to be Clive, I'm sure. And Carol, smiling sideways, not looking at her, had known she could not, would have to say 'you' now, for always, be for ever picking her way round the problem. She huddled into her school coat, stiff with cold, her knees raw red between the top of her socks and hem of her skirt, and fingered again the ticket in her pocket, checked the brown suitcase in the rack, in which were her holiday clothes, her good tweed skirt and her two jerseys and the tartan wool dress bought today by Aunt Frances – Frances – with money sent by her father from India. The money had meant complicated arrangements of cheques and deposit accounts and Frances, irritated, queueing at the bank, glancing at her watch. Money from the bank in Calcutta, hot and crowded, rupees not pounds and shillings. Don't think of it, she told herself, the tears pressing again behind her eyelids, don't think of India. But it came, as it never ceased to do, clamorous with smells and sounds and what-used-to-be, and she sat, miserable with longing, watching the lights of Suffolk villages twinkle through the tattered black-out paint.

Frances, in her corner, was wedged beside a young soldier with hair so short his head seemed almost shaven, and battledress that smelled of damp and sweat; she had flinched away from him, Carol could see, turning to the window, reading her London Library book. She looked up, caught Carol's eye, and said, 'Ipswich in another few minutes now – lovely thought!'

I've put you in the spare room, she had said earlier, not in with Marian, I thought you might rather be on your own, and Carol, who had feared to be classified with her cousins, as a child, had been relieved. She did not know how to be with children, what to say, they made her feel awkward, inadequate. But I don't know how to be with grown-ups either, she thought, there is no one I talk to, I am quite by myself, it is as though I was some kind of thing there is only one of. At school she was not unpopular, but had no friends; she never walked with her arm round someone else's waist, or gathered over the tepid radiator in the form room, warming her hands and whispering. The other girls alarmed her; they were so worldly-wise, so cushioned by their confidence in how things were done, how to talk and act and respond. The school bewildered her, with the jungle of its customs and taboos. She remained uninitiated, an outsider, doing her best to use the right language, show the right interests, have the right emotions. She collected, as the others did, photographs of the royal family cut from newspapers; she stared at the battered fashion magazines passed from hand to hand, exhaustively discussed and analysed. At night, she lay silent in bed, hearing their whispers of cinemas and London musicals, and India created and re-created itself in the darkness, and she could hardly bear it. It set her apart from them, she knew; it was not quite the thing, to have been born in another country. It was not good to be different.

She knew it, and felt inadequate; there was nothing she could do about it, nothing could make her one of them. Sometimes, not often, they asked her about India, but their curiosity was brief, it would evaporate within minutes. She would be talking – of the house, the garden, the heat, the people – and they would be gone, their attention switched, back with their own concerns. The other thing they never mentioned. The girl who had shown her round, her first day – one of the prefects – had said, 'Bad luck about your mother, Carol,' and she had known that it was unmentionable, death you did not talk about, like God, or love.

She had learned how she ought to be, what was expected, and was quietly pleased that she had learned so much. She made fewer mistakes now, was more acceptable. She was managing.

The train slid to a stop. Frances opened the door, and steam oozed up between carriage and platform, cold air gushing in, and country voices, voices all related to one another, Carol could hear. Accents. There was a girl at school who had an accent; that was not good either, she too was apart. Her parents did not pay, it was said, she had the Scholarship. Listening, in streets, on buses, Carol felt dizzied, sometimes, by voices: different, the same, connected. Like the babel of tongues in an Indian bazaar. You have to know who you are, she thought, who other people are, or it is impossible, you do everything wrong. Often I do not know who I am.

They got out, festooned with parcels. If you could take the children's stocking presents, Frances said, and Nigel's train-set, I can manage the Fortnum's bag and the curtain stuff. And Clive will get the cases, no hope of a porter of course, not these days.

Clive had come up almost at once, out of the darkness, and Carol thought wildly: do I kiss him or not, I can't remember, is it all relations, or not men ones? But he solved the problem himself by holding out a hand, and they shook awkwardly, and yes, she said, I had a good term, and yes, it is lovely to think it's nearly Christmas.

In the car, bumping through the East Anglian night, Frances recounted the day. London was awful, she said, I can't tell you, the shops so crowded, such a struggle on the buses, but I got everything, nearly everything, there was a problem with John's school things, they hadn't the games socks in yet . . . She sounded tired, but triumphant, like a huntsman at the end of the day, the job done. The road shone wet black in the car headlights and the fields that slid by were ribbed with snow; it was bitterly cold. A frost tonight, Clive said, Marian's cold seems a bit better – oh, and Mrs Binns left a pie in the oven for supper, she said give it another half hour or so, after you get back.

They were close, easy, in their concerns, the running of their lives. Once or twice, remembering, they passed questions to her, or comments, over the back of their seats. Is it this summer you do School Cert., Carol, or next? This village is called Kersey, the church is so pretty, you'll have to walk over one day and have a look.

They arrived, and the house seemed to burst, spilling out into the night like a ripe fruit; light, voices, the small shapes of children running and leaping beside the car. Dogs barking. Wireless music. The country night lay black and still and freezing all around, and here was this confident, unassailable place, waiting. The children bounced and shrieked. Did you find the balloons? they cried, and have you got my ribbon, and are there any sweets? Mummy! they shrieked, Mummy! And Frances was hugging and recounting and saying, oh, and here's Carol, say hello to Carol.

Hello, they said, and then their voices were back on that note of excitement and demand, and everyone was going into the house, shutting out the darkness – the endless snowy fields, the black roads.

She woke early in the morning, perished with cold. She had got up in the night to put on her underclothes beneath her pyjamas, and then her jersey on top, and still had lain frozen in the bed, curled knees to chest, the rest of the bed an icy pond. She listened to the noises of the house expand around her: the children's scampering feet, their voices crooning to cats or dogs, the rattle of a boiler being filled, Frances and Clive talking in the bedroom. It was an old, wooden house; it rang and echoed. Presently she got up and went to the bathroom that Frances had said she should share with the children. It smelled of flannels and damp and toothpaste; there was a full pottie in the corner. She stripped to the waist as you had to do at school, and washed under her arms, up her neck, over the growing breasts that she felt must be so obvious, that slopped and bounced under her jerseys.

She dressed and went downstairs. On the bottom step there was a dog, a great golden lion-headed thing, lying right across it. She stood there, not knowing what to do, and it did not move, but looked at her and away again. And then one of the children – Nigel, the youngest – came from some room and saw her and said, 'Are you frightened of her?' And before she could answer he had gone running into the kitchen and she could hear him shout, 'Daddy! She's frightened of Tosca – Carol's frightened of Tosca.'

She could hear them laughing. Frances said, 'I expect she's not used to dogs, darling.' She came out and tugged at the dog's collar, still laughing, saying what a stupid, soft old thing she was, wouldn't hurt a fly, you mustn't mind her. And Carol could think of no reply: she was not afraid of dogs, liked them, but in India a dog may be rabid, you do not go near a strange dog, never. It was instinctive, now, the hesitation, a conditioned response, just as at night, always, she thought, for the rest of her life, she would feel unsafe without the shrouding security of a mosquito net.

Clive was in the kitchen, nursing a cat. He stroked and tickled it, talking baby-language to it so that Carol was both embarrassed and fascinated. There was something wrong, apparently, it was ill. 'Poor Mr Patch,' crooned Clive. 'Poor pussy. Poor patchums,' and the children gathered round soft with sympathy, offering it tit-bits. 'We are a terrible animal family, I'm afraid, Carol,' said Frances, frying bacon. 'Everybody is mad about animals. The children will show you the pony after breakfast.'

She trailed with the children, in a wind that cut through her mack, clutched her bare knees, was shown the garden and its secret places, the hens, the rabbit hutches, the pony, the orchard. And then they became involved in some game of their own and she came back into the house alone and stood at a loss in the kitchen, where Frances mixed things and talked to a woman washing up at the sink.

'This is Carol, Mrs Binns,' she said. 'My niece, you know.' And Carol felt herself appraised, not unkindly, not critically, just with the shrewdness of a person who liked to see what was what, how things were.

'You'll be much of an age with my Tom, I should imagine,' said Mrs Binns. 'Fourteen he was, in October. We'll have to get you together. He's at a loose end, in the holidays, Tom, there's no one much his age, not nearer than the village.'

At school there were girls who had, or who were rumoured to have, boyfriends. The reputation gave them an aura, of daring but also of distinction; they too were set apart, but in a desirable way. They had moved on a little, on and up. Carol knew no boys, had not, she thought, spoken to one since long ago, since nursery days on another continent. She stared at Mrs Binns in alarm.

'Mmmn,' said Frances. 'What a good idea,' and Carol, puzzled now, saw that for some reason it was not. But Mrs Binns, saying, 'Well, you must look in at the cottage, dear, your auntie'll tell you where it is,' had turned now to the table and taken up the pink and pimpled carcase of a chicken. 'I'll do this for you, Mrs Seaton, shall I?'

Frances looked at the chicken with distaste. 'Yes, please, if you would. A beastly job. I'd be sunk without you, I really would.'

Mrs Binns laughed. She stood at the sink, rummaging with deft, knowledgeable hands in the chicken's insides. 'It's a matter of what you're used to. I did my first bird when I was – oh, younger than Carol here.' Appalling things slid from within the chicken and lay on the draining-board. Frances, Carol saw, had turned firmly away, busy with her pie-dish. Carol said, 'In India you buy chickens live. They hang them up by their feet in the bazaar, in bunches.'

'How absolutely horrid!' Frances exclaimed; her voice was tense with emotion. Mrs Binns, halted in her work, looked up. Frances went on, vehemently, 'That is what is so awful about those places – they are so foul to animals. One really cannot stand it. I remember going to Morocco, before the war, and it simply spoiled the holiday, the way they treat the donkeys and things. You had to walk about

54

trying not to notice – it was wretched, we were so glad to come home.'

Mrs Binns said in neutral tones, 'It's not nice to see, cruelty to animals.' She swilled the chicken out under the tap and put it on a plate. 'His dad give Tom a gun for his birthday, for rabbiting, but he told him he's to use it properly, no maiming things, he's to see there's a clean death.'

Frances's face was set in disapproval. 'Mmmn. Isn't fourteen a bit young for a gun?'

Mrs Binns was packing the chicken with stuffing now. Crumbs of it fell from her fingers and lay on the table, smelling of herbs, of summer. 'Rabbits are terrible round us now – had all my cabbage. He's the makings of a good steady hand, Bob says – Tom has. Three he got, last week.'

'Mmmn,' said Frances again. She got up, putting away flour and fat. 'Could you do the bedrooms next, Mrs Binns, and then I think the dining-room windows need a going over.'

At lunch, Frances and Clive talked of Mrs Binns. Clive said that she was a card, quite a character, and tales were recounted, remarks that Mrs Binns had made, her opinions, her responses. They were told with affection, with indulgence – much, Carol noted, as the children were spoken of in their absence. 'But,' said Frances, 'I cannot approve of that boy being given a gun. They *will* start them off slaughtering things so early, people like that, I hate it.'

Marian said in stricken tones, 'Does he kill rabbits, Tom? Oh, *poor* rabbits . . . Mummy, can't you tell him not to?'

'No, I can't, darling, it's not up to me. There, don't think about it – I don't expect he does it much. Finish up your sausage and then you can get down.'

One girl at school got letters from her boyfriend. It was known, and envied. She took them away and read them alone, in the cloak-room, and later could be seen, pink-faced and giggling, poring over selected passages with her best friend. Carol said, staring at the bowl of frost-nipped chrysanthemums in the middle of the table, 'Mrs Binns said I could go over to her cottage sometime.'

There was a silence. Clive picked up the cat and blew softly into its fur, murmuring to it. 'Poor Mr Patch,' he mumbled. 'How are your insides today – how's your poor tummy?'

'Yes,' said Frances. 'Well, just as you like, Carol.' She began to clear the table. 'I think a walk this afternoon, to the village and back, I need some things from the post office, anyway.'

The landscape was black and white under huge white skies – black ploughlands striped with white runnels of snow, criss-crossed with the dark lines of hedges, trimmed with the stiff shapes of trees. They walked along a road bordered by fawn-coloured rushes and grasses, each one starred and bearded with frost; icy wind poured through the skeletal hedges; there was a chain of crisp puddles along the uneven surface. The children skittered ahead, sliding on the ice, darting off into the fields on brief excursions. Clive and Frances walked arm in arm, Carol a few paces behind. Their talk and occasional laughter came back to her in irrelevant, incomprehensible snatches. I am so cold, she thought, colder than I have ever been, colder even than I am at school, will I ever be warm, how do people get warm, ever, in their lives? In India, in childhood, she had been too hot; always, one was sticky with sweat, looking for a place out of the sun. I cannot remember that now, she thought, I have no idea, really, how it was, it is like something in a book, something that happened to someone else. The gap had lengthened between her and the others; Frances, looking back over her shoulder, called, 'Not far now – we shall have to get you used to walking, Carol.'

At the house, in Frances's sitting-room, on the desk, there was a photograph of her and her brother, Carol's father, in youth. Around seventeen or eighteen. It was a bad photograph, muzzy, and Carol had not at first recognized the faces. Then, her father's familiar features had somehow emerged, but displaced and distorted; the boy in the photograph was him, and yet not him. She thought of this, and of herself; her hands, thrust into the pockets of her school coat, were rigid with cold; it was three o'clock in the afternoon, there was no reason, it seemed to her, why this day should not go on for ever. She stumped behind Frances and Clive, through the sphere of that silent, suspended landscape; it is so lovely here in summer, Frances had said, quite perfect, you must come in August, in the holidays.

At nights, at school, the other girls planned and recalled; the long thin room in which she slept with eight others was filled with dis-embodied voices, whispering in the dark of holidays past and holidays to come, of what they had done and what they would do. The limbo of the term was put away; they roamed into other times, other places. And Carol lay silent; to roam, for her, had too many dangers. Recollection must be checked; that way lay disaster. And the other way? She had nothing there, either, to offer; no plans nor expectations.

The children came running from a field, solemn-faced and import-ant, with a dead bird they had found, a lapwing, bright-plumaged and uncorrupt, its eyes closed by filmy lids. Marian was on the brink of tears. Her father took the bird and they huddled round him, quiet and comforted, as he dug a grave, lined it with leaves, buried the body, marked the place with a ring of berries collected from the hedges. 'I don't expect it *felt* anything, Mummy, did it?' begged Mar-ian. 'It didn't *hurt* it, did it?' And Frances said, 'No, darling, it would be just like going to sleep, it would hardly know anything about it.'

In the village, Frances bought things in the warm, cluttered post office that smelled of soap, matches and bacon; the children fingered and fidgeted, their voices shrill and confident. 'This is my niece Carol,' Frances explained, 'who is here for the Christmas holidays.' And the shop lady, petting the children, giving them each a toffee from a personal store behind the till, hesitated, the open tin in her hand, as also did Carol hesitate; we neither of us know, she thought in despair, what I am, if I am a child or not. The shop lady reached a decision, good or bad, and put the tin back on its shelf, unproffered.

On the way back, Marian pointed suddenly over the fields and said to Carol, 'That's Mrs Binns's cottage, down that track: they've got chickens, and a dog called Toby.'

Carol stared over a grass field, patched with unmelted snow; smoke filtered from a chimney, barely darker than the sky; washing hung limp on a line in stiff geometric shapes of sheets, towels, shirts with outstretched arms.

On Christmas morning she lay in bed hearing the children open their stockings in their parents' room across the corridor; their high-pitched voices alternated with their parents' deeper ones like a series of musical responses, statement and commentary. She heard their feet pattering on the bare boards, the dogs barking in excitement; the animals too had Christmas presents – bones wrapped in scarlet crepe paper, beribboned rubber mice. The day proceeded through a series of ceremonies and rituals: after breakfast we have presents under the tree, before church we telephone grandmother, in the afternoon we walk to Clee Hill. Frances said, 'I forgot to tell you, Carol – tomorrow our old friends the Laidlaws are coming. Mark is fifteen so he will be someone for you, I thought – it is dull for you, being always with the younger ones.'

The children did not like her, she knew. At first they had been shy, the small boys arch, trying to appeal as they would appeal to a grown-up. But they saw her now for what she was, neither fish nor fowl, not exempt like them from adult obligations, but without adult privileges either. Sharp-eyed, they noted her position as a class-less person, without position, and exploited their own the more; if she would not join in their games when they wanted her to, they complained to Frances, and Carol felt her aunt's resentment, unstated but none the less evident. I have a hundred things to do, her silent back said, the least you could do is help to amuse them for a while. They danced around Carol, more agile in every way; they made her feel lumpish of mind and in body.

The prospect of Mark filled her with apprehension. He is at Marlborough, said Frances, he is awfully clever, he has such nice manners, we have always liked him so much.

They came, the Laidlaws; there were kisses and handshakes and the house was filled with talk, with people at ease with one another. Mark, Carol furtively noted, had longish hair that flopped over one eye and was dressed as a man – tweed jacket, grey flannels, grown-up tie. He sat next to Frances at lunch and talked with what Carol saw to be charming attention, listening when listening should be done, taking the initiative when that was appropriate. After lunch he played with the children – an absurd game of crawling on the floor, romping, and he was in no way diminished by it, it made him seem more grown-up, not less so. And Frances beamed upon him.

He had said to Carol, 'Where do you go to school?' She had replied to this. He had asked her how many School Cert. subjects she was doing and she replied to that too. And then there had been a silence, she had searched wildly for something to fill it, and seen that he wanted to get away from her, to get back to the others, that she did not interest him. 'It must have been awfully exciting, growing up in India,' he said. 'What was it like?' and India swirled in her head, a kaleidoscope of sights and sounds and responses, and there was nothing she could say. 'Yes,' she stammered. 'It was . . . I mean . . . Yes, I . . .', and felt Frances's gaze upon her, observing, regretting. 'Have you ever seen Gandhi?' he asked, and she shook her head.

Later, in the evening, Frances said, 'The Laidlaws are having a small party for Mark, at the New Year, but of course you will be gone by then, Carol – they were so sorry.'

It snowed in the night. She drew her curtains and saw the landscape powdered over, not deeply, but shrouded as it were, in a state of suspension once again, motionless. The children, outside, were rushing about trying to scoop up enough for snowballs or snowmen; they came in wet and querulous, their hands scarlet with cold. Their exhilaration disintegrated into tears and fretfulness; Frances was irritable. Later, she had letters to write, and the children wanted to go to the village, to buy sweets. Carol can take us, they cried, and Frances, relieved, said yes, of course, Carol can take you – wrap up well; don't let them run on the road, Carol.

They met him on the way back. She was walking behind the children, who were quiet now, amiable, tamed by chocolate. He came down the track from the cottage, the gun crooked over his arm, and they arrived together precisely at the gate. Marian said, 'Hello, Tom.'

He nodded, 'Hello.' And then he looked at Carol and smiled, and quite easily, without her eyes sliding away to left or right, without a problem, she smiled back. He said, 'Mum told me you were stopping with your auntie.'

The children wanted to see the gun. But their curiosity was tinged, even at this remove, with Frances's disapproval. In silence they watched him demonstrate its workings; his thin fingers clicked this and pressed that, ran over the sleek metal, caressed the polished butt. He was immensely proud of it; in his light voice, not yet broken, a boy's voice, but with its sudden odd lurches into manhood, he described the make and model. It was not a toy, it was real, serious, it marked him. It told him what he was. 'My dad gave it me for my birthday. My fourteenth. He reckoned you can learn to use a gun, then, when you're fourteen, it's time.'

The children were restive, moving away. Come on, they said, let's go, it's cold, let's go home.

Tom turned to Carol. 'I'll be going out tomorrow morning, shooting. Early, when it's getting light. Sevenish. You could come if you like.'

She said, 'Yes, please', before she could stop to think. 'Right,' he said. 'Come by the cottage then, and we'll go.'

She walked back to the house amazed; things like this did not happen, it was astonishing, she could hardly believe it.

It was in the cold, wakeful reaches of the night that it struck her she should have told Frances, asked Frances. But now it was too late. Frances was asleep: at seven – before seven – she would not be about. And suppose she said no, or even just implied no? I have to go, Carol thought, I must go, it is the only thing that has ever happened to me.

She woke again long before dawn and lay looking at her watch every few minutes. When it said half past six, she got up, making as little noise as possible, and dressed in all her warmest things. But she was warm already, for the first time in days, weeks, it seemed, and when she crept down the stairs, and opened the back door the air outside was tinged with mildness, she thought. The wind that met her face was not so keen, and the snow, in the drive, had melted. Only in the lee of the hedges it lay still in thickish drifts.

It was almost dark. The sky was streaked with light in the east; dark clouds lay like great fish along the horizon. She walked down the road and there was no one else in the world, except her; she was alone, and it was quite all right, she felt confident, at ease with things, she walked briskly with her hands in her pockets and there was beauty in the landscape that wheeled around her, she could see that. It was still and quiet, clenched in its winter state, but there was a flush of reddish brown on the plough, where the snow had melted, and the bare shapes of the trees on the skyline were of amazing delicacy, they held the suggestion of other times, the ripeness to come, summer.

She hesitated outside the cottage door; there was an easy murmuring of voices from inside, and the chink of crockery, and smells of toast and something frying. And then a man came out, at that moment, in old jacket and muffler, his trousers clipped ready for a bicycle – Tom's father, presumably – and told her to go on in, Tom wouldn't be a moment.

Mrs Binns gave her a cup of tea, but she could not eat the food offered; she felt in her stomach all the instability of before a journey, before an event. But it was good, it was the best thing she had known, beyond things which must not be remembered, things from other times. Tom said little; he attended to the gun with oil and a rag and a stick, and when he had done, he got up and said, 'We'll be off now, Mum,' and Carol rose too, in a state still of amazement. She felt quite comfortable, quite in place. I have a friend, she thought, and could hardly believe it.

He led her over the fields, up a shallow hillside. Out of the cottage, he became talkative. He told her about the ways of rabbits, and how you must go after them downwind, towards their burrows, towards the slope where he knew they would come out to graze around now. He had shot two, he said, the week before, and Carol said, no, three your mother said, and he corrected her, carefully – two it was, one I missed, I told Mum, she got it wrong. I'm not good with sighting, he said, seriously, not yet, and I've got a shake in my wrist, I'll have to work on that, and she nodded, intent, and stared at his wrists. They were bony wrists, white-knobbed, sticking out from the frayed sleeve of his too-short jersey. His hair was cut short, almost cropped, like the soldier in the London train. He spoke with the accent of the place, this place to which he belonged, where he had been born, where his parents had been born; sometimes she could not quite follow what he said. She thought confusedly of this, as they climbed the hill, the ground wet and springy under their feet: of her own speech, which was quite different, and of the place where she had been born, none of whose many tongues she spoke. Once, climbing a gate, he gave her the gun to hold for a moment; she felt the sting of the cold metal on her hands, and cradled it gingerly, with reverence. They reached the side of the field where, he said, the rabbits would come. It ran downhill from a small copse, and she could see the brown markings of burrows at the top. He edged cautiously along the ditch until he came to a place in long grass where they could lie and wait. 'They might have heard us,' he said. 'We'll have to sit tight a bit, and they'll come out again.'

They lay flank to flank on the wet grass. She could feel its damp and cold creep through to her skin, and the faint warmth of his body beside hers. Their breath steamed. Occasionally they whispered a little; it was better, though, he said, to stay quiet. He seemed to expect nothing of her; if she had not complied, if she had infringed the rules in any way, he did not let her know. He let her hold the gun again, and she peered down the long barrel into the field and saw, suspended cinematically beyond it, the cropped turf with its dark enigmatic holes and scrapings of rich earth and pockets of snow. He said, 'They're a long time about it, usually they come out quicker than this, once you've sat quiet a bit,' and she could feel the tension in him; the rabbits mattered, they were the most important thing in his life just now. She said suddenly, amazed at her own temerity, 'What is it like, killing something, do you like it?' And turning to look at him, saw with shock that a slow tide of colour had crept up his face.

'I don't like them dying,' he said, mumbling with his head to the ground, so that she could hardly hear. 'I hate that. The first time I came out with my dad, I felt sick, I didn't want to do it. I couldn't say, not to him. He gave me the gun, see, for my own. Now it's all right. They die quick, it's over just like that.' He looked at her, his face still red. 'It's not for the killing, it's not for that.'

She nodded. There wasn't anything to say. And then suddenly he touched her arm, pressed his fingers down on her coat, and she looked out towards the field and there was movement on the turf, something brown shifting against the green – two, three of them. One sat up, nosing the wind, and she saw its pricked ears, and, as it turned, the white scut. He lifted the gun, aimed; she was clenched in excitement, breathless. And then he pressed the trigger, and the noise was startling, louder than ever she had imagined, but in the second before, in a fraction of a second, something had happened out there and the rabbits had bolted, homed back on their burrows, gone. The field was empty.

She said, '*Oh* . . .' He sat up, breaking the gun apart angrily, unloading. 'Won't they come out again?'

He shook his head. 'Not for hours, maybe. That's done it, that has. Something scared them.' His hands were shaking, she could see that, they had been shaking earlier too, when he lay still on the grass, aiming. Now he seemed almost relieved. 'Come on,' he said. 'Have to get back. Mum'll be wondering.'

They ran down the field; there was no longer any need to be quiet. At the gate he showed her how he could vault over it, and she, who was unathletic, who lumbered hopelessly around the games pitch at school, found that she could do it also; there was no end, it seemed, to the surprises this day held. There are bits of me I know nothing about, she thought, I am not so clumsy after all, I can talk to people, I can feel part of something. The sky was crossed and recrossed by ragged flights of birds. 'What are they?' she asked. 'What kind of bird is that?' and he told her that those were rooks, and these on the plough, in the field, were lapwings, surprised at her ignorance but uncritical. 'Mum said you grew up somewhere else,' he said, 'somewhere foreign,' and she talked about India; she brought heat and dust and the sound of the place on to this wintry Suffolk field and it was painless, or almost so.

At the corner of the track to the cottage he asked her if she would like to come out again the next morning; she had half-expected this and yet not dared to hope. Such coincidence, in the normal way of things, of what you would like and what was available, did not happen. She said, 'Yes please,' and thought it sounded childish, and blushed.

Back at the house, she was amazed to find it past breakfast-time, Frances clearing the table, the children staring as she came in at the kitchen door, Clive reading a letter. Frances sounded annoyed. '*There* you are, Carol, we were beginning to wonder, where have you been?'

She had prepared nothing, given no thought to this moment. She stood, silent with confusion, and then one of the children said, 'She's been shooting rabbits with Mrs Binns's Tom. We heard him ask her yesterday.'

Frances swept things off the table on to a tray. 'Oh, really. I can't imagine why you should want to, Carol, I must say.'

'Did he kill any rabbits?' said Marian.

Carol muttered, 'No.' She could feel her face scarlet; the day, and all that it had held, died on Frances's kitchen floor; she felt dirty.

'Goody,' said Marian. 'Can I go out now?'

Clive had not spoken; he had put down his letter and was playing with the dog, gently pulling its ears, mumbling to it; Carol, catching his eye by accident, saw it go cold, excluding her. 'Well,' he said to the dog, 'walkies, is it? Walkies for a good girl?' The dog beamed and fawned and swished its feathered tail.

All that day was sourly flavoured with Frances's disapproval; nothing was said, but it hung in the air at lunchtime, in the afternoon, over tea. Mrs Binns did not come, for which Carol was grateful; there would have been references, Tom would have been mentioned, and that she could not endure.

In the afternoon there was a letter from her father, enclosed in one to Frances. She read it by the drawing-room fire, and it seemed to come not from another country but from another time; his familiar handwriting, speaking of the house, the garden, neighbours, referred to things that no longer were, they had perished long ago. 'Poor Tim,' said Frances, reading her own letter. 'He is so anxious to get home, pack things up out there. It must be trying for him, but it is not long now, he has booked his passage.' Carol read that the bulbuls had nested again in the bush outside the laundry, that the cannas were a lovely show this year, that the rains had come early; it was as though he were frozen in another age, her father, in an imagined world. She asked, in sudden panic, 'Will he really be here this summer, here in England?' And Frances, preoccupied now with the demands of the children, of the hour, said that of course he would, he was bound to, the house was sold, the furniture to be packed and shipped. If you are writing to him, she went on, you had better put it in with mine, and save the stamp.

Lying awake, after everyone else had gone to bed, Carol knew that she would go with Tom in the morning. She had thought about it, on and off, all day; she felt grubby, condemned by Clive's cold eye, by the children's indignation. '*Poor* rabbits,' Marian said once. 'I think it's beastly. Horrid Tom,' and she had answered nothing, being without defence. Now, staring at the dim square of the window, she knew that she would go, had to go, whatever they thought, whatever happened. Guilt clutched her; she lay sleepless for most of the night.

He was waiting for her at the bottom of the track. 'Hello,' he said, 'I thought you weren't coming,' and his innocence compounded her guilt. She carried now the burden not only of what she was doing, but of the fact that he did not know what they were doing, did not know that what they did was wrong, despised by decent people.

They climbed the hill again. It was raining; the wind blew wet sheets into their faces and they walked with heads down, not talking much. At the gate Tom did not vault but climbed over; Carol noticed how thin his legs were, childishly thin, like his bony wrists. Walking behind him, she observed that his hair made a ducktail at the nape and that the cleft had the softness, the look of vulnerability that the back of a small boy's neck has. She saw, for a moment, the ghost of the child that he had recently been; Mark Laidlaw's stocky frame had suggested the man from whom he stood at one remove. She thought of her own body, which seemed always to scream out in conflict – the alien, uncontrollable breasts, the pudgy hands and face, the scar on her knee that remembered a fall when she was ten. Her body held her back; at the same time, it dragged her inexorably onwards.

At the place where they had waited before, he gestured her down into the grass. They lay again side by side, staring through rain-studded greenery at the point in the field where something might happen. The time passed slowly; it stopped raining and a weak sun shone opalescent behind the clouds. Occasionally, they murmured to each other. 'Taking their time again,' he said. 'Hope I'll have better luck today.' And she nodded and murmured yes, hope so, and ssh! look, isn't that one? no, it's just a thistle, sorry. Something had lifted, things had eased once more, guilt had been put to flight; Frances, Clive and the children no longer hovered behind her shoulder. The crystal globes of water on the grass blades shivered with a thousand colours; the dried head of a summer flower held between delicate stalks a miniature of the landscape beyond skyline trees, clouds; the sun on the back of her hand was a breath, a promise, of warmth.

And then, together, they saw it on the grass beside the burrow; a moment ago it had not been there and now suddenly there it was, quietly munching grass, bobbing away a yard or so, sitting up to sniff the wind.

He raised the gun, hesitated for what seemed far too long, fired.

The rabbit bucked into the air. Bucked, and at the same time screamed. The sound was hideous; it rang over the field, obscene in the quietness of the morning. She cried, 'You got it! You hit it!' and they jumped up together and ran across the grass.

And saw, together, at the same moment, that the rabbit was not dead. It lay threshing and writhing and as they came near it screamed again, humanly, like a hurt child, and they pulled up short and stood there in horror, a few yards off, staring. Blood welled from its ear; it writhed and twitched.

Tom was shaking. His voice was high-pitched, out of control, 'I got to do something. You got to kill them, when that happens, you got to finish them off.'

She said, 'Oh, I don't want to see!' and turned away, her hands over her eyes, but then turned back, moments later, and he was standing above the rabbit, white-faced, and the rabbit bleated again, and arched its back, and kicked. He said, 'I don't know what to do. I've seen my dad do it: you have to break their necks. I don't know how to do it.' He was distraught.

She covered her eyes again.

When she looked back, he had the rabbit in his hands, and the rabbit was limp. Blood dripped from it. He put it on the ground and it lay still. He was shaking violently. He moved away a few paces and sat on the grass, turned from her, and she could see his whole body tremble. She felt sorry for him, and yet at the same time exasperated. She could not help him; they were quite separate now, it was as though they did not know each other; the whole fragile structure of confidence, the sense of being at ease with the world, had been destroyed with the rabbit. She saw Tom, wretched, and could think only: I am wretched, too, I hate myself, and what we have done, and what people must think of us for it.

He got up, without a word, and began to walk away down the field, and wordlessly she followed him. He carried the gun all anyhow, not with pride, cradled over his arm; it looked, now, disproportionately large, as though it had grown and he had shrunk.

At the road he turned to her. 'Don't say anything about what happened – not to my mum.' She shook her head. 'Cheerio, then.'

'Goodbye.'

It was raining once more. She trudged towards the house; she was shrivelled with guilt. They did not know what had happened, could not know, but she felt that the very look of her announced the incident; she carried still, in her head, the rabbit's scream.

They were having breakfast. As she came into the kitchen silence fell and the children looked expectantly towards Frances.

Frances said, 'You'd better have something to eat, Carol'; her voice was not friendly. When Carol was sitting at the table she went on, 'It would have been a good idea, you know, to mention that you were going out with Tom Binns again. Clive and I are responsible for you, while you are here.'

Carol stared at the table. 'I'm sorry,' she said.

Clive had not looked once at her. He kept his back half-turned. Now, he busied himself giving milk to the cat. He poured the creamy top from a bottle into a saucer and put it by the stove. 'There, Mr Patch,' he murmured. 'There. Come on then, puss.' The kitchen was filled with well-loved, well-tended animals.

'Did Tom kill a rabbit?' said Marian in her small, clear voice.

Scarlet-faced, Carol noted the bordered tablecloth: red flower, cluster of leaves, spray of berries, red flower again. 'Yes,' she muttered.

'Children,' said Frances, 'you can get down now and go up and do your teeth. Oh, and tidy your bedroom, please, Marian darling.'

They went. Clive said he thought he would just go now and do the hens and the pony before he went into Ipswich. He went.

Frances began to clear the table. The room was charged with feeling; once, she dropped a cup, and swore. Carol sat, the rabbit's scream still in her ears, behind and above the sounds of the children upstairs, of Frances running water at the sink, of the cat lapping milk.

Frances slapped plates on to the draining-board and spoke again, her voice assured and tinged with indignation, 'What I cannot understand – what Clive and I cannot understand – is why you should *want* to. I daresay it has been a bit dull here for you given that the children are a good deal younger and I am frightfully busy what with little or no help these days, not like it was for people before the war, but we've tried to find things for you to do and had Mark Laidlaw over who I thought would be just right for you, so I simply cannot understand why.'

The room spun; Frances's voice roared. Carol wrung the

tablecloth between her shaking fingers and burst out, 'He didn't mean to. Tom didn't mean to – he meant to do it like his father said, a clean death, not hurting it, and something went wrong, it wasn't. He felt awful about it. I don't think he'll go shooting again. *I* don't want to, not ever. I hated it. It was beastly, the rabbit being hurt like that.' She fought back tears.

Frances turned from the sink; she was staring now, in surprise, across the kitchen table. She said, 'What rabbit? What do you mean? I'm not talking about shooting rabbits, Carol, which is really neither here nor there, lots of people round here shoot rabbits and of course one wishes they wouldn't but there it is. I'm talking about why you should want to go off doing things with someone like Tom Binns, as though he were a friend or something, when surely you must realize that it really won't do. I don't know what Mrs Binns was thinking of, suggesting it, she is normally such a sensible woman.' She paused, and then went on, 'I know it has made things difficult for you, growing up out there in India, sometimes it is a bit confusing for you here, I daresay, but surely you must see that a boy like Tom Binns . . . well, it really doesn't do, you should know that, Carol.' The rabbit's scream died away; in its place there came, all innocent and unaware, Tom's voice of yesterday, explaining the workings of the gun. She stared at her aunt in bewilderment and thought: I don't know what you are talking about, I knew I had done one thing and now you are saying I have done another. It came to her suddenly that there was no way, ever, that she could oblige everyone, could do both what was expected of her, and what her own discoveries of what she was would drive her to do; she would have to learn to endure the conflict, as her body endured the conflict of what she had been and what she was bound to be, like it or not.

A Long Night at Abu Simbel

In Cairo they had complained about the traffic and at Saqqara Mrs Marriott-Smith and Lady Hacking had wanted a lavatory and blamed her when eventually they had to retire, bleating, behind a sand-dune. She had lost two of them at Luxor airport and the rest had sat in the coach in a state of gathering mutiny. Some of them were given to exclaiming, within her hearing, 'Where's that wretched girl got to?' At Karnak the guide hadn't shown up when he should and she had had to mollify them for half an hour with the shade temperature at 94°. On the boat, a contingent had complained about having cabins on the lower deck and old Mr Appleton, apparently, was on a milk pudding diet, a detail not passed on to the chef by the London office. She knew now that not only did she not like foreign travel or tour leading but she didn't much care for people either. She continued to smile and repeat that they would be able to cash cheques between five and six and that no, she didn't think there was a chiropodist in Assuan. When several of them succumbed vociferously to stomach upsets she refrained from saying that so had she. They sought her out with their protests and their demands when she was skulking in a far corner of the sun deck and throughout every meal. In the privacy of her cabin she drafted her letter of application to the estate agent in Richmond where there was a nice secretarial job going.

At Edfu the woman magistrate from Knutsford was short-changed by a carpet-seller, to the quiet satisfaction of some of the others. At Esna Miss Crawley lost her travellers' cheques and Julie had to go all the way back to the temple and search, amid the pi-dogs and the vendors of basalt heads and the American party from Minnesota Institute of Art (biddable and co-operative, joshing their ebullient blue-rinsed tour leader). They all called her Julie now, but on a note of querulous requirement, except for the retired bank manager, who had tried to grope her bottom behind a pillar at Kom Ombo, and followed her around suggesting a drink later on when his wife was taking a nap.

None of them had read the itinerary properly. When they discovered that they had an hour and a half to wait at Assuan for the flight to Abu Simbel they rounded on her with their objections. They wanted another plane laid on and they wanted to be assured that they wouldn't be with the French and the Japanese tours and Lady Hacking said over and over again that at least one took it, for goodness' sake, that there would be adequate restaurant facilities. She got them, eventually, into the plane and off the plane on to the coach, where the guide, Fuad, promised by the Assuan agency, most conspicuously was not. She went back to the airport building and telephoned; the Assuan office was closed. The man at the EgyptAir desk knew of no Fuad. She returned to the coach and broke the news in her most sprightly manner. The American coach and the French coach and the Japanese coach, smoothly united with their Fuad or their Ashraf, were already descending the long road to the temples in three clouds of dust.

They said their say. The coach driver spat out of the window and closed the door. They bumped across the desert. Lake Nasser lay to their right, bright blue fringed with buff-coloured hills. Those who had sufficiently recovered from their irritation at the non-appearance of Fuad exclaimed. Those who had not continued loudly to reiterate their complaints. The coach driver pulled up at the top of the track down to the temple site. They disembarked. Miss Crawley said she hadn't realized there was going to be even more walking. They straggled off in twos and threes and stood, at last, in front of the blindly gazing immensities of the god-king. Mrs Marriott-Smith said it made you think, despite everything, and Miss Crawley found she had blistered both feet and the chartered surveyor's wife was sorry to tell everyone she couldn't, frankly, see a sign of anywhere to eat. They stood around and took photographs and trailed in the wake of the guided and instructed French and Japanese into the sombre depths of the temple and when they were all out of sight Julie left them.

She walked briskly up the hill to where the American coach, its party already aboard, was revving its engine. She got on and went with them back to the airport, where, with a smile, she deposited an envelope containing twenty-two return halves of Assuan-Abu Simbel-Assuan air tickets with the fellow at the EgyptAir desk. She then boarded the plane, along with the American party. They were shortly joined by the Japanese and the French. The plane left on time; it always did, the stewardess said, truculently, glancing out of the window at the solitary airport building tipping away beneath.

The Magitours party continued to devote themselves to the site. They gathered in front of the stone plaque unveiled by Gamal Abdul Nasser as a memorial of international collaboration for preserving a human heritage. The other tours were now wending their way up the track to the coaches. 'Peace at last!' said Lady Hacking. 'I don't know which drive me dottier – those American women screaming at each other or the French pushing and shoving.' Mr Campion, the senior police inspector, being in possession of an adequate guide-book, assumed the role of the absent Fuad and briefed them on Rameses the Second and on the engineering feat involved in hoisting the temples to their present position. The party, appropriately humbled by the magnitude of both concepts, moved in awe around the towering pillars of the temple and the equally inhuman twentieth-century shoring-up process within the artificial hillside. They all agreed that it was frightfully impressive and well worth coming for. Those still suffering from internal disorders were becoming a little fidgety, and Mrs Marriott-Smith was longing for her dinner, but on the whole the mood was genial. They emerged from the temple and sat around admiring the lake, tinged now with rose-coloured streaks as the late-afternoon sun sank towards the desert. Some of the women put their woollies on; it was extraordinary how quickly it got chilly in the evenings. Mr Campion read out more from the guide-book. None of them paid any attention to the distant hootings of the coach driver, at the top of the hill. Someone said, 'That damn girl's vanished again.'

The coach driver, hired for so long and no longer, hooted for five minutes. Then, in the absence of any instructions, he threw his cigarette out of the window and drove his empty coach back to the depot.

The sun had almost completely set when the first of them reached the airport building. The stragglers, including the grimly stoical Miss Crawley, now hideously blistered, continued to arrive in dribs and drabs for another quarter of an hour. It had been a good two miles. It was Mr Campion who discovered the envelope with the flight tickets, shoved carelessly to one side of the EgyptAir desk. And it was another ten minutes or so, as the party slowly gathered around him, subdued now and in a state of mingled fury and apprehension, before the penny dropped. 'I simply do not believe it,' said the chartered surveyor's wife, over and over again. The EgyptAir official, subjected to a barrage of queries, shrugged, impassive. Those on the edges of the group, who could not quite catch what was going on, pushed closer, and as the enormity of their plight was conveyed from one to another, the murmurs grew louder. Mr Campion, determinedly keeping his cool, concentrated on the EgyptAir fellow. 'When is the next plane, then?' There was not another plane; the last plane left each evening at five-thirty.

'Then,' said Mr Campion with restraint, 'You'll have to call Assuan, won't you, and have them send up another plane.' The EgyptAir official smiled.

'Oh, rubbish,' said Mrs Marriott-Smith. 'Of course they can send another plane. Tell him not to be so silly.' The EgyptAir official

shrugged again and made a phone call with the air of a man prepared, up to a point, to placate lunatics. The outcome of the call
was clear to all before he put the receiver down.

'All right, then,' said Lady Hacking. 'We shall just have to endure.
Ask him where the local hotel is.'

The police inspector, a man accustomed to matters of life and
death, did not bother to reply. The woman's manner had been getting on his nerves for days anyway. He simply pointed towards the
long windows of the airport building, overlooking a vista of desert
enlivened here and there with a scrubby tree or a skulking pi-dog
and sliced by the single runway. The sand, now, was lilac, pink and
ochre in the sunset. The rest of the group also followed Mr Campion's pointing finger.

'Heavenly colours,' said the Knutsford magistrate. She had
tended to display artistic sensibilities since the first morning in Cairo
Museum.

The dismay, now, was universal. 'I don't *believe* it,' said the chartered surveyor's wife. 'You'll damn well have to,' snapped her
husband. The group, with appalled mutterings, surveyed the uncompromising reality of the airport hall. There were half a dozen rows
of solid plastic bucket seats in bright orange, welded to a stone floor
with a thick covering of dust, two or three plastic tables, and a soft-
drinks counter attended by a young boy who, like the EgyptAir
official and the several cleaners or porters, watched them now with
mild interest. There was also the EgyptAir desk, on which the official
had placed a grubby sign saying CLOSED, some tattered posters on
the walls of the Taj Mahal and Sri Lanka, and a great many overflow-
ing rubbish bins. Those who had already sped into the ladies' lavatory
had found it awash at one end with urine and attended by a woman
who handed each client a dirt-spattered towel and stood expectantly
at their sides. Lady Hacking pointed accusingly at the swilling floor;
the woman nodded and indicated one of the cubicles from which
fumed a trail of sodden toilet paper: 'Is no good.'

'Then *do* something,' said Lady Hacking sternly.

It was now six-thirty. The group, with gathering urgency, had converged on the soft-drinks counter. It was Miss Crawley, a late-comer, who revealed that all that was left were half a dozen cans of 7-Up and four packets of crisps. Those in possession of the only three packets of sandwiches and the single carton of biscuits sat watching, in defiance or guilt according to temperament. 'There are thirteen of us,' announced Miss Crawley loudly, 'without anything at all.' The principle of first come first served was in direct collision now with some reluctant flickerings of community spirit. The two retired librarians offered a sandwich to Mrs Marriott-Smith, who accepted it graciously; they did not offer, it was noted, to anyone else. The temperature had now fallen quite remarkably. The few who had coats put them on; most people shivered in shirt-sleeves and light dresses. The architect who had served in Libya in 1942 reminisced, as he had done before – too often – about the desert campaign. The chartered surveyor's wife told everyone that bloody girl would be bound to get the sack, if that was any comfort. Miss Crawley, with a sigh, took a book from her bag and began ostentatiously to read. A clip-eared white cat lay on one of the plastic tables, luxuriantly squirming. The Knutsford magistrate reached out to stroke it; the cat flexed its claws and opened a red mouth in a soundless mew; Miss Crawley observed without comment.

Outside, it became dark. The EgyptAir official was no longer there. Those sufficiently interested – and resentful – pin-pointed a bungalow at a far corner of the airfield in which lights cosily glimmered. The soft-drinks boy continued to slump at his counter and the ladies' lavatory attendant emerged and squatted on the floor outside. The one remaining porter or watchman came to squat beside her, smoking and exchanging the occasional desultory remark. They ignored the Magitours party, who were now dispersed all over the hall in morose clumps, sitting on the upright bucket seats or leaning against the EgyptAir counter. The architect tried, unsuccessfully, to get together a foursome for whist. Those who were unwell sat near the lavatories, grim-faced. The Knutsford magistrate offered the cat a crumpled ball of newspaper; it lashed out a paw and she withdrew her hand with a squeak.

'I hope it's not rabid,' said Miss Crawley with interest. 'You have to expect that, in places like this.' The magistrate examined her hand, on which beads of blood had appeared. 'Oh *dear . . .*' said Miss Crawley. 'I wonder if it's worth putting on some antiseptic.' The magistrate, glaring, applied Kleenex.

It was at around nine-thirty that the feelings of those without provisions of any kind became insupportable. The mutiny was provoked by the revelation that the surveyor's wife was in possession of a cache of oranges, Ryvita and Garibaldi biscuits which she now attempted furtively to distribute among those of her choice. The murmurings of those excluded became impossible to ignore; Mr Campion, eventually, rose to his feet, crossed the hall and had a brief and gruff word with the surveyor's wife, who bridled angrily. He then cleared his throat and announced that given the circumstances some kind of a kitty situation as regards food might be a good idea. This produced a small assorted pile which Mrs Campion, with evident embarrassment, divided up and carried round on a tray borrowed from the soft-drinks counter. The several sick said they didn't want anything, prompting further complex and minute division. These comings and goings caused a considerable diversion – so that it was some while before anyone – including his wife – noticed that there was something wrong with old Mr Appleton. He sat slumped down in his seat, intently muttering and emitting, from time to time, a sort of bark that was neither laughter nor a cry of distress. His wife, with as much embarrassment as concern, leaned over him, murmuring exhortations. Presently one of the librarians bustled across with a bottle of mineral water. Aspirins were also produced, and a variety of throat lozenges.

'Poor old chap,' said the Knutsford magistrate. 'Mind, I've been thinking all week he was ever so slightly gaga. What a shame.'

Others declared that they weren't surprised – this was enough to unbalance anyone. 'You know what it makes me think of?' said the Knutsford magistrate. 'That place in Orkney – Maeshowe. Anyone been there?' No one had; those for whom she had already over-done the widely travelled bit returned emphatically to their books or their magazines. 'Oh, it's quite extraordinary – you really should go. BC three thousand or something but the fascinating thing is these Viking inscriptions by some sailors who spent the night there in a storm and one of them went barmy.' There was a silence. The cat, writhing seductively, wrapped itself round the magistrate's calf; she pushed it away with her bag.

'How does your hand feel?' enquired Miss Crawley.

'Perfectly all right,' said the magistrate with irritation. She watched the cat, which sat lashing its tail. Miss Crawley lowered her book and eyed it. 'Of course, all the animals out here look unhealthy. What *is* that on its mouth?'

At eleven o'clock the only functioning ladies' lavatory packed up, a circumstance causing a frail-looking and hitherto silent woman to burst into ill-concealed sobs. Someone else's husband admitted some amateur plumbing proficiency, rolled up his sleeves and braved the now softly rippling floor. 'Good chap,' said the police inspector loudly.

The attendant at the soft-drinks counter wrapped himself up in a tartan rug, lay down and was seen to fall instantly into deep and tranquil sleep. 'Lucky sod,' said the architect. 'Mind, we used to be able to do that, back on the Halfaya Ridge.'

'Oh, do shut up about the Halfaya Ridge,' said Mrs Marriott-Smith, her voice inadequately lowered. The architect, a more sensitive man than was superficially apparent, and who had shared a genial lunch-table with her and Lady Hacking only yesterday, sat in bristling silence. 'Ssh, dear,' said Lady Hacking. 'Of course, these people aren't made like us physically. It's something to do with their pelvises. Haven't you noticed how they can squat for hours?'

'What absolute nonsense,' muttered the police inspector's wife. Lady Hacking swung round, but was unable to identify the speaker.

The party, by now, had divided into those determinedly enduring in as much isolation as possible and those seeking – tacitly – the faint comfort of collective suffering. One or two had tried to clean up a section of the floor and lie down upon it, inadequately cushioned by newspapers and the contents of handbags, but soon gave up. A few people, drawn to authority, had settled themselves around Mr Campion, as though in wistful belief that he might yet effect some miracle. Old Mr Appleton continued to mumble and bark; his wife, now a little wild-eyed, plied him with mineral water.

Mrs Marriott-Smith said, 'Oh my goodness, it *can't* only be half past midnight . . .'

'Tell you what,' said the chartered surveyor's wife. 'We should do community singing. Like people stuck on Scottish mountains.' She giggled self-consciously. 'Don't be so damn silly,' muttered her husband. Miss Crawley, lowering her book, stared with contempt: 'A peculiarly inappropriate analogy, if I may say so.' No one else spoke. The chartered surveyor's wife got out a powder compact and dabbed angrily at her nose. A detached observer, arriving now at Abu Simbel airport, could not have failed to detect something awry. The complex lines of hostility and aversion linking the members of the Magitours group were like some invisible spider-web, grimly pulsing. Apart from the small group of acolytes around Mr and Mrs Campion, the bucket seats, in their uncompromising welded lines, were occupied in as scattered a manner as possible. Married couples were divided from other married couples by an empty seat or two. Solo travellers like Miss Crawley and the Knutsford magistrate sat in isolation. The two retired librarians had fenced themselves off, pointedly, with a barrier of possessions spread over two unoccupied seats. Old Mr Appleton's barking and muttering had cleared a substantial area around him; he appeared, now, to be asleep, his jaw sagging. From time to time someone would cough, shuffle, murmur to spouse or companion. An uneasy peace reigned, its fragility manifest when someone grated a table against the floor. 'Some of us,' said Lady Hacking loudly, 'are trying to get what rest we can.'

It was at one-forty-five that Mr Appleton, apparently, died. He sagged forward and then toppled to the ground with a startling thud, like a mattress dropped from a considerable height. His wife, for a moment or two, did nothing whatsoever; then she began, piercingly, to shriek.

Everyone stood up. Some, like the Campions, the Knutsford magistrate and the librarians, hurried over. Others hovered uncertainly. Miss Crawley, moving to a position where she could see what was going on, said loudly that one must assume a stroke, so there probably wasn't a lot to be done but in any case, there was no point in crowding round. Those trying to offer assistance had split into two groups, one devoted to Mr Appleton, the other admonishing his wife, who continued, with quite extraordinary vigour, to scream. 'Hysterics,' said Mrs Marriott-Smith. 'Something I know all about. We had a girl for the children who used to do it, years ago. Someone should slap her face – it's the only thing.'

Mrs Campion, her arm round Mrs Appleton's shoulders, was imploring her to be quiet. 'It's all *right*. Everyone's doing what they can. Do please stop making that noise. *Please.*' Mrs Appleton paused for a moment to draw breath, glanced down at the prone body of her husband, and began again. 'Be quiet!' ordered the inspector. 'Stop that noise!' The librarians and the magistrate were arguing about whether or not to turn Mr Appleton over. 'I tell you, I *know* about this sort of thing – he shouldn't be moved.' 'Excuse me but you're wrong, I know what I'm doing. Is he breathing?' 'I don't think so,' said the magistrate, her words unfortunately falling into a momentary respite in Mrs Appleton's screams, and serving to set her off again nicely.

The soft-drinks attendant had unfurled himself from the tartan rug and, along with the lavatory attendant and the porter, stood watching with interest. 'Tell them to get a doctor,' said Lady Hacking. 'I should think that's the best thing to do.'

'Shut up, for Christ's sake, you stupid woman,' said the police inspector. There was a startled silence; even Mrs Appleton, briefly, was distracted. Lady Hacking went brick red and turned her back. The chartered surveyor's wife burst into frenzied laughter. The Knutsford magistrate, kneeling over Mr Appleton, looked up and snapped that she didn't frankly see what there was to laugh about just at the moment. Mrs Appleton had been led to a seat somewhat apart and was being damped down, with some success, by Mrs

Campion. Mr Campion, having picked up the receiver of the phone on the EgyptAir desk and listened for a moment, was trying to convey to the porter that the EgyptAir official must be summoned. 'Is sleeping,' said the porter. 'Office closed.' 'Give him some baksheesh,' advised the architect. The police inspector, a big man, ignored this; he leaned forward, seized the porter's jacket in either hand, and violently shook him. The lavatory attendant uttered a shrill cry of outrage.

'Frightfully unwise,' said Mrs Marriott-Smith loudly. 'That simply isn't how to deal with these people.' Interest, now, was diverted from the Appletons to the EgyptAir counter.

The porter, muttering angrily, picked up the phone, and, presently, was heard to speak into it. 'Tell him to bloody well get over here at once,' said Mr Campion, 'and bloody well get on to Assuan for us.'

'The man doesn't understand English,' said Miss Crawley.

'At least some of us are trying to *do* something,' hissed the magistrate. 'Which is more than can be said for others.'

Miss Crawley stared, icily: 'There's no need to be offensive.'

Lady Hacking, tight-lipped, was sitting stiffly while Mrs Marriott-Smith spoke in a mollifying undertone. 'I have no intention,' said Lady Hacking loudly, 'of getting involved. One simply ignores such behaviour, is what one does.' The chartered surveyor's wife gazed at her, beady-eyed.

The porter had put down the phone and was loudly reiterating his grievances. 'All right, all right, old chap,' said the engineer. 'We've got the message. Calm down.' Mrs Appleton continued keening; Mrs Campion, still in attendance, was becoming visibly impatient. The woman who had been reduced to tears by the collapse of the surviving ladies' lavatory was again quietly weeping. 'I just want to be at home,' she kept saying. 'That's all. I want to go home.'

At this point Mr Appleton twitched convulsively and made an attempt to roll on to his back. 'He's coming round,' announced the magistrate. 'Good grief! I thought he'd croaked, between you and me.' The librarians, with cries of encouragement, heaved him into a sitting position.

The porter, shrugging, looked meaningfully at Mr Campion: 'Is OK now.' 'Go to hell,' said the police inspector, advancing towards Mr Appleton, who was heard to ask where he was. 'Don't tell him,' advised the engineer. 'It'll be enough to knock the poor fellow out again.'

Mrs Appleton, supported by Mrs Campion, was led across to her husband and began attempting to brush the dust off his trousers and jacket while reproaching him for giving everyone such a nasty shock. The old man, ignoring her, allowed himself to be helped up into a seat; he stared round, wheezing. 'That's the ticket,' said the police inspector, patting him on the shoulder.

The EgyptAir official arrived, tie-less and with one shirt-tail untucked. The porter fell on him in noisy complaint. The police inspector, cutting in, took him aside. 'Spot of baksheesh might save the situation,' said the architect. Mr Campion continued, in quiet but authoritative tones, to explain that a member of the party had been taken ill, and was undoubtedly in need of medical attention, but that fortunately the immediate crisis seemed to have passed. 'Man not dead,' stated the EgyptAir official, aggrievedly. 'No, I'm happy to say,' said Mr Campion.

And when, presently, dawn broke over the desert and a grey light crept into the airport building the scene there was one of, if not peace, at least an exhausted truce. A few of the Magitours party, done for, were in restless sleep; the others, raw-eyed, sat staring out of the windows at the reddening desert or braved the lavatories to attempt whatever might be done by way of physical repairs. The librarians graciously offered cologne-soaked tissues. A few people ventured outside for a breath of air and even wandered a little way along the road to the temples, at the far end of which those stone immensities, in their solitude, were contemplating yet another sunrise.

And when, three hours later, the first flight from Assuan decanted its passengers the arrivals found the place occupied by a party of people grim-faced but composed. Members of a Cook's tour bore down on them: 'I say, is it true you've been here all night? It must have been ghastly!' Those who saw fit to respond were deprecating. 'The odd little contretemps,' said Lady Hacking graciously. 'But on the whole we muddled through quite nicely.' Miss Crawley, in sepulchral tones, warned of the condition of the lavatories. The librarians, gaily, said it had been a bit like an air-raid in the war, if you were old enough to remember. Mrs Appleton, supporting her husband, who was demanding a morning paper, valiantly smiled. The wan appearance of the party was defied by an air of determined solidarity, even perhaps of reticence. 'The thing was,' said the Knutsford magistrate, 'we were all in the same boat, so there was nothing for it but to grin and bear it.' The exclamations and queries of the Cook's tour members were parried with understated evasions. Mrs Marriott-Smith assured the new arrivals that the temples were absolutely amazing, unforgettable, no question about that. 'Absolutely,' said the police inspector heartily. 'Extraordinary place.' There was a murmur of agreement and, as the Cook's tour filed towards their coach, the Magitours party, rather closely clumped together, made their way across the sand-strewn tarmac to the waiting plane.

A World of Her Own

My sister Lisa is an artist: she is not like other people.

Lisa is two years younger than I am, and we knew quite early on that she was artistic, partly because she could always draw so nicely, but also because of the way she behaved. She lives in a world of her own, our mother used to say. She was always the difficult one, always having tempers and tantrums and getting upset about one thing and another, but once mother realized about her being artistic she made allowances. We all did. She's got real talent, the art master at school said, you'll have to take care of that, Mrs Harris, she's going to need all the help she can get. And mother was thrilled to bits, she's always admired creative people, she'd have loved to be able to write or paint herself but having Lisa turn out that way was the next best thing, or better, even, perhaps. When Lisa was fifteen mother went to work at Luigi's, behind the counter, to save up so there'd be a bit extra in hand for Lisa, when she went to art school. Father had died three years before. It worried me rather, mother going out to work like that; she's had asthma on and off for years now, and besides she felt awkward, serving in a shop. But the trouble is, she's not qualified at anything, and in any case, as she said, a delicatessen isn't quite like an ordinary grocer or a supermarket.

I was at college, by then, doing my teaching diploma. Lisa went to one of the London art schools, and came back at the end of her first term looking as weird as anything, you'd hardly have known her, her hair dyed red and wearing black clothes with pop art cut-outs stuck on and I don't know what. It was just as well mother *had* saved up, because it all turned out much more expensive than we'd thought, even with Lisa's grant. There was so much she had to do, like going to plays and things, and of course she needed smarter clothes, down there, and more of them, and then the next year she had to travel on the continent all the summer, to see great paintings and architecture. She was away for months, we hardly saw anything of her, and when she came back she'd changed completely all over again – her hair was blonde and frizzed out, and she was wearing a lot of leather things, very expensive, boots up to her thighs and long suede coats. She came home for Christmas and sometimes she was gay and chatty and made everybody laugh and other times she was bad-tempered and moody, but as mother said, she'd always been like that, from a little girl, and of course you had to expect it, with her temperament.

Mother had left Luigi's by then, some time before, because of her leg (she got this trouble with her veins, which meant she mustn't stand much) but she started doing a bit of work at home, for pin-money, making cushions and curtains for people: she's always been good at needlework, she sometimes says she wonders if possibly that's where Lisa's creativity came from, if maybe there's something in the family . . .

It missed me out, if there is. Still, I got my diploma (I did rather well, as it happens, one of the best in my year) and started teaching and not long after that I married Jim, whom I'd known at college, and we had the children quite soon, because I thought I'd go back to work later, when they were at school.

Lisa finished at her art college, and got whatever it is they get, and then she couldn't find a job. At least she didn't want any of the jobs she could have got, like window-dressing or jobs on magazines or for publishers or that kind of thing. And can you blame her, said mother, I mean, what a waste of her talents, it's ridiculous, all that time she's spent developing herself, and then they expect her to be tied down to some nine-to-five job like anyone else!

Lisa was fed up. She had to come and live at home. Mother turned out of her bedroom and had the builders put a skylight in and made it into a studio for Lisa, really very nice, with a bare polished floor and a big new easel mother got by selling that silver tea-set that was a wedding present (she says she never really liked it anyway). But then it turned out Lisa didn't do that kind of painting, but funny things to do with bits of material all sort of glued together, and coloured paper cut out and stuck on to other sheets of paper. And when she did paint or draw it would be squatting on the floor, or lying on her stomach on the sofa.

I can't make head nor tail of the kind of art Lisa does. I mean, I just don't *know* if it's any good or not. But then, I wouldn't, would I? Nor Jim, nor mother, nor any of us. We're not experienced in things like that; it's not up to us to say.

Lisa mooched about at home for months. She said she wouldn't have minded a job designing materials for some good firm – Liberty's or something like that – provided there was just her doing it because she's got this very individual style and it wouldn't mix with other people's, or maybe she might arrange the exhibitions at the Victoria and Albert or the Tate or somewhere. She never seemed to get jobs like that, though, and anyway mother felt it would be unwise for her to commit herself because what she really ought to be doing was her own work, that's all any artist should do, it's as simple as that.

Actually Lisa did less and less painting, which mother said was tragic, her getting so disillusioned and discouraged, such a waste of talent. Mother would explain to people who asked what Lisa was doing nowadays about how disgraceful it was that the government didn't see that people like her were given the opportunities and encouragement they need. Goodness knows, she'd say with a sigh, it's rare enough – creative ability – and Mrs Watkins next door, or the vicar, or whoever it was, would nod doubtfully and say yes, they supposed so.

And then Bella Sims arrived and opened up this new gallery in the town. The Art Centre. Before, there'd only been the Craft Shop, which does have some quite odd-looking pictures but goes in for glass animals and corn dollies and all that too; Lisa was vicious about the Craft Shop. But Bella Sims's place was real art, you could see that at once – lots of bare floor and pictures hung very far apart and pottery vases and bowls so expensive they didn't even have a price on them. And Lisa took along some of her things one day and believe it or not Bella Sims said she liked them, and she'd put three of them in her next exhibition which was specially for local artists. Mother was so thrilled she cried when Lisa first told her.

Lisa was a bit off-hand about it all; she seemed to take the attitude that it was only to be expected. She got very thick with Bella Sims.

Bella Sims was fiftyish, one of those people with a loud, posh voice and hair that's just been done at the hairdresser and lots of clunky expensive-looking jewellery. She scared the wits out of me; and mother too, actually, though mother kept saying what a marvellous person she was, and what an asset for the town. I didn't enjoy the preview party for the exhibition, and nor did Jim; I was expecting Judy then, and Clive was eighteen months, so I was a bit done in and nobody talked to us much. But Lisa was having a good time, you could see; she was wearing all peasanty things then, and had her hair very long and shiny, she did look really very attractive. She met Melvyn at that party.

Melvyn was Bella's son. He taught design at the Poly. That meant he was sort of creative too, though of course not a real artist like Lisa. He fell for her, heavily, and who could blame him I suppose, and they started going round together, and then quite soon they said they were getting married. We were all pleased, because Melvyn's nice – you'd never know he was Bella's son – and we didn't realize till later that it was because of Francesca being on the way. Mother was rather upset about that, and felt she might have been a bit to blame, maybe she should have talked to Lisa about things more, but frankly I don't think that would have made any difference. Actually she worried more about Lisa not being able to paint once the baby was born. She was pleased, of course, about

Francesca, but she did feel it might be a pity for Lisa to tie herself down so soon.

Actually it didn't work out that way. Lisa got into a habit almost at once of leaving Francesca with mother or with me whenever she wanted some time to herself – she was having to go up and down to London quite a lot by then to keep in touch with her old friends from college, and to try to find openings for her work. I had my two, of course, so, as she said, an extra one didn't make much difference. It did get a bit more of a strain, though, the next year, after she'd had Jason and there was him too. Four children is quite a lot to keep an eye on, but of course mother helped out a lot, whenever her leg wasn't too bad. Bella Sims, I need hardly say, didn't go much for the granny bit.

Lisa had Alex the year after that. I've never understood, I must say, why Lisa has babies so much; I mean, she must *know*. Of course, she is vague and casual, but all the same . . . I've had my two, and that's that, barring accidents, and I'm planning to go back to work when I can, eventually. I daresay Lisa would think that all very cold and calculating, but that's the way I am. Lisa says she doesn't believe in planning life, you just let things happen to you, you see what comes next.

Alex had this funny Chinese look from a tiny baby and it took us ages to cotton on, in fact I suppose he was eleven months or so before the penny finally dropped and we realized that, to put it frankly, Melvyn wasn't the father.

It came as a bit of a blow, especially to poor mother. She went all quiet for days, and I must admit she's never really liked Alex ever since, not like she dotes on the others.

The father was someone Lisa knew in London. He was from Thailand, not Chinese, actually. But in fact it was all over apparently sometime before Alex was born and she didn't see him again.

Melvyn took it very well. I suppose he must have known before we did. In fact, Melvyn has been very good to Lisa from the start, nothing of what's happened has been his fault in any way. Not many men would have coped with the children like he has, right from the beginning, which he had to because of Lisa being away quite a bit, or involved in her own things. Truth to tell, he was better with them, too. It's not that Lisa's a bad mother – I mean she doesn't get cross or impatient, specially, she just doesn't bother about them much. She says the worst thing you can do is to be over-protective; she says mother was a bit over-protective with her. Bella Sims had some fairly nasty things to say; but then soon after that she sold the gallery and moved back to London and we never saw any more of her. This was the wrong kind of provincial town, apparently; art was never going to be a viable proposition.

Things got worse after Alex was born. Lisa went off more and more. Sometimes I'd find we had the children for days on end, or Melvyn would come round, pretty well at the end of his tether, saying could we lend a hand, Lisa was down in London seeing about some gallery which might show her stuff, or she'd gone off to Wales to see a woman who was doing the most fantastic ceramics.

It was after the time Francesca wandered off and got lost for a whole day, and the police found her in the end and then it turned out Lisa had been somewhere with Ravi, this Indian friend of hers, that things rather came to a head. Lisa and Melvyn had a row and Lisa brought all the children round to me, late one night, in their pyjamas, and said she was so upset about everything she'd have to go off on her own for a few days to try to think things over. Jim had flu and I'd just got over it myself so I was a bit sharp with her: I said couldn't Melvyn have them, and she said no, Melvyn had to teach all next day, which was probably true enough. And anyway, she said, they're my children, I'm responsible for them, I've got to work out what to do. She was wearing a long red and blue thing of some hand-blocked stuff, and lots of silver bracelets, and she looked exhausted and very dashing both at the same time, somehow; the children were all crying.

So I took them, of course, and she was gone for a week or so. We talked things over while she was gone. Jim and I talked, and Jim said (which he never had before) that he thought Lisa ought to pull herself together a bit, and I had to agree. It was easier with her not being there; somehow when Lisa's with you, you always end up feeling that she really can't be expected to do what other people do, I actually feel bad if I see Lisa washing a floor or doing nappies or any of the things I do myself every day. It does seem different for her, somehow.

And mother talked to Melvyn, who'd been round to find out where the children were. Mother was very sympathetic; she knows what living with Lisa is like; we all do. She said to Melvyn that of course Lisa had been silly and irresponsible, nobody could deny that. She told Melvyn, with a little laugh to try to cheer things up a bit, that there'd been occasions when Lisa was a small girl and was being particularly wilful and tiresome that she'd been on the verge of giving her a good smack. And then, she said, one used to remember just in time that there is a point beyond which she – people like her – simply cannot help themselves. One just can't expect the same things you can from other people.

I don't know what Melvyn thought about that; he didn't say. After the divorce came through he married Sylvie Fletcher who works in the library; I was at school with her and she's very nice but quite ordinary. Mother always says it must seem such a come down after Lisa. They've got a little boy now, and Melvyn takes a lot of trouble to see Francesca and Jason (and Alex too, in fact) as much as he can – and it *is* trouble because he has to trail down to London and try to find where Lisa's moved to now, unless it's one of the times Jim and I are having the children, or mother.

Mother and I had to talk, too. I'd gone round there and found her up in Lisa's old studio, just standing looking at a great thing Lisa had done that was partly oil paint slapped on very thick and partly bits of material stuck on and then painted over; in the top corner there was a picture of the Duke of Edinburgh from a magazine, sideways on and varnished over. I think it must have been meant to be funny, or sarcastic or something. We both stood in front of it for a bit and mother said, 'Of course, it is very good, isn't it?'

I said I honestly didn't know.

We both felt a bit awkward in there; Lisa has always been very fussy about her privacy. She says the one thing people absolutely have no right to do is push themselves into other people's lives; she is very strong for people being independent and having individual rights. So mother and I just had a quick tidy because the dust was bothering mother, and then we went downstairs and drank a cup of tea and chatted. Mother talked about this book she'd been reading about Augustus John; she's very interested in biographies of famous poets and artists and people like that. She was saying what a fascinating person he must have been but of course he did behave very badly to people, his wife and all those other women, but all the same it must have been terribly exhilarating, life with someone like that. You could see she was half thinking of Lisa. I was feeling snappish, the children were getting me down rather, and I said Lisa wasn't Augustus John, was she? We don't really know, do we – if she's any good or not.

There was a silence. We looked at each other. And then mother looked away and said, 'No. I know we don't. But she just might be, mightn't she? And it would be so awful if she was and nobody had been understanding and helpful.'

Lisa came back for the children once she'd found a flat. She'd had her hair cut off and what was left was like a little boy's, all smoothed into the back of her neck; it made her look about sixteen. Lisa is very small and thin, I should say; people always offer to carry suitcases for her, if you see her doing anything involving effort you automatically find yourself offering to do it for her because you feel she won't be able to manage and anyway it makes you feel guilty watching her.

She said the hair was symbolic; she was making a fresh start and getting rid of the atmosphere that had been holding her back (I suppose she meant poor Melvyn) and actually everything was going to be good because Ravi's father who was an Indian businessman and quite rich was going to buy a little gallery in Islington that Ravi was going to run and she was frantically busy getting enough stuff together for an exhibition.

The gallery didn't last long because it kept losing money and after a bit Ravi's father, who turned out to be quite an ordinary businessman after all and not as sensitive and interested in art as Lisa

had thought, said he was cutting his losses and selling up. In fact
Ravi and Lisa weren't living together by then anyway because Lisa
had realized that the reason her work wasn't really right was that
she'd always been in cities and in fact what she needed to fulfil herself properly was to get away somewhere remote and live a very
simple, hard-working life. Actually, she thought, pottery was the
right medium for her, once she could scrape up enough for a wheel
and everything.

Mother helped out with that, financially, and Lisa took the children down to this place in Somerset where a man she knew, someone
quite rich, had this big old house that was a sort of commune for
artists, and for parties of young people to come and study nature
and the environment. We went down there, once when Lisa wanted
us to take Alex for a bit, because he'd not been well and she was
finding it a bit of a strain coping with him. There was certainly a lot
of environment there, it was miles from anywhere, except the village, and there wasn't much of that, so that there seemed to be
more artists than ordinary village people. It was a hot summer and
Lisa and the rest were going round with just about no clothes on,
more like the south of France than west Somerset and I rather got
the impression that some of the older village people didn't like it all
that much, and there was an outdoor pop festival one weekend that
went on to all hours, and this man who owned the place had made
the church into an exhibition room for the artists. It was one of
those little grey stone churches with old carvings and so on and it
looked queer, all done out inside with huge violent-coloured paintings and peculiar sculptures. Lisa said actually it was frightfully
good for these people, to be exposed to a today kind of life, they
were so cut off down there, and to be given the sort of visual shock
that might get them really looking and thinking.

Eventually Lisa began to feel a bit cut off herself, and there'd
been some trouble with the county child care people which Lisa
said was a lot of ridiculous fuss, it was just that Francesca had got
this funny habit of wandering off sometimes and actually it was
good that she felt so free and uninhibited, most people *stifle* their

children so. Francesca was six by then, and Jason five. Jason had this bad stammer; he still has, sometimes he can't seem to get a word out for hours.

Lisa came home to mother's for a bit then, because rents in London were sky-high and it would have meant her getting a job, which of course was out of the question, if she was going to keep up her potting, and the weaving she had got very keen on now. And at mother's she had the studio, so it might work out quite well, she thought, provided she kept in touch with people and didn't feel too much out on a limb.

Jim and I had Alex more or less permanently by then; we are very fond of him, he seems almost like ours now which is just as well, I suppose. It is just as well too that Jim is the kind of person he is; Lisa thinks he is dull, I know, but that is just her opinion, and as I have got older I have got less and less certain that she gets things right. In fact, around this time I did have a kind of outburst, with mother, which I suppose was about Lisa, indirectly. She had gone down to London to keep in touch with people, and there had been a business with Francesca at school (sometimes she steals things, it is very awkward, they are going to have the educational psychologist people look at her) and I had had to see to it all. I was feeling a bit fed up too because what with Alex, and having so much to do, I'd realized it wasn't going to be any good trying to go back to work at the end of the year as I'd planned. Maybe you should be like Lisa, and not plan. Anyway, mother was telling me about this biography of Dylan Thomas she'd been reading, and what an extraordinary eccentric person he was and how fascinating to know. Actually I'd read the book too and personally I don't see why you shouldn't write just as good poetry without borrowing money off people all the time and telling lies.

Once, when I was at college, one of the tutors got this well-known poet to come and give a talk to the second-year English. He had glasses with thick rims and a rather old-fashioned-looking suit and frankly he might have been somebody's father, or your bank manager. He was very friendly and he talked to us in the common-room afterwards and he wasn't rude to anyone. I told mother about it, later, and she said she wondered if he was all that good – as a poet, that is.

And I suddenly blew up when she was going on like this about Dylan Thomas. I said – shouted – 'T. S. Eliot worked in an office. Gustav Holst was a bloody schoolteacher.'

Mother looked startled. She said, 'Who?' She's less interested in musicians.

I said crossly, 'Oh, never mind. Just there's more than one way of going about things.' And then the children started squabbling and we were distracted and the subject never came up again, not quite like that.

Lisa got a part-share of a flat in London with a friend; she had to be down there because there was this person who was talking of setting up a craft workshop for potters and weavers and that, a fantastic new scheme, and she needed to be on the spot for when it came off. It was difficult for her to have the children there, so Francesca stayed with mother and the two little ones with us. Francesca settled down well at school and began to behave a lot better, and Jason's stammer was improving, and then all of a sudden Lisa turned up, as brown as a conker, with her hair long again, and henna-dyed now, and said she'd met these incredible Americans in Morocco, who had this atelier, and she was going to work there and learn this amazing new enamelling technique. That was what she ought to have been doing all along, she said, if only she'd realized, not messing about with pots and fabrics. She was taking the children with her, she said, because growing up in an English provincial town was so stultifying for them, and it was nice and cheap out there.

She took Alex too, but after six months she suddenly sent him back again with a peculiar German friend of hers; we had to collect him at Heathrow. He kept wetting the bed apparently and although Lisa isn't particularly fussy about that kind of thing she said she had the feeling he wasn't very adaptable.

And so it goes on. She came back from Morocco after a couple of years, and there was a spell in London when a rather well-off Dutch person that we thought she was going to marry bought her a house in Fulham. For six months Francesca went to a very expensive school where all the teaching was done in French, and then the Dutch person went off and Lisa found the house was rented, not paid for like she'd thought, so she came home again for a bit to sort things out, and Francesca went to the comprehensive.

And then there was Wales with the Polish sculptor, and then the Dordogne with the tapestry people, and London again, and back here for a bit, and the cottage in Sussex that someone lent her . . .

The last time she was here she had a curious creased look about her, like a dress that had been put away in a drawer and not properly hung out, and I suddenly realized that she is nearly forty now, Lisa. It doesn't seem right; she is a person that things have always been in front of, somehow, not behind.

Mother and I cleaned out her old studio, the other day. Mother has this feeling that Francesca may be talented, in which case she will need to use it. We dusted and polished and sorted out the cupboard with Lisa's old paintings and collages and whatnot. They all looked rather shabby, and somehow withered – not quite as large or bright as one had remembered. Mother said doubtfully, 'I wonder if she would like any of these sent down to London?' And then, 'Of course it is a pity she has had such an unsettled sort of life.'

That 'had' did not strike either of us for a moment or two. After a bit mother began to put the things away in the cupboard again, very carefully; mother is past seventy now and the stooping was awkward for her. I persuaded her to sit down and I finished off. There was one portfolio of things Lisa did at school, really nice drawings of flowers and leaves and a pencil portrait of another girl whose name neither mother nor I could remember. Mother put these aside; she thought she might have them framed and hang them in the hall. Holding them, she said, 'Though with her temperament I suppose you could not expect that she would settle and at least she has always been free to express herself, which is the important thing.' When I did not answer she said, 'Isn't it, dear?' and I said, 'Yes. Yes, I think so, mother.'

Bus-Stop

The 73 bus, plunging from the heights of Islington down Penton-ville Road towards King's Cross, put on a burst of speed between the traffic lights. The conductor, collecting fares from the standing passengers, smiled indulgently: a private smile, and hardly detect-able in any case below the lush droop of his yellow-white moustache. He was a big man, a shambling figure with a stoop, the London Transport jacket even more ill-fitting than most, hanging lankly on him, the trousers sagging and supported by a broken belt.

'Any more fares then? King's Cross next stop!'

The diction was upper class – Edwardian upper class at that, a whiff of long-retired statesman about it; indeed, his whole head, if you isolated it from the grey uniform jacket and the paraphernalia of the ticket-machine, was that of, say, some city magnate, the kind of face that features in *The Times* above a brief note about an appointment to chairmanship of a bank or building society. Any incongruity, though, attracted no interest; a good many of the bus passengers, indeed, were foreign in any case and perhaps impervi-ous to such subtleties. A Scandinavian couple wanted South Kensington and were redirected on to a 30. The lower deck thinned out at King's Cross and the conductor went to stand for a moment at the end of the aisle, leaning against the driver's window, his very large feet braced against the floor, stooping slightly to keep an eye out of the window and humming to himself. He had an expression of benign detachment, but there was also something faintly *louche,* a suggestion, the merest hint, of afternoon drinking clubs, of the odd flutter on the horses.

At Euston he came loping down the aisle to help a woman with a pushchair. As the bus halted at the Park Crescent traffic lights he restrained an elderly man from getting off – 'Not the stop, watch it! Just hang on till we get across the lights.' In Gower Street he remonstrated with a bunch of teenagers pushing their way up the stairs against the descending passengers. He ran an orderly bus, it was apparent. At the Great Russell Street stop he paused a full minute or so before ringing the bell to direct a party of Japanese to the British Museum; a querulous fist knocked on the panel of the driver's window. 'All right, all right,' he muttered amiably, reaching for the cord. The bus swung round into the seedier wastes of New Oxford Street, leaving behind it the grace of Bloomsbury, its cargo constantly mutating – raincoated map-laden tourists, bright-eyed shoppers, girls with rainbow hair, a West Indian woman with a tiny staring doll-like baby propped over her shoulder.

At the bottom of Tottenham Court Road there was a surge from a waiting queue, sending the conductor racing up the stairs to check empty seats on the upper deck. The lower deck filled up completely. A plump woman in her late sixties, fur-jacketed, forged her way panting to one of the seats up front. The bus proceeded in fits and starts along Oxford Street; the conductor moved down the aisle, collecting fares.

When he reached the fur-jacketed woman she said, 'Barkers, please', delving in her purse. Then she looked up, met the conductor's gaze fair and square, and gave a gasp that caused heads to turn.

'Hello, Milly,' said the conductor. 'Fancy seeing you. Barkers – forty, that'll be.'

The woman found, at last, speech. 'George!' She clutched a pound note in a gloved fist, staring transfixed.

The conductor glanced back at the platform, rang the bell for the request stop. 'How's Philip, then?'

'George . . .' whispered the woman. 'I don't believe it. Oh my God, how could you . . .'

'Come on, Milly,' said the conductor with a trace of impatience. 'How could I what? Forty, please.'

The woman closed her eyes for a moment and hugged the jacket about her. She turned to the conductor, spoke in shocked hushed complicity; 'Oh my God, George, what would Shirley say . . .'

'Look, turn it down would you, Milly.' The bus lurched, stopped. 'Oxford Circus! Anyone for Oxford Circus?' Passengers jostled on and off. 'I'll come back, Milly. Forty, to Barkers.' He made for the platform, gave an arm to a woman with a stick, stowed another pushchair for a mother, swung up the stairs.

When he was on the top deck, sorting out two English-less Spaniards wanting Harrods, the bell urgently rang. Someone shouted up, 'Oy – there's a lady been took ill down here.' The conductor, with a sigh, hurrying but unfussed, made his way down. The bus had come to rest alongside a jeans shop; music gushed into the street. There was an atmosphere of unrest on the lower deck. People craned and stared; at the front two women had stood up. The conductor pushed his way through.

'What's up, Milly?'

She was leaning forward, her head in her hands. Her voice rose faintly from beneath her hat, from amid her furs.

'The shock, George . . .'

'Oh, come off it,' said the conductor briskly. 'It's a job, that's all. What d'you expect? Can't pick and choose at sixty-one. I'm fine.'

'It's not you I was thinking of.' Querulously. 'You were always difficult, George. Poor Shirley . . .'

The passengers rustled and peered. A singer screeched from the jeans shop. 'Look,' said the conductor, 'you'd better get off, Milly, if you're feeling under the weather. I'll stop a taxi.'

She raised her head. 'She'd turn in her grave, I tell you.'

A girl now pushed her way up the aisle; a girl in her mid-twenties, blonde neat hair to her shoulders, also in London Transport grey. 'What's the matter, George?'

'Nothing. Small problem, that's all. Leave it to me, there's a good girl.'

'What's up, luv?' said the girl.

Milly transferred, now, her attention. She stared suspiciously. 'What's she doing? What does she want? She's never the . . .'

'She's the driver. Now d'you want to get off or don't you, Milly? We can't stay here.'

She closed her eyes again. 'I simply do not believe it. The *driver*. A girl that age.'

'What's wrong with that?' said the girl angrily. 'I'm qualified. Who is she, anyway?'

'My sister-in-law. Take no notice.' The conductor gave her a pat, headed her back down the aisle. 'Come on, let's push off. I'll sort things out.' Voices, now, were wanting to know what was going on. People were crowding on to the stationary bus. The conductor fought his way back to the platform. 'Full up! Sorry – full up on this one. Another behind.' The bus leapt forward, dislodging one or two of those standing. 'Watch it! Hang on there. Anyone for Selfridges? Selfridges next stop!'

Marble Arch and Park Lane siphoned off at least half the passengers. The conductor unfurled a pushchair for the West Indian woman and chucked the baby under the chin. He directed two Arabs to Grosvenor Square. He allowed himself, as the bus entered the long haul down Park Lane, a brief glance over into the park. Then he vanished to the upper deck. 'Any more fares, then, please . . .'

When he came down the bus had stopped at the lights. He reached, at last, Milly. 'All right, Milly, forty please.'

She held out a pound note between finger and thumb. 'What Philip will say, I dare not think. I simply dare not think.'

'Don't tell him then,' said the conductor amiably. 'But you won't be able to resist, will you, Milly? Make your day.' He tore off the ticket, held it out. The lights changed. The bus, a broad unoccupied stretch of road ahead, rushed forward.

Milly clasped the rail in front of her with both hands and drew in her breath sharply. 'Does she want to kill us all, that girl?'

'Oh, stuff it,' said the conductor. 'The girl's perfectly competent.'

'What's a girl want to do a job like that for, I'd like to know.'

'Rubbish, Milly. Plenty of women driving buses in the war.'

'That was different.'

He shrugged.

She took out a powder compact, bravely. 'You've got me shaking all over, George. When I saw you I thought I was dreaming. I said to myself, it's impossible, it can't be.'

'Oh, put a sock in it.' He turned back down the aisle. 'Hyde Park Corner! Next stop Hyde Park Corner!'

The clientele of the bus, Knightsbridge now within sniffing distance, had undergone a sea-change, shifted up-market, blossomed with leather and fur. 'Knightsbridge for Harrods!' called the conductor. 'Hold tight now!' He propped himself on the platform as the bus swung round the maelstrom of traffic and up Grosvenor Place, ran a huge hand round his shirt collar, curbed a woman trying to jump off at the lights. He contemplated, pensively, the green spread of the park as the bus halted throbbing on the corner; he marshalled passengers on and off at the next stop. The bus was now polyglot; it chattered in French, Italian, Arabic, unidentifiable tongues.

The next time he reached Milly she was waiting. A lengthy transaction over a five-pound note for which he had to find change gave her her moment. 'To set off on a simple ordinary little expedition to Barkers' sale for sheets and pillowcases – I'm staying with Mary Hamilton for a couple of days, not that you ever had a civil word for her, I remember – just any ordinary shopping excursion, and find your own brother-in-law handing you your bus ticket, it's beyond belief, simply beyond belief. And the bus driven by a chit of a girl, the sort of girl that should be doing a decent job behind a counter, not risking all our lives . . .'

'Leave the girl out of it, Milly,' said the conductor. He showered silver into an outstretched palm. 'Fifty, sixty, eighty, one pound. Thank you, madam.'

'And that frightful grey jacket thing . . . With a *number* on you. Shirley would *weep*.'

'Leave Shirley out too, d'you mind, Milly. Any more fares then? Albert Hall next stop!'

'And when I think of that gorgeous little house in Sunningdale, and Shirley's lovely drawing-room with the chintz three-piece . . .'

'I shouldn't,' he advised.

'Well, at least *she's* spared this.'

'That's right, Milly.'

'I'll never get over it. Never. I'll not sleep a wink tonight, I can tell you that now.'

'Get old Philip to give you a nice shot of whisky. Does marvels.'

The bus, cruising alongside the park, was relaxed now, easy, down to a dozen passengers, taking time off. Albert brooded in his Memorial; the Broad Walk swept grandly upwards; tulips stood in ranks. A woman heading for Oxford Street discovered she was going in the wrong direction; 'Oh, what rotten luck,' said the conductor, pulling the cord for the request stop. He stood on the platform, tugging at his moustache, watching a posse of shrieking French schoolchildren on the pavement. He turned to the interior of the bus; 'High Street Ken! Barkers next stop!' The French schoolchildren invaded at the traffic lights; 'Watch it, there! Only the lights – hold on, please.' The park was left behind; traffic gripped the bus; the pavements bloomed with racks of clothes, a field of Agincourt in crimson, puce, lilac and blue denim. He thumped upstairs to sort out the schoolchildren, rampaging overhead.

When he got down again the lower deck had filled. He arrived at Milly. 'And *how* old is that girl?'

'Milly, you've missed your stop.'

'A chit of a creature! One feels like writing to the papers.'

'I thought you wanted Barkers, Milly.'

She stared ahead, in transports of outrage.

'All right, then,' he said. 'That'll be another twenty pence, if you're stopping on the bus. And twenty more at Earls Court Road.'

She surfaced, glared, gathered herself into her coat, rose. 'I'm getting off. And there's no need to smile like that, George. I don't find anything amusing about this, nothing amusing at all.'

He agreed that it was not amusing. He escorted her down the aisle, handed her on to the pavement. She stood for a moment, stumpy, upright, befurred, affronted; 'I'm shattered, George. I simply do not know what to say.'

He inclined his head. 'Sorry about that, Milly. You've done your best, I'd have thought.'

'I'll never bring myself to use this route again.'

'Come, now, no need to go to those lengths.'

A blonde head appeared from the window of the driver's cab. 'What's up, George?'

'Nothing,' he called. 'Let's go.' The blonde head vanished; the bus quivered and moved. 'Cheerio, then, Milly. All the best to Philip.' A hand, a small hand, stuck now from the driver's window, thumb up. Milly, on the pavement, gave one hard, dismissive stare and turned away to the consoling certainties of Barkers' sale. The conductor stood braced on his platform, the bus plunging ahead for Hammersmith and the terminus.

The Crimean Hotel

Caroline Oakley had taken to foreign travel after the death of her husband, who preferred to spend holidays on the Cornish coast or in the western Highlands.

Caroline had had no complaints at the time, but after the first two or three searing years of widowhood she began to feel that she must take herself in hand and make a determined effort to live more positively. Travel was one of the tasks she set herself. She visited Italy and Greece, on group excursions with friends, and then became more ambitious. She joined the local Literary and Philosophical Society not for intellectual reasons but because she learned that it organized annual foreign tours; the trip for this year was to Yalta, on the Black Sea, to visit Chekhov's house. Caroline had seen *The Cherry Orchard* several years ago and had once had a collection of the short stories out of the library. One of them, she remembered, was set in Yalta – something about a lady and a dog; at the time she had been baffled and faintly irritated by it, the dog seeming in the event irrelevant.

But Chekhov, in a way, was neither here nor there. The interesting thing would be to go to the Black Sea, a place that had almost fabulous overtones, like Shangri-La or the Hanging Gardens of

Babylon. And it was in Russia, which was of course intriguing and then there were other associations – Florence Nightingale, the Charge of the Light Brigade. It would be well worth the subscription to the Lit. and Phil. and the enforced company of some of its members. In any case Caroline was by temperament a passive traveller, preferring to have arrangements made for her and thus be able to sit back and experience without the bother of decision and negotiation.

It was early September when the eighteen-strong group from Middleton Lit. and Phil. arrived at Simferapol airport in an Aeroflot Ilyushin. The inside of the Ilyushin had been exactly the same as the inside of any other large jet aircraft, down to the piped Muzak and the nets on the backs of seats for advertising material (though these were empty). The air hostesses had been dumpier than usual. Nothing felt, yet, at all alien. The group stood around on the tarmac commenting on the balmy sunshine and were processed through immigration and customs and eventually into an Intourist coach, carefully counted and recounted by the Intourist girl. Caroline, tired after the flight and disinclined for conversation, found herself a seat alone at the back and watched the landscape roll past: enormous harvested fields which presently gave way to mountainous country with vineyards and plots of sweetcorn. She felt melancholy and a little bleak and thought continuously of her husband. The first days of a holiday usually had this effect on her; Florence or Athens were overlaid by St Ives or Glenelg and she would move around within a capsule of recollection, staring out through the glass at the unreal world beyond.

The rest of the party were somewhat dismayed, upon arrival in Yalta, to find that their hotel was an immense cliff-like structure, commanding impressive views of the sea and the coast but fourteen storeys high and with a thousand rooms. The entrance lobby was a vast shiny-floored concourse in which scores of people milled about talking German and the languages of eastern Europe and looking like the holiday crowds of any other resort. The Middleton party gathered around their luggage while the Intourist girl went to claim the room keys; the county librarian, the only member of the Lit. and Phil. to have read carefully the information on the brochures they had been given, kept pointing out that they had in fact been told about the hotel. Most people, though, distracted by photographs of palms and bougainvillaea and nineteenth-century villas, had skipped the less evocative stuff about modern touristic facilities and formed a picture of some pleasant local *pension* with bosky courtyard. Still, as they kept saying to each other, there's a lot to be said for mod. cons. and reliable food.

Caroline Oakley, before she went to bed, stood on her balcony (a rather sickening drop below, at which she was careful not to look) and watched the light fade from the sky above the dark shapes of the mountains that rose so sharply from the sea. One of these mountains, seen from the coach, had had a bare rock surface towards its summit on which was a just-visible inscription in red paint; this had been translated by the guide – it said, apparently, 'Glory to the Party'. The Lit. and Phil. had joked about this; 'Catch me climbing Snowdon to write "Vote for Thatcher!"' said someone. The county librarian observed tartly that that was hardly an appropriate parallel. Caroline, in her capsule, had paid little attention; now, in the soft warm night air, she was filled for the first time with the sense of being in another country. On the next balcony, a deckchair scraped and someone said something in a tongue she did not recognize; music seeped up from far beneath; lights twinkled along the coast. The sea was quite flat and still, a shade darker than the sky, and split by a wide shimmering belt of reflected light from a huge yellow moon.

She tried to remember exactly when the Crimean War had been and what it had been about. Who was against whom, and who won? All she could recall was Florence Nightingale and the Light Brigade. She had read a book on Florence Nightingale fairly recently. Written from a feminist position, it had left Caroline rather more affected by the unenviable situation of men at that time. The descriptions of the sufferings of the soldiers were something you could not forget – typhus, cholera, gangrene, those hideous suppurating wounds. The mud and the cold; the sick and wounded laid out in rows like corpses; the operations without anaesthetic. As you read of all that, it was no wonder that you ended up paying little attention to what it had been all about or who won. Now, that seemed irrelevant – like the dog in Chekhov's story.

She looked down, gingerly, at the forecourt of the hotel, where Intourist buses roosted under a floodlight. Sevastopol, she supposed, must be somewhere further along the coast. Perhaps they would be taken there.

They were not to be, as it turned out. The Intourist girl said it would not be interesting. They would visit, on various days, the Livadia Palace where the famous conference took place, a vineyard, the Botanical Gardens and, of course, Chekhov's house. They were urged to take full advantage of the hotel's facilities – the saunas and massage rooms, the theatre in which there would be concerts of Ukrainian folk music, and the private beach accessible by lift.

Caroline went to the beach with other members of the party on the first morning. The lift, plunging precipitately down through the cliff, disgorged them into a tunnel just like the approach to a tube station – a curious way in which to go bathing. Once outside, the prospect was uninviting: narrow concrete promenades with rows of changing cubicles and shower-rooms, from which steps led down to a strip of shingle beach on which many people sat or lay upon wooden boards. The Lit. and Phil. party changed into swimming costumes and descended to the shingle, where they equipped themselves with boards and sat in the sunshine.

The sea, flat and motionless, was studded with heads and torsos. People swam round in circles or simply stood, chest deep. Beyond them the smooth grey expanse reached away to the horizon, quite empty – no white sails, no power boats. The Intourist girl, now wearing a flowered bikini, reiterated facts and figures about the development of the coast as a place of rest and recreation for the Soviet people. Caroline, gazing at that bare inactive sea, said, 'People don't go sailing?' The Intourist girl replied that Russian people were not very interested in boats.

'How odd,' said Caroline.

'No. Not odd. Just they are not interested.'

Caroline got up and made her way down to the water. The function of the wooden boards became apparent; the pebbles were quite excruciatingly painful to the feet, like walking on blunt knives. Lurching from side to side she achieved the water, which was tepid and full of very small inoffensive jellyfish that brushed against her thighs as she waded out. The sea slopped around her, lethargically; she sank into it, swam for a little and then trod water. All around her other heads stuck up. She turned away from the beach and stared out across the empty sea, the horizon now seeming very close, as though you could reach out and touch it. She wondered how far away Turkey was.

The afternoon was devoted to Yalta itself – a tour of the town on foot to be followed by the visit to Chekhov's villa. Shepherded by the Intourist girl, they walked slowly along the front amid decorous crowds, noting the absence of transistor radios, litter and hooliganism. People patiently queued at a funfair for dodgems and the big wheel; rows of teenagers sat on a wall, looking at the sea. They seemed to walk for a long time; the sea-front was more extensive than anyone had realized.

Caroline, falling behind the others at one point, and separated from them by the crowd – there really were a great many people – found a man alongside and was startled to realize that he was speaking to her: 'American?'

'English.'

There was a pause. 'I like very much England,' he said.

'Really?' said Caroline with interest. 'You've been there, then?'

He was a big burly man, balding, tanned, neatly dressed in clean white shirt and drill trousers. A large chrome watch glittered on a hairy arm; he evoked, for some indefinable reason, the sea. And indeed it emerged that he had worked as engineer on a refrigerator container ship plying the North Sea and frequently calling in at Hull, which accounted for his knowledge of England. He was recently retired and lived near Gorky. Still walking side by side, jostled by the thickening crowd (they were approaching the central square) they talked of Hull ('Very nice people – very kind – I am visiting in many houses of friends'), of the circumstances of Caroline's visit to the Crimea, of the man's situation, which perturbed her a little – an inadequate pension, food shortages, problems about accommodation which he had to share with a sister ('We are not always liking each other very much, I am afraid'). His openness surprised her.

They had caught up, now, with the rest of the group. Caroline explained her companion's familiarity with England; the conversation became more general; the Intourist guide said, 'And now we are making our visit to Chekhov's villa.' To Caroline she added, 'I think this is a very boring man, we must get rid of him.' 'No,' said Caroline. 'He's rather nice.' 'I do not think so,' said the girl. 'Good, here is our bus. Get on, please.'

The man, when Caroline looked out of the coach window, had vanished into the crowd. The woman beside her, wife of a prominent Middleton headmaster, said, 'How interesting – someone turning up like that and talking English. Hull, of all places!' Her husband leaned across the aisle: 'Mind you, their language teaching is a sight better than ours, it seems to me. But that chap had learned his on the job, one gathered. You had quite a chat, Mrs Oakley?' 'Yes,' said Caroline. 'We did.' The coach was squeezing through narrow streets; large Edwardian houses sheltered behind high walls and foliage; people clutching plastic carrier bags were queueing beside a lorry that had tipped a heap of potatoes on to the pavement.

The Chekhov villa was reached by way of a museum displaying memorabilia and photographs. Letters in glass cases; early editions of the works; a very long black coat, a pair of gloves, a handkerchief. A photograph showed the writer wearing what appeared to be that very coat, standing with two dogs beside a large watering-can. The dogs, prick-eared curly-tailed creatures, stared alertly at the camera; Chekhov looked sad. Caroline examined it for a couple of minutes, wondering if the dogs related at all to the dog in the story. She found their beady, interested eyes, gazing at one from eighty years ago, curiously moving. So, in some humdrum way, was the watering-can. The Intourist girl was recounting, in an uninterruptible monotone, the story of the last years of Chekhov's life: the tuberculosis, the exile to Yalta's beneficial climate, his loneliness separated from Olga Knipper and his Moscow friends. The Middleton party moved respectfully through the villa, fenced off by velvet ropes from the desk, the dining-table, the favourite chair. Caroline, alone for a moment in a small room overlooking a tree-filled garden within which little winding paths disappeared into greenery, could hear nothing but the creak of a floorboard and a clock ticking. She thought of long aching afternoons in an empty house.

That evening in the hotel a vocal group appeared in the immense dining-room; conversation was blotted out by the crash of amplified music. The Lit. and Phil., grimacing, ate without speaking, while rainbow shafts of strobe lighting swept across them. Caroline went to bed early with a headache and lay awake for a long time. She felt as though she had been sleeping in this room for many weeks. Its landscape was infinitely familiar: the matching orange-patterned curtains and bed spread, the cheap veneer dressing-table, the glass-topped chest, the squat fifties-style armchair. Above, below and on all sides were a thousand similar rooms, like the cells of a honeycomb, each with its embedded occupant or occupants, lying there dreaming in assorted languages. Eventually she got up, put the light on and fetched a book from her suitcase. Before getting back into bed with it she stood for a while looking at the map of the Soviet Union thoughtfully supplied by the hotel in a folder along with the list of charges for laundry, hire of a refrigerator, use of the sauna, etc. She saw a great shapeless mass cementing Europe to China; there were the familiar almost cosy outlines of Scandinavia, the Germanies, Austria, Hungary, Yugoslavia, neat and small, and then this immense sprawl of space – emptier and emptier of place-names – reaching across the top of the world with India and the Malaysian archipelago dangling from it. She put her finger on the Crimea and thought: there am I.

They visited the Botanical Gardens. They tasted Crimean wines at a vineyard. They walked or plunged in the lift down to the beach and swam in that tepid sea. People kept saying Russia somehow wasn't at all as one had imagined. On the fourth day they climbed once again into the coach to be taken to the Livadia Palace, scene of the conference. The Intourist girl recited recent history to them, doggedly, through the megaphone. Harold Innis, the headmaster, became irritated, interrupting *sotto voce*: 'Yes, yes, my love . . . we're not complete ignoramuses.' Inside the palace the party stood before glass cases and inspected the signatures of Roosevelt, Stalin and Churchill; the conference table, at the far end of an expanse of parquet, looked deceptively homely, like something you might have breakfast at. 'There is now exhibition of photographs,' announced the girl. 'This way, please.' 'Well, I don't know . . .' said Rosemary Innis. 'I'm not that mad about photography. I may just slip out and enjoy the gardens a bit.' 'Everyone comes, please,' said the girl sternly. 'It is very interesting. You will wish to see.'

They were war photographs. Caroline, absorbed, moved from one grey scene to another: a towering mound of German helmets, a man sitting head in hands beside the shot bodies of his wife and daughter, people digging in the rubble of Berlin, an aircraft embedded in the façade of an eighteenth-century Belgrade house, the lunar landscape of destroyed cities. A great bleakness crept over her; when someone spoke she could not reply but moved away to the window. Outside, some small children ran round and round on the gravelled paths of the palace gardens. One of the photographs had shown people sunbathing amid the ruins of Sevastopol. Caroline thought again of an illustration in that book about Florence Nightingale; soldiers laid out on stretchers, row upon row of them, mummy-like with bandaged arms, legs, heads.

They came out into the sunshine. 'We walk a little, I think,' said the Intourist girl. 'It is very nice to walk in these gardens.'

It was indeed. Caroline, though, still chilled by the photographs and feeling tired, sat down on a bench, saying to the guide that she would wait there until the rest of the party finished their tour. 'I think you will not like to be alone,' said the girl. 'It is better you come also.' 'I'll be fine,' said Caroline firmly. 'Please . . .' The group moved away among the trees.

It was hot. She lay back, her head against a tree, and closed her eyes. After a few moments, though, the sense of a presence made her open them. A man was standing over her – sprung, apparently, from behind the tree for there had been no one near when she sat down. He wore only a pair of bathing-shorts and glistened with sweat. It was, she realized with amazement, the man from the promenade at Yalta – the English-speaking engineer. He was smiling broadly.

'Good morning.'

'Good morning,' said Caroline.

'I am very pleased to be seeing you again.'

She continued to stare at him, quite nonplussed. He carried a rolled bathing-towel under one arm which he shook out and applied vigorously to his shining bronzed torso.

'I am very hot. I have done much walking. I may sit down?'

'Yes – of course.'

He sat beside her on the bench. 'You have enjoyed your visit to the Livadia Palace?'

'Well . . . I'm not sure that enjoy would be quite the right word. It's certainly very interesting. Those war photographs are rather . . . disturbing.'

'Ah . . .' He appeared to ponder. 'I too have seen.'

There was a silence. 'Where were you in the war?' Caroline asked. Wondering, at once, if this was tactless.

It was not, apparently. He began to talk with animation about his service on a destroyer in the Barents Sea off Murmansk. Caroline sat listening in the sunshine; around her carefully tended trees and shrubs shifted in the breeze and a squirrel ran across the grass. Images flickered before her eyes – figures in oilskins battling along tipping decks, bearded faces iced with spray – derived, she realized, from old Pinewood Studios films. When he stopped speaking she said, 'I'm afraid I find it almost impossible to . . .' – not to imagine, that was wrong, imagining was what one did, so ineptly – '. . . to have any idea of,' she ended lamely.

'You are child in the war, I think?'

'Well . . . adolescent. I was at a boarding school in Devon.'

'Please tell me how that was. You were happy?'

'It's hard to say. I missed my parents a lot. I was only eleven when I went there. I suppose it was like many adolescences – happy some of the time, rather wretched at others.' The school re-created itself and hung invisible around them in the Crimean park: expanses of shiny linoleum, Spam, powdered egg, the smell of metal polish, the thin high cries of girls playing hockey. The man was gazing at her with kindly, puzzled brown eyes: 'Wretched?' 'Miserable. Unhappy.' He nodded, 'I am like so too. I am very difficult as boy, my mother say. I think perhaps boy is more difficult than girl, always? Yes?' 'I've never had children, so it's something I'm a bit ignorant about.' 'I too have not children – not wife either. I would like wife, several times, but it is not good life for woman, husband always going away on ships. So I am not marry.' 'Married,' said Caroline. 'You did not marry or you were not married'; really! she thought, how pompous! And blushed. 'I am sorry – I speak English very badly.' 'No you don't,' Caroline exclaimed. 'You speak it very well – extremely well. And I don't speak a word of Russian.'

The man lit a cigarette. 'We are coming from very different countries.' She glanced at him, wondering.

He waved the cigarette – at distant mountains, at the hammer and sickle rippling above the wedding-cake palace. Sparks of sunlight snapped from his chrome watch-strap. 'You are not seeing young sailor on a destroyer. I am not seeing this school in . . . where it is?'

'Devon. Yes – I understand what you mean. But in a way isn't it a more general difficulty. I mean . . . ' – she groped, surprised at herself – '. . . in fact even where people one knows well are concerned, my husband even, you see he used to go to an office every day – he was a solicitor – and after he died, I realized I had very little idea of what it was *like* for him. Really like. He wasn't a person who talked a lot about himself. It upsets me sometimes, now – feeling that I had so little idea.' She couldn't think what had come over her – talking like this to a complete stranger.

'Russian people are talking more about themselves, I think.'

'Are they? Well, I should imagine that's a good thing.'

'I am not talking so much because there is my sister only to listen and she has heard much already. Here now are your friends coming again.'

'Yes,' said Caroline. 'So they are.' The Lit. and Phil., herded by the Intourist girl, straggled from the woodland path.

'I am going now.' He stood up. 'Perhaps we meet again on the beach. I am swimming there tomorrow early. Before breakfast. Do you like to swim before breakfast?'

Caroline did not look at him. 'I do quite like swimming before breakfast,' she said. He walked away. She picked up her bag and rejoined the group. 'Miles of trees with little labels,' said Rosemary Innis. 'You were wise to stay behind.' 'I say!' exclaimed her husband. 'Wasn't that the same chap we talked to in Yalta?' 'Yes,' Caroline replied. 'It was.' 'What an extraordinary coincidence! I suppose it *was* a coincidence?' 'I don't know,' said Caroline. 'Do you think it was?' The Intourist girl, restive, was trying to head them towards the coach.

Caroline sat at the front, a position that gave you the best view. Within the coach's shell of tinted glass you moved between sea and mountains, gazing dispassionately down at people, houses, cars, knowing that you would never see them again: the place passed by like a film, unreachable and impinging only on the vision. You saw it but did not feel it. Indeed, since the coach was air-conditioned you forgot even that it was hot outside.

There were only two more days to go. The Lit. and Phil. had fallen by now into small interior groupings; Caroline found herself frequently with the Innises. 'I've enjoyed it,' declared Rosemary, at dinner that evening. 'But I don't think I'd want to come back. Once is enough. It's another country all right – I mean in a way that others aren't.' Her husband turned to Caroline, 'I've been thinking about that chap again. Very odd – him turning up like that. I mean – things may not always be quite what they seem. You don't know what he may be after. It's probably innocent enough – spot of hard currency, that sort of thing. Or it may be more complicated. I'd steer clear, if I were you, if he shows up again.'

'But how could he possibly have known we'd be at the Livadia Palace at that moment?' said his wife. 'Surely it was coincidence?'

Harold Innis shrugged. 'I daresay.'

After the meal they wandered for a while in the warm darkness of the hotel grounds, amid polyglot crowds. Moonlight glittered on the sea, as it had on the first evening; the hotel, a white cliff packed with light, rose against the black mountainside; music thumped from one of its several discos. It had been built, apparently, ten years ago but its positive occupancy of the night seemed immutable, solid and confident in a different way to the Tsarist palaces along the coast. It was as though complacent nights like this, moonlit and stormless, reached away forwards and backwards in an uninter-rupted succession, giving the lie to those photographs and to the Sevastopol soldiers on their stretchers.

Caroline got up at half past six. There was no one waiting for the lifts; she descended alone to the vast entrance hall, where cleaning women operated huge polishers. She walked down the winding cliff path to the beach; a few swimmers bobbed in the water and joggers pounded up and down the promenade. She sat on the beach and presently, when she looked up, there he was coming down the stone steps, a bathrobe over his swimming costume.

They went together into the sea and swam out. He was a strong swimmer, forging through the water with a purposeful breast-stroke, holding back from time to time to allow Caroline to keep up. Turning, she saw the beach now disconcertingly distant and felt slight panic: 'I think this is as far as I'd better go – I've not done much swimming lately.' He said, 'It is quiet, this sea, it has not strong how do you call it? Forces?'

'Currents,' said Caroline. 'But even so '

Back on the beach they dried themselves off. 'I am finding at last a map of England,' he said. 'It is not easy but at last I am finding a person who has. So I see Devon where is this school is at one end so' – he drew in the air a shape, and stabbed – 'there'.

The sea was almost empty, and the beach: a couple of lazily bobbing heads, someone a few hundred yards away doing press-ups on the shingle. They were alone. 'I looked at a map too,' said Caroline. 'To find Murmansk. I hadn't realized how very far north it is. Almost in the Arctic Circle.' She turned to him; he had nothing with him except for his towel and the bathrobe. She had only her towel and the dress she had now slipped on over her damp bathing costume. If either of us could be thought to have something to give to the other or something to receive, she thought, then it is clear by now that we haven't got it. We neither of us have anything but towels, bathing costumes and whatever is in our minds.

He said, 'I think you are going back to your home tomorrow?'

'Yes.'

He too now turned and faced her. 'I am,' he stated, 'a man who is very much lone.'

'Lonely,' she said. 'We say lonely, not lone.' She got to her feet and stood looking down at him. 'I am lonely too. Quite a lot of the time. So I do understand. And now I think I had better go.' She held out her hand. He rose, took it, and they stood there thus until Caroline took a step backwards, turned away and began to climb the stairs to the promenade. When she was half-way up she looked back. He was still there, sitting on his board and gazing at the sea. The sun was up now, and the heat of the day beginning to concentrate. Caroline climbed on towards the hotel which now, at nearly half past eight, was spilling scantily clad people on to the concrete concourses which surrounded it.

Corruption

The judge and his wife, driving to Aldeburgh for the weekend, carried with them in the back of the car a Wine Society carton filled with pornographic magazines. The judge, closing the hatchback, stared for a moment through the window; he reopened the door and put a copy of *The Times* on top of the pile, extinguishing the garish covers. He then got into the driving seat and picked up the road atlas. 'The usual route, dear?'

'The usual route, I think. Unless we spot anything enticing on the way.'

'We have plenty of time to be enticed, if we feel so inclined.'

The judge, Richard Braine, was sixty-two; his wife Marjorie, a magistrate, was two years younger. The weekend ahead was their annual and cherished early summer break at the Music Festival; the pornographic magazines were the impounded consignment of an importer currently on trial and formed the contents of the judge's weekend briefcase, so to speak. 'Chores?' his wife had said, and he had replied, 'Chores, I'm afraid.'

At lunch-time, they pulled off the main road into a carefully selected lane and found a gate-way in which to park the car. They carried the rug and picnic basket into a nearby field and ate their lunch under the spacious East Anglian sky, in a state of almost flamboyant contentment. Both had noted how the satisfactions of life have a tendency to gain intensity with advancing years. 'The world gets more beautiful,' Marjorie had once said, 'not less so. Fun is even more fun. Music is more musical, if you see what I mean. One hadn't reckoned with that.' Now, consuming the thoughtfully constructed sandwiches and the coffee from the thermos, they glowed at one another amid the long thick grass that teemed with buttercup and clover; before them, the landscape retreated into blue distances satisfactorily broken here and there by a line of trees, the tower of a church or a rising contour. From time to time they exchanged remarks of pleasure or anticipation: about the surroundings, the weather, the meal they would eat tonight at the little restaurant along the coast road, tomorrow evening's concert. Richard Braine, who was a man responsive to the moment, took his wife's hand; they sat in the sun, shirt-sleeved, and agreed conspiratorially and without too much guilt that they were quite glad that the eldest married daughter who sometimes accompanied them on this trip had not this year been able to. The daughter was loved, but would just now have been superfluous.

When they arrived at the small hotel it was early evening. The judge carried their suitcase and the Wine Society carton in and set them down by the reception desk. The proprietor, bearing the carton, showed them to their usual room. As she was unpacking, Marjorie said, 'I think you should have left that stuff in the car. Chambermaids, you know . . .' The judge frowned. 'That's a point.' He tipped the contents of the box into the emptied suitcase and locked it. 'I think I'll have a bath before we go out.' He lay in the steamy cubicle, a sponge resting upon his stomach. Marjorie, stripped to a pair of pants, came in to wash. 'The dear old avocado suite again. One day we must have an avocado bathroom suite at home.' The judge, contemplating the rise of his belly, nodded; he was making a resolution about reduction of the flesh, a resolution which he sadly knew would be broken. He was a man who enjoyed food. His wife's flesh, in the process now of being briskly soaped and scrubbed, was firmer and less copious, as he was fully prepared to concede. He turned his head to watch her and thought for a while in a vague and melancholy way about bodies, about how we inhabit them and are dragged to the grave by them and are conditioned by them. In the course of his professional life he had frequently had occasion to reflect upon the last point: it had seemed to him, observing the faces that passed before him in courtrooms, that confronted him from docks and witness boxes, that not many of us are able to rise above physical appearance. The life of an ugly woman is different from that of a beautiful one; you cannot infer character from appearance, but you can suspect a good deal about the circumstances to which it will have given rise. Abandoning this interesting but sombre theme, he observed his wife's breasts and muscular but not unshapely thighs and the folds of skin upon her neck and remembered the first time he had seen her with no clothes on. She turned to look at him; 'If you're jeering at my knickers, they're a pair of Alison's I grabbed out of the laundry basket by mistake.' Alison was their youngest, unmarried daughter. 'I hadn't really noticed them,' said the judge politely. 'I was thinking about something quite different.' He smiled. 'And don't leer,' said his wife, flicking him with her flannel. 'It's unbecoming in a man of your age.' 'It's a tribute to your charms, my dear,' said the judge. He sat up and began to wash his neck, thinking still about the first time; they had both been embarrassed. Embarrassment had been a part of the pleasure, he reflected. How odd, and interesting.

It was still daylight when they drove to the restaurant, a violet summer twilight in which birds sang with jungle stridency. Marjorie, getting out of the car, said, 'That veal and mushroom in cream sauce thing for me, I think. A small salad for you, without dressing.'

'No way,' said the judge.

'I admire your command of contemporary speech.' She went ahead into the restaurant, inspecting the room with bright, observant eyes. When they were sitting at the table she whispered, 'There's that same woman we met last year. Remember? The classy type who kept putting you right about Britten.'

The judge, cautiously, turned his head. 'So it is. Keep a low profile.'

'Will do, squire,' said Marjorie applying herself to the menu. 'Fifteen all?' she added. 'Right?'

'Right,' said her husband.

Their acquaintance, leaving before them, stopped to exchange greetings. The judge, mildly resenting the interruption to his meal, left the work to Marjorie. The woman, turning to go, said, 'So nice to see you again. And have a lovely break from juries and things.' She gleamed upon the judge.

He watched her retreating silk-clad back. 'Rather a gushing creature. How the hell does she know what I do?'

'Chatting up the hotel people, I don't doubt. It gives you cachet, you note, your job. Me, on the other hand, she considers a drab little woman. I could see her wondering how I came by you.'

'Shall we enlighten her? Sheer unbridled lust . . .'

'Talking of which,' said Marjorie. 'Just how unprincipled would it be to finish off with some of that cheese-cake?'

Back at the hotel, they climbed into bed in a state of enjoyable repletion. The judge put on his spectacles and reached out for the suitcase. 'You're not going to start going through that stuff *now* . . .' said Marjorie. 'At least have one whole day off work.'

'You're right,' he said. 'Tomorrow will do. I'll have that Barbara Pym novel instead.'

The judge, waking early the next morning, lay thinking about the current trial. He thought, in fact, not about obscenity or pornography but about the profit motive. He did not, he realized, understand the profit motive; he did not understand it in the same way in which he did not understand what induced people to be cruel. He had never coveted the possessions of others or wished himself richer than he was. He held no stocks or shares; Marjorie, once, had been left a small capital sum by an aunt; neither he nor she had ever been able to take the slightest interest in the financial health of her investments. Indeed, both had now forgotten what exactly the money was in. All this, he realized, was the position of a man with a substantial earned income; were he not paid what he was he might well feel otherwise. But he had not, in fact, felt very much otherwise as an impecunious young barrister. And importers of pornography tend, he understood, to be in an upper income bracket. No – the obstacle, the barrier requiring that leap of the imagination, was this extra dimension of need in some men that sought to turn money into yet more money, that required wealth for wealth's sake, the spawning of figures. The judge himself enjoyed growing vegetables; he considered, now, the satisfaction he got from harvesting a good crop of french beans and tried to translate this into a manifestation of the profit motive. The analogy did not quite seem to work.

The profit motive in itself, of course, is innocuous enough. Indeed, without it societies would founder. This was not the point that was bothering the judge; he was interested in those gulfs of inclination that divide person from person. As a young man he had wondered if this restriction makes us incapable of passing judgement on our fellows, but had come to realize at last that it does not. He remembered being involved in an impassioned argument about apartheid with another law student, an Afrikaner; 'You cannot make pronouncements on our policies,' the man had said, 'when you have never been to our country. You cannot understand the situation.' Richard Braine had known, with the accuracy of a physical response, that the man was wrong. Not misguided; simply wrong. A murderer is doing wrong, whatever the circumstances that drive him to his crime.

The profit motive is not wrong; the circumstances of its application may well be. The judge – with a certain irritation – found himself recalling the features of the importer of pornography: a nondescript, bespectacled man memorable only for a pair of rather bushy eyebrows and a habit of pulling an ear-lobe when under cross-examination. He pushed the fellow from his mind, determinedly, and got out of bed. Outside the window, strands of neatly corrugated cloud coasted in a milky-blue sky; it looked as though it would be a nice day.

The Braines spent the morning at Minsmere bird sanctuary; in the afternoon they went for a walk. The evening found them, scoured by fresh air and slightly somnolent, listening to Mozart, Bartok and Mendelssohn. The judge, who had never played an instrument and regarded himself as relatively unmusical, nevertheless responded to music with considerable intensity. It aroused him in various ways; in such different ways, indeed, that, being a thorough and methodical man, he often felt bemused, caught up by the onward rush of events before he had time to sort them out. Stop, he wanted to say to the surging orchestra, just let me have a think about that bit . . . But already he would have been swept onwards, into other moods, other themes, other passions. Marjorie, who played the piano in an unspectacular but competent way, had often suggested that the problem might be solved at least in part if he learned to read music.

She was no doubt right, he thought, wrestling now with a tortuous passage. When I retire; just the thing for a man reduced to inactivity. The judge did not look forward to retirement. But a few moments of inattention had been fatal – now the music had got away from him entirely, as though he had turned over two pages of a book. Frowning, he concentrated on the conductor.

Standing at the bar in the interval, he found himself beside their acquaintance from the restaurant, also waiting to order a drink. Gallantry or even basic good manners required that he intervene. 'Oh,' she said. 'How terribly sweet of you. A gin and tonic would be gorgeous.' With resignation, he led her back to where Marjorie awaited him.

'Your husband was so sweet and insistent – I'm all on my own this evening, my sister had a splitting headache and decided not to come.' She was a tall woman in her early fifties, too youthfully packaged in a flounced skirt and high-heeled boots, her manner towards the judge both sycophantic and faintly roguish. 'I was reading about you in *The Times* last month, some case about people had up for embezzling, of course I didn't understand most of it, all terribly technical, but I said to Laura, I *know* him, we had such a lovely talk about Britten at the Festival.'

'Ah,' said the judge, studying his programme: the Tippett next.

'I'm Moira Lukes, by the way – if you're anything like me names just *evaporate*, but of course I remembered yours from seeing it in the paper.' She turned to Marjorie. 'Aren't you loving the concert?'; patronage discreetly flowed, the patronage of a woman with a sexual history towards one who probably had none, of a lavishly clad woman towards a dowdy one. The judge's antennae slightly quivered, though he was not himself sure why. Marjorie blandly agreed that the concert was superb. 'Excuse me,' she said. 'I'm going to make a dash to the loo while there's time.'

The judge and Moira Lukes, left alone, made private adjustments to each other's company: the judge cleared his throat and commented on the architecture of the concert hall; Moira moved a fraction closer to him and altered the pitch of her voice, probably without being aware that she did either. 'You must lead such a fascinating life,' she said. 'I mean, you must come across such extraordinary people. Dickensian types. I don't think I've ever set eyes on a criminal.'

The judge thought again of the importer of pornography. 'Most of them are rather mundane, when it comes to the point.'

'But you must get to know so much about people.' She was looking very directly at him, with large eyes; a handsome woman, the judge conceded, rather a knock-out as a girl, no doubt. He agreed that yes, one did get a few insights into the ways in which people carry on.

'Fascinating,' said Moira Lukes again. 'I expect you have the most marvellous stories to tell. I envy your wife no end.' The large eyes creased humorously at the corners; a practised device, though the judge did not recognize this. 'In fact I think she's a lucky woman – I still remember that interesting chat you and I had last year.' And she laid on his arm a hand, which was almost instantly removed – come and gone as briefly as though a bird had alighted for a fleeting second. The judge, startled in several ways, tried to recall this chat: something about when *Peter Grimes* was first performed, or was it *The Turn of the Screw*? The interest of it, now, escaped him. He cast a quick glance across the foyer in search of Marjorie, who seemed to be taking an awfully long time. Moira Lukes was talking now about the area of Sussex in which she lived. Do, she was saying, look in and have lunch, both of you, if you're ever in that part of the world. The judge murmured that yes, of course if ever they were . . . He noticed the rings on her hand and wondered vaguely what had become of Mr Lukes; somehow one knew that he was no longer around, one way or the other. 'The only time,' she said, 'I've ever personally had anything to do with the law was over my rather wretched divorce.' The judge took a swig of his drink. 'And then actually the lawyer was most awfully sweet, in fact he kept my head above water through it all.' She sighed, a whiff of a sigh, almost imperceptible; thereby, she implied most delicately, hung a tale.

'So I've got rather a soft spot for legal people.'

'Good,' said the judge heartily. 'I'm glad to hear you've been well treated by the profession.'

'Oh, *very* well treated.'

No sign of Marjorie, still. Actually, the judge was thinking, this Moira Whatshername wasn't perhaps quite so bad after all, behind that rather tiresome manner; appearances, inevitably, deceive. One got the impression, too, of someone who'd maybe had a bit of a rough time. 'Well, it's a world that includes all sorts, like most. And it brings you up against life, I suppose, with all that that implies.'

The respect with which these banalities were received made him feel a little cheap. In compensation, he told her an anecdote about a case in which he had once been involved; a *crime passionnel* involving an apparently wronged husband who had turned out in fact to be the villain of the piece. 'A mealy-mouthed fellow, and as plausible as you like, but apparently he'd been systematically persecuting her for years.' Moira Lukes nodded sagely. 'People absolutely are not what they seem to be.'

'Well,' said the judge. 'Yes and no. On the other hand, plenty of people give themselves away as soon as they open their mouths.'

'Oh, goodness,' said Moira Lukes. 'Now I'll feel I daren't utter a word ever again.'

'I had in mind those I come across professionally rather than in private life.'

'Ah, then you think I'm safe?'

'Now, whatever could you have to conceal?' said the judge amiably. A bell went. 'I wonder where Marjorie's got to. I suppose we'd better start going back in.'

Moira Lukes sighed. She turned those large eyes upon him and creased them once again at the corners. 'Well, this has been so nice. I'm sure we'll run into each other again over the weekend. But do bear in mind that I'm in the East Sussex phone book. I remember that case I read about was in Brighton – if you're ever judging there again and want a few hours' retreat on your own, do pop over and have a drink.' She smiled once more, and walked quickly away into the crowd.

The judge stood for a moment, looking after her. He realized with surprise that he had been on the receiving end of what is generally known as a pass. He realized also that he was finding it difficult to sort out exactly what he felt about this; a rational response and his natural judgement of people (he didn't in fact all that much care for the woman) fought with more reprehensible feelings and a certain complacency (so one wasn't a total old buffer just yet). In this state of internal conflict he made his way back into the concert hall, where he found Marjorie already in her seat.

'What on earth happened to you?'

'Sorry,' she said cheerfully. 'There was an awful queue in the ladies' and by the time I got out it wasn't worth coming to find you. How did you make out with our friend?'

The judge grunted, and applied himself to the programme. The lights went down, the conductor reappeared, the audience sank into silence . . . But the music, somehow, had lost its compulsion; he was aware now of too much that was external – that he could achieve no satisfactory position for his legs, that he had slight indigestion, that the chap in front of him kept moving his head. Beside him, he could see Marjorie's face, rapt. The evening, somehow, had been corrupted.

The next morning was even more seraphic than the one before.

'Today,' said Marjorie, 'we are going to sit on the beach and bask. We may even venture into the sea.'

'That sounds a nice idea.' The judge had thought during the night of the little episode with that woman and, in the process, a normal balance of mind had returned; he felt irritated – though more with himself than with her – that it had interfered with his enjoyment of the concert. It was with some annoyance, therefore, that he spotted her now across the hotel dining-room, with the sister, lifting her hand in a little finger-waggling wave of greeting.

'What's the matter?' said Marjorie, with marital insight.

'Oh . . . Her. Well, I'll leave you to hide behind the paper. I'm going upstairs to get sorted out for the beach.'

He was half-way through the Home News page when he felt her standing over him. Alone. The sister, evidently, had been disposed of.

'Another heavenly day. Aren't we lucky! All on your own? I saw your wife bustling off . . .' She continued to stand, her glance drifting now towards the coffee pot at the judge's elbow.

I am supposed, he thought, to say sit down and join me – have a cup of coffee. And he felt again that quiver of the antennae and knew now the reason. Marjorie does indeed bustle, her walk is rather inelegant, but it is not for you to say so, or to subtly denigrate a person I happen to love. He rattled, slightly, his newspaper. 'We're off to the beach shortly.'

'Oh, lovely. I daresay we'll go down there later. I wonder . . . Goodness, I don't know if I ought to ask you this or not . . .' She hesitated, prettily, seized, it seemed, with sudden diffidence. 'Oh, I'll be brave. The thing is, I have this tiresome problem about a flat in London I'm buying, something to do with the leasehold that I simply do not follow, and I just do not have absolute faith in the man who's dealing with it for me – the solicitor, you know – *could* I pick your brains about it at some point?'

The judge, impassive, gazed up at her.

'I don't mean *now* – not in the middle of your holiday weekend. My sister was noticing your address in the hotel register and believe it or not my present flat is only a few minutes away. What would be lovely would be if you could spare an hour or so to look in for a drink on your way home one evening – and your wife too of course, only it might be awfully boring for her if you're going to brief me. Is that the right word? Would it be an imposition? When you're on your own like I am you are so very much at the mercy of . . .' she sighed – 'people, the system, I don't know what . . . Sometimes I get quite panic-stricken.'

I doubt that, thought the judge. He put the newspaper down. 'Mrs Lukes . . .'

'Oh, Moira . . . please.'

He cleared his throat. 'Conveyancing, as it happens, is not my field. Anything I said might quite possibly be misleading. The only sensible advice I can give is to change your solicitor if you feel lack of confidence in him.'

Her eyes flickered; that look of honest appeal dimmed suddenly. 'Oh . . . I see. Well, I daresay you're right. I must do that, then. I shouldn't have asked. But of course the invitation stands, whenever you're free.'

'How kind,' said the judge coolly. He picked up his paper again and looked at her over the top of it; their eyes met in understanding. And he flinched a little at her expression; it was the look of hatred he had seen from time to time, over the years, across a courtroom, on the face in the dock.

'Have a *lovely* day,' said Moira Lukes. Composure had returned; she gleamed, and wrinkled her eyes, and was gone. Well, thought the judge, there's no love lost there, now. But it had to be done, once and for all. He folded the paper and went in search of Marjorie. She was packing a beach-bag with costumes and towels. The judge, unlocking the suitcase, took out a stack of the pornographic magazines and pushed them into the bottom of the bag. 'Oh, lor,' said Marjorie, 'I'd forgotten about them. Must you?'

' 'Fraid so. The case resumes tomorrow. It's the usual business of going through them for degrees of obscenity. There are some books too.'

'I'll help you,' said Marjorie. 'There – greater love hath no woman . . .' The beach was agreeably uncrowded. Family parties were dotted in clumps about the sand; children and dogs skittered in and out of the surf; gulls floated above the water and a party of small wading birds scurried back and forth before the advancing waves like blown leaves. The judge, who enjoyed a bit of unstrenuous bird-watching, sat observing them with affection. The weather, this particularly delectable manifestation of the physical world and the uncomplicated relish of the people and animals around him had induced a state of general benignity. Marjorie, organizing the rug and wind-screen, said, 'All right?'

'All right,' he replied. They smiled at each other, appreciating the understatement.

Marjorie, after a while, resolutely swam. The judge, more craven, followed her to the water's edge and observed. As they walked back up the beach together he saw suddenly that Moira Lukes and her sister were encamped not far off. She glanced at him and then immediately away. Now, at midday, the beach was becoming more occupied, though not disturbingly so. A family had established itself close to the Braines' pitch: young parents with a baby in a pram and a couple of older children now deeply engaged in the initial stages of sandcastle construction. The judge, who had also made a sandcastle or two in his time, felt an absurd urge to lend a hand; the basic design, he could see, was awry and would give trouble before long. The mother, a fresh-faced young woman, came padding across the sand to ask Marjorie for the loan of a tin-opener. They chatted for a moment; the young woman carried the baby on her hip. 'That sort of thing,' said Marjorie, sitting down again, 'can still make me broody, even at my time of life.' She too watched the sandcastle-building; presently she rummaged in the picnic basket and withdrew a plastic beaker. 'Turrets,' she explained to the judge, a little guiltily. 'You can never do a good job with a bucket . . .' The children received her offering with rewarding glee; the parents gratefully smiling; the sandcastle rose, more stylish.

The judge sighed, and delved in the beach-bag. 'To work, I suppose,' he said. Around them, the life of the beach had settled into a frieze; as though the day were eternal: little sprawled groups of people, the great arc of the horizon against which stood the grey shapes of two far-away ships, like cut-outs, the surface animation of running dogs and children and someone's straw hat, tossed hither and thither by the breeze that had sprung up.

The judge and his wife sat with a pile of magazines each. Marjorie said, 'This is a pretty gruesome collection. Can I borrow your hankie, my glasses keep getting salted over.'

The judge turned over pages, and occasionally made some notes. Nothing he saw surprised him; from time to time he found himself examining the faces that belonged to the bodies displayed, as though in search of explanations. But they seemed much like any other faces; so presumably were the bodies.

Marjorie said, 'Cup of tea? Tell me, why are words capable of so much greater obscenity than pictures?' She was glancing through a book, or something that passed as such.

'That, I imagine, is why people have always gone in for burning them, though usually for quite other reasons.'

It was as the judge was reaching out to take the mug of tea from her that the wind came. It came in a great wholesome gust, flinging itself along the beach with a cloud of blown sand and flying plastic bags. It sent newspapers into the air like great flapping birds and spun a spotted football along the water's edge as though it were a top. It lifted rugs and pushed over deckchairs. It snatched the magazines from the judge's lap and from Marjorie's and bore them away across the sand in a helter-skelter whirl of colourful pages, dropping them down only to grab them again and fling them here and there: at the feet of a stout lady snoozing in a deckchair, into the pram of the neighbouring family's baby, on to people's towels and Sunday papers.

Marjorie said, 'Oh, *lor* . . .'

They got up. They began, separately, to tour the beach in pursuit of what the wind had taken. The judge found himself, absurdly, feeling foolish because he had left his jacket on his chair and was plodding along the sand in shirt-sleeves (no tie, either) and tweed trousers. The lady in the deckchair woke and put out a hand to quell the magazine that was wrapping itself around her leg. 'Yours?' she said amiably, looking up at the judge, and as she handed him the thing it fell open and for a moment her eyes rested on the central spread, the *pièce de résistance*; her expression changed, rubbed out as it were by amazement, and she looked again at the judge for an instant, and became busy with the knitting on her lap.

Marjorie, stumping methodically along, picked up one magazine and then another, tucking them under her arm. She turned and saw that the children had observed the crisis, abandoned their sandcastle and were scurrying here and there, collecting as though involved in a treasure hunt. The mother, too, had risen and was shaking the sand from a magazine that had come to rest against the wheels of the pram. As Marjorie reached her the little girl ran up with an armful. 'Good girl, Sharon,' said the mother, and the child – six, perhaps, or seven – virtuously beamed and held out to Marjorie the opened pages of the magazine she held. She looked at it and the mother looked at it and Marjorie looked and the child said, 'Are those flowers?'

'No, my dear,' said Marjorie sadly. 'They aren't flowers,' and she turned away before she could meet the eyes of the young mother.

The judge collected a couple from a man who handed them over with a wink, and another from a boy who stared at him expressionless, and then he could not find any more. He walked back to their pitch. Marjorie was shoving things into the beach-bag. 'Shall we go?' she said, and the judge nodded.

It was as they were folding the rug that Moira Lukes came up. She wore neatly creased cotton trousers and walked with a spring. 'Yours, apparently,' she said; she held the magazine out between a finger and thumb, as though with tongs, and dropped it on to the sand. She looked straight at the judge. 'How awfully true,' she said, 'that people are not what they seem to be.' Satisfaction flowed from her; she glanced for an instant at Marjorie, as though checking that she had heard, and walked away.

The Braines, in silence, completed the assembly of their possessions. Marjorie carried the rug and the picnic basket and the judge bore the beach-bag and the wind-screen. They trudged the long expanse of the beach, watched, now, with furtive interest by various eyes.

Beyond the Blue Mountains (1997)

The Slovenian Giantess

'Definitely you must see this castle,' said Eva. 'It is very historic.'

The rain fell in thick curtains. They had driven up a narrow, twist-ing road down which water gushed. Eva drove leaning forward to peer through the streaming windscreen. They were now in the cas-tle car park, ostensibly waiting for a break in the weather. Eleanor had proposed that they abandon the venture and go for lunch in the hotel down below, by the lake.

'No, no. The castle is essential. What is some rain!' Eva laughed. 'In England it never stops raining, I thought. I was in London last year to work at the British Library and it was every day – rain, rain, rain.'

'There are occasional periods of respite,' said Eleanor.

Eva opened the car door. 'Come on. We must be brave. It is not so far to walk, I think.'

The castle perched on the highest point of the crags that reared above one shore of the lake. Seen from down below, jutting out of the pinkish-grey rock and the dark mantle of trees, it looked like some carefully considered scenic device, a set piece for the enjoy-ment of observers in the recently constructed lakeside resort complex – hotels, restaurants, conference centre and boutiques. Eva and Eleanor, walking awkwardly close together in order to share an umbrella, stumbled up the stony path that led to the castle entrance. There was no one else about; the car park had been empty.

'Maybe it's shut,' said Eleanor.

'No, no. Always these places are open.' There was a big wooden door set into the outer wall of the castle precinct at which Eva now hammered.

Rain crashed on to the umbrella. After a minute or so a custodian appeared, looking surprised, and watched without interest the ritual scuffle over who was to pay.

'I am the hostess,' said Eva firmly. 'In England, another time, it will be your turn.'

This was what Eleanor feared. Eva was a lecturer at the University of Zagreb and Eleanor was not sure that she liked her that much. Around forty, a few years older than herself, Eva was a somewhat frenzied woman with a mane of wiry black hair and a professional interest in anglophone women writers of the early twentieth century. She had battened on to Eleanor throughout the three days of the conference. This expedition to the lake on the final afternoon was at her insistence. The concluding sessions left Eleanor with four hours to spare before check-in time for her flight back to London. When Eva discovered this she had proposed a trip to the mountain lake. 'You will have your luggage with you and then I take you straight to the airport.'

Eleanor had demurred, partly on account of a certain lack of enthusiasm for Eva's company, but also because it was clear that a longish drive would be involved. By that time the countdown to departure would have begun and the airport would be exercising its magnetic pull. She had not much faith in Eva's time sense, or indeed in her battered little car. She had made excuses, but Eva would have none of it. 'You don't trust me, Eleanor. You think I will not get you to your plane.' And so decency had required a gracious acceptance and now here they were, plodding round the ramparts of this gothic monument in the father and mother of all downpours with the lake below barely visible through grey veils of rain. Never mind, thought

Eleanor, never mind. All part of life's rich pattern. By 6.30 I'll be on BA 354 to Heathrow. Home by eleven, with any luck.

'Ah,' said Eva. 'Here is the entrance. Now we go in and get dry. In England of course you have plenty of castles. I should like next year to do a trip. Perhaps we go together and you will be my guide.'

They toured the rooms. The furnishings were tapestries, much stricken with age, and vast blackened cupboards, tables and settles. There were some perfunctory showcases of china, coins and objets d'art. Eva translated the explanatory leaflet. 'Yes, this is very historic. From the eleventh century, with many rebuildings. Where we are now is from the seventeenth. Here is the fine view of the lake. And it is raining not so much now.'

They looked over a cliff face down which Serbs and Croats had apparently been throwing one another for hundreds of years. The castle's past, inextricably entwined with that of the region, was characterized by violence and implacable tribal feuding. It had changed hands each century, it seemed, to the accompaniment of further slaughter. Eleanor, contemplating the grey-black water, the sweeping pine forests and rain-sodden rocks, had a feeling of being in the bloodstained heartlands of Europe with history hanging like some dreadful miasma of pollution.

Eva's footsteps came clattering back from the next room. 'Come – here is something most interesting.'

In the centre of the room was an oblong wooden pen of sand on which lay a huge skeleton. 'Here is the skeleton of the Slovenian giantess,' said Eva. 'She is from the tenth century, it says. And beside her is her necklace and the head-dress she wore.'

'Heavens – she certainly was tall! Seven foot, do you think?'

'We will see. I am five foot eight.' Eva got down and lay on the floor alongside the skeleton. Eleanor stood and looked at them both – the immense bony frame of this survivor of the tenth century and Eva, a Croat of the twentieth. Eva lay there, her arms stiff at each side of her, in a dark blue double-breasted coat with brass buttons and knee boots with high heels, still clutching her handbag. 'Well?' she said.

Eleanor was quite disoriented by the sight. She stared down.

'Well?' said Eva again. 'Is she seven feet?'

'At least. A bit more, I'd say.'

Eva got up and dusted herself off. 'And now definitely the rain is not so bad, so we will drive to the hotel for lunch. And we will talk about where I can apply for a study grant in England next year.'

Yes, thought Eleanor, I suppose that is what we're here for, if the truth were told. No, that's a disgraceful thought. She is merely being hospitable to a visitor.

Given the choice, it was not Eva with whom she would have struck up an acquaintance. Indeed it could be said that Eva had scuppered her chances with the one appealing man of around her own age on the conference, a Henry James scholar from Sarajevo called Boris. Every conference has its Lothario and Boris was probably that, a fact of which Eleanor had been well aware, but in the artificial circumstances of three-day cloistered proximity, who cares? Boris had been drily entertaining and initially distinctly attentive, but every time she found herself with him Eva hove in sight with cries of greeting and muscled in on the conversation, killing it stone dead. Boris, tilting a sardonic eyebrow, would drift away.

The conference was a biennial forum on English literature studies held by teachers of the subject in Yugoslavian universities. Eleanor herself was one of only half a dozen British delegates, included presumably to leaven the mixture. Everyone else knew one another rather too well. She had given her paper on Virginia Woolf and then settled into the audience in the Hall of Culture presided over by a relentlessly autocratic professor from the host university. 'No speaker will address the conference for more than thirty minutes please. We will then have twenty minutes for discussion and five minutes for concluding remarks from the chair . . .' Eleanor had listened to presentations on 'The Macedonian response to the Movement poets' and 'The Serbo-Croat reception of the Sirens episode in *Ulysses*' and the event had come to seem more and more surreal. For outside the lecture hall no one talked of anything but the patently more compelling matter of the imminent break-up of Yugoslavia.

'You must understand that Yugoslavia is not a country but a cultural salad,' said Boris, on the first occasion that they talked. 'Is this your first visit?'

It was. She felt humiliated by her ignorance, by the assorted fragments of information that stood in for knowledge or understanding of this place and of these people. What she heard bore no resemblance to the dispassionate accounts of newspaper reports. She felt her own detachment from their concerns and with it an unsettling guilt, as though she were watching distant wars on a television screen.

And then on the second morning Eva came into the breakfast room and made straight for her. 'I have some bad news for you, Eleanor. Your Mrs Thatcher is defeated.'

Eleanor stared. It was early in the morning, she had slept badly and the domestic political situation was far from her mind.

'She is not any longer the prime minister. She is thrown out.'

'Oh, good,' said Eleanor.

Eva was astonished. 'But this is surely very bad for your country. She is a great leader.'

Boris had just brought Eleanor another cup of coffee. He sat down.

'Well, some of us don't feel that,' said Eleanor.

Boris laughed.

'Anyway, this is what has happened.' Eva shrugged. 'It is the first item on the news, before even what the Serbs are saying. And I cannot see what is so funny, Boris. For Eleanor this is a very historical moment.'

'Ah, but Eleanor does not feel that it is,' said Boris. 'History is a question of perspective, I suppose. The downfall of Mrs Thatcher will not much affect Eleanor's life.'

Eva helped herself to one of Eleanor's pieces of bread. 'Do you mind? I will get more in a minute. Boris is being clever – you should pay no attention.'

'Actually I think he's right,' said Eleanor. 'It's the difference between our politics and . . . those in other places.'

'Such as here,' – Boris gave Eva a bland smile and addressed himself to Eleanor – 'where we may be about to be exposed to rather more history than we would like. Usually history is what happens somewhere else and at some other time. It should be avoided at all costs, or kept at a low temperature, as you manage to do in England.'

Eva snorted. 'This is a very silly conversation, I think. Are you coming for the dinner at the Greek restaurant tonight, Eleanor? We could then talk some more about my article on Virginia Woolf's feminism.'

At which point Boris had slid away, with a regretful little grimace at Eleanor.

And now here she was, crammed into Eva's car, hurtling around this menacing landscape on a day of intermittent cloudbursts, already in her mind slotted once more into her own life, picking up the letters on the doormat (there wouldn't be many – she'd only been away four days), unpacking the case, thinking about the week ahead. It was still term time – she had a heavy teaching load and had had to cancel two seminars and a lecture in order to get to this conference. She considered ways of making these up, as the car plunged down the narrow road to the lakeside.

'This hotel is built quite recently,' said Eva. 'It is all newly laid out. They are hoping to attract foreign tourists and conferences.'

The entire lakeside resort had a doleful air of incompletion and abandonment. The pedestrian shopping precinct was a miniature townscape of empty windows and unpeopled walkways. The skating-rink and putting-green were closed. There was hardly anyone around. Eva led Eleanor into the hotel, which was equally deserted. They made their way through vast lounges in which oversized sofas and chairs bleakly confronted one another, and thence into a dining-room, one wall of which was a great sheet of glass overlooking the lake. Waiters wearing tuxedos converged upon them, proffering wine lists and urging them to make their selection from the cold buffet at the other side of the room.

Surveying this spread, Eleanor was again seized with a sense of the surreal. Whole salmon garnished with skewered twists of cucumber and lemon. Other cold fish, piped with rosettes of mayonnaise. Ranks of different kinds of salad, platters of sliced meats. Little bowls of caviare on ice.

'All for us?'

'Perhaps they are expecting some conference,' said Eva. 'Here maybe we will share the bill, shall we? Go Dutch – is that right?'

They returned to their table with heaped plates. The weather had improved and the lake was fully visible now, dimpled by light rain, sweeping away to a dark, distant backcloth of trees. Eleanor felt disembodied, only tenuously present, on loan to this place for a few hours, courtesy of British Airways. She had felt much like that throughout the conference. Occasionally the map of Europe would form itself in her head. She would see the familiar outline, pay tribute to the distances. This place was nearly a thousand miles from London, but of course it was not that. It was as far as the half-hour in the airport and the wander round the duty-free shops, the three-hour flight with the read of the papers and a book, the meal, the brief doze. That was the reality, not this eerie sense of an elsewhere in which she was present only as a transitory ghost. In dreams, you can experience that sense of licence – this is only a dream and therefore I can do as I wish and cannot be brought to book. She was here in the same spirit. Prick her and she would not bleed.

Perhaps that is why people behave out of character as soon as they leave their own country, she thought. Have love affairs with Italian waiters, sleep around at conferences. She had not herself done either of these things but it did occur to her now that her resistance might not have been so great had Boris become pressing. Under normal circumstances she liked to take her time about sexual commitment, so this perception was interesting. She even felt a mild regret. She glanced at her watch. Only two and a half hours now till check-in time.

Eva was talking about her family. Her widowed mother in Zagreb. Her brother who had a successful import and export business, threatened now by the impending collapse of Yugoslavia.

A word, thought Eleanor, just a word. You can't make a country out of a word. And for her, she realized, this place was a preconception built around that word – present in the mind as an arbitrary sequence of images. A ragged procession of refugee women and children following the partisans into the mountains. These mountains? Tito – a stocky figure with shiny boots, crammed into a uniform that bristled with epaulettes and buttons, a grin like the Cheshire cat. Derring-do British officers parachuting into the partisan camps – Randolph Churchill, Evelyn Waugh. As irrelevant surely as the Sirens episode in *Ulysses*. Sarajevo. The Archduke Ferdinand. The single shot that plunged Europe into war, or so one understood. None of this had any connection with the acreage of white napery around her, the bored waiters, the lake with its torrential pine forests, the castle of the Slovenian giantess.

Eva was now talking of an uncle, her mother's brother, who had emigrated to the United States immediately after the war and had recently returned on a visit, for the first time. A dismaying visit, it emerged.

'Eleanor, he did not even speak good English,' Eva confided. 'After forty years over there. He has been always with an enclave of Croatian émigrés in Cleveland, working just as a garage mechanic. My mother was . . . embarrassed by him. His manners. His way of speaking. My family is quite different now. My mother was head teacher of a big school. My brother is well known in business. But he was . . . well, from another world. He was twenty-one when he left. And still all he can talk about is the war. The war, the war, the war. For us it is long ago now, the war. It is finished, done with. He has mended cars in Cleveland all his life and thought of nothing but the war, him and his friends.'

'Why did he emigrate?'

'There were problems for some people, back then. Others trying to settle old scores. You know . . . He did not feel safe. They said he had some connection with the Ustashi.'

'Did he?'

'I don't know,' Eva shrugged. 'If so . . . he was very young. But the point is, all that is gone now, for people like us. Finished. We have moved on. But he had not. In the end it was hard to talk to him. My mother was relieved when he went back to the States.'

'Had you met him when you were doing your doctorate over there?'

'No, no,' said Eva, a trifle irritably. 'I was in Pittsburgh. It would have been much too far to visit him.' Their plates had been removed and the waiters were now trying to interest them in the dessert trolley. Eva abandoned her family and wrenched the conversation firmly in the direction of her own prospects of a research grant at a British university. Eleanor had a certain satisfaction in explaining that the Thatcher years had made such largesse hard to come by. She promised to make inquiries.

The meal completed, Eva made a meticulous division of the bill and looked at her watch. 'Excellent – we have still plenty of time. I shall take you to see the waterfall.'

'Well . . . maybe I should be getting straight to the airport now.'

'No, no. You will only be sitting about there – it is half an hour from here, that is all. And the waterfall is not to be missed. We can drive to a place not far away and then it is a short walk up the mountainside. I have been many times.'

The road climbed up from the lake even more tortuously than that to the castle, doubling back on itself in hairpin bends. It was not much more than a track, in any case. The rain had given way now to a thickening mist.

Eleanor said, 'Is this where the partisans were, in the war?'

'Probably. They were in many places. Certainly near here is where there was a massacre by the Germans, I think. Look, this now is where we leave the car.'

'It's going to start getting dark soon, Eva. Are you sure it isn't far?'

'Not far at all. This is the way over here, look . . . It is a well-known beauty spot.'

But not in the middle of November, thought Eleanor dourly. It was distinctly chilly now and the air was thick with moisture. She tied her scarf round her head and followed Eva up the steep shaly path, slippery from the rain, which wound up between the trees. Eva, in her high-heeled boots, was having difficulty. Eleanor, pointing this out in hopes of a reprieve, was brushed aside. At any moment they would reach the waterfall, Eva assured her. 'Hush . . . I think I can hear it already.'

For nearly twenty minutes they scrambled up the mountainside. Then Eva stopped. 'It is possible I have taken the wrong path. I think perhaps we go down some way and see if we have missed a turn.'

Eleanor said, 'I really do feel it would be wise to head for the airport now, Eva.'

'No, no. We are very close, I promise.' Turning, Eva began a hasty and hazardous descent. Within half a dozen paces she had fallen. Her left foot slipped and twisted and she was on her back on the rain-sodden path.

It was quickly apparent that damage had been done. As soon as Eva tried to get up she became faint. Eleanor squatted beside her on the path, supporting her. 'Just keep still for a minute. You've probably winded yourself.'

'I am all right. Look, I can get up now . . .' But there was a yelp of pain. 'My ankle . . .'

'Keep still,' said Eleanor. She improvised a pillow with their two handbags and unzipped Eva's boot. 'Does that hurt?'

It did. And the ankle was beginning to swell. Broken or merely sprained?

'I try to stand,' said Eva. 'Look, it is not so bad . . .' And immediately fainted.

Eleanor ministered. She found some skin freshener in her handbag and rubbed it on Eva's forehead. Oh God, she thought, what a thing to happen . . . Presently Eva came to. She stared at Eleanor. 'I am not so good. You will have to take the car and go to get some help. Here – the keys are in my pocket.'

'Eva,' said Eleanor, 'I'm afraid I can't drive.' And have always rather prided myself on the fact, she reflected grimly. Felt myself a touch radical, original. Environmentally chaste.

Eva closed her eyes. 'Ah . . .' She opened them. 'I am afraid that you may miss your plane.'

'That's the least of it,' said Eleanor heroically. 'The main thing is to get you down from here. Let's try once more and see if you might be able to walk if you lean on me and we take it very slowly.'

They tried. Eva all but passed out again.

'I'm going to have to leave you and find some help,' said Eleanor. Hell and damnation, she thought. Shit. She saw the airport departure lounge, the reassuring departure board: BA 354 London Heathrow. The light blinking: BOARDING.

'I made perhaps a mistake to go to the waterfall,' said Eva. 'I am sorry, Eleanor. This is most inconvenient for you.' She was now extremely white.

'Never mind. Now look – can you wriggle as far as that pile of leaves there? You'd be a bit more comfortable.'

Eva was laid out by the side of the path. For the second time Eleanor stood looking down at the woman's supine form – the buttoned coat, those boots, her now ashen face. I knew this would happen, thought Eleanor, somehow I knew it. It was built into the day from the moment we walked into that castle. But it is not a major catastrophe. Eva's injury is a minor one. I have missed a plane, that is all. What I have to do is follow the path and then the road. Sooner or later there'll be a car. The driver of which probably won't speak any English.

She tore a page from a notebook on which Eva wrote a message of explanation and appeal. She still looked extremely seedy but was rallying sufficiently to instruct Eleanor on a quicker way down from the car park. 'The road will take so long, and there will be no cars coming up here now. There is a path from where we left the car, for people who walk up to the waterfall. It is steep but much more quick, down to the big road where there will surely be cars.'

Eleanor hesitated. 'Well, I'll see how dark it's getting by the time I'm at the car park.'

'Do not fall . . .' came Eva's voice, as she departed.

Eleanor achieved the car park within ten minutes. And there

indeed was the suggested path, with a wooden sign indicating the lakeside village. Clearly this would be a much quicker route than the tortuous hairpin bends of the road. The path looked definite enough, if a trifle steep, and it was still only early dusk.

After a few minutes of somewhat precipitate descent the path became rather less well defined, encroached on by undergrowth. Not much used, it would seem. Eleanor considered turning back. But then, after another minute or so, she found herself confronted by a bifurcation, one arm of which opened up in a distinctly more promising way and must surely be the descent to the main road. To go back now would be to lose a lot of time.

This branch of the path was steeper yet. Now and again she had to cling on to overhanging branches to steady herself. Good thing she had flat shoes on, not ludicrous boots like poor Eva. She glanced at her watch: 5.45. Check-in 6.15. Not a hope in hell.

It was distinctly murky now. And the path was getting more and more precipitous. I don't like this, she thought. This is crazy, I should have stuck to the road. The image in her head was the nirvana of the airport lounge, the reality which had somehow been snatched from her and replaced by this unpleasant, wet and darkening mountainside.

She struggled on. And now, to her horror, the path forked again. One route wound off to the left, the other continued steeply downwards. Oh God – which? Damn you, Eva – I should never have let you land me with this bloody path.

The path leading down seemed the most logical route, if the least inviting. Steeper and steeper. She was constantly slipping and sliding now. Trees closed in around her. The light was fading all the time.

She slithered down and down. The path began to level off. Eleanor's spirits rose – the road could not be far. The trees were too thick to see ahead, but at any moment they would surely start to thin out. She listened hopefully for cars.

Instead, there came the sound of rushing water. The forest did indeed thin out – to show a fast-flowing stream, into which the path led, to emerge on the other side and rise up a further tree-hung hill-side. She had descended into a gully rather than to the road.

Her stomach was churning. It would be dark within fifteen minutes or so. She knew that she was starting to panic. Think, she told herself. Think what to do. To go back the way she had come was the safest in the sense that she was bound to end up back at the car park, but this would involve a horribly steep climb in darkness (why the hell didn't I ask Eva if there was a torch in her car?). The way ahead was unpredictable but considerably less steep. It seemed likely that the gully was just a fold in the hillside and that the path would yet descend to the road. The stream was narrow enough to jump.

She would go on.

When it was so dark that she could barely see ahead at all she knew with awful certainty that she had made the wrong decision. She should be at the road by now and was not. The path had climbed, and then began a reassuring descent, but now it was climbing once more. It was raining again. She was wet, exhausted and nearing despair. At one point she lost the path when undergrowth swept across it, and she realized only just in time that she had started to plunge off into the forest. She scrambled on with her eyes all the time on the faintly pale surface of the stony track. She no longer thought of the comforting interior of BA 354, where she should rightly be. Occasionally she saw Eva lying on a pile of leaves in the dark somewhere above and beyond. Once when she peered at her watch she realized that she had been walking now for over an hour. She was dizzy with fatigue and when she seemed to hear a horde of shuffling feet around her she thought that she was hallucinating until the sound turned to the drip of water from the trees above. But the sense of unreality that she had experienced over the last few days was gone. She knew now that she was here, in this place, on this implacable hillside, hundreds of miles from home and that there was no bland assurance of stepping back into her own life. She understood that reality is what is happening to you, not what you anticipate. She perceived also, with a clarity she had never known, that there are realities which for most of us are beyond imagination.

And with this perception came fear – fear such as she had never known, fear that seemed to come pouring from the trees to snatch her up and take her stumbling on and on into the wet whispering darkness. She was invaded by fear, a fear beyond all reason. She knew only that she had to go on – to go on and to get away. She no longer thought of the plane, she no longer thought of Eva, only of her own desperate plight and this terrible shroud of trees that closed in on her and from which she would never escape.

Later that night, much later, an electrician returning home after a drinking session with a friend was puzzled to see a stumbling swaying figure by the side of the road. A woman. A woman with a scarf tied round her head. For a moment he felt a creep of unease and superstition, as though something of another time might have come crawling from these forests in which, everyone knew, dark things had come about. And then he saw that she was waving and shouting and he pulled up alongside, wound down the window and heard her gabble incomprehensibly. It was one o'clock in the morning, his mind was on his own warm bed and the wife who would want to know where the devil he had been. This sodden figure weaving about in the mist seemed like some effect of the drinks he'd put down, but when she thrust a piece of paper at him he took it and peered at the scrawl. Then he gestured the woman into the passenger seat, turned the van round and headed for the road to the waterfall, while his passenger sat there shivering.

'And how did you and your friend get yourselves into this fix?' he inquired, not unkindly. But all the woman would do was shake her head and mutter, an alien apparition sprung from the night.

In Olden Times

She lived by the clock. Her days were apportioned, hour by hour, parcelled up into time at work, time for sleeping, time for house cleaning, for shopping, time for the children. An hour, a half-hour, ten minutes. Time for love-making; time for ironing, for cooking, for taking a bath. A crisis meant time borrowed from one sector and forever owed – the entire week flung out of order by an emergency visit to the surgery, or a faulty washing-machine or car that would not start. And each day was punctuated by the rigorous, inescapable blasts of the whistle: 7.30 (evening) – leave for work; 8.45 (morning) – arrive home from work; 8.50 – Tim leaves for work. Take children to school; sleep till 1; clean, wash, shop, fetch children from school. Attend to children – laugh, chat, listen. Glimpse, for a moment, the parallel but alien universe in which the girls live, Katie and Linda, aged seven and eight, a place in which time was pliable, wayward, in which an hour could be a day, the clock could stop still or whirl unrestrained, in which you could be quite unfettered by chronology, stepping from moment to moment, not knowing if it were morning or afternoon.

'It's all rush, rush, rush with you people nowadays,' said old Mrs Arthur, her regular patient. 'When I was your age we took life as it came. We didn't try to cram forty-eight hours into twenty-four. Going to give me a bath tonight, Marion, are you?'

She was an agency nurse and worked nights; Tim, her husband, was an accountant, and worked days. They passed each other twice daily, like ferries plying to and from a harbour. On Saturday nights she did not work, and they made love, luxuriously. Sometimes they had a quick go mid-week too, in between Tim getting home and her leaving – in haste with the bedroom door locked while the girls were watching telly.

She did sums in her head, continuously – as she drove, as she peeled potatoes, as she brushed her hair or cleaned her teeth. The mortgage plus the insurance plus the electricity the gas the telephone the holiday money. Tim's salary plus my pay. Five hundred and ninety-six in the building society. The housekeeping plus the children's dinner money plus the boiler repair bill plus Katie's new shoes. Figures flew around inside her head, neat in columns, plus or minus, or jumbled and spinning, unrestrained and unstoppable.

'Never satisfied,' said old Mrs Arthur. 'That's what's wrong with people today. Videos and those computer things and I don't know what. I had a three-piece when I got married, and a new gas cooker, and thought I was well off. Now it's want, want, want.'

She made the girls a dolls' house out of a tea-chest – anguished secret hours with plywood and saw and hammer and tacks and battered fingers. Wallpaper remnants, carpet offcuts and real pictures on the walls, in tiny photograph frames. She was the good mother. All right, so they didn't have holidays in Spain or Greece, but they had a dolls' house. They had a mother who fetched them from school, who helped them with their homework, who paid attention.

'We're learning about the olden days this term,' they told her. 'Old-fashioned times. The Victorian times. We're going to do a project. And we're going to have a Victorian day and it'll be a Victorian school and we'll be children in old-fashioned times.'

'Goodness!' she said. 'Well!'

There was always a half-hour missing in the day, somehow – mislaid, gone astray. At night, at Mrs Arthur's, cat-napping in a sleeping-bag on the couch, getting up two-hourly to check the patient, she would still feel out of breath, as though she had run a race and failed to keep up.

She was a State Registered Nurse. She knew many things; she had many skills. She could inject and dress and dose; she could lift and turn, fetch and carry. She could alleviate pain; she could save life. She could also sand floors and strip walls and hang paper and apply paint or distemper. She could change a washer or fit a plug. She could cut hair, make a soufflé, assemble within fifteen minutes and without notice the materials with which to construct a rag doll like children had in olden times, to take to school tomorrow morning. Everyone's got to bring one, Mum, so can we do it now, before tea?

Tim went to evening classes to learn car maintenance and thus save on garage bills. He was not a technically competent person, not the sort of man who is always about the place with spirit-level and power drill, who swarms confidently up stepladders. He would peer disconsolately into the car's innards, the manual in his hand, frowning and fiddling. She felt an ache of pity, and wanted to help, but knew she would probably do no better. The car was a tyrant, and a saviour. It gobbled money, lost value, would eventually have to be replaced; and they could not do without it. Should it break down, then the whole delicate precise timetable of the day was destroyed – laid waste by long waits for buses, the trudge across town to the children's school or to the shops. As she drove, she was always on edge for those ominous little sounds – a squeak, a rattle, an alien note to the engine, the heralds of disaster. The car was five years old, vulnerable, on the brink of decline. She was locked into hatred of it, and dependence, as in some stale habitual marriage.

'You've lost the use of your legs, you young people,' said Mrs Arthur. 'I walked two miles to school when I was a child, two there and two back. And when I was a working girl I'd take the tram. We never thought to drive a car, back then.'

On Mondays and Wednesdays and Fridays she went to Mrs Arthur, who was semi-paralysed after a stroke. Mrs Arthur's daughter, who coped for the rest of the week, thus achieved three nights at home with her family. Marion would have a quick chat with the daughter in the hall, coming and going: two women in a hurry, in tacit complicity, knowing with unerring insight what the other's life was like, so that they could talk in shorthand – a coded exchange about children, and time and money and the way of the world. Colluding, buoying one another up.

On the other nights she worked at a geriatric nursing home, in twilit wards filled with sighing and coughing and the sudden authoritative tap of footsteps as the duty nurses attended to a call or a crisis.

In the mornings, at home, when she slept in her own room with the curtains drawn and the windows outlined by a hard edge of light from the insistent day beyond, voices from the street would invade her dreams, as she cruised just below the level of consciousness. Inhabiting that surreal dream world in which there is no logic, in which time is not sequential but episodic, in which anything is possible, she would hear the voices as nagging or peremptory reminders of an elsewhere, filling her with unease, with the sense that there was something she should be doing, somewhere she should be going. And then she would wake, subject at once to the tyrannous schedule of the day.

In Victorian times, the children reported, people worked in factories all day long, little children too. All day in horrid black rooms and they never played in the sunshine and they didn't go to school or learn anything. If you'd been born then you might have worked down a coalmine, Mum, pulling a cart like horses did. Honestly. Their eyes blazed with indignation. It wasn't all lovely in olden times, like people think, they told her.

She was happy, she believed. In fact she knew that she was happy. Occasionally – when she had a moment – she counted her blessings, as her mother used to advocate. Tim, the girls. All of them in good health. The house, the car, the washing-machine. She considered the house, which was like many, many other houses. Well, yes – the house was a blessing. Plenty of people do not have any house at all. The car, the washing-machine? Well, up to a point.

Just occasionally, she was able to identify happiness. She saw it made manifest, and perceived what it was. It was Linda belting towards her from the school gates, it was Katie laughing in the bath, it was Tim's face when they made love. It could be quite other things, too, quite different things – a blue and green May morning, starlight, the sun on your face. You could identify it – with hindsight, it always seemed. What you could not do was cost it, count it, add or subtract it. Catch and keep it. Interestingly, it seemed to have little to do with cars or washing-machines or, indeed, houses.

'When I was young,' said Mrs Arthur, 'there was none of this pollution. We had proper countryside, back then, with flowers and birds, and you could walk the length of the High Street without seeing a car. And there were real summers, back then, with sunshine end to end. No need to go traipsing off in aeroplanes to get a suntan.'

'And they made little boys be chimney-sweeps,' said Katie and Linda. 'They sent them up hot chimneys and sometimes they got stuck. And lots of children died of illnesses because there was dirty water and they didn't have good food and baby clinics. And it was all smoky and smelly and foggy. But when we have our Victorian Day it's not going to be like that. We're going to pretend it's an old-fashioned school like lucky children went to, and we're going to dress up and be the children.'

'Well!' she said. 'What fun!'

Each day was a course that she had to negotiate. She would look along the channel of the hours, each morning, with narrowed eyes, calculating the hazards, the tricky bends. Sometimes she had a clear run. On other days she stumbled her way through, betrayed by each obstacle, prey to a malign confederacy of ailing children, failed machinery, missing car keys. All days were the same, and entirely different.

Time was hours, which added up to days, and days which clustered to become a week. She saw it as an element, like air or water. The element in which she moved, through which she fought her way.

'Scrub my back, dear, would you?' said Mrs Arthur. And she would rub the flannel down skin that was flabby here and papery there, quite different from the plump, springy surfaces of her children. She always had her hands on bodies, it seemed – she was an expert on the smooth feel of thighs, the protuberance of feet, the way a breast hangs or a buttock curves. She could date flesh at a glance: time incarnate.

All days were the same, and different, and then every now and then there would arrive a day that was in a class of its own, that pointed up the nature of all her days. Such as the day before the Victorian Day.

Which began like any other.

'Off now, are you?' said Mrs Arthur, barely awake, squinting up bleary from the bedclothes. 'I'll see you when I see you, then. Take care. Give yourself a break, you need it.'

It was crafty, that day. It pulled its punches, to start with. No traffic jam at the bridge, for once, green lights all the way down the High Street, home seven minutes earlier than usual. Time for a cup of tea with Tim; time to sew a button on Katie's shirt before school.

Then the day began to snarl. Rain, bucketing down. Katie falling in a puddle outside the school – mud-splashed, weeping.

She decided to shop on the way home, get that done. She weathered the check-out line, achieved the cashier, watched her pile rung up, groped for her purse – and knew then that she had left it on the seat of the car after finding the coin for the meter. A set-back, but relatively low on the scale of things – just a low hurdle, a treacherous bend in the road. (Leave shopping stacked at check-out; fetch purse from car; lose twenty minutes and forfeit ten-minutes-with-paper-and-cup-of-coffee when back at the house.)

But, back at the house, the day had its fangs properly bared. She put the washing in the machine, switched on, and water promptly gushed all over the floor. Inspection revealed a rotted lining. She removed the washing from the machine, dried the floor and rang repair firms, none of which could come till the day after tomorrow. She did the washing by hand. By now it was a quarter to twelve and she knew that she would not get her morning nap that day. Well, all right. Not the first time, and she had snoozed last night, on and off, between getting up to check old Mrs Arthur, turn her, take her the bed-pan. The mid-morning coffee she had not had could become an early lunch break. She put the kettle on.

The kettle remained cold and silent. She checked the plug, the switch: no progress. Now she felt that surge of impotent anger that had to be resisted, that got you nowhere. She fetched the screw-driver, dismantled the plug and found a blown fuse.

And no, of course there was not a spare fuse in the drawer where such things as spare fuses should be.

She weighed up the choices: get in car, drive to High Street, search for parking space, etc., or walk to corner shop which may or may not stock fuses. Fifteen–twenty minutes and certain fuse against four minutes and very possibly no fuse. She decided to live danger-ously and gamble.

But lo, suddenly the day had relented, gone soft, turned a blind eye on her! For the corner shop did indeed have fuses – 3 amp, 5 amp, take your pick.

Back home, she set about installing the fuse and reassembling the plug (on no account mislay tiny screws, which would never again be found). The cup of coffee was now within sight.

The phone rang. A neighbour, whose toddler has fallen and gashed his forehead; an edge of panic to her voice . . . 'I don't know if I should take him to the Casualty or not, could you come and have a look, Marion, sorry to ask but . . .'

Abandon plug (put screws in empty matchbox). Hasten to neigh-bour's house.

The gash is not disastrous but warrants a precautionary visit to the Casualty. And of course the child's mother has no car to hand so the only neighbourly course is to offer to drive her there. 'Really it's no bother. I've got a couple of hours at least before I have to get the girls from school.' (No – revise that – a half hour has evaporated since last she checked her watch. An hour and a half.)

A rough passage to the hospital: traffic jam in the High Street, a lorry unloading in what should have been a nifty short cut, the toddler fretting and the mother agitated. At last she got to the Casualty, saw them to the reception desk, set off home. But now she was not in good shape: that muzzy feeling in the head, heart going a little too hard and too fast, limbs fizzing as though lightly aerated. Calm down, Marion. Slow up; take it easy. But it was nearly a quarter to three now, and the girls must be picked up at half past. Also, there was something odd about the car, was there not? A dragging feel, a wobble to the steering.

She made it to the house, with sinking stomach to add to the leaden head and aerated limbs. Pull yourself together, Marion, it's only a flat tyre.

Only.

Scurry, now. Five to three, and she will have to walk to the main road, wait possibly ten minutes for the bus. She should make it to the school gates in time, but gone is the chance for that cup of coffee and the planned quick preparation of vegetables for the evening meal.

Twelve minutes, not ten, at the bus-stop. The girls already outside the school when she arrived. More walking, more waiting, more bus. Home at 4.20. Ah well.

And then it happened. 'Oh . . .' they said. 'Oh, Mum, it's the Victorian Day tomorrow. Didn't we tell you? Well, it is. And we're all to have mob caps and pinafores. You can make them out of old sheets, Mrs Sanderson says. You cut out a round, Mum, and machine it round the edge and then pull it up round the middle and it makes a frilly mob cap. It's easy-peasy. And you make the pinnies like this – look, she's drawn a pattern. And she said if your mum hasn't got a machine tell her she can just hem them round. OK? Mum?'

They gaze at her happily – excited, trusting.

'I see,' she says. 'Yes. Well. I wish you'd told me this yesterday. Or the day before.'

'Sorry, Mum,' they said. 'We forgot. We thought we had.'

So . . . Quick search of the airing-cupboard, to find a sheet old enough to be condemned. Get out the ancient Singer, once her mother's, which has not been used for many a long year, since she decided in early youth that dressmaking was not for her. At least the girls are tranquil elsewhere, busy on some concern of their own. One can get on unimpeded.

She cut out circles for the caps, squares for the pinnies. So far, so good. But, oh God, a cup of tea would be a help! That bloody plug. It won't take a moment to fix it.

'Katie! You haven't touched the matchbox I left on the kitchen table, have you?'

The matchbox is now incorporated into a sofa that they are making for the dolls' house. Hence the tranquillity. The screws? They gaze at her again, in guilt and anxiety. Oh . . . they say. We didn't think you wanted them . . . We're not sure where they are.

One could, of course, take a plug off something else, there being, inevitably, no spare one. One could return to the corner shop, which might still be open.

What one will in fact do is renounce the cup of tea.

Back to the sewing-machine. Find the white cotton; fit reel and spool; thread needle (the last one in the little box, incidentally). All set, at last.

Well, the machine seems to be working, anyway. Working fine, indeed. Halfway round the rim of the first mob cap in a trice. Nothing to it. Easy-peasy. This will not be too bad. Her head is perhaps throbbing a little less, too, and the limbs not fizzing quite so furiously.

And then the needle broke. A sickening little crack . . . and a stump without a point.

For a minute she sat there, simply staring. She could hear Linda calling out from the next room, asking, 'Is it nearly supper time?'

And presently the girls came to investigate the silence. They stood at the door, transfixed. And when she looked up she saw herself reflected in their eyes – their faces stiff with shock, aghast at the sight of their mother in tears, at the view of a woman they hardly recognized, weeping over a sewing-machine and a heap of white sheeting.

The Clarinettist and the Bride's Aunt

The best man did not dance with the bridesmaid; the bridesmaid was four and a half and the best man had other fish to fry. The bridegroom's former girlfriend cruised the reception, dressed to kill, attracting much interest and staking out territory for months to come. The bride flew hither and thither, a froth of white silk and billowing skirts, kissing and smiling. The bridegroom took his jacket off quite early on, while they were all still seated at long tables in the big gilded and beflowered ballroom of the country-house hotel. Gradually, the contained decorum induced by the church service fell away. Long before the jazz band arrived there were jackets off all around and children were scooting up and down the room, getting under the feet of the waitresses.

The wedding guests were a fine confusion of age and circumstance, the entire association of two people's lives, acquisitions by birth and by choice, gathered together thus amid the white napery and the lilies and the champagne buckets, most of them wearing unaccustomed clothes and wondering who everyone else might be. There were teachers and nurses and financial consultants and computer programmers, there were a ballet dancer and a journalist and a motor-cycle courier and a member of Parliament and a wine merchant and a hairdresser and many others. Between them, they reached away in all directions, a kaleidoscope of the time and the place from which they sprang. There were those who had scarcely begun and those who were nearly through, and those who hung out in bedsits and those whose homes would fetch half a million. They wore Austin Reed suits and Levis and leather jackets and suits from Oxfam shops, silk outfits from Jaeger and skin-tight Lycra and Monsoon dresses and two-pieces from Marks & Spencer. Each homed in upon familiar faces and eyed the rest, passing judgement. Only the bride and groom knew everyone. They presided, the stars of the event, the catalysts, the rationale for this medley which was both random and entirely ordered. This man was here because his wife was the groom's cousin, that girl was here because she had once worked with the bride. Most of them would never set eyes on one another again.

The jazz band arrived when the meal had ended, after the toasts and the speeches, when coffee was being served and people were drifting around, visiting other tables, trooping out to the cloakrooms. They arrived without fuss, were suddenly there, at one end of the room, chatting to one another and setting themselves up with a sort of unobtrusive assurance. They were a seven-piece band, all male, veering towards middle age, the trombone player and the pianist in their sixties. They filled that end of the room with the brassy shine of their instruments and their calm, purposeful presence. People did not so much notice them as become aware of them, and when they began to play it was without fuss or flourish but with the relaxed power of those who know exactly what they are about, and know also that they are doing it very well indeed. It was as though everything moved on to a different plane, as though the whole event changed gear.

They played 'Canal Street Blues' and 'Ace in the Hole' and 'Louisiana'. People got up and danced. Children bounced around on the polished floor. The wedding party proceeded beneath the level of the music in a cheerful burble and a ceaseless swirl of comings and goings. The bride's parents toured the room, paying especial attention to the old, the very young, and those who seemed to have nobody to talk to. The bridegroom's cronies hived off into a noisy group of shirt-sleeved and tieless young men and thin long-legged girls who laughed a lot. Babies wailed and were fed or swept off for a nappy-change. Those few guests who knew good jazz when they heard it gave the music three quarters of their attention and missed much of what was said to them, occasionally causing offence.

The bride's aunt, Susan Hamilton, was one of these. She had not at first noticed the arrival of the band, busy exchanging polite nothings with a relative, but when they began to play she felt at once a thrill of appreciation. Oh yes, she thought, oh yes. She disengaged herself tactfully from the relative and moved to a seat where she could see the band more clearly. She noted that unforced power, the fluency of people who are on top of the job. This was the real thing all right. The trombone player was amazing. They were into 'Snake Rag' now. Very nice too. The clarinettist took a solo.

And as he did so she saw who he was. This man, ten feet away from her, playing the clarinet like nobody's business, was the one-time love of her life, the first and only. James Carlisle. Him.

Older. Of course. Thicker. Slight stoop. Wearing white shirt, dark trousers, red-striped waistcoat, and still playing jazz clarinet fit to break your heart. Just like back then in smoky cellars choked with students and awash with rot-gut cheap wine. Better, indeed. He'd been good, back then. He was stunning, now.

Well, she thought. Well. She gazed. She felt the incredulous smile that spread across her face.

Halfway through the solo he saw her. He looked directly at her and continued to do so. His playing did not change, his expression did not flicker, but he played now, she became complacently aware, directly to her. For her. He played and she listened and they looked at one another, for what seemed a very long time. The number came to an end. The leader of the band announced that they would now take a short break. And the clarinettist, still looking directly at the bride's aunt, cocked his thumb in the direction of the double doors that opened into the gardens.

They met at the top of the flight of steps leading down on to an acreage of brilliant lawn. 'Breath of fresh air, I thought . . .' said James Carlisle.

They proceeded down the steps and arrived at a bench overlooking the grass. They sat down, and set about a mutual examination. The years did not fall away – oh no. Rather, they gathered around them in an interesting haze, a mysterious screen of untransmittable experience. Here we are, each thought, the same and not at all the same.

'I won't say I'd have known you anywhere,' he observed. 'It was the way you had your head on one side. You always did that in the Union cellars. Head on one side. Slightly critical expression.'

'I didn't spot you at once. Only when you started playing. In the street, we'd have walked past each other, I imagine.'

'Well, what luck,' he said.

'I take it this isn't what you do? I mean, day in day out . . .'

'Would that it were. I'm a statistician by trade. This is a spot of moonlighting. Ditto for most of us. Our trombone player is an antiquarian bookseller. And what brings you here?'

'I am the bride's aunt.'

James Carlisle laughed.

'And why is that funny?' she inquired.

'Just that I would never have thought of you as being anyone's aunt. But I can quite see how these things happen.'

'Oh, they do indeed. Before you know where you are.'

'Nice girl, is she?'

'Delightful. My favourite niece. I have three.'

At the far side of the sweep of grass a bride was posing for a photograph, a swirl of white against the green.

'More photos?' said Susan. 'I thought they'd done all that.'

'This is not your bride. Different outfit, if you look. There's another wedding going on in the annexe over there. It's absolutely the thing these days – marriage. We're booked up for weeks to come. Not that we take just anything, I'll have you know. We pick and choose a bit.'

'How did Natalie and David get to hear about you?'

'Let's see now . . . Oh yes – the bridegroom knew a bloke whose girlfriend had been at a wedding we did and got chatting to someone in the band.'

'And so here we are today . . .'

'So here we are today. Quirk of fate.'

'Do you ever see any of that crowd?' she asked. 'From back then.'

'I do not. You?'

'Nobody. One loses touch, somehow.'

Each considered, for an instant, the impenetrable mass of the intervening years, and decided to let them be.

'I like your dress,' said James.

'Thank you.'

'I've become a connoisseur of wedding outfits. You see some pretty odd gear, I can tell you.'

'How many do you chalk up, then? Weddings.'

'This time of year – height of the season – you can reckon on one a week.'

'Gracious . . .' she said.

'And do they know what they're at, one asks?'

She shot him a look. Something glimmered, it would seem, from that impenetrable mass.

'Let no man put asunder . . .' he continued. 'Well, there'll be a fair amount of putting asunder, I don't doubt. Nothing personal, of course – I daresay your nice niece is all set for eternal bliss. Just statistics, that's all.'

'Statistics . . .' she said. 'Of course, when it's going on, you never feel quite like a statistic.'

He, now, shot a glance.

'Married yourself, are you?' he inquired, after a moment.

'Not now. Up till three years ago I was.'

'Me too. Not – I mean.'

There was a silence. They gazed reflectively at the photographic session in the distance. The bride and groom, flanked now by the complementary pairings of their parents.

'How about I take our glasses in for a top-up?' said James Carlisle.

'Have we time?'

'Plenty of time.'

She watched him go up the steps, holding the empty champagne glasses. The same, and not at all the same. Well, well. Just fancy.

There came to her, now, various images from back then, frozen like clips from a film, images which presumably he shared and upon which it seemed wiser not to dwell. She fended these off, observed the distant group (now marshalling recalcitrant bridesmaids) and thought about pairings.

Back in the days of the Jazz Club and the Union Cellars there had been pairings – definitely there had been pairings. But it had been tacitly understood that these were transitory, temporary, that they were for the term, or for a week or two, or just for the evening. And, likewise, there were those who were couples, and were known and recognized as such, but it was known and recognized equally that couplings could become uncoupled, with the greatest of ease and quite possibly with no hard feelings.

'Goodness . . .' she thought, knowing what she now knew. How was it done? What innocence. What primal innocence.

The pairings, back then, had been pairings of mutual convenience and intellectual pairings and sporting pairings and pairings of undisguised carnality. From time to time a girl got pregnant and vanished from the scene, amid commiserations. Very rarely, a couple got married, prompting shock and unconcealed disapproval. They then went to live in squalor in a bedsit or flat and nobody visited them. Marriage was not at all the thing, back then. Definitely not.

Except that, eventually, after a few years, many of them got married. Not to one another but to completely different people encountered in the real world of job applications and mortgages. Others, of course, did not, for various reasons.

James Carlisle returned, with glasses of champagne. He had fended off his colleagues, been introduced to bride and groom and shaken the hand of the bride's mother. The bride's mother was a little distracted at that moment, looking round for her sister, whom she did not seem to have seen for some while. She hoped Susan hadn't got stuck with someone tiresome.

He sat down again. 'Marriage,' he said, 'is an act of such extraordinary optimism.'

'Too right.'

'The young, of course, tend to be optimistic. And so they damn well should.'

'Were we? I can't remember.'

'It's not something one remembers – a state of mind. It's precise things you remember.'

'True,' she said. She carefully did not look at him, now, but gazed out over the grass. The photo session was over; the bridesmaids were whooping it up like foals, to the detriment of their dresses.

'Hm . . .' He had decided, evidently, to drop that. 'Yes, well . . . Actually, I'm deficient in that area, myself. Tell me something – I didn't ever propose marriage, did I? Back then.'

'Good heavens, no,' she said.

'You'd have slapped me in the face, no doubt.'

'Well . . . It would have seemed a distinct breach of manners, I think.'

'I'm glad I behaved myself, then.'

'Oh . . .' she said. 'You were splendid, always.'

'You were pretty good yourself,' said James Carlisle.

They looked at each other, now, and hugely grinned.

'Dear me,' said Susan Hamilton. 'This won't do at all. Surely you should be getting back to your duties?'

'All in good time.'

'And I have not yet done my stuff with the in-laws. Nor with Natalie's boss nor my sister's best friend. What are you going to play, after the interval?'

'What would you like us to play?'

'It's hardly up to me.'

'If that's how you feel I'll have to trust to my memory. I think I still know your tastes.'

And so, in due course, they left their bench, and the fresh air, and returned to the wedding. The band struck up. Couples took to the floor. The bride danced with her father. The bride's mother, anxiously inspecting the room, caught sight of her sister once more, sitting a little apart, being talked at by the groom's parents, and thought that Susan was looking extremely . . . vibrant. She knew that look, but could not quite put a finger on it.

The wedding continued. The cake was cut. The best man achieved a couple of objectives. The groom's former girlfriend consolidated ground. The bridesmaid began to flag, tearfully, and was removed. The older guests drifted to the perimeter of the room and became spectators. The band played on; the dancing became more energetic; outside the windows, twilight gathered. And all the while, above and beyond the music, isolated amid the chatter and the comings and the goings, the clarinettist and the bride's aunt watched each other – thoughtful, speculative and alert.

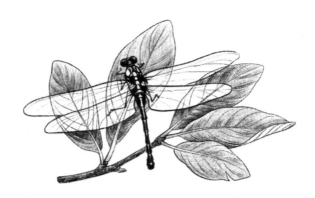

Marriage Lines

The Dawsons, who were having their marriage counselled, glared at each other across their counsellor. The counsellor, known to them as Liz, was a small plump woman who might have been thought attractive had any concessions been made by way of becoming clothes or a flattering haircut. As it was, her manner and appearance spoke of responsibilities heavily borne and an implacable confidence in her own judgement. She treated the Dawsons with maddening patience and impartiality, as though they were children in a nursery school whose behaviour was wayward but inevitable. Her bland attention to their complaints implied that she had heard it all before, that they were in no way unique or especially blighted, and that nothing could jolt her from her complacent consideration of their various sources of discord. She drove Ben Dawson to a frenzy. Sometimes the ferocity of his feelings about Liz quite distracted him from his irritation with his wife and the matter in hand.

'And another thing,' Prue Dawson was saying, 'I thought it was settled that when we disagree about how to handle a situation over the children we don't give conflicting instructions but we sit down and talk it over. And now only yesterday you walk in and completely undermine what I've already sorted out. That business with Nicky about the ballet shoes and next Tuesday.'

Liz turned to Ben. 'Do you have a problem with that, Ben?'

This was Liz's favourite question. Or comment, or way of moving on, or whatever it was. So far it had been clocked up five times in this session.

'Yes,' he said sourly. 'Or it wouldn't have been mentioned, would it?'

'Would you like to tell us about this, Ben?' Liz continued.

'No, to be honest. For two reasons – I should find it unspeakably boring, and Prue would get more annoyed than she is already. I daresay you might get something out of it, but I'm not sure what.'

Liz fixed him with her most neutral gaze. 'Thank you for sharing that with us, Ben.'

It occurred to Ben, not for the first time, that he might simply walk out. The only thing that stopped him was that such a move would undoubtedly be interpreted to his disadvantage and held against him. Principally by Liz.

He stared at the floor, which was the only place to look if you were not to catch someone else's eye. The chairs were arranged in a semicircle, so that Liz sat between her clients. They were chairs of an awkward lowness, forcing the occupant to sit with legs stuck out straight ahead, in a parody of relaxation. The only window was covered by a blind, to exclude reminders of ordinary life in the world beyond. The room was profoundly claustrophobic, which was presumably the intention. Concentrate, it said. Bare your soul. Expose yourself. Go on – wallow in it.

He said, 'Do you mind if we talk about something else now?'

Liz gave Prue the glance of measured impartiality. 'How do you feel about that, Prue?'

'I don't care one way or the other,' said Prue. 'Incidentally,' she added, speaking across Liz to Ben, 'in the end it turned out the wretched ballet shoes were the wrong size. I'll have to get another pair. God knows how, before Tuesday.'

'Are you married, Liz?' said Ben, after a moment. 'Or have you been?'

Liz dealt him a chilly smile. 'That's irrelevant, Ben, isn't it?'

'No, I don't think it is, really. It's a question of credentials. I mean, to advise us you have to have some experience of our situation, don't you?'

'Let's just say I'm in a relationship,' said Liz. The tone of stern professional neutrality once more.

If I hear that dire word again I'll scream, thought Ben. 'Good,' he said. 'Join the club.' He looked at Prue. 'I daresay I could take her to get some shoes tomorrow. I could leave the office early.'

'Oh, right,' said Prue. 'Thanks.'

Liz cleared her throat. She shuffled the papers on her lap. These actions, the Dawsons now knew, meant that she felt the focus of attention had strayed and that she needed to establish control. 'I've noticed that you both mention work quite a bit today. Maybe that's an area we should cover. Ben, could I ask you what you feel about Prue's work situation?'

'What do you mean – what do I feel about it? Are you asking if I think she's got a good job, or a suitable job, or are you asking if I think she ought to be working in WC1 rather than WC2, or what, for heaven's sake?'

Liz reflected, eyeing him. At last she said, 'It's interesting that you seem to be getting a bit overexcited, Ben. Do you want to say anything about this?'

'Only that I wish you'd use language with rather more precision.'

Liz turned to Prue. 'What do you feel about Ben's attitude here?'

'Actually I think he's got a point,' said Prue.

Ben shot his wife a look of surprise.

'You think he has a problem with your work situation?' said Liz encouragingly.

'No, I mean I think he's right about language. Sometimes we all have a problem over what it is exactly we're trying to talk about.'

Ben experienced a gust of something suspiciously like affection. 'In point of fact,' he said, 'work is not a prime area of dissension. I entirely approve of Prue's job. I think she's good at it. I try to be supportive.'

'Hm . . .' said Prue.

'Well, all right. I agree I was a touch unreasonable about the Leeds trip. Next time I'll shut up. But . . .' – he addressed himself to Liz – '. . . by and large and on the whole work is not something we have rows about. I appreciate that Prue's work is important to her, and that she does it well. I don't resent that. I don't suspect her of sleeping with her colleagues, either.'

Liz's expression of shrewd appraisal meant, he now recognized, that he had said something of deep significance. 'I wonder why you said that, Ben?'

'It was a joke. A rather stupid joke. I was trying to lighten things up a bit.'

'But you said it. There's some sort of sexual tension there, then?'

'Oh, Christ . . .' said Ben wearily.

Prue said, 'Actually there isn't. That's something else we're not in fact quarrelling about. We don't suspect each other of having it off with someone else.'

Liz faintly smiled. She shook her head slightly. 'In fact, Prue, I'm going to suggest that next time you have a full psychosexual session. Doctor Chambers handles that.'

'I thought you were our counsellor?' said Prue.

'Not for psychosexual. That's a separate area.'

'I'm surprised,' said Ben. 'This is interesting. You're suggesting then that the sexual element of marriage is a thing apart? I'd have thought that was a trifle unorthodox.'

'I'm not trained for psychosexual, that's all.'

'You specialize in straight domestic wrangling and childrearing disputes, is that right?'

There was a silence. Liz now wore her expression of personal distaste modulated by infinite professional patience. 'Ben, I'm going to have to say that I think you have a serious attitude problem. This is not something to make jokes about.'

'That wasn't a joke,' said Ben. 'It was a conversational style. And I was asking a question.'

Liz turned to Prue. 'Do you have a problem with the way Ben talks, Prue?'

'No,' said Prue. 'Not particularly.' There was a distinct edge of irritation to her voice. 'Possibly it takes a bit of getting used to.'

Liz frowned slightly. 'Has this adjustment been difficult for you?'

'No,' said Prue. She glanced rather wildly at Ben, who grimaced. Prue looked at him again and then away, quickly. 'No, that's not the point. Actually it's one of the things I like about Ben.'

'I see.' Liz was now registering muted disapproval.

'There are quite a lot of things I like about Ben,' Prue went on determinedly. 'And in fact I think there are things he likes about me.'

Liz sighed. 'Prue, we're getting off course again, aren't we?'

'Well, I must say I don't quite see . . .' Prue began.

'Compatibility is irrelevant, is it?' said Ben.

Liz turned to him. She was impregnable, he saw. He read in her face absolute complacency and an unswerving rectitude. 'Ben,' she was saying, 'I think we're in trouble again with your basic attitude. I feel that . . .' Language oozed from her, smothering him.

It came to him with sudden clarity that there was something dreadfully awry. He could not imagine how they had arrived in this room, locked into eerie collaboration with this dispiriting woman. He recognized with elation that Prue's discomfort matched his own feverish impatience. He got to his feet. He said, 'Liz, thank you for trying to help us, but speaking for myself I feel there's nothing further I can contribute. I don't know about Prue, but . . .'

Prue also had risen. 'Yes,' she said. 'Me too, in fact. Thank you very much, Liz, but . . .'

They fled. They stepped into the street, still trailing their unfinished excuses. They headed for home, side by side, bolstered by the familiar private apposition of disagreement and collusion which seemed now a protection rather than a constraint.

The Cats' Meat Man

She opened the front door and there he was on the step, wearing a white coat. Like someone behind the deli counter in Tesco, she told her daughter later. Not as clean as it might have been, either – the coat.

'Yes?' she said.

'Do you like good food?' he gabbled. 'Interested in good food, are you?' She saw the van now, parked in her little bit of driveway. A small blue van. 'Chicken Kiev. Lasagne. Prawns. Dover sole.' He had a white pasty face in which his sloe dark eyes darted about like fish in a tank – looking here, there, everywhere except at her. 'Beef Stroganoff?' he urged. 'Fond of Beef Stroganoff at all?'

'No,' she said. 'Not really. I eat vegetables mostly. And egg dishes. Eggs Florentine. Do you know that? With spinach.'

Freeze-dried, he told her. It's the new process. Not just frozen – air-dried. Or air-blown, did he say, or airbrushed. Something like that. Anyway, not just straightforward frozen, she explained to her daughter. More up to date than that.

It was six o'clock. Probably he hadn't made a sale all afternoon, she thought. Dead on his feet now, and still having to burble on about air-dried and Beef Whatsit. The people at the farmhouse wouldn't have taken anything, that was for sure, and the Holly Cottage family were away on their holidays and old Mrs Hammond wouldn't have so much as answered the door.

'Do you know what you've reminded me of?' she said. 'The cats' meat man. When I was a child. He'd come down the street with his handcart, ringing a bell. And you'd see all the cats come out, all along the row, and hang around. He'd have this great big wet red slab and he'd cut off a slice for you. Sixpence. And lights, he'd have. I'm not sure what bit of an animal that is. Have you any idea?'

The man looked in her direction. His eyes continued to twitch this way and that. 'I couldn't say. We don't do any of those. Just prime T-bone steak. £4.50 each. Beautiful quality.'

'I haven't got £4.50 to spare, I'm afraid. That's as much as I spend on food in two or three days.'

He was opening up the back of the van now. 'Individually packaged,' he was saying. 'All ready to store in your freezer.' She saw tier upon tier of metal trays in which were stacked flat cardboard boxes. He took one out and opened it up: she saw neat overlapping fillets of fish. 'Lemon sole. £6.50.'

'Too much,' she said firmly. 'I suppose I could run to a few fish fingers.'

'We don't do those.' He sounded sulky now. That'll get you nowhere, she thought. Smile and smile, if you're a salesman – that's the trick. But he was wiped out, you could see that. He swayed as he stood there waving his packets of this and that.

'It was the same cats' meat man right up till I was fifteen,' she said. 'We never knew his name. We went through several cats, they'd come to grief one way or another, but always the same cats' meat man. Big fellow that could cut up meat like nobody's business.'

He stared at her. No, not stared – looked her way and his eyes went on flickering around. Not a straightforward sort of a man, she rather thought.

'Oh, all right,' she said. 'I'll have one of those Chicken Kiev things. Just the one portion. I'll get my purse.' She paused. He looked as though he was in a daze now. Oh, for heaven's sake, she thought, show a bit of Christian charity, Eileen. 'If you'd like to come in for a minute, I've got a pot of tea made. You look as though you could do with a cup.'

He muttered. Wouldn't mind . . . or something like that. Not – That's very kind of you. Oh, well.

He trailed after her into the house. She put him in the basket chair in the kitchen. The tea had gone cold. 'I'll make a fresh pot,' she said. 'This is no good to man nor beast. Won't take a minute. This'll be your last call today anyway, I should think.'

He muttered again.

She filled the kettle, rinsed out the pot. 'My father did house to house for a bit,' she said. 'Selling vacuum cleaners. This was before the war. He was a warehouse clerk really, but he lost his job and then you had to take what you could. I suppose it's like that again now.' There wasn't much milk in the jug so she went through into the larder to get some more from the fridge. 'And then the war came,' she said. 'And solved that problem at least. Plenty of jobs for everyone then. Not that I'd suggest that again as a solution.' She looked across at him and he'd fallen asleep, if you please. Fast asleep in her chair with his head poked forward on his chest and that grubby white coat open to show a T-shirt with a Mickey Mouse on it. Scruffy sports shoes on his feet. My father wore a suit, she told him. Suit and tie and a clean shirt every day. And his shoes polished so you could see your face.

She poured herself a cup of tea and drank it reading the local paper. The free one that came through the door. The paper seemed to be mostly about food too. Pizzas brought to your door and Indian takeaways and three-course family lunch at the Red Lion for £5.99. She read all about this, and skimmed the Used Car column and had a look at the Property Section and still the man slept. She drank a second cup of tea, glancing at him occasionally. This is all very well, she thought. Another five minutes and I'll wake him. His mouth was open now, not a pretty sight.

She needed to go to the loo, so she got up and went upstairs. She took her time and made a bit of a noise up there, on purpose, running taps and so forth. That would get him moving, with any luck.

She came down and he wasn't there. She looked at her bag, on the dresser, and saw that neither was her purse. And she noticed at once that the small jug was gone off the dresser and the carriage clock from the mantelpiece. She stood for a moment and her daughter hovered in the air in front of her, mouthing things. Were you completely out of your mind, Mum? Letting a perfect stranger into the house. Asking him in.

Oh, be quiet, you, she said. All right, all right.

She went outside, round the corner into the driveway and the van was still there. He was sitting in the driving seat, fiddling with something. She saw at once what had happened.

She walked up and looked at him through the open window. Whiter than before he was, if possible, pasty white and his eyes flickering as he kept turning the key in the ignition. Click, whirr. Click, whirr.

'Oh dear,' she said. 'What a nuisance for you.'

He muttered. Swearing. She could see that from his face, though she couldn't catch the words. Click, whirr. Click, whirr.

She watched, interested. 'Oh dear,' she said again.

Click, whirr. His eyes swivelled in her direction, then away, then back. Frantic, he was.

'Better come back in,' she said. 'Then we can ring the garage at the crossroads. They'll come out and have a look at it, I daresay.'

He swore again. Got out of the van, opened up the bonnet and stared into the van's innards. Poked at a wire. Took out a plug and put it back again. He didn't know t'other from which, you could see that.

'Suit yourself,' she said. 'But you can use the phone if you want to.'

He straightened up and eyed her. Not knowing how to take it. Wondering. Mum! shrieked her daughter. Oh, be quiet, she said. I wasn't born yesterday. Watch this.

He said something about a spanner.

'I'd have thought you'd have a toolkit with you,' she said sternly. 'Come back in then and I'll have a look.'

He followed her inside. 'I'll have to go upstairs,' she said. 'That sort of thing's in the landing cupboard. You may as well have that cup of tea now. Sit down.'

He looked relieved. He thought she hadn't noticed. The purse, the jug, the clock. She put the kettle on and went upstairs. When she came down with the spanner he was in the chair again. She made the tea and poured him a cup. This time he said thank you. She sat down herself, and watched him. Sweating, he was. She could see his skin glistening. She'd seldom come across such an unhealthy look. Her mother always used to say you can tell at a glance if a person's constipated. She knew now what was meant. All that expensive food in the back of the van and there he was looking like death warmed up.

'Fish is all very fine, I suppose,' she said, 'but too much red meat never did anyone any good. All that steak you've got out there. Fresh fruit and vegetables – that's what I go for myself.'

'It's nothing to do with me, is it?' he said. 'It's the firm's, not mine. Nothing to do with me what lines they decide to put out. Sell it on commission, that's all I do.'

'You don't reckon that much with the BeefWhatsit, then?'

'I didn't say that.' He was cross with himself now, knew he'd overstepped the mark. 'It's all good stuff.'

She studied him. 'Been doing this long?'

He shook his head. He didn't want to talk, but he was trapped. By the tea, the spanner, by what he thought she didn't know. 'I had a fast-food business. I used to do the lay-bys. Buffalo Bill's Pull-In – hamburgers and that. Had to pack it in.'

'What a pity,' she said. 'Why?'

She understood him to say something about a problem with his accountants. He got out a filthy bit of Kleenex and wiped his face. Pouring sweat he was, and she wouldn't have called the room hot – just nicely warm. She watched him thoughtfully. He was breathing in a funny way, too.

'One thing I should tell you,' she said. 'It's not silver, that jug. It's Britannia metal. I doubt if it's worth much. More tea?'

He twitched violently. His eyes went mad. She wondered if he'd make a run for it. And then I'll be left with a van full of steak and prawns. Air-dried or whatever it is. Either that or he's a different type altogether and he'll get out a knife and go for me.

She felt a bit queasy, thinking that. Somewhere, her daughter was wailing I told you so.

He put the teacup down with a crash. But he didn't get up. He sat there making a sort of panting noise. He was green now, rather than white, like mouldy bread.

'You know,' she said, 'I don't think you're feeling very well today, are you?'

He stared at her. 'Be all right in a minute,' he said thickly. He swayed.

'Well, it's your choice, but if I was you I'd cut my losses and get on the phone to that garage.' She thought she'd put that rather well. He could work out for himself what was meant by losses. Not that he looked as though he was up to working anything out just at that moment. No knife, she decided, he's not the type. Thanks be. So you can stop squawking, she told her daughter.

He clutched his throat and made a sort of gargling noise. And then he keeled over. He slumped forward and if she hadn't come across and propped him up he'd have toppled forward on to the floor. His eyes rolled up till she could see only the whites and for a moment she thought he'd died until she realized she could still hear him breathing, in that gasping way. She considered him. If a person's fainted you put their head between their knees, but she didn't somehow feel that was the problem here. She wondered if she was seeing a heart attack. But he wasn't more than thirty or so, by her reckoning. It's the likes of me who have heart attacks, she thought, not someone his age.

She waited a couple of minutes and when he showed no sign of rallying she picked up the phone.

She didn't go out to the van until the ambulance had come and gone, and him with it, strapped to a stretcher in a red blanket. The ambulance men had been noncommittal, and had become even more so when they discovered the patient was neither here nor

174

there to her, as it were. At first they'd assumed he was her son, until she'd put them right, rather sharply. After that it was just a matter of bundling him off and she'd never know, she realized, if it was heart or terminal indigestion or what.

She found her purse and the jug and the clock under the passenger seat of the van, wrapped in a couple of sheets of the *Sun*. She also found the address and phone number of the food company on an invoice pad under the dashboard and left a message on their answering machine to tell them where their van was and to request them to remove it first thing tomorrow morning.

She then returned to the van and opened up the back. She pulled out the metal trays, one by one. She took several packs of Chicken Kiev, some Dover sole and something called Vegetarian Lasagne, which might suit her. Think of it as a parking charge, she told the food company. Then, as an afterthought, she took four portions of Beef Stroganoff. Her daughter and the daughter's boyfriend, who were coming to lunch on Sunday, wouldn't know what had hit them.

The First Wife

At his niece's wedding Clive Harper fell in love with his first wife. At least that was what it felt like. There she was, not seen for many a long year, and he found himself in a turmoil. He stood staring at her through the chattering groups. Mary. Older, greyer, but unaccountably alluring. He was startled by his own response. Women of his own age did not appeal to him, generally speaking. His present wife was ten years younger.

It had not occurred to him that Mary might be at the wedding. He now remembered that she had always kept up with his brother and sister-in-law, with whom he himself was not on particularly close terms. He was looked upon with slight disapproval, which amused him. Well – they would, wouldn't they? He contrasted with satisfaction his own vigorous and varied life and their staid and complacent routine. Moreover, his brother was always taken for the eldest, though he was in fact four years younger than Clive. Gratifying, that.

Clive surveyed the room. A dull gathering, on the whole. Neighbours, old friends, the statutory sprinkling of relatives. Gaggles of young – the niece's cronies. There was only one person here he wanted to talk to.

He watched her being patiently nice to an ancient aunt of his. Mary had always been good about that sort of thing. He edged nearer, to inspect more closely. She hadn't seen him yet. She of course would be expecting him to be here, so there was not for her the element of surprise. She presumably anticipated a meeting. And the very fact that she was here must mean that she . . . wanted to see him? He felt a further thrill of interest.

She was looking handsome – distinctly handsome. She seemed somehow more positive than the Mary he remembered. There she stood, a tall woman in a light green suit, with greying hair becomingly arranged, a creamy silk scarf knotted at her neck. Good legs, elegant shoes. Clive noticed this sort of thing about a woman. Mary had not used to dress thus, in the old days. He observed the pretty Victorian brooch on the lapel of her jacket and her unusual silver earrings. No rings on her hands. A warm, responsive smile on her face as she talked to this importunate aunt.

He was overcome with a quite desperate sense of loss. There she stood, who once had been entirely his, and who no longer was. She seemed a reinstatement of his own past, of his own unattainable youth. A miraculous reincarnation – tangible and present. All he knew was that he had to be near her, had to talk to her, had to have her turn that smile upon him.

He quite forgot that he had left her, all those years ago, because he was suddenly aware that she had begun to look old. Someone had said jokingly that she looked like his mother. A young mother, mind, the person had added hastily – but the damage was done. Clive had gone home in a state of jitters, and a month later he had left Mary and moved in with Michèle, who was twenty-four and half French, an irresistible combination.

He was terrified of age. The terror had begun – oh, back in his twenties when he had looked around and realized with surprise and dismay that there were others younger than himself. His thirtieth birthday had risen up and smashed into him like a rock in a tranquil sea. He was incredulous. Thirty? Me? And then he had rallied and told himself that thirty was nothing, thirty was fine. Well – no great disaster, anyway. But he found himself looking in the mirror more often, and watching the faces of his contemporaries to see how he was doing by comparison. And every now and then there would come one of those moments of chilling realization. Thirty-six. Thirty-nine – Christ! Forty.

He was forty-one when he left Mary. She had never understood his fits of terror. She had made light of his panic, when she perceived what he felt. Look, she had said, so what? You're getting older. So am I, so's everyone. She simply didn't understand. She had no conception of those awful seizures – the cold fear in the stomach. No, no – this can't be happening. Not to me. To other people, maybe. Not to me.

And now he was fifty-nine. Sometimes, in dark moments, the awful fact reared up and sent him reeling. But he had learned, over the years, how to keep it all at bay. Activity was the thing. Fill the days, the evenings. Travel. Go out. Be with others. Talk, laugh. He made sure to surround himself with younger people. When his old friends showed signs of becoming a touch decrepit he slid away from them. And of course Susan, his present wife, was not yet fifty.

The arrangement with Michèle had not lasted long. Indeed, he could barely remember Michèle now. She had had many successors, over the years. Little affairs – never intense enough to rock his marriage (one must have a base, a calm centre), just something to keep the adrenalin flowing. He had to have that constant frisson of interest – the anticipation of a discreet meeting, the flattery of a new face turned attentively to his.

And now – astonishingly, bewilderingly – here was Mary's face with all the allure of some stranger sighted and marked down. She was still talking to the aunt, still had not seen him. He thought with a pleasurable tingle of how she might respond when she did. How would he look to her? He was glad he had put on his rather dashing new shirt. Susan had pulled a face, for some inexplicable reason – had got out a plain white one and proposed that instead. Thank God, though, that Susan had woken with what looked like incipient flu and had decided to cry off the wedding. What luck.

He would have expected that by now Mary would be wondering if he was here, would be casting furtive glances round the room. She did not. She continued with her patient attention to the aunt until some acquaintance joined them, when she took the opportunity to slide gracefully away. But still she did not search for him. She walked over to his brother and sister-in-law and stood talking and laughing with them in a casual intimacy that had Clive in a sudden fret of jealousy.

He tried to remember what news of her had reached him over the last few years. She had never remarried. There had been a relationship that had lasted for some while but he knew that it was over now. She was alone, he was sure of that – if she were not he would have heard. She lived alone and worked in hospital administration, a career on which she had embarked after their marriage broke up.

Long ago now, all of that. He could no longer remember very precisely the sequence of events. Just that catastrophic remark by some acquaintance, and his jitters. Michèle hoving upon the scene with her beguiling youth. The way in which he himself had flailed between guilt and the panic-stricken knowledge that he was going to do what he subsequently did. He had to – it had been inevitable. And there had been outrage. His brother and sister-in-law had not spoken to him for a year. One or two friends had dropped him. And of course Mary had been badly hurt. He could see that now, could feel compunction. He had behaved badly – he would be the first to accept that.

And now was his chance – not to make amends but to initiate a new, rewarding relationship. This was so very much what he needed, he suddenly realized. Not some transitory flirtation with an agreeable newcomer, but a dependable, mutually supportive liaison with the person he had once known best in the world. It need not affect his marriage in any way. The thing would be tactfully concealed, and provide a marvellous private uplift for them both. He was amazed still at the excitement the sight of her had induced in him.

His brother and sister-in-law had been distracted by other guests. Mary was alone. It was time to act. She was already moving away.

He arrived at her side. 'Well! . . . It's wonderful to see you, Mary.'

At the sound of his voice she turned her head. There was no surprise on her face – indeed no identifiable expression at all. 'Hello, Clive.'

'Well!' he said again. He put everything into the look he gave her. He was good at that kind of tacit eloquence, he knew. His look conveyed admiration and regret and pleading anticipation. It told her that he admired her appearance, that he thought she seemed years younger than he knew her to be, that he had a thousand things to say to her, that he needed time in which to say them. It told her, in effect, that he had fallen in love with her. Clive had himself been on the receiving end of such looks in his day and knew them to be instantly unsettling. He waited for Mary to display unsettlement.

She did indeed seem taken aback. She was silent for a moment, apparently studying him. Then she said, 'I gather poor Susan's got flu.'

This was not the direction in which he meant them to go. He dealt quickly with Susan's flu and tried to bring things back to a more personal focus. He asked where she was living, and was told. Good – now he could get her address and phone number from the directory. He inquired about her work, and was given a dispassionate account of what she did. She was quite high-powered, he recognized. This also was disorienting, like her dress and manner. The earlier Mary – his Mary – had been a more self-effacing person. But this authority was undoubtedly part of her new appeal. A woman of her time, he thought approvingly. Good for you. He finished what he was saying – something about his own present doings – and gazed at her again with unashamed admiration. Let her know what he was feeling, what he was thinking.

She seemed a touch restive. She glanced over his shoulder, sipped at her drink. She was affected by him, no doubt about that. He had disconcerted her. Now, perhaps, was the moment to make a direct approach.

'Could we perhaps . . . meet?' he said.

She hesitated. And now that wretched aunt was heading for them.

'Mary,' she was crying. 'Mary – I quite forgot to give you my new address.'

Clive gave his first wife his most beseeching smile. 'Soon? I'll call you. All right?'

She seemed about to speak, hesitated again. And then the aunt was there, chuntering on. Clive touched Mary's arm for a second and left them.

He could understand her hesitation – he could sympathize entirely. She didn't know how to respond. She mistrusted her own feelings, perhaps – was confused by the whole encounter. He would wait a couple of days, and then phone her. No – he would write a brief note first, maybe send some flowers, phone the day after that.

For the rest of the afternoon he made perfunctory conversation with others while trying to keep Mary within his sights. He did not manage to speak to her alone again, and when he searched for her to say goodbye she had already gone. Never mind, the groundwork had been done.

He decided against the flowers – a banal touch, that would be. He wrote her a letter – short but intense. He told her how deeply moved he had been at seeing her. He hinted delicately at years of regret. He implied a sense of void in his own life. He included one or two veiled references and muted jokes which referred back to their life together. He concluded by saying that he wanted very much to see her. Perhaps they could meet for lunch or dinner? He would phone her next week.

She did not reply. He had anticipated this – naturally, she would not wish to seem precipitate. He called, and was confronted with an answerphone. He rang off without leaving a message, and tried again the next evening. Still the answerphone. This time he spoke. He proposed lunch in three days' time. He named a restaurant. If he did not hear from her he would take it that this was acceptable and would look forward with immense pleasure to seeing her.

He arrived slightly late at the restaurant, stymied by traffic. Handing his coat to the waiter, he looked round anxiously – no sight of her. Good – it would not do to have kept her waiting. And then the waiter said, 'A lady came earlier, sir. She left you this note.'

Clive stared at the man. He took the envelope. He felt a trickle of fear. He sat down, pulled out a single sheet of paper, and began to read.

Dear Clive: No, thank you. Not lunch nor anything else. I wonder what makes you think I should wish to? Well – empathy was never your strong point.

Your letter implied a certain desolation – nicely understated but poignant none the less, which was no doubt the intention. A state of mind with which I have been deeply familiar. However, I am not I feel the right person to offer solace. I'm sure you will find someone more receptive, unless you have entirely lost your touch, which everything suggests that you have not.

Thank you for your compliments – most acceptable to a woman of my age. You haven't changed all that much yourself, though more I fear than you would like. The signs of a desperate rearguard action are plainly visible. You seem anxious to remind me of the old days, so I'm sure you won't mind if I presume on former intimacy and make a point or two. The hair en brosse is not a good idea, and I wouldn't tint the grey bits if I were you – it shows in a strong light. Also, the puce shirt is unwise on a man of your age and figure. I do hope Susan's flu is better. Poor thing. Yours, Mary.

'Would you care for an aperitif, sir?' the waiter was saying.

The Butterfly and the Tin of Paint

This is a story about a tin of paint and a prime minister. It seems also to be an eerie reflection of the butterfly effect. The butterfly effect illustrates chaos theory – that intriguing explanation of physical events which proposes that a very small perturbation can make things happen differently from the way they would have happened if the small disturbance had not been there. Thus, a butterfly in the Amazon forest flaps its wings and provokes a tornado in Texas. Other variations have the butterfly in Adelaide and the storm in Sussex, but the implications are the same and we don't need to know what kind of butterfly it was either.

The irritating thing about the butterfly effect as a theory is that you are never given an account of the progression from the wing flap to the tornado. The butterfly moves a wing and generates presumably a current of air. Then what? This is where scientists do not always deliver the goods. Real life, on one hand, and fiction, on the other, leave nothing unexplained. There is a reason for everything, in life as in art. Whether this story is life or art or neither is for the reader to decide. One thing is certain: it is not science.

The tin of paint was a trade size drum of Dulux Gloss White. It had been acquired by a decorator called Pete who was painting and wallpapering the bedroom of some people called Ambrose who lived in Fulham. The Ambroses do not come into this story. They are an absence, though a significant one, because if they had not elected to have their bedroom redecorated none of these events would have taken place. They were absent – on holiday in the Algarve – when Pete began work on their bedroom one Tuesday morning and even more mercifully absent when, at 8.35, he stumbled and kicked over the open tin of Dulux Gloss White.

The paint gushed in a viscous flood all over the Ambroses' bedroom carpet, which Pete had not covered with plastic sheeting as an efficient decorator should. He stared in horror and then rushed around the house looking for cloths. After another fifteen minutes he realized that more drastic remedial measures were called for. He leapt into his van and drove off in search of a hardware store that could supply carpet cleaning materials. He was in a total panic, because his wife had just had a baby and he desperately needed the money from this job. When eventually he located a promising-looking shop and drew up outside it on a yellow line his panic made him do something he had never done before. He left the van unlocked and tore into the shop, his head full of queries about carpet cleaning techniques.

Pete's negligence was noted by a seventeen-year-old opportunist called Lennie who was standing outside the shop drinking a tin of Coke for breakfast, with nothing in particular in mind for the foreseeable future. Lennie knew exactly what to do under these circumstances. He whipped open the bonnet of the van, started the engine and was into the driving seat and off while Pete was still discussing paint removers with the assistant in the hardware shop. Lennie's plan was to nip straight to the estate where he knew some of his friends would be hanging out, also with no specific plans for the day, go through the contents of the van to see what was resaleable and then all have a bit of a joyride down the M4.

He had been driving for only three or four minutes when he

heard the banshee wail of a police car. Lennie's response to a police siren was instinctive – he simply slammed his foot on the accelerator. As it happened, the police car was about quite other business and knew nothing of Lennie or the van. Lennie hurtled round a corner, lost control of the steering and the van skidded into the back of a builders' lorry which was temporarily parked outside a café while the driver got himself a cup of tea.

Lennie did the sensible and expedient thing. He abandoned the van and disappeared. By the time the lorry driver came roaring out of the café there was a driverless white van with broken windscreen and crumpled bonnet embedded in the tailgate of his lorry.

The van was immobilized and had to be prized away by a breakdown truck. The only serious damage to the lorry was a burst back tyre. The lorry driver set about changing the tyre, seething with rage. He was already well behind schedule and would catch merry hell from his employer, who was on site awaiting delivery of the load of planks in the back of the lorry. After half an hour the van had been removed and the tyre changed. The driver bounced back into his cab and revved off at some speed. In his haste to get going he had not noticed one further piece of damage. The impact of the van had snapped one of the tailgate locks and loosened the other, so that it was no longer securely fastened.

The lorry driver, anxious to make up for lost time, hurtled through south London with the load of timber jouncing furiously behind him and slamming into the insecure tailgate each time he accelerated. The surviving lock eventually sprang apart in a one-way street down which he sped in search of a short cut. The planks broke free and shot out into the road. Three taxis which were also taking advantage of what was in fact a well-known rat run piled up behind the spilled planks and the stationary lorry and were at once neatly trapped by a brewer's truck which turned off the main road just in time to plug the street completely. The lorry driver climbed down from his cab and began wearily to retrieve the planks while the taxi-drivers sat in their throbbing vehicles and listened to Capital Radio.

The street was still blocked when an apprentice taxi-driver who was on a moped doing the knowledge tried to edge past the brewer's truck. He was practising the run from Gray's Inn Road to the Elephant and Castle, which should by rights take him along here. Seeing that this route was out of the question just now he swerved back into the main road in search of an alternative way and swung round a corner into the next side road, rather too fast, at the same moment as the Filipino houseboy of a foreign diplomat stepped off the pavement.

The Filipino houseboy was exercising the diplomat's two young Rhodesian ridgebacks. The dogs were on leashes but even so not sufficiently under control. One of them shot out of the gutter as the moped turned the corner, utterly disconcerting the apprentice taxi-driver, who mounted the kerb and ended up in a tangle on the pavement with the Filipino, who let go of the leashes in the confusion.

The Rhodesian ridgebacks were delighted. It is not a lot of fun being hauled around the streets on the end of a leash when you are nine months old and bred to a peak of perfection. They shot off like bats from hell, careered the length of several streets and fetched up in a garden square where they roamed around for a while until they spotted a cat furtively crossing the road. They homed in on it at thirty miles an hour.

The cat raced up the trunk of a chestnut tree and sat quivering in a fork fifteen feet above the dogs, who ran up and down excitedly for a bit and then got bored and wandered off, thus dropping out of the story, as do the apprentice taxi-driver and the Filipino houseboy. Actually, the Rhodesian ridgebacks turned up soon after in Brompton Road, where they caused a major traffic incident and thus triggered several other chaos sequences with which we cannot be concerned. The apprentice taxi-driver and the Filipino struck up an acquaintance which developed in a rather interesting way, but we cannot be deflected by that either, I'm afraid.

The cat was a young Burmese which belonged to the ten-year-old daughter of a divorced fashion designer who lived in the square. The child looked out of the window and spotted her darling mewing pathetically from the fork of the chestnut tree in the square gardens. Mother and daughter rushed out with a tin of sardines and a broomstick.

Fifteen minutes later the two of them were still standing at the foot of the tree, fruitlessly calling the cat and proffering sardines on the broomhead. The kitten wept and clung to the tree. The fashion designer, who had a client due shortly, began to get restive. The daughter became hysterical. At this point their next-door neighbour, a rather well-known theatre director, came out of his house intending to pick up some milk from the corner shop. Seeing this imbroglio, and being a decent fellow, he volunteered to fetch his extending ladder and retrieve the cat. The offer was accepted with gratitude.

The theatre director climbed the ladder and grabbed the cat, which promptly bit him, thus making him lose his balance. He slipped, slid awkwardly to the ground and broke his ankle. The cat was fine.

The director was due shortly at a rehearsal of the play he was currently directing. From the Outpatients Department of Charing Cross Hospital he used his mobile phone to notify all concerned that the rehearsal would have to be called off. The leading lady made noises of false regret and moderately genuine sympathy. In fact she could not have been better pleased. She had just embarked on an amorous involvement with a famous playwright, of whom she was not seeing enough owing to pressure of work commitments. As soon as the director was off the line she called her lover to announce that – surprise, surprise – she had a free day ahead. The playwright was delighted and proposed lunch at their favourite restaurant. The actress set about making herself look even more delectable than she did already and in due course was seated in a discreet corner of the restaurant gazing into the eyes of the playwright.

Their presence was noted by a journalist who made a point of visiting that particular restaurant at regular intervals to see who was consorting with whom. He worked for a tabloid newspaper and was even more devoid of moral scruples than others of his kind – a majestic example of the breed, shall we say. He watched the play-wright holding hands with a lady not his wife, identified her with interest, and when they left he decided to follow them. The trail led him to the entrance to an apartment block in a side street not far away, where the couple vanished, presumably into the actress's apartment for an afternoon of dalliance.

The journalist called up his paper and told them to send along a photographer. He had better things to do himself than hang around any longer, but one of the boys could stake the place out and maybe get a nice pic to go with tomorrow's story if and when the pair emerged.

Thus it was that a bored photographer was huddled on the step of the apartment block entrance at six o'clock that evening, wearing a grubby sweater and holding out an empty tin, with his camera discreetly stowed behind him, pretending to be a street beggar. He did not at first recognize the prime minister when the latter ran swiftly up the steps and pressed the Entry-phone bell to one of the apartments. The photographer simply shook his tin and chanted, 'Spare any small change?' Then he looked at the prime minister again and did a double take.

The prime minister ignored him. He was used to such figures and indeed had uttered many public pieties about the problem of youth-ful vagrancy. In any case he had other things to think of right now. It is not easy for a prime minister to carry on a sexual liaison. They are busy men, apart from anything else. But where there is a will there is a way, and the prime minister had perfected a system of clandestine visits to the object of his attentions which had worked efficiently for many months now. The lady in question was the for-mer wife of a political associate, an attractive enough woman but not one to set the world on fire and many would be surprised that he saw her as worth the risk. But there is no accounting for passion, as we all know. Suffice it that it is probably true to say that our man was the first prime minister since Lloyd George to conduct an undetected adulterous relationship.

The prime minister had left his car discreetly parked around the corner, and his security guard with it. The story was that he was paying a duty call on an elderly relative. Whether or not the chauffeur and the guard fell for this routine is not known. Necessarily each visit was brief, given the prime minister's schedule – an hour or so, at the best of times.

He rang the bell. The photographer listened intently. He heard the prime minister's voice – quite distinct and familiar – saying simply, 'It's me.' And then he heard another voice, unmistakably female, somewhat amplified by the Entry-phone: 'Hello, darling.'

The photographer rose to his feet, faint with excitement. He saw the prime minister vanish into the apartment block. The photographer stood there for a few moments, quivering like some sleek carnivore that has scented prey, and then he began to plan the days ahead, which might stretch into weeks. He would need time, patience and equipment. The hidden mike, the concealed camera. Well, we know the arrangements, don't we?

In the event he struck gold within a fortnight. The prime minister resigned a few days later. The nation's press carried on the front page similar photographs of his expressionless face, seen in profile through the window of the car which bore him to the Palace.

Pete, the decorator, saw it on the front of his copy of the *Sun* as he went to work in the Tube, but he did not pay it much attention. Prime ministers come and go, and in any case he had problems of his own. The insurance company had not yet paid out on the van, the Ambroses were back and their bedroom carpet was a write-off.

The Purple Swamp Hen (2016)

The Purple Swamp Hen

I am the Purple Swamp Hen. *Porphyrio porphyrio*, if you are into taxonomy and Latin binomials. And, let me get this clear, I am *Porphyrio porphyrio porphyrio*, the nominate sub-species, not to be confused with the Australasian lot – *P. p. melanotus*, or the Indonesian crowd – *P. p. pulverulentis*. And others. No, indeed; we are talking species definition here, the enduring stuff, and thus I endure – founding father, the Mediterranean nominate. I am eternally defined, thanks to Linnaeus, himself stuck in the seventeenth century, and we would have been rather beyond his range – we've never bothered with Scandinavia nor indeed with the Americas, they have quite enough species of their own, by all accounts. That said, our range is extensive, and it seems that in conservation terms we are, in a general sense, of Least Concern – in your time, that is. Though I'm glad to say that we – the home team, the Mediterranean Purple Swamp Hen – require strict protection on account of habitat loss, hunting and pesticide use.

Wondering where all this is going? Have patience. You'll get your story. You know me. You know me on the famous garden fresco from Pompeii – somewhat faded, a travesty of my remarkable plumage, but nevertheless a passable portrait. You all exclaim over those frescos: the blues and greens, the precise depiction of flora and fauna. Oh, look! you cry – there are roses, and ferns, oleanders, poppies, violets. And oh! there's a pigeon, a jay, a swallow, a magpie. You don't cry – oh! a Purple Swamp Hen, because the vast majority of you can't recognize one. You eye me with vague interest, and pass on. It's just like a garden today! you cry.

No, it isn't. Wasn't. I am – was – in this garden because it was a Roman garden and the Romans kept us there for ornamental purposes. Occasionally they ate us, but more often they didn't. We decorated the place, alongside the statues and the fountains. That's one distinction, though the tradition persists, I believe – those creatures called peacocks – but I regard us as unique in terms of horticultural decor. But, make no mistake, the garden of Quintus Pompeius, where I passed my time, was nothing like any garden you've ever known.

It hosted fornication, incest, rape, child abuse, grievous bodily harm – and that's just Quintus Pompeius, his household and his associates. We fauna simply got on with the business of copulation and reproduction; far more imaginative, *Homo sapiens*. The climate of the Bay of Naples was warm (and going to get a lot warmer, but we'll come to that), and they liked to be out of doors as much as possible. Eat out, sleep out, wash the dishes, pluck a pigeon, gossip, quarrel, wallop an old slave, fuck that pretty new one, plot, scheme, bribe, threaten. Get drunk, utter obscenities, vomit in the acanthus.

I saw it all. I heard it all.

Let me fill you in on the general situation that autumn, in the household of Quintus Pompeius. Livia, wife of Q. Pompeius, has a new hairstyle. Major event – oh, yes. Fetching curly strands around the forehead. The new hairstyle is appreciated by Quintus, and even more so by Livia's lover, Marcus Sempronius, business associate of the husband, who does not know of this further family arrangement. Quintus himself is deeply embroiled in politics; he wants to be elected to the city council, to become a magistrate, which means an intensive process of persuasion, bribery, boasting and general manipulation of what passes for democracy in Pompeii. Of his children, his eldest son, Titus, aged eighteen, is theoretically employed in the family winery but spends most of his time hanging out downtown with his friends. His younger sister Sulpicia helps her mother chivvy the slaves around. The two youngest children, aged five and six, occupy themselves in the garden – making mud pies, digging for worms, catching grasshoppers, pulling the wings off butterflies. Chasing Purple Swamp Hens.

Quintus and his son Titus both have their way with the new slave girl, Servilia, whenever they feel like it. Nobody would question their right to do so. Servilia is fourteen years old.

Servilia washes dishes. She also sweeps, empties chamber pots, carries water, and is being trained to help Livia with her toilette. She is not as yet very good at this, and gets cuffed a lot.

Other slaves, too, do all these things. The whole place is in a ferment of activity, morning till night, from the fetid stew of the kitchen area to the relative fresh air of the garden. People everywhere – fetching, carrying, getting in each other's way, shouting, being shouted at. The atrium fills up with those who have come to see Quintus Pompeius – to cut a deal with him, get rooked by him, curry favour with him, sign up to some propitious arrangement. He may take a turn in the garden with one or two of these, which is how I knew that he was cornering the market in Etruscan wine imports, that he was spreading salacious rumours about a fellow candidate, that he owed money in various directions and resisted payment, that he was owed in various other directions – and was uttering dire threats.

Thus, the daily life of the household. And of scores of other households in the city – prosperous households, the households that called the shots. Elsewhere, much the same took place, on a lesser scale – among those engaged in selling bread and oil and grain and fruit and fish and meat and dormice and sea urchins. Plus the provision of various services, including of course sex. Not so much garden life, there; horticulture the preserve of the well-heeled.

All the same to me – master, mistress, slave. Egalitarian – my outlook. Detached, you might say. A forensic interest in the practices of this curious species.

Let us take some instances of attitude and behaviour.

They find it perfectly acceptable that one lot possesses another lot. So, half the inhabitants of the city wait upon the other half; a section of them are commodities, to be bought and sold like a loaf of bread or a flagon of wine.

We – we swamp hens, swallows, golden orioles, sparrows and all else – eat in order to survive. No more and no less. They eat to excess, with deplorable consequences. Eating as entertainment it would appear to be. Along with the lavish consumption of wine, which has this humiliating effect on them. Except that they apparently find it enjoyable rather than humiliating.

Quintus Pompeius is a wine magnate. Was, was . . . I keep forgetting. Preserved into your time on that fresco, floating timeless, I have somewhat lost my grip on chronology. Quintus P. is ashes now, or rather, he is a featureless grey cast, stared at by innumerable visitors to the site of his demise.

My demise also? Certainly not. Wait. We'll get to that.

The Q. Pompeius wine business is both manufacture and distribution. It procures grapes, it processes them, stores the product and then enables inhabitants of the city to get legless as often as they wish or can afford to do so. An ideal trade – the bottom is never going to fall out of wine. The human race is fuelled by it, one observes.

This, then, was the set-up: the family, the household, the supporting business. All coasting along as normal in the run-up to that climacteric event of which you already know.

Livia took an almighty risk. She entertained her lover, Marcus Sempronius, in a secluded part of the garden while Quintus Pompeius was out of the way, visiting a political supporter. Entertainment in every sense of the word; I heard the moans and groans and passed by with disdain.

Sulpicia, her daughter, was courting the son of a neighbour. They too made full use of the garden. Lucius, a Greek slave who was the principal cook, was engaged in a feud with Sextus, the Libyan thug responsible for janitor duties; these two brawled outside the kitchen, where Servilia scoured pans and occasionally fetched up as collateral damage.

Servilia is of interest. She was a recent acquisition, spotted by Quintus P. and bought off a friend, for whom she was surplus goods. I am no connoisseur of the human female but it would seem that she was appealing. Other males of the household eyed her up, but were wise enough not to encroach. As far as I was concerned, she was just another presence, until a particular morning which made her of interest.

The children had been chasing me. This happened, not infrequently. I kept well away, when they were in the garden, and if they did get near and start molesting, I am quick on my feet and could be off pretty smartly. On this occasion, I was unwary. They crept up, and the boy had me by the neck.

'Pull its feathers off!'

'Kill it!'

'Let me have it!'

They squabbled. I lost a tail feather.

'I saw it first! I want it!'

'Kill it! Let's kill it!'

She must have heard, Servilia. She came over. She remonstrated. She said that their parents might not wish me killed. The children told her to get lost.

And then she reached out, prised me out of the boy's hands, and let me go.

I flew up on to the fountain.

We looked at each other, bird and girl.

'Thanks,' I said.

'My pleasure,' said she.

No language passed, but perfect understanding. Something I had not come across before with that species.

The children rushed off to their mother, and reported Servilia for un-slavelike conduct. Livia was not much interested, preoccupied with a fear that Quintus might be on to her activities with his associate. Also, a swamp hen is garden decor, nothing like as valuable as a

Herm or a statue of Bacchus, but still worth preserving. We are not that fecund. We don't breed easily. My mate and I had not done well that year; two eggs addled, the surviving chick picked off by a cat.

My mate? Oh, yes. Have I not mentioned her?

This happened a few days before the event, the final hours. During which time things warmed up in various ways at the villa of Quintus Pompeius. Never exactly a haven of tranquillity, it became the scene of violence and recrimination.

The Greek cook and the Libyan thug had an almighty dust-up, as a result of which the thug suffered a black eye, and the cook several broken ribs, which put paid to cooking duties for the time being. A thug is always replaceable, but a good cook is an essential commodity, so the thug got a further pasting, by order of Quintus P.

The carcass of a kid destined for a banquet disappeared from the kitchen. Other culinary material had gone missing before and it was suspected that an assistant cook, another recently acquired young slave, was purveying goods to an associate in the city. He was questioned, with some brutality, and accused the guard dog, occasionally let off its leash. Since it was not feasible to question the guard dog, the slave was further interrogated and eventually admitted guilt. He was beaten and despatched to the slave market.

A couple of days later the banquet took place, replacement kid or kids having been acquired, along with much else. The whole place reeked of cooking, slaves rushed about sweeping and scrubbing, the couches in the triclinium were laid out with covers and cushions. I knew what we were in for – a raucous evening, inescapable because the triclinium gives on to the garden so that even if one roosted at the furthest corner, the noise could not be avoided nor, indeed, the occasional guest coming out for a breath of fresh air or a quick vomit.

And so it was. Lamps lit everywhere, night turned into day. Slaves staggering to and fro with dish after dish, wine poured and poured and poured again. Talk, shouts, boisterous laughter. Now and then someone burst into song. Eventually I gave up any attempt to roost and took up a position in a clump of irises beside the path. Various bits and pieces were falling from the dishes that came from the kitchen, some of which were tasty.

Thus it was that I observed the furtive meeting between Livia and her lover Marcus, both of them taking temporary absence from the gathering on some pretext. A passionate embrace behind the fountain, noted by me, and, unfortunately, by Quintus Pompeius who had also risen, in order to give directions to the slave in charge of wine supply.

He saw. They knew that he saw.

Nothing said. Not then.

Later, much was said. A short while later, when the guests had dispersed. Marcus Sempronius was one of the first to leave, looking preoccupied. My guess is that he was to find that various useful arrangements with Quintus P. were now history. What passed between Quintus and his wife was audible throughout the villa, for some while. He roared; she bleated excuses. He clouted her; she shrieked. Slaves lurked nearby, interested and appreciative. The children woke up and wailed. The guard dog barked. It was nearly dawn before the place quietened down. Then swallows dipped into the fountain, the golden oriole began its song – somewhat repetitive, I've always thought, but preferable to human cacophony.

That evening reverberated, over the next few days. Quintus Pompeius was now in a thoroughly bad temper, which meant that everyone had to watch their step. Those seeking his attention in the atrium found him terse, dismissive, intolerant. Any slave who put a foot wrong got biffed. Those who didn't got shouted at anyway. The children, bouncing up to him, discovered that he didn't like children any more. Livia cowered in the cubiculum.

A bad atmosphere then, at the Villa Pompeius. A presage of things to come? They might well have thought so; a credulous lot, the human race. If there were some propitiatory sacrifices, some attempt to pacify the gods, I was not aware.

The first earthquake came at midday. Not a particularly strong one – a mere shudder by comparison with some. A garden Herm fell over – hideous head of Hercules – some kitchen crockery was smashed. People exclaimed – a bit of shouting, but not much excitement. Earthquakes are not uncommon here. This one did not cause undue alarm and it was soon over.

And then another, two days later. Longer, stronger. Rather more comment this time; the gods are angry, they said to one another – or, more practically, better stand clear of the building till it's over.

I do not like earthquakes. We do not like earthquakes – swallow, dove, oriole, sparrow, and rat, mouse, cat, dog, the animal kingdom. An earthquake makes you uneasy, restive. The stability of things has been questioned, in every way.

We ride them out, usually. Take cover. Batten down till it's done.

This was different. I knew. I knew when I felt that second heave, that ripple of the earth beneath my feet. The acanthus wildly waving. Bricks tumbling from a wall. I knew that this would end, but was also a beginning. Something more would happen.

I spoke. We can be noisy, we swamp hens, when it is appropriate. We can be loud. I called my mate. Come, I said. Out, out, out.

I was near the kitchen, where also was Servilia. I flew up on to a wall. My mate joined me.

'Go!' I said to Servilia. 'Get away from here. Just go. Go, go, go.'

Bird to girl. Again. She looked at me. She heard. She understood.

I saw her put down the dish she was scouring, look around, get to her feet. I did not wait. We're off, I said to my mate. Now. We flew.

We circled the city. I needed to get my bearings, see which way to go.

We flew. Fast. Low. And, as we flew, I saw a great black cloud had risen above the mountain, a cloud like some immense pine tree reaching up into the sky.

We flew higher, above the city, up and beyond. The air was thick, stuff falling from above. And there was movement now below, people on the road, carts, horses, people leaving the city.

I saw a girl running. Away from the mountain, away from that black cloud. Running, running.

On that day, of all days, there would be no attention paid to a runaway slave. May she have run far.

As we flew. Far, far. Away from the mountain, until there was no more falling stuff, and that terrible black cloud was distant. And then, at last, in a good marshy place, where there was no garden, no fountain, no presiding Herms, but water, reeds, the kind of habitat appropriate to *Porphyrio porphyrio*, we came to earth again. And there we settled, and bred, as have my descendants, thus ensuring the survival of the species from that benighted age into your own. Where things are done differently, but it is not for me to proclaim progress, or otherwise.

Abroad

Fifty years ago there were peasants in Europe. France was full of them – Spain, Portugal. Greece had the very best – prototype peasants. As for Macedonia, places like that – you were spoiled for choice. Ploughing with oxen and a sort of prehistoric plough. Heaving water out of wells, carrying it picturesquely on the head in a pitcher. Washing their clothes in the river, drying them in colourful swathes on the banks. Driving their donkeys to market, with interesting goods in panniers. Small boys herding goats on rocky hillsides. Women hoeing fields. Old men grinding maize. Landscapes peppered with peasants, doing what peasants do, wearing proper peasant clothes – women in long skirts and aprons, men with black waistcoats and baggy trousers.

In England we didn't have peasants. Just the rural working class. Farm workers. Not the same. Not colourful, not picturesque. They had tractors and mains water. They dressed from the Co-Op.

We were artists. Tony and I. We needed subject matter. We needed arresting, evocative subject matter. So we needed Abroad. Anyone artistic needed Abroad in the 1950s. You needed the Mediterranean, and fishing boats pulled up on sandy shores. Olive groves under blue skies. Romanesque churches. Market squares with campanile and peasantry. Sunflowers, cactuses, prickly pears, cypresses, palms. We needed scenery; we needed well-furnished scenery. Particularly we needed peasants. Real, earthy, traditional peasants.

I sketched. Tony both sketched and photographed. A sketch would be worked up later into an oil painting, back home. The photos were prompts, reminders; that girl with the great load of washing on her head could be used in due course – such a graceful stance.

Abroad was cheap – relatively cheap. We were skint, and you could potter around Spain or Greece for weeks on a few pesetas or drachma or whatever. One was always in a muddle with the money – what this scruffy note was worth, or this fistful of coins – and then pleasantly surprised when some old dear was apparently offering B & B for tuppence ha'penny, or so it seemed. Mind, not B & B as we think of it; more like a bare room with an iron bedstead and a jug and basin, and some crusty bread and coffee in the morning. But all so authentic. We wouldn't have gone near a hotel or a *pension*, even if we could have afforded it. We wanted to be seeing things as they saw them – the locals. I've still got a sketch I did of one of those old dears – all in black, head to toe, brown wrinkly face, and so grateful for whatever we paid. Portuguese, I think. Or possibly Italian. Or was that in Yugoslavia?

We were young – early twenties. We'd met at art college, set up together, decided to get Abroad, as much as possible, for as long as possible. Abroad then was just Europe; now it's everywhere – Sri Lanka, Thailand, Barbados, wherever. But in the 50s Abroad meant the Continent, and that was that.

Tony was so good-looking. Those sort of rather ravaged good looks, even at twenty-two or so – thin face, dark brown eyes, dark brown hair flopping over his forehead, dark brown body too because we were so much in the sun. Abroad's lovely sun. And he was very much the artist: French beret, check shirt with the sleeves rolled up, linen slacks.

And me? I was pretty arty too, back then. Jeans, when jeans were hardly known. Bra top, bare midriff. Sloppy Joe sweater when chilly, fair hair to my shoulders, tied back with a pink cotton hanky. The hair is neither long nor fair these days. Went mouse, then grey, and shoulder-length won't do at eighty. Oh, well; I dare say Tony has worn a bit, too. Wherever he is. If he still is.

Attractive? Yes. I was. We were a somewhat arresting couple, I'd say. Sketching away in little Greek fishing villages or beside some Spanish field, with the fishermen heaving nets or whatever, and Spanish peasants picking and cutting and digging and generally getting into nice poses that you could quickly rough out for future use. There'd be plenty of banter directed at us, that of course we couldn't understand, all perfectly amiable, and lots of smiles and flashing white teeth as well. Peasants always seemed to have rather good teeth. Except for the old ones. Shortage of teeth, then. Thank heaven for modern dentistry. Mine aren't too bad.

Mind, we did sometimes realize that we weren't seeing things as the locals saw them. There was the day of the life class. Somewhere in France. Tony had decided he wanted to do some life drawing. We were in the depths of the countryside, we had had a picnic by a field. 'Come on,' he said. 'Life class.' So I had stripped off and I was sitting there, posing and sunbathing both at once, and Tony had his sketch pad out, when all of a sudden this – well, peasant – appeared. The farmer, I suppose. And roared at us. Shouted and yelled. And then stormed off, and next thing a couple of gendarmes arrived. I'd got my clothes on by then. So we were down at the police station explaining for hours. No charges, but don't do it again.

There could be problems about money, too. Peasants seemed to be over concerned with money. All that careful counting out of coins, in the markets; endless bargaining over the equivalent of a farthing or two. Goodness, farthings . . . I've almost forgotten them – odd that the word swims up. We always got the coins confused. If you accidentally gave too little there'd be an end to the flashing white smiles and a flood of abuse instead. Not so picturesque, suddenly. You learned to tread carefully, where money was concerned; a bit of an obsession, apparently, in those circles.

We weren't having to worry about money all that much.

Everything so cheap. We could eke out what we'd brought for weeks on end, and if we found we had absolutely miscalculated, or we wanted to stay longer, well – there could always be an emergency telegram home. Mummy and Daddy would come up with something – grumbling a bit. I was supposed to be on an allowance, and not overspend, and they were a tad tight-lipped about Tony, and us not being married, or even thinking of it, but they were in favour of Abroad. Mummy felt it was so educational. So if we ran short it would just be a question of a post office, and an arrangement with some bank, when we'd found one. Not all that thick on the ground, often, banks; peasants seem to do without them.

I shouldn't keep saying peasants. Sounds patronizing. People. Country people. Thing is, they were – in a way that doesn't exist any more. No peasants in Europe now. I know – I've been there. No long skirts, black waistcoats, oxen, prehistoric ploughs. Banks all over the place. I don't know where young artists are to go nowadays.

Right – people. Peasant being merely a technical term. Nicely different people, which was what we liked about them, apart from the subject potential. Not boring English. England was so boring in the 1950s. Everyone agreed about that, even Mummy and Daddy. They went Abroad as much as they could, too, though a different Abroad from ours: Italian Riviera, and French châteaux. You didn't holiday in Wales or Cornwall, in the 1950s – not if you could possibly help it.

Not boring English, and not speaking English. That was part of the appeal – not knowing what people were talking about. Just that chatter of Spanish or Greek or whatever. You were on the outside, not involved, just looking on, which is what you were there for. We had a bit of French, from school, but that didn't get you far. Peasant French was something else. Sorry – country people French.

Goodness – how we got around. It amazes me, now, looking back. We never cared for being stuck in one place, so it would be into the car and off – when the car was behaving, that was. Old Hillman. Ancient Hillman – proper old banger. Many punctures, many stops while the radiator boiled. Many failures to start unless pushed. Places like Greece and Yugoslavia, we used buses; elsewhere, the car. Blissfully empty roads – you tootled along on your own, deep in France or Italy or wherever. A few of those old Citroëns – *deux-chevaux* – the occasional pick-up truck, lots of bikes. Garages as infrequent as banks, which could be a problem when the Hillman was playing up, or when we'd forgotten to get petrol. You always carried a can, in case.

But the point was to be carefree, independent. Artists can't be hampered by the *dailiness* of ordinary life – Tony felt strongly about that. Doing the same things each day, forever bothered about money. Art has to be freed from all that. Everything was very *daily*, in Europe, back then – daily life was what we were looking at constantly, what we were sketching. Subject matter, said Tony, that's the point. He was very serious about his work – more experimental than I was, more abstract, very much a colourist. He had tremendous promise – everyone said so. He was going to be the next Graham Sutherland, Paul Nash. I think it hasn't worked out like that. I'd have heard.

We weren't getting on quite so well that summer. We disagreed in Brittany, argued our way down to the Auvergne, made it up somewhere around the Pyrenees, squabbled again in Catalonia. Issues about where to go next, and how long to stay here or there, plus the Hillman was being really tricky. I said I was tired of Spain. Tony said we've hardly *touched* Spain – amazing landscapes, super people, so *visual*.

The last time he'd say *that*.

Actually, we were on good terms, the day we came across the wedding party. We'd driven deep into the back of beyond, miles from any town, hardly any villages even, just isolated farms, fields of this and that, hillsides with goats. So I had laughed and agreed. Only problem was the Hillman, which kept coughing and spluttering and stalling. We stopped, to give the tiresome thing a rest, and did some sketching beside a pasture with cows wearing bells, got the car started again, with difficulty, and then a mile or so further on suddenly there were all these people.

A farmhouse, and a long table outside with eats and drinks, and this party going on – everyone done up to the nines, and the younger ones dancing, and the bride and groom very obvious. She was about my age – Spanishly gorgeous, long black hair, glittering eyes.

We slowed down. Slow was all the Hillman cared to do at that point, anyway. But we were both thinking the same thing . . . must draw this. Tony was reaching for his sketch pad before he was out of the car.

We stopped a little way away. Tried to be unobtrusive. Sat on a stone wall by the road. Did quick sketches: that old fellow at the end of the table, the woman pouring wine, those girls dancing.

Unobtrusive? Two people couldn't turn up in a car out of nowhere without being noticed. Children came over, peeked at our sketches, ran back giggling. A woman brought two glasses of wine, indicated that we could join the party.

We did. We went and sat by the table, accepted a bite of this, a taste of that, sketched some more. Big smiles all round.

What luck! The real thing, so authentic.

Tony drew the bride. He was good at a likeness; she came out well. Much approval – laughter, and the sketch passed from hand to hand.

Artista?

Yes, we said. Yes. *Artista.*

Bueno! Muy bueno!

Then the bride's mother wanted her portrait done. And a sister. Tony obliged, though I could see he was getting a bit bored with this. It was like being one of those people who sit around at Piccadilly Circus with an easel, doing bespoke likenesses. Not his scene.

After a couple of hours we decided to move on. You can have enough of authentic, eventually. So lots of smiles and handshaking, and we headed back to the car.

It wouldn't start. Ignition dead. Terminally dead.

Our situation had been observed. Some of the men came over and set about giving us a push.

That usually did the trick. Not this time.

Somebody opened up the bonnet, peered inside. Much tutting and frowning. Others looked, expressed dismay.

Garage? we said. *El garage?*

Laughter. Gesticulations. We got the message. The nearest garage was twenty-five kilometres away.

The father of the bride had taken over a leadership role. The farmer, evidently. Big, burly man with a forthright manner. Some sort of conference took place – everyone talking at once – and then he seemed to be offering a plan. He gestured towards the old pick-up parked by the farm, one of the only two vehicles in sight. The other was a battered little car that didn't look any healthier than ours. The means of transport around here was evident: mule, cart, and bike.

Some rope was fetched. The idea, it seemed, was to tow the Hillman to this distant garage.

We beamed. *Gracias, gracias.*

A pause. Unmistakable indication of what was needed. *Dinero. Peseta.* Money.

Ah, we said. *Sí, sí.*

Trouble was, we were pretty well out of cash. Not a long-term problem – we had travellers' cheques. But we'd been meaning to find a bank for the last couple of days, and then never did.

We got this across. *Banco*, we said. We get to a *banco* and then we have *dinero*. No problem.

Yes, problem. Money up front. Surprising how clearly the farmer got that across.

Oh, come on, said Tony. Surely they can trust us? When the car's fixed we get to a bank, and bring him what's needed. We go with the bloke in the pick-up and then stay with the car till it's done.

He explained, all smiles. Pointed to car, to pick-up, indicating time on his watch. 'Then – *banco!* Then – come back here! *Aquí! Dinero!*' He displayed our travellers' cheques, which provoked derision.

No. No and no. *Aquí.* Stay here.

The pick-up had been driven up and the Hillman roped behind. Tony sighed: 'Well, if that's the way they want it. How long's this garage going to need, I wonder?'

El garage? Cuanto tiempo?

Much shrugging and rolling of eyes. You were talking days, several days. A week.

By now we were getting a bit fed up. Evidently we were going to spend rather more time with authentic Spanish country life than we'd reckoned with. And the warmth had rather gone out of our welcome. Treatment had become distinctly brisk. Do this, come over here. We got our stuff out of the car, as indicated, watched the Hillman bump away behind the pick-up, carried the haversacks, easels, sketchbooks, painting equipment over to a barn where, the farmer's wife proposed, we should sleep. Hay bales. Chickens for company. Oh, well. We'd have a tale to tell, at least.

The farmer was taking a thoughtful interest in our paints. Picking up tubes of colour, fingering brushes. He looked at Tony, with a sort of smile. Speculative smile.

'*Artista. Bueno!*'

He beckoned. We followed him into the big farmhouse kitchen. Flagged floor. Huge old black stove. White-washed walls. To which he pointed. Then to himself, to his wife, to others who had now crowded in.

'*Niente dinero – pintura.*'

'Oh, for heaven's sake!' said Tony.

This, it seemed, was the deal. You haven't got any cash to pay up front for taking your car twenty-five kilometres to the garage, getting it fixed, and bringing it back, so you can pay in kind. A nice fresco on our kitchen wall – group portrait of the family. Take it or leave it – except that leave it wasn't an option.

Tony painted all through the next day. He painted the farmer, as central figure. He painted the wife, alongside. He painted the bride, who had gone to live just a couple of fields away, it turned out. He painted the bride's two little sisters.

There was criticism, at points. The farmer wanted his money's worth. This face not so good, do it again. More colour here. Put the family dog in there.

Tony painted on, the following day. The son. An old granny, brought in for the occasion on a cart. A couple of aunts.

'It's like *The Last Supper*,' he said. 'And I'm not bloody Leonardo, am I?'

He was given a glass of wine, presumably to keep his strength up. Food was provided twice a day; basic food – coarse bread, soup, bit of hard cheese, a chunk of sausage, a tomato. Authentic, you had to call it. Same as they were eating themselves.

And me? I was not painting – oh, no. I had been measured as an *artista*, it appeared, and found wanting. There were other plans for me.

I fetched water. The well was some way away from the house. You pumped with a sort of iron handle thing. It made your arm ache. Then you carried the buckets. I hadn't known before that water is *heavy*. Several trips, over the course of the day. 'Bueno,' said the farmer's wife. I suppose she did this, normally.

I made use of the water, as instructed. I washed clothes, in a tub. Scrub. Scrub some more. Rinse. Hang out to dry.

Bueno, bueno. And here's another lot. Do those now. When you've fetched more water.

The kitchen floor. Scrub again. On hands and knees. I scrubbed around Tony's feet, as he worked. I said, 'What if we just refuse? Say we're damn well not going on like this.'

'He'll just say – OK, push off, get lost. We're miles from any-where. We haven't got the foggiest idea where they've taken the car.'

I said, 'We haven't been very clever, have we?'

Tony stared at his fresco, teeth clenched.

'And you've got the best of it,' I said. 'At least you're painting. Just try doing this.'

'Frankly,' he said, 'I never want to bloody paint again.'

'*Andale!*' snorted the elderly uncle who was posing for his place in the line-up. Irritable interjection – get on with it.

On the third day I went out into the fields with the bride's sisters. We were on weeding duty. Stuff growing; you weeded everything that wasn't the right stuff. Bent double. Back aching. Hot. The girls chattered and laughed. I didn't.

Everybody was being perfectly nice to us, but brisk. Firm. Our position was made quite clear. You have to earn your keep. Pay for the trouble we've taken.

El garage? we said, glumly. *El auto? Cuanto tiempo?*

Shrugs. Three more days, maybe. Four? Five? The farmer's son, driver of the pick-up, who had taken the Hillman to the garage, indicated difficulties. Much trouble, many problems.

After weeding duty came . . . more weeding duty. Different stuff growing in another field. Again, weed everything not the right stuff. When finished weeding – fetch water. And – oh, *bueno*, if you've got nothing to do now you could clean and chop these vegetables for the soup.

I said to Tony, 'I told you we'd had enough of Spain. We should have ditched the Hillman and gone to Greece.'

'Right now, I'd rather like to go to Brighton.'

His fresco now covered most of their kitchen wall, a study of the extended family. People had been brought in by the day, not a second cousin left unturned. Now, it seemed, they had run through the lot. Not the end of Tony's work, though, as the farmer indicated. Backdrop required. Put in the farm buildings – here, see? Behind, like this. And animals – cow, goat. *Bueno, bella pintura*. He had taken to standing over Tony, observing every brushstroke, expressing approval – or not.

I learned how to pluck a chicken. Ugh. The chicken was a treat for Sunday lunch, a scrawny thing. It served ten people. You didn't get much chicken.

El garage? El auto? Pathetic, we were.

Pronto, pronto.

I had blisters on my hands. Hoeing, that was. Hours of it, where they grew their vegetables. And sore knees. At night, on the hay bales, we bickered.

'If you'd listened to me, we'd be in Greece now.'

'I kept saying – look, we really should find a bank before we go any further.'

'You didn't.'

'I damn well did.'

'*Artista!*' I said. It sounded like a term of abuse.

He sighed. 'Let's not fight. Sorry.'

'OK. Sorry.'

We made it up, observed by the chickens.

Another day.

And another, on which there was activity. A man stopped by, driving a battered lorry. Who had, it seemed, some message for the farmer. Long exchange, much bonhomie. The man departed. Discussion between farmer and son. Uncles appear, and join in. Finally, we are summoned.

El auto – terminado! The car is ready. Everyone most genial – smiles all round, as though this were a personal achievement.

Great! we say. Fantastic!

Vamanos, then.

We were to be taken in the pick-up by the son. We collected our stuff, said our goodbyes. Long spiel from the farmer's wife, amiable but with, you felt, a bite there. You may have learned a thing or two, was the gist of it, I think.

Gracious farewell to Tony from the farmer, as from a patron who might well provide a reference, if required. Tony took a photo of the fresco. Black and white, of course, in those days, and it came out very murky, when we had it developed. I wonder if he's still got it.

We drove to the village where the garage was, bumping around in the pick-up. And there, indeed, was the Hillman, now viable, as was demonstrated. Starting up without protest, engine running nicely. Two new tyres.

The bill.

Ah. Of course, we said. *Sí, sí.*

The pick-up and its driver had departed. Whatever made us think the garage repair bill might have been covered by our labours at the farm?

We produced the travellers' cheques, with brave confidence. *El banco?* Looking around, cheerfully, as though there might be one just over there, by the grocery store and the homely bar.

A stony glance at the cheques, from the mechanic. *Banco?* What *banco? Dinero, por favor.*

It came to both of us that life might be about to become even more daily than it had just been. We looked at each other. A fresco on that white-washed wall at the back of the garage? Nice portrayal of truck, pick-up, old car or two?

And me? Heave tyres around, like that boy over there? Wash forecourt. Wash trucks.

'No,' I said.

Negotiation, we realized. There was a way. *Where* was there a bank?

Twenty kilometres, it emerged, eventually, in the nearest town. And yes, all right, the mechanic would come with us in the Hillman, we would cash our cheque, pay him, and return him to the garage. The bill to be adjusted to take his time into account.

And so it was. On the way, this man became rather more amiable. He had noticed our painting equipment in the back of the car.

'*Artista?*' he enquired.

We said that, yes, we were indeed *artista.*

He laughed. Continued, after a moment: '*Dinero?*' Laughing again.

Much money in that, is there?

No, said Tony. *Niente dinero.* At least – *poco dinero.* So far.

The mechanic gave him a friendly slap on the shoulder. Amuse yourself then, mate.

We arrived at the bank, paid off the mechanic, returned him to his garage.

I don't know if we were both thinking the same thing. We never really discussed it. The trip rather disintegrated after that. We headed for Portugal, but it had lost its charm; we found we didn't any longer much care for rural life, and made for cities. Tony suddenly found street scenes inspiring.

I was thinking about money, and how one had somehow underrated it. I thought about peasants – sorry – counting out every coin in those markets. Stronger stuff than I had thought, money.

Back in England, we sort of drifted apart. I haven't heard of Tony in years.

I've carried on painting, of course. Norman has always made a point of saying, 'My wife's an artist, you know.' There's a *cachet*, no question. He brings home a packet, as a barrister, so it's been neither here nor there if I sell things or not – we don't need the money. I'm glad I realized when I was young that actually money signifies. I've been able to – well, organize my life so much better.

Who Do You Think You Were?

In west Somerset in 1787 a young woman who could not read or write, but knew fine how to skin a rabbit or pluck a fowl, forged her way through autumn mud from Rodhuish to Withycombe, where she would fetch the old red rooster from her aunt Mary Ann. The rooster was destined for the pot, and has no further part in this story, except that as it was handed over, squawking, both Sarah and her aunt experienced a most unusual sensation, like a mild electric shock (a concept that would have baffled them).

Aunt Mary Ann said, 'A goose walked over my grave.'

Sarah was busy subduing the rooster, and tucking it under one arm. In her other hand she carried the basket that had contained a fresh loaf and some potatoes, fair exchange for the rooster. She shivered, though she hadn't been feeling cold, and said she'd be off back, there was rain to come. The rooster made one final protest, Aunt Mary Ann went into her cottage, and Sarah Webber walked on into the rest of her life.

In London in 2015 another young woman stares at a screen. She scrolls through names, a cascade of names; she frowns, she taps, she pulls up a further name torrent. She makes a note on a pad beside her laptop. She scrolls again, and lo! she spots a most satisfactory connection. She pounces, makes a further note, and then she decides to call it a day. She closes the laptop. She is twenty-four years old, and is engaged in postgraduate work; she would be hard put to it to pluck a fowl, let alone skin a rabbit.

Caroline puts the laptop into her briefcase, the laptop that knows everything, or most things, and in which the past is stored, by way of a thousand names, tens of thousands of names, hundreds of thousands. The laptop knew about the relationship between Mary Ann Crowhurst and Sarah Webber, though possibly not about the red rooster.

It is the end of the working day, for Caroline Gladwell. She works in the Reading Room of the British Library, because she may have need of its resources, though much of the time she is making use of the omniscient laptop. She is doing an MA in Economic History, of which a component part is the dissertation on a subject of her own choice. She has chosen to research her own family history, back to the early seventeenth century, in order to demonstrate the directive force of economic circumstance on individual lives. She will show why unemployment in the shipbuilding industry impelled this ancestor to leave Portsmouth, why opportunities in domestic service brought that one to Cheltenham. At the moment she is tracing forebears of her mother's, who appear to have been stuck generations deep in the West Country, being born, marrying, dying, within a relatively small area. Agricultural labourers for the most part, and it would seem that conditions were favourable enough to allow of staying put.

Caroline is pleased with her choice of subject for the dissertation which, she feels, lends colour to the sometimes grey backcloth of economic history. Persons, people – the real people who are the drivers, the facilitators, often the victims, of economic developments. Names – she can cite them – the Johns and Georges and Alberts, the Elizas and Alices and Janes – whose toil has contributed to a climate of prosperity, or otherwise. She will pinpoint certain names, evoke their circumstances, and tether them with a detailed account of their particular occupation – the dissertation will be richly informative about bricklaying, needle-making, baking, brewing and much else. It will bring the past alive – make it relevant. Caroline is intensely concerned with history – she is hoping for a career in academic life – and she sometimes feels that the past is seen simply as an object of study, that its very reality is ignored, the fact that it happened, that these people lived and died. The populace within the laptop.

Next year Caroline will get married. Caroline Gladwell will become Caroline Fox, though of course she will not use Alan's name, generally speaking, but will remain Caroline Gladwell. In this she is very different from the young women whose names have scrolled down in front of her, and for whom marriage meant immediate abandonment of their birth name. They became their husband's appendage, for ever after. A change that is a signifier for the times, she thinks, as she gets a number seventy-three bus to head for home. Our times. Now, which is so much not then.

Home is a one-bedroom flat in Stoke Newington, for which Caroline and Alan pay a wicked amount of rent. The flat is the ground floor of an insignificant two-storey Victorian terrace house which would once have housed a lower-middle-class family of modest means, and is now worth around a million pounds. If Caroline and Alan were to buy their flat from the landlord they would have to pay half a million or so for sitting-room, bathroom, bedroom, kitchen, broom cupboard and minuscule entrance hall; that is of course out of the question.

Alan is quite favourably placed in economic terms. He is on the lowest rung of the civil service ladder, at the Home Office. If he beavers away for the requisite number of years, and climbs accordingly, he will eventually be in a position to hang his hat on a pension. Caroline herself has no such certainty, not yet, but with her MA under the belt, to add polish to her First, she will be equipped for a decently paid teaching job, even if she doesn't make academia.

The flat feels chilly; it is November. The days are closing in. Caroline puts the heating on, draws curtains, unpacks the shopping she picked up on the way. Lemon garlic roasted chicken thighs for supper.

Over which, presently, she and Alan exchange their days. He has had a slight run-in with a superior, and would have liked to give him a piece of his mind, but was sensible enough not to do so. Alan is pragmatic, clever, and usually cheerful; he is stockily built, has large and compelling brown eyes, and Caroline loves him inordinately.

She tells him about today's search. 'And then suddenly everything clicked into place. I realized that a Mary Ann Crowhurst was the aunt of a Sarah Webber, and I could fit that family tree together.'

'Your Somerset peasants?' says Alan.

'Agricultural workers.'

'Hodge,' says Alan. 'The generic term for nineteenth-century labourers. No names, just a tribe of Hodges.' He too read history at university, and has acquired arcane pieces of information.

'And that's what I'm doing,' says Caroline triumphantly. 'Filling in the names.'

They smile fondly at each other across the lemon garlic chicken. Alan is thinking that Caroline's face is a perfect heart shape, and that it is quite unfair for a girl to be so pretty and also so bright. Caroline is savouring the moment; if she were a cat she would be purring.

Caroline says, 'It is almost creepy that these people are my forebears. That there's a *connection*. Genes. DNA. And that nobody, so far as I know, has ever done this before. Reached back, and made the links. Touched them, as it were. I am their future.' She was silent for a moment. 'It feels quite odd. You identify, almost.'

'You can't really identify. It's impossible. Their circumstances are so different. The mind-set – the assumptions, the expectations. Think of it – the age before antibiotics, sanitation – people likely to be clobbered by anything and everything.'

She stared at him. 'All the same . . .'

'And,' he went on, 'most appropriately – it's that programme tonight. Do you want to see it?'

Alan is referring to the television programme *Who Do You Think You Are?*, in which some celebrity is confronted with their family

history, usually to be startled by the revelation of an ancestral con-
vict, or slave owner. Reality genealogy.

And so, later, they watch with amusement as a well-known actor
learns that his great-great-great-grandfather was imprisoned for
body-snatching. As compensation, there is another distant grand-
parent who died in the workhouse. Penury is always a badge of
honour.

'They didn't get that from the parish records,' says Alan. 'The
body-snatcher.'

'No, of course not. They have to investigate further if someone
looks interesting. As do I.'

Indeed. When Caroline can identify a name that invites enquiry –
on account perhaps of their trade, or their sudden movement from
one place to another, or even an early death – she tries to acquire
further information. This is where she may have to leave her comfort zone in the British Library Reading Room, and hive off in
pursuit of unfamiliar archives. She may try to find a particular street,
even a house, a gravestone. Actually, all this is quite good fun –
heading off to places she has never been to before, engaging with
helpful people in some archive, taking to unfamiliar streets and
spotting survivals. Oh – here's the terrace in which so-and-so lived,
still standing, no longer a slum, all gentrified now. And yes, here is
the gravestone I'm after, giving substance to a name on a list. She
really did live and die.

At the moment Caroline is in pursuit of a descendant of those
West Country Hodges/peasants/agricultural workers, a man who
seems to have broken out and headed off to Bath. Why? What was
he doing there? Did he marry, have children?

In Bath in 1840 a young man worked on a building site. A railway
station was being built, though the young man was barely aware of
the ultimate purpose of his labours. Suffice it that he had daily
work, and daily pay – superior to the circumstances he had known
where he was born and grew up, where there might be work, and a
meal on the table, but very well might not. Today, he would be

called an economic migrant, though he has migrated merely across a county.

He is in fine fettle, on this spring morning, heaving barrow-loads of golden Bath stone, and thinking of his Eliza, to whom he was married only yesterday. He thinks of the moment when the priest declared them man and wife, when he experienced what felt like a great surge of being – an affirmation of his very existence. And he thought of what Eliza said, after: 'I came over all funny, Tom, when he said that – "man and wife".' And he had known that she must have shared this momentary euphoria. Eliza is Bath born and bred; her father is an innkeeper, and Tom and Eliza have rooms over the inn, where, in due course, they too will breed.

In London in 2015 Caroline Gladwell spots a marriage entry that homes in on her wandering Hodge and most satisfactorily establishes that, in 1840, he was married in Bath to Eliza Fulbrook. She places Tom and Eliza at the head of a new family tree, in expectation of the births for which she will search in due course. Caroline suspects that Tom had been drawn to Bath by the work opportunities offered in the construction industry – Brunel's new railway station for instance – and she will now do some research on that. She thinks of this as colouring in – giving background, substance, to the stark recital of names. A name can then bloom a little – it can conjure up the image of a person: Tom Webber can become a robust young man labouring amid the dust and clamour of a nineteenth-century building enterprise.

Caroline thinks a lot about age – ages – as she pursues one name and another. Infant mortality, early deaths, the relative rarity of those who make it into their eighties. Death hovered, two hundred years ago, even one hundred years ago. Caroline has four octogenarian grandparents, doing quite nicely, bar various hip or knee problems.

Caroline herself is young, in today's terms. But would have been seen, more, as mature, a couple of hundred years ago – a hundred, even. Perceptions of age shift, as expectation of life lengthens. One third of the children born today will live to be a hundred.

My own, perhaps, she thinks. Goodness! Disappearing off into the twenty-second century. She and Alan plan to start a baby in a year or so, after their spring wedding. Another signifier for the times, she reflects (scrolling through some Bath births of the 1840s, in search of Tom Webber's progeny) – child born untypically in wedlock, when actually, nowadays, most are not. And born according to schedule (all being well . . .) instead of arbitrary, possibly unwelcome.

Ah! She has found it – a son born to Tom and Eliza in 1841. Within wedlock, by a comfortable few months.

Caroline now accelerates the nineteenth century. She whisks through time, disposing of decade after decade, until in due course she has nailed down the descendants of Tom and Eliza Webber, unto the fourth and fifth generation, forging ahead into a new century. Not her mother's direct ancestors, but a branch line and interesting in itself for economic flexibility; male Webbers abandon the building trade and become grocers, brewers, and in one instance a funeral director.

But at lunchtime Caroline closes her laptop, consigns the past to another day, and steps out into the present, away from the British Library and in the direction of Oxford Street. She's taking an afternoon off; she has a date with a friend, to consider wedding dresses. Rosie is also getting married next year. Weddings are almost a cult, for their generation. People marry with a flourish, in their late twenties or so, often having been together for several years.

Caroline remarks on this to Rosie, as they inspect an acreage of white and ivory silk, tulle, organza, in the bridal department.

'Why do we do it? My mum says in her day most of her friends just sneaked into a registry office, and then had a family lunch somewhere. She and my father didn't bother till I was nearly two.'

'My parents never have.' Rosie works in a bookshop, would like to get into publishing. She is short and dark, a foil to tall fair Caroline. 'What about this one? Too frothy for me.'

'I don't want froth either. So why do we?'

'Because each other does, I suppose. I've been to five this year already. You've got to retaliate. This one?'

'No – I don't want to look half-naked. My parents were still in recovery, I imagine – my mum had nearly died.'

'Having you?'

'Yes. Everything went horribly wrong. First I was stuck, and then she had a haemorrhage. And infection too – she was very ill after.'

'Scary . . . Mostly it seems to be a doddle, nowadays. Sue Parker – remember Sue? – she went shopping in Brent Cross the next day. This?' Rosie brandishes a beaded confection.

'You're joking . . . Utterly bling.'

They are getting tired of wedding dresses, and retreat to the coffee shop.

'I'm saturated in marriages,' says Caroline. 'Researching. Marriage after marriage. But it's just names and dates. You want to know more. What did she wear? I had a great-great-great-someone or other yesterday in Bath. Eliza. You find yourself imagining them.'

'Write a historical novel. Be the next Hilary Mantel. Cutting-edge stuff nowadays.'

Caroline shrugs. 'I can't think like that.' She wants to explain that what she reads in lists, entries, bare references, has come to reflect some alternative reality. Nothing to do with fiction. But it would be hard to put into words without sounding fey, and in any case Rosie has moved on to other matters: a flat she and her partner covet but cannot afford, a job interview next week, the person they caught nicking books in the shop. 'Actually, in a way, I couldn't help feeling – good on him. More high-minded than your run-of-the-mill shoplifter.'

They consider this ethical point over another coffee, and part company. Having got nowhere with the matter of wedding dresses, as Rosie observes.

'Perhaps we don't take marriage seriously enough,' says Caroline. 'An excuse for an event, rather than a rite of passage.'

They agree to pillage the wedding department at Selfridges, on some other occasion.

Somewhere in London, in 1821, a young woman is giving birth. She is in the final stages of labour, but the child is awkwardly placed. It (she, as it happens) is presenting feet first; the labour has been arrested, hour by hour, the woman is weakening, dying. Eventually the midwife decides to risk manual extraction, plunging her hand into the uterus to grasp the child by the feet and pull – a procedure potentially harmful to both mother and child, but needs must, in this instance.

The child is dragged forth. Wonderfully, she cries. The mother is beyond speech or crying. And the placenta has not been delivered. The doctor, summoned earlier, now arrives, late, hurrying in from the busy street, and at once rummages for the placenta.

Two days later, Maria Gladwell dies.

Elsewhere in London, in 2015, Caroline arrives back at the flat later than usual, and voluble about her day's work.

'I got so involved today. Guess what – I've found myself, as it were! Caroline Gladwell. How weird is that?'

Alan considers that it is not all that weird. Caroline was, after all, a popular name in the 1820s. Caroline – his Caroline – has explained that she was now pursuing her father's ancestry, and had arrived at this woman, a Maria Gladwell, who died in childbirth in 1821, the child, Caroline, having survived.

'I suppose so. But it did rather jump out at me. And the mother dying.'

'But your mother didn't,' says Alan.

'Only because of twentieth-century obstetrics.'

Caroline had decided to follow up that entry in the family tree with a short discursion on the conditions of childbirth in the late eighteenth and early nineteenth centuries. She has already read fairly extensively. In the early 1800s, she has learned, one in eight childbirths ended with the death of the mother. Maria Gladwell was one of those, then: a statistic.

The entry that Caroline had found stated only that she died in childbirth – which had led her to the confirming entry of the birth of her daughter Caroline two days earlier. What happened in the interim? Well, Caroline speculated, Maria had very likely contracted puerperal fever, in the absence of basic hygiene – the notion of hand-washing in a solution of chlorinated lime was not introduced until the 1840s. And many things could have gone wrong during the birth, which would nowadays be addressed by a forceps delivery, or an emergency Caesarean. Or, if the child was known to be awkwardly positioned, a Caesarean would have taken place automatically.

'She died,' Caroline continues, 'because she was giving birth in 1821 and not, like my mother, in 1991.'

'And what happened to your namesake?'

'That's what I must find out.'

Finding her own name had startled Caroline rather more than she admitted. Your name is your identity. She had thought about this, coming home on the bus. I know who I am because I know my name. I don't know who these people all around me are because I don't know their names. You read of people who have forgotten their name because of accident, or illness, and they are displaced, adrift, in need of help. The medics come running. You are not allowed to be without a name. Your name confirms that you exist, that you are you, that you can stand up and be counted.

And she had my name, back then.

Of course there are always people who have the same name as someone else, thousands of them. There are no doubt other Caroline Gladwells today – I may have walked past one in the street. And that feels a bit funny, too. But somehow not as weird – disturbing, even – as a person dead a long time ago.

How did she live? Marriage? Children? When did she die?

There is a new flavour now to this piece of research, Caroline finds. This oddly personal element. A kind of fortuitous intimacy. She is both intrigued by this and a bit disconcerted. Wrong-footed, as it were, as though the great neutral resource into which she taps had suddenly answered back. Spoken.

She gets down to it the next day. She has sited this Caroline within a new family tree. The interesting thing will be to see if she is a direct forebear, to find her children, and theirs, and see if they can be fined down to a great-grandparent, say.

First, she needs a marriage. But can find none. Oh.

So . . . To the deaths. And then she has it.

Caroline Gladwell died in 1847, aged twenty-four.

Twenty-four.

The rest is stark. An instance of the bald entry that sometimes accounts for a death that is out of the ordinary.

'Struck by a coach.'

Caroline stares at this. Around her, the Reading Room is going about its business, impervious, while the screen in front of her delivers its news.

Struck by a coach. Killed.

It occurs to Caroline that this could indeed have been news at the time. The search does not take long. Sure enough, in an issue of a London paper a few days later than the death date, there is the item: '. . . tragic accident . . . death of a young woman . . . stepped into the path of an oncoming coach . . . onlooker who rushed to try to pull her back said she appeared distracted, perhaps unwell . . . coachman much distressed.'

Caroline reads this. Once. Twice. The brief item is somehow resonant. She reads it yet again. She wants at once to tell Alan about this. Twenty-four. How weird indeed . . . She starts a search through the other London papers of the period for further coverage, but finds none, and as she does so, she begins to feel – well, rather ill. Shaky. Not herself at all. Flu or something coming on. Oh, I really don't feel too good.

She decides to go home – it is gone five, anyway. She gathers up her things, and leaves the Library. She crosses the open space outside in the darkening early evening, heads for the bus stop, and then feels really quite dizzy. Taxi, she thinks, taxi for once – I'm just not well.

She stands on the pavement, searching the pounding traffic for a free taxi. Stands with aching head, feeling quite unsteady. Traffic roars past, buses surging down the bus lane, steady stream beyond. Oh, to get home. Oh, taxi, please. And there at last is the orange light she needs, free taxi, out in the traffic, about to go past.

She steps from the pavement, waving. And as she does so everything happens at once: she is hearing horses' hooves, thundering hooves, but it is a seventy-three bus that she has not seen, that is almost on her, and in that instant arms have grabbed her by the shoulders, someone is pulling her back, the hooves are fading, she is hearing the screech of brakes, she is back on the pavement, a man has her by the arm – a burly, efficient man saying, 'You all right? You bloody nearly . . .'

'I'm all right,' she says. 'This time I'm all right. This time. Thank you.'

Old as the Hills

Here she is. Stick. Which I don't need yet. That patrician way of surveying a room – she hasn't seen me. I shan't wave. Let her find me. She's worn well – oh, yes. Apart from the stick. Doesn't look eighty. Do I? She's not done up, but understated stylish. Good coat, arresting scarf. Neat hair – all over silver grey, not pepper and salt like mine. No glasses – surely she used to? Oh, she'll have had the cataract op.

You are in my head, Celia. Multiple versions. Multiple Celias. Is this one the first time I set eyes on you? If so – or if not – I still am. Still seeing you across a different room. Blue dress, summery blue, talking to . . . oh, I've no idea who. Laughing. And then you look over towards us, you smile. At Hugh, I later realize. Much later. And you wander over to us, still smiling, and it seems that you and Hugh have met before. 'Celia,' he says to me. 'Celia Binns.' A name I'll get to know. The blue dress has a crisp white collar, a nipped-in waist. You are slim, at thirty-six.

Not now. She is a touch overweight, I'm glad to see. Snap.

Ah, she's seen me. The stick raised a little, in recognition. Faintest of smiles.

She approaches. Slow, with entitlement, forging through the tables. People looking up as she passes. She knocks someone's jacket off the back of his chair; he leaps up – apologizing, by the look of it. Of course – not her fault.

And here she is.

'Jane!'

Yes, I am Jane. I know that. 'Hello, Celia.'

'I haven't been to this place before.' She is removing her coat; a waitress materializes at once, to take it, pull out her chair, flourish a napkin across her knees.

I say that I have been here once. It had seemed all right. She has settled in, is considering me. She is thinking that I look all of eighty, that I have jowls, pouchy eyes, that I ain't what I used to be.

Or maybe she isn't. She says, at once, 'So you decided to miss the funeral. Delicacy?'

'Norovirus,' I say. Which is the truth. She can believe it, or not – her choice.

'Ours all sat together. People thought that was so nice.'

Ours. My children, her child – his children. My grandchildren, her grandchildren – his grandchildren.

'Quite a line-up. The youngest ones behaved impeccably. My Sophie. And that small lad of yours.' She picks up the menu. 'I shall probably go for something salady. Not a great eater, these days.'

Grief? Or concern about obesity? Not that she is anywhere near obese. Just rather stout, like me.

We choose. We order. We refuse wine (did I see her hesitate for a moment?) and sip mineral water. I ask if she is going to stay in that house. That large, expensive house.

'Of course. Why wouldn't I? All our things . . . I'd hate to part with anything. And so many memories.' A little sigh.

Indeed. We all have those.

'Dear me,' she says. 'Long time since we saw each other, Jane. Maisie's wedding?'

I correct her. Another funeral, which I did attend.

'Oh yes – his mother. I'd forgotten you came. Good of you, considering. I'm sure Hugh appreciated that.'

Oh, he did. If an air of deep embarrassment and confusion equals appreciation.

There he is, and why am I surprised that he is older, has some grey hair, a different face. Me too. And you, Celia, and you. Elegant in black, neither embarrassed nor confused. Running things. Meeting and greeting. Presiding over the funeral bakemeats.

You are sixty. As am I. Well into middle age, and you carry it off well. As a successful gallery owner should. I am successful too, in my own sphere, but university administrator is less conspicuous.

You have forgotten, you say (you say . . .), but I have not. I am there still in some stratum of the mind, supported by my Maisie, my Ben, observing your Toby, screwing myself up for strained exchange with Hugh. Observing Hugh.

You stand in gracious conversation with some relative and remain thus in my head, competing with this subsequent Celia, Celia now, Celia seated, eating salade niçoise.

'Not before time, one felt,' says Celia. 'But perhaps you got on better with her than I did.'

I am noncommittal. Actually, I had problems too. Seems we have that in common.

'Odd to think she wasn't much older than we are now. But there it is. We're as old as the hills, aren't we?' She grimaces.

Old as the hills. And young as all those other Janes and Celias that crowd the mind. And Hugh. And Hugh.

He cannot bring himself to say it. He has to bring himself to say it. Long ago. And now. Now and forever.

'Jane,' he says. 'Jane, I've got to tell you . . .'

And I know. He need not bother.

'Celia Binns' I say.

★

'One never thought it would happen, old age,' says Celia. She is tucking into the salade niçoise, I note. 'Just something that happened to other people.' She laughs. 'You were more realistic, I imagine.'

'I tend to be realistic,' I say. 'Something I've learned.'

She gives me a sharp look. Wonders if I am making a point. Well, yes, Celia.

'One can only try to make the best of it, I suppose. The occasional treat. I'm going on a little cruise next month. Hugh and I had planned to do that at some point.' She sighs again.

I am impassive.

'He was so stoical. Right to the end. I know you'd want to hear that.'

Would I? But impassive seems inappropriate here. I nod.

'Treats,' says Celia. 'And physiotherapy. I have a wonderful physio. But maybe you're in better nick than I am. I'll have to have a hip done.'

I mention my torn shoulder tendon, to keep abreast of her. Celia says she believes the best shoulder man is at the Royal Free. A friend of hers went to him.

'You know,' she says, 'I'd go back to the forties, if I could have my time again. Forget youth – nothing but *Sturm und Drang*. The forties were good. Fifties not at all bad, either.'

Celia at fifty. Yes, that memory slide comes up at once: Celia at my Ben's wedding, her hat trouncing all other hats, being tactfully unobtrusive but nevertheless emphatically there, impossible to miss. Hugh and Celia. Celia and Hugh. I am used to that, by now, but forever not. It is always an affront. So at my son's wedding I am affronted.

'Eighties are an outrage,' says Celia. 'What have we done to deserve this?'

I do not care for this implied community. I say that as far as I am concerned we are rather lucky to be living where and when we do and thus to have got to be eighty at all.

Celia pulls a face. 'Lucky? I don't feel particularly lucky.'

I regret the word. Not quite what I meant. I say so. 'Statistically lucky,' I say.

She laughs. 'Well, I don't feel like a statistic either. Just myself in a condition that I never anticipated.' She puts down her knife and fork; she has demolished the salade niçoise. 'And usually the oldest person in the room. Though not right now – there's a real old codger over there. Ninety if a day. Boring the socks off his granddaughter, by the look of it. That's what one is afraid of. Boring the socks off. Are you bored, Jane?' That smile. The Celia smile.

I am not bored, oh no. I do not return the smile (who could compete?), but ask after her grandchild (his grandchild) Sophie, who has had health problems. I am not, as it happens, particularly concerned about Sophie, but one should observe the proprieties.

Sophie is much better, it seems. 'And, incidentally,' says Celia. 'I imagine you've had the lawyer's letter. About the legacies. Same for all of them.'

I have. I say that my Ben will be glad of his – he is in his first job, low-paid, and saving for a car.

'Oh, that rings a bell. Being young and strapped for cash. I remember being twenty-one and lusting – *lusting* – after a dress I couldn't possibly afford.'

No image surges forth. I did not know Celia at twenty-one. Nor did Hugh. She would hove upon the scene all in good time. Bad time, you could say.

'Did you get it?' I ask.

'Oh, yes. I found a way.' She laughs.

Of course.

The waitress is wondering if we would like desserts. Celia says she could manage something if I would join her. We opt for the lemon cheesecake.

And then . . . 'Why am I here?' says Celia. 'Surely not for the pleasure of my company?'

I have been waiting for this.

'Satisfaction,' I say.

Celia considers me. 'Handbags at dawn? Isn't it a bit late for that?'

The pleasantries are done. This is more like it.

'Why Hugh?'

'Well,' she says. 'Why not Hugh? I was high and dry – my previous attachment had foundered. There had to be someone.'

'Someone else's husband.'

'Unfortunately. But not entirely unusual, Jane. And he could have resisted.'

Indeed, indeed. Point taken, Celia.

'And you thought – Jane will get over it, people do.'

She inclines her head: possible agreement. 'You found your Chris before too long, after all.'

Indeed, again. Quick on her feet, Celia. Level pegging at the moment, it would seem.

'I always liked Chris,' says Celia thoughtfully. 'Hugh didn't, for some reason.'

I am rather pleased to hear that. Affinity would not have done.

But this is beside the point.

'How is he?' says Celia. 'You should bring him over one day, now that . . .'

Oh no. Oh no, Celia.

'He has sciatica and a prostate problem,' I say.

A moue of sympathy from Celia. She will not press the invitation.

Back to business. 'No compunction at all?'

Celia reflects. 'Well, not really, I'm afraid. After all, I was in love,' she adds sweetly.

Oh, come on. 'Of course,' I say. 'Which explains everything.'

Celia sighs. 'Jane – it's history, all this.'

I say that I have always thought history to be of great relevance.

'Oh, I can't think like you,' says Celia. 'You're so well educated.'

The waitress appears. Would we like coffee?

Celia would kill for a coffee, it seems. So would I, I find.

After a moment, Celia says, 'Am I supposed to say I'm sorry?'

I have considered this. 'No, because you're not, so it wouldn't mean anything.'

'Then . . . Satisfaction?'

I tell her that perhaps confrontation would be a better word. 'It's called the elephant in the room nowadays. What is never spoken of. Forty-two years ago you helped yourself to my husband.'

Celia gazes at me. 'Absolutely. I can't deny that. Not an unprecedented situation, but I can see you feel that is irrelevant.' She wears a benign smile, but her eyes are steely. It is each for herself now.

And that is fine by me. This has been a long time coming. Forty-two years. I have plenty to say.

So has she.

We get down to it. At last.

Our coffee comes. The waitress hopes we have enjoyed our meal. The restaurant is emptying. People are getting up, putting coats on, passing our table with an indulgent glance and smile: two elderly friends lunching, having a chat about old times. Bless.

The Weekend

The Dennisons were on their way to spend the weekend with the Sanderbys. At the Sanderbys' new Cotswold second home. Philip and Vanessa Dennison; Nick and Jill Sanderby. And Martha Dennison, who was eight, and sat in the back of the car, silent.

'All right, darling?' said Vanessa. An eight-year-old who has been silent for a considerable time is suspect. Car sick?

'I'm OK.'

'Sure?'

Martha was understood to say, quietly, that she didn't really want to go and spend the weekend at the Sanderbys' new house.

Vanessa, no longer concerned, spoke of country walks and a little bedroom of her own.

'There'll be no one to play with. You said they haven't got any children.'

Vanessa mentioned a possible television in this customized room. And Martha's new colouring things. She herself was not on a mission of potential pleasure but a sortie into alien territory. Alien, and probably challenging.

An Aga, she thought. Bet you an Aga. And a wet room.

Woodburning stove and en suites to every guest room and dresser with interesting old china and floodlights in the driveway.

Philip was an academic. Academics do not have second homes in the Cotswolds, with or without Aga, wet room, en suites. Philip and Nick had been at college together, since when their paths had diverged.

Vanessa had Googled Nick. Google spoke of him as 'millionaire City lawyer'. Google is dispassionate, so this could not be read as respectful nor condemnatory. Vanessa knew how she read it. Philip and Nick had met up at some alumni gathering recently, when this weekend proposal had been floated, and followed up with a florid card of invitation from Jill: '. . . so longing to see you, and now the house is all kitted out at last we can entertain *properly*.'

'She hardly knows us,' Vanessa had said. 'Display of circumstances, that's what this is. His mega-bucks pay packet and their country mansion.'

Philip shook his head, vaguely. He and Nick had been quite good friends, back in that alternative world of youth. Academic high fliers, both of them; college aristocracy.

Vanessa continued: 'Does she do anything, Jill?'

Philip said that Nick had talked of her agency. 'It organizes parties, I think. Events of one kind and another.'

'Oh, *gawd*.' Vanessa worked as a copy-editor for a publishing group. She was able to feel dismissive: who needs party organizers? A rubbish occupation.

'Oh, well,' she had said. 'We may as well go. See how the other half lives.'

And now, according to the sat nav, here they were. Driveway with scrunchy gravel, yes. Not mansion, exactly, but substantial honey-coloured house swathed in wisteria.

A million plus, thought Vanessa. Of course. And there's the Range Rover.

Philip was a scholarly man who took no interest in house prices. He saw mauve flowers, a large red car, and Jurassic stone, wouldn't it be, round here? Yes, oolitic limestone. Palaeontology was not his subject, but he tended to know things.

The front door opened. Here were Jill and Nick, enthusiastically greeting.

'And Martha! Hello, Martha! There's a darling little room for you – the Rose Room, we call it, because I went mad with rose-covered wallpaper.' Jill seized bags. 'Is this hers? Come on in.'

No welcoming Labrador, thought Vanessa. That's an omission. Grandfather clock, yes. Open fireplace with stash of logs. Flower arrangement – but are those not *bought* flowers?

Allocation of rooms. Martha went to her window and looked out over a garden. Huge garden. With a separate sort of secret little garden at the end where a swing hung from the branch of a tree. The swing moved; it swung a bit, to and fro.

There was tea in the kitchen. The sort of kitchen anticipated; I have to stop looking and bristling, thought Vanessa. She talked brightly of the drive down here: 'Really not bad traffic at all.' Nick said that in the Range Rover they reckoned to get back to town in two hours max. Philip talked about oolitic limestone and wondered if there had been a quarry nearby. Jill and Nick looked blank. Jill said they were lucky, there was a really good little deli in Chipping Campden. 'You'll sample it tonight.'

Martha ate chocolate cake, in silence.

Later, there was a tour of the garden.

'Except that it isn't, yet,' said Jill, waving at expanses of shabby lawns, overgrown bushes, grass-infested paving. 'All in hand, though. There's an excellent local firm, and they've done a lovely plan – complete overhaul. Starting work next month – it's going to be rather something.' The party wandered through the damp grass, Vanessa concerned for her thin shoes, Jill talking about a laburnum walk, a sunken rose garden.

'And this funny little space at the end,' she continued. 'I'm not quite sure what they've got in mind for that.' She led the way through a high yew hedge. A couple of huge old apple trees. Sprawling bushes. Even longer and damper grass.

Martha was looking at the swing.

'I wonder if it's safe,' said Jill. 'I'm not too sure about that, darling.'

Philip tugged at the ropes; the sturdy branch of the apple tree hardly moved. He bounced the seat up and down. 'Seems all right. D'you want a go, Martha?'

Martha was very still, looking at it. She shook her head.

'Fruit area down here,' said Jill. 'Yes, that's what they're thinking of. Get it all dug over and have raspberries and all that sort of thing. Come along now – it's getting on for drinks time.' She murmured to Vanessa and Philip that she had rather imagined that Martha did not stay up for grown-up dinner. Vanessa said that was indeed so. Just a bit of early supper, if that's not a bother.

A weekend visit like this revolves round eating, thought Philip. Dinner tonight, breakfast, lunch . . . He was already realizing that there was really no longer much to talk to Nick about; young Nick seemed some other being. He found Jill a bit exhausting.

They returned to the house. 'The chaps can have a natter in Nick's study,' said Jill. 'And we'll sort out some supper for Martha, shall we?'

Nick's study had an immense fitted bookcase with nothing much in it except for some law books. Large desk; computer, printer, iPad. Couple of leather armchairs.

They sat. Nick talked about the establishment of a branch in Hong Kong, for their firm: 'I dare say I shall find I need to go and check up on it once or twice a year. I love Hong Kong.' He spoke of a complex recent case. At length.

Philip thought about parliamentary enclosure in the eighteenth century, his current preoccupation. He was good at mental retreat, practised it in prolonged departmental meetings, and occasionally at home, when Vanessa was on a roll about something.

He became aware of silence. 'Extraordinary,' he said. 'Fascinating.'

Nick smiled complacently. 'And we won, of course. Anyway . . .' He seemed, now, to be flailing a bit. 'How's life in academia? Working on something?'

Philip thought of talking about parliamentary enclosure, and

decided against it. A mere handful of people were likely to be interested in his eventual article, in any case, and Nick would not be
among them. He slid sideways into an account of problems with
increasing student numbers, and the university's new building programme. He wondered how Vanessa was getting on.

In the kitchen, Vanessa and Martha were watching Jill muster an
omelette and some salad. 'And then there's ice-cream in the freezer.
Can she?' – to Vanessa.

Vanessa said that she could. She hated this kitchen, from its rich
green Aga (of course) through the row of copper pans slung from
one wall, and the butcher's block, and the dresser with pretty Victorian china (of course) and the shelf of Le Creuset casseroles in
every size and shape. She hated it because she wanted it.

Martha said, 'Our kitchen isn't like this.'

Jill laughed. 'Well, this is a *country* kitchen.'

Vanessa said that Martha would be ready for bed as soon as she'd
had her supper. 'Won't you, darling?'

Presently the two of them climbed the stairs to the Rose Room
and its attendant bathroom. Martha had a bath. Vanessa said, 'I'm
afraid it's a bit dull for you here. Never mind – home tomorrow
evening.'

'I like the garden,' said Martha.

'I've got to get ready for dinner now. Our room is just along the
passage, if you want anything in the night.'

Martha said she thought she would be all right.

Drinks outside, before dinner.

'Do you think a hot tub on the terrace would be completely naff?'
said Jill. 'I would rather love one.'

Philip wondered what she was talking about. Vanessa had no
opinion. She was considering whether to drink as much as possible
and become mercifully oblivious, or whether to hold back in case
drink prompted some unwise remark. By the time they went in for
dinner she was somewhere in between these two positions.

Philip was still interested in this matter of local stone. He tended
to wrestle with a subject. 'A lot of the Oxford buildings came out of

these quarries, I believe. And there's some special slate – Stonesfield, I think. Yes, Stonesfield. Does this house have a Stonesfield slate roof?'

'Oh, I imagine so,' said Jill. It sounded as though that sort of roof was the thing to have. 'Of course, we were incredibly lucky to get the house. They tend to get snapped up. But we did the snapping – the previous owners were in a hurry to sell – they'd had a child die and just wanted to get away and live somewhere else. Tragic, of course, but a bit of luck for us. We jumped in with an offer rather over the asking price, and here we are.' She beamed across the table, over the gravad lax starter.

Definitely more wine, thought Vanessa. It's the only way. She reached for her glass, emptied it.

Jugged hare, there was next. 'Of course, I didn't jug it myself,' laughed Jill. 'The local deli does these really good frozen meals. A godsend, when we arrive from town after a hectic week.'

Please don't let's hear about your hectic week, prayed Vanessa. But they did: some event at the O2, and a wedding at the top of the Shard. Philip retreated to parliamentary enclosure; Vanessa toyed rather obviously with her empty glass. Nick opened another bottle.

The jugged hare gave way to a fruit salad. Vanessa excused herself: 'I must just pop up and see Martha's all right.'

She found Martha asleep. She had fallen asleep easily. The room seemed quite companionable, as though somehow she was not alone.

Vanessa returned to the party, finding that she had to take extra care on the stairs. No more wine, she thought. It's probably done the trick now anyway. She allowed the conversation to lap around her rather than join in and risk being either irrelevant or provocative. She was nicely sleepy, in any case.

Eventually, the evening ended. Upstairs, in their room, Vanessa said, 'I'm completely sloshed. It was the only thing to do, wasn't it? Are you?'

Philip yawned. 'Mildly so. Is it that bad here?'

'Yes,' said Vanessa.

'One feels rather out of place, certainly. Sorry to have let you in for it.'

'Never mind.' Vanessa could afford to be generous, in an alcoholic haze. 'I dare say he was perfectly all right when he was young. You couldn't know how he would develop. Or who he would marry.'

Philip sighed. 'We don't seem to be on the same wavelength. No doubt he's thinking the same.'

'Let him. All we have to do is get through tomorrow. We can leave smartly at five or so – plead Sunday evening traffic.'

Next morning, Vanessa found that the comfort of alcohol had soured into a hangover. She dragged herself down for breakfast and drank a lot of coffee. Jill was unrelentingly bright, enthusing about the lovely sunny day, the fresh croissants from the village shop, the prospect of lunch out at a local eaterie. 'More gastro than pub, if you see what I mean. Amazing chef.' The morning could be spent '. . . any way you like. Nick got the Sunday papers along with the croissants. Or a walk, if anyone wants.'

Martha spoke up, surprising her parents. 'Can I go in the garden?'

'But of course.' Jill beamed. 'Do whatever you like there.'

Philip said that he would quite like a walk. As he had feared, Nick declared that he would join him. Jill would stay here to keep Vanessa company.

The morning proceeded. Vanessa's planned retreat into the Sunday papers was sabotaged by Jill's constant interventions and tendency to read out loud some item she had come across: 'Do listen to this . . .'

At one point Vanessa went to check up on Martha, wading again through the damp grass. She found her sitting on the swing, looking as though somehow interrupted. No, Martha said, she didn't want any juice. Or a biscuit. She was fine.

Vanessa returned to the terrace. Jill said, 'What a good little thing she is, amusing herself on her own like that. I heard her *laughing* just now.'

'She's had to learn to, as an only.' Vanessa regretted this at once, expecting interested comment, or some revelation about Jill's own childlessness, but Jill merely embarked on an account of recent visitors, whose child had been an absolute pain.

The men returned. Time for the lunchtime excursion. Martha, summoned, asked if she could stay here.

'By yourself?' snapped Vanessa. 'Of course not.'

Martha began to say something. Fell silent. Remained so throughout the meal in the pub. Her parents were also subdued. Philip had heard about another case of Nick's, in unremitting detail, over several fields and through an otherwise delightful bluebell wood. Vanessa now knew that Jill had a resident housekeeper in London ('Spanish, brilliant, quite simply keeps the show on the road for us') and that her clothing needs were attended to by a personal shopper ('She sources everything and saves me all that traipsing around – I can give you her name').

Lunch ended. Vanessa felt gastronomically assaulted. Philip had indigestion. Back at the house, there were more Sunday papers and desultory chat on the terrace. Martha vanished.

And, at last, the moment came when Vanessa could decently propose departure. She went upstairs to pack up their things, and came down in rather better spirits.

She put their bags in the hall and went out on to the terrace. 'Martha! Martha! We're going now.'

Jill was saying that they must come again some time. 'We're rather booked up for the rest of the summer, but it's lovely here in autumn.' Nick was proposing lunch at his club, to Philip: '. . . must get together again at some point.'

'*Martha!* Philip, could you go and round her up?'

Philip wandered off into the garden. Vanessa stood about, exchanging niceties. Philip returned, towing an apparently reluctant Martha. There were goodbyes all round. The Dennisons piled into the car. The Sanderbys stood waving. Gravel crunched under the tyres. 'Goodbye, goodbye.'

'Whew,' said Vanessa.

'Sorry,' said Philip.

'Never mind.' Generosity could again be afforded. 'Part of life's rich pattern.' Vanessa turned to Martha. 'All right? Sorry it wasn't much of a weekend for you.'

'Oh, we had a really nice time.'

Vanessa swung round. 'We . . .'

'You told me they didn't have any children,' said Martha. 'So who was the girl in the garden?'

Point of View

The Scriptwriter is wrestling with the question of POV. Point of View. She has these three characters shut up in a room together, engaged in a discussion which must reveal, at the same time, their relationships with one another, aspects of their individual histories, and the current state of play in all three lives. To do this, she needs to display the scene from different points of view. The characters in question are in the nineteenth century. This is a costume drama series – it is hoped that it will trounce *Downton Abbey*. So there is the added complication of the nineteenth-century POV, which does not come naturally to the Scriptwriter but must be seamlessly suggested.

The Scriptwriter is Lauren Stanley, and right now, as she sits at her desk, wrestling, everything is seen from her POV. The screen of the laptop in front of her, the view of the street out of the window above. And, especially, thoughts which are distracting her from work, thoughts about a real-life connection which keep shoving aside these fictional concerns. She is a bit – well, quite a lot – worried about her relationship with her partner, Paul. It occurs to her that real life is a single POV affair, or rather, a matter of myriad conflicting POVs.

The relationship is not in crisis, but in poor health. It has a bad case of flu, from which it may well recover, but it is in need of care and attention. Lauren thinks of it in that way, as though it were some delicate substance – the Relationship. She is concerned about it.

Is Paul concerned?

Ah – this is where POV comes in. She does not know if Paul is concerned, if he is aware that things are not good, or, if he is aware, whether he is concerned. Or just not bothered, possibly. Is he thinking: so we're not getting on . . . well – whatever.

Paul is a research chemist. He works for a big pharmaceutical company. A pharma, you say nowadays. His work is about as remote from Lauren's as could be, a matter of substances and reactions, hypotheses and results. No nonsense about what he said or she said or who did what, when, where and to whom. No hint of a POV.

They met at the wedding of a mutual friend. Oh, cliché, cliché. Met, got talking, took a shine to one another, met up a week later, took further shine, the gulf between their occupations no impediment whatsoever, met up again, and again, went to bed, went to Venice for a weekend, were spoken of as a couple, moved in together. Lauren, Paul, Harry and Archie.

Harry is Paul's thirteen-year-old son. Archie is Lauren's cat. Paul has been married (he is somewhat older than Lauren) – Harry is the detritus of the marriage and is actually only with them alternate weekends and some of the school holidays, though it sometimes seems longer than that to Lauren. When she and Paul first got together Harry was a charming – well, mainly charming – six-year-old. Thirteen is less charming. Most of Harry's time is spent with his mother, who lives in Maidenhead, and exerts a malign influence from there.

Archie is a ten-year-old neutered tabby. He has had no previous relationship.

Lauren has. Two. Eighteen months and three years. She has been assuming for some time that she and Paul are a fixture, which is why the Relationship's onset of flu is a worry. She considers the symptoms each day, testing them for progress. Better? Or worse?

Paul fails frequently to give her that quick kiss before he goes off to work.

He seldom enquires about *her* work, which he used to do.

Sex, when it happens, feels perfunctory.

All that is worse.

Better was when he did remember her birthday. When he and Harry brought a choice takeaway supper back for them all after they had been to a football match. When he reached out for her hand in the car last week.

But worse are all these times he has nothing to say. When he comes home late (could he be having an affair?). When he seems not to care whether she is around or not.

She does not really think he is having an affair. Paul just is not that sort of man (but anyone could suddenly become that sort of man, couldn't they, if subject to a *coup de foudre*?). And he hates crisis, upheaval. The end of his first marriage shattered him. That Relationship suffered some kind of terminal flu, it seems. He prefers not to talk about it.

The Scriptwriter homes in on her three characters, determinedly. She has one of them move to the fireplace, and turn angrily to her sister saying . . . Saying what?

Lauren wonders if Paul really has these departmental meetings that make him late home – very late – every Tuesday. He probably does. Paul is deeply involved in his work. This is a much more likely scenario than some woman tucked up in an adulterous flat.

The Scriptwriter frowns, stares at her screen, types: 'Charlotte (angrily): That is untrue, Emily. I have never spoken ill of you – I have *not*, I have *not*.'

Lauren compares life with Paul now to life with Paul, say, a year ago. Surely he talked to her more then? Surely sex was more enthusiastic? There was more companionship: going to see a film, a walk in the park. Last weekend he didn't want to come for a walk with her, stayed home reading the paper.

The Scriptwriter tells Emily to reply. Emily is silent.

Lauren sifts the last week for some positively companionable, even affectionate, moment. Paul patted her on the shoulder when asking what was for supper. An email he sent from the office to say what time he would be home had a couple of Xs at the end. He has never been one for endearments, so absence of a 'darling' or two means nothing.

The Scriptwriter sighs, closes the screen, and consigns her characters to the depths of the laptop.

Lauren considers their respective personalities; pronounced differences are perhaps relevant. She knows that she is more volatile, more excitable, more prone to panic or dismay. None of these defects are present to excess, but they are not reflected in Paul's personality. Paul is phlegmatic. He is even-tempered, inclined to caution, rational, conscientious, persistent.

So, given what seems a certain apposition, is she just fussing? Is it just that Paul doesn't react like she does, so seems distant?

No. Because if always a bit calm and cool he has become more so. Much more so.

Are they an otherwise mismatched couple? Paul is tall, gangly, with a long thin face, glasses. Lauren is short, inclined to plump, with (she considers) a reasonable face, quite pretty even, perfect eyesight.

No, appearance is irrelevant.

Are their living circumstances unsatisfactory? Well, not really. They moved into the Finsbury Park flat three years ago, after a prolonged engagement with London house prices, and are very pleased with it; their bedroom, a small one for Harry, Lauren's study, sitting-room, bathroom, kitchen with high cabinet on top of which Archie usually roosts, paws neatly folded, surveying them. No, the flat is fine.

Problems with their extended families? Paul's mother is widowed; Lauren gets on well with her, they visit regularly, Eileen comes to them for Christmas. His only sibling, a sister, lives in Australia but relations have been entirely amicable on her occasional visits.

Lauren also has a sister, of whom she is fond. Paul has always seemed to like her well enough, and her husband. Sally recently had her second child, and Lauren was careful, when last she and Paul went there, to refrain from any enthusiastic reaction or comment; no 'Oh, isn't he lovely!', no pleas to be allowed to hold him. Indeed, she remembers making some breezy remark on the way home to the effect that Sally was in danger of becoming a complete baby bore: 'Rather her than me!'

Paul does not want them to have a child together. His silence on the matter has made that clear to Lauren.

Lauren is thirty-six. Before too long it would be too late anyway. So she has bitten the bullet, told herself if that is the way it is, then that's the way it is, get over it, get a life.

No, families pose no problems. And the baby issue . . . The baby issue is her problem; she has never confronted Paul, sensing how he feels, never made anything of it, has not risked wrecking this good, solid relationship. He has Harry – well, a share of Harry; she can understand that that is enough, for him.

And she has her work, her absorbing work, which is enough for her, isn't it? She has her work, she has a much-loved partner, she has a choice flat in a sought-after area of London, she has good health, a stable bank balance, and an assertive cat who is winding round her legs right now not out of affection but because he wants food.

Lauren feeds Archie: Whiskas, one pouch.

There, she tells him. You are not a baby substitute, and never were. I am fond of you, but in a perfectly balanced, merely cat-loving way.

Archie eats.

Later, Lauren feeds Paul: chilli con carne, followed by a fruit salad.

Paul eats, but with expressed appreciation. Chilli con carne is a favourite of his. He pours them each a glass of wine.

Archie, with practised agility, has leapt to the top of the kitchen cabinet and settled himself, observing them without apparent interest.

Paul has had an exacting day. Now, back home, he is trying to put these things out of his mind and concentrate on . . . chilli con carne, a glass of Sauvignon, the sight of Lauren, in that grey stripy top and the amber pendant he gave her for Christmas.

Paul loves Lauren. His POV, right now, is of the person he loves, eating her supper, talking about something someone said in the supermarket. Fine, you might think. What more could a man want?

Except that it is not fine. Not quite. Because there hovers around Lauren an absence. There is something missing. A someone.

Paul knows that Lauren does not want to have a child with him. That is clear from the fact that she has never raised the matter, from the merrily disparaging remarks she makes about her sister's new baby. All right. All right, if that is the way she feels. But for him, there is this hovering absence. This wistful wishing. It has made him a bit offhand with her lately – he knows that.

Lauren says, 'I never understand how Archie gets to the top of that cabinet. It would be, for us, like jumping about twenty feet.'

'Well,' says Paul, 'he is differently constructed. Constructed to leap. But yes, it always does seem rather an achievement.'

'I've watched him. One jump up on to the counter. Then he sort of eyes the top of the cabinet, and there is this effortless lift-off. And he arrives. If there is reincarnation,' Lauren goes on, 'I'm coming back as a domestic cat.'

'In order to be able to jump on top of kitchen cabinets?'

'Because it's the most luxurious, unthreatened life going. Everything you need supplied. No dangers. Nothing demanded of you.'

Paul considers. 'Limited, then, one might say. No challenges or achievements – except access to high places.'

'That's anthropomorphism. Animals don't think in terms of challenges or achievements. Survival is all. And reproduction, of course. Poor old Archie. Snipped in youth. No genetic drive for him.'

'Then he is spared,' says Paul.

Something in his voice makes Lauren look more intently at him. 'Spared?'

Paul shrugs. 'A maddening compulsion, I imagine. Necessitating indiscriminate sexual pursuit and mortal combat with rivals. We're lucky to have more contained feelings.'

'Yes,' says Lauren. 'I suppose we are.'

There is a silence. An odd silence, somehow – no, not pregnant, inappropriate word. Loaded, perhaps.

The freight that this silence carries seems to fill the room. A thought freight emanating from him, from her.

Paul thinks of children. Not of specific children, not of his Harry, but of abstract children. The concept of children. The reproductive drive, he supposes sourly. Somehow, it doesn't feel quite like that. It feels less ruthless, more considered, more *human*.

Lauren does not so much think as experience. First, she experiences the baby issue that she thought she had managed to tamp down. It comes surging up: disturbing, dismaying. Then, looking at Paul, she seems to begin to experience something quite different: she is not just looking at Paul but looking out from him. It is as though her POV has suffered fission, and become double. She sees Paul but she also sees herself, a Paul's-eye view of herself, and she understands that she is lacking, that there is an absence, that he wants more of her, that there should be more of her.

'Do you?' she ventures, at last.

'Do I what?'

'Have . . . have feelings that way?'

He gazes at her. He is all POV.

'Well, yes,' he says. 'I do.'

If she could levitate, she would. She would rise up in joy, sail round the room, rejoice, rejoice.

Lauren says, 'Actually, me too.'

There is a silence. Paul reaches for the wine, fills their glasses. 'I had no idea. You've never . . .'

'Said. Nor have you.'

'I thought you . . .'

'Didn't want to?' says Lauren. 'And I thought *you* didn't.'

Paul's expression is a turbulence of surprise, delight, confusion, pleasure. And he is not that kind of man. He is a calm man, phlegmatic. It occurs to Lauren – the Scriptwriter surfaces now, for a moment – that if she were writing this scene the POVs would be rampant, competing.

'I've been *so* . . .' She shakes her head. 'So not *realizing*.'

'And I'm afraid I've been . . . well, I'd got a bit glum about it.'

The POVs, at this point, are no longer rampant but are holding hands, united. And so, too, are Lauren and Paul. Holding hands across the kitchen table, smiling, planning, anticipating. Archie, perhaps sensitive to a change in kitchen atmosphere, drops down from his perch. But no, he is prompted not by sensibility but opportunism. The pan from which Lauren served the chilli con carne is on the side, not entirely empty. And something tells Archie that people are not, right now, paying attention.

Archie eats.

Licence to Kill

'Coat,' she said. 'No, the red one, please.'

The girl got the red one, stood there with it.

'Scarf, please. Grey scarf.'

'Shopping list!' said the girl. Pouncing, triumphant.

'Put butter. I forgot. And J-cloths.' She was eighty-six, and forgot much. The mind was porous; some things lodged, others did not.

The girl wrote. And drew a cat with whiskers, back view of. And a smiley face. She was eighteen. Might try that Aussie shampoo. Might go to Oxford Street with Lindy, at the weekend.

They went out of the front door. Cally said, 'Shall I do the mortise lock, Pauline?'

'Yes – do it.' The agency had asked if she would rather be Miss, and she'd said not. Hospitals don't now, either, one had noticed. Neither here nor there, as far as she was concerned, so long as they knew who you were.

Slow and careful on the steps, for her. Cally jumped the last three, stood at the bottom checking her phone, remembered she wasn't supposed to when working, shoved it in her pocket. She said, 'Shall we get a coffee when we're in Marks?'

Pauline considered. Coffee, and one might need a loo before this shopping expedition is done. There's the bank, and Boots.

'Mmn. Maybe.' You plot, daily. Face down circumstance. Measure out your life with . . . not coffee spoons – pills. Line them up with breakfast, lunch, supper. Never mind mermaids, and lilacs in bloom, and all that stuff. He hadn't a clue. In his twenties, wasn't he? It's pills, and have I phoned the surgery, and did I pay that gas bill, and have I got my debit card?

Have I?

She delved in her bag. Ah – there. Shall I eat a peach?

'Peaches,' she told Cally. 'Stick them on the list.'

'You said they never got ripe, last time.'

'I'll persist. Dare. Maybe we will have a coffee, too.'

In the bank, Cally had to put the number into the cash dispenser for her. Not easy to see them, now.

Cally said, 'That bank person's staring at me. Thinks I'm up to no good. Using your PIN.'

'I'd better give him a smile. There. He's lost interest – I am not under coercion.'

'Mind,' said Cally. 'If you were going to nick someone's card and march them to the bank, they'd hardly just go along with it and stand there watching.'

'They might if they'd lost their marbles. What he was thinking, perhaps.'

'Three twenties and two tens. I've put them in the purse. And the card. Here . . . Boots next?'

I can look at the shampoos while she's waiting for her prescription, she won't mind. That's the thing about this job – there's spare time, sort of. Easy, and spare time, and this Pauline's fine, not like her in Brunswick Gardens – do this, do that, and never a thank you. Ninety-five, that one is. How can a person be ninety-five years old?

They found a chair for Pauline, by the prescription counter.

'Yes – go and browse. I shall be here for some time, I can see.'

And time is no longer of the essence. It is baggy stuff, disposable, no need to preserve, allocate. Actually, that's a legal term, isn't it?

Of the essence. To do with contracts. In non-legal life you just mean the need to hurry.

I have hurried, she thought. I have been hurried. Now, I no longer hurry. Days are capacious, to be idled through. Butt ends of my days. Oh, for heaven's sake, enough of that stuff. Mental sediment – all that was once read. Extraordinary, the accretion of it all. What one has done, what one vaguely knows. The arbitrary archive.

The pills came. Whole bag of them. The ones to be taken before a meal, the ones after, the ones with. The pharmacist inspected the haul: 'I think you're familiar with all these?'

'Tiresomely familiar.'

The pharmacist was young, Asian, pretty. Delicate small hands folded the bag shut and passed it to Pauline. Nice smile.

'Thank you.'

Science A levels. Degree also, I think. The world will always need pharmacists. Wise girl. In fact, will need them more and more, with the expanding horde of the likes of me. Dispense pills, or make them – that's the business to be in.

Cally had returned, with Boots bag.

'Satisfactory?' said Pauline.

'I'm trying a new shampoo.' And black nail polish, but she wouldn't care for that.

Marks & Spencer was the serious challenge: Pauline's grocery requirements. They began to work along the aisles. A slow process. Pauline was a judicious shopper. She peered, considered.

Cally pushed the trolley. She drifted, in the head, eyed people, fished for her phone, remembered and put it back. She needed to text Lindy, and Mum – that would have to wait. Nice – that girl's jacket. Zara? Oh yuck, that kid with a runny nose. If I have children . . .

She thought briefly of these unimaginable children. Binned them. Too far away. Well, out there somewhere, but not of interest just now.

Saturday night? Nothing fixed up. Lindy? Or that Dan? They were in Vegetables. 'Where do these beans come from?' said Pauline.

'Kenya.'

'Ah. Large carbon footprint, then. Still, I want some.'

Kenya. One had a spot of bother once in Mombasa. Had to use the whole bag of tricks. I'd know him now – the face. And the name. But I can't put a tag on that woman I met last week. 'Mustard,' she told Cally. 'I forgot that.'

'OK. We'll get there. You've still potatoes and salad things.'

'Right. And use your phone while we're having coffee. That's fine by me.'

'Oh,' said Cally. 'There's no need. I . . .'

'I noticed you wanting to, dear,' said Pauline. 'Tea break coming up.'

Embarrassed, Cally focused on lettuce. Many forms of lettuce.

'Do you like the mixed baby leaves?'

'No, let's have those Little Gems. Absurd name. Small lettuces, they are.'

'My dad grows them, I think. Gardening's his thing. I used to like helping him but I've gone off it. The worms and stuff. I'm more of an indoor person.'

'So what's in mind for the long term? You don't want to be dancing attendance on old women indefinitely.'

'Oh, no,' said Cally. 'I mean . . . well, I mean I really like it, of course, but . . .'

'But with all options open. Quite right.'

When I was her age, thought Pauline, the options were confusing. They always are. Who'd be young? Everything wide open, which means that the not chosen is discarded. Junked. I have junked being policewoman, interior decorator, estate agent, High Court judge, Home Secretary.

'I'm wondering a bit about nursing,' said Cally.

'Only a bit?'

'I'm not sure about blood. I've not been awfully good with that.'

'I imagine you get inured to it,' said Pauline. 'But if in doubt, maybe look elsewhere.'

'I like cooking. My mum thinks perhaps a catering course. City and Guilds there is. Hospitality and Catering.'

'Nice idea. Distinct possibility. Now, where are the potatoes?'

'Over here. Is it baking you want?'

'Jersey Royals. Or are we in the wrong time of year?'

Yes. Spring, they are. And this is autumn. For a moment I was untethered. Adrift in time. Alarming. But now I am hitched again to a Tuesday in October, and in need of a rest. 'We'll head for the coffee place,' she said. 'My knee is complaining. Grab a bag of small potatoes and find us somewhere to sit.'

Cally organized a table, queued up for two coffees, rejoined Pauline.

'Good. We've earned this.' Pauline took a sip of her coffee.

'Hot. Have to leave it a minute. You do your texting now – rest period.'

Feeling a little exposed, Cally told her mother she was in Marks with the Albert Street lady, who was OK, nice in fact, and I'll let you know about Sunday this evening. She arranged Lindy for Saturday. She nudged Dan. She drank her coffee.

'Yes,' said Pauline. 'Why don't you investigate this catering idea. Might lead to all sorts of things. Oh, it's such a teaser – the road not taken. Do you know that poem? "Two roads diverged in a wood, and I / I took the one less travelled by." Hackneyed, rather, now, but he had a good point.'

'I expect you were a teacher, Pauline, were you?' said Cally kindly.

Pauline finished her coffee. 'No, dear. I was a spy.' She collected her bag, her stick. 'Well, we'd better get on, I suppose.'

They got up. Cally followed Pauline. She saw her looking much as she had before. Really old. Those thick glasses. The stick. But looking also . . . different. She was talking about chicken now, Pauline. Something about how she roasts a chicken with tarragon and lemon.

Cally stared at the chicken carcasses. 'Licence to kill?' she ventured.

'Well, yes. But it wasn't called that. There was a euphemism. Find me the small size, could you – I can never finish the medium ones.'

'Were you . . .' said Cally. 'Did you spy sort of on your own?'

'No, no. It's an organizational operation. Have you heard of MI5 and MI6?'

Cally said that she had.

'Well, then. And it's less James Bond than you'd think. Office work, to an extent.' Pauline examined a proffered chicken. 'That one will do nicely.'

Office, and what one might call exit periods. Most of which are still there with absolute clarity. Not in chronological order, and richly peopled. Oh, people above all – a filing cabinet of faces. One was always good at filing faces, of course.

They had reached oil and dressings. 'Which mustard?' asked Cally. 'And we want olive oil.'

Like onions, she thought. A person is. Layers. And you haven't a clue. You just look at the top. An old person's just an old person, you think. Anyone is. Her there in that awful pink skirt too short for her, my mum's age she is. And him with the dreadlocks.

She said, 'Did you . . . spy . . . go spying . . . in lots of far-away places?'

'A good Italian oil, I like,' said Pauline. 'And a lemon-flavoured one.'

Chimborazo, Cotopaxi . . . In fact one never made it to either of those. Nor yet Popocatépetl. But Mogadishu . . . No, this lass doesn't need to know about that episode in Mogadishu. Or Kinshasa.

'I suppose I did. It tends to be a global procedure. But forget speedboats on blue Bermuda waters or car chases in Singapore. More, waiting about in train stations and meeting up with people one would have preferred to avoid.'

'I'd like to travel,' said Cally.

'Said to broaden the mind. Though that depends rather on the condition of the mind in question. I have known some well-travelled minds that were nicely atrophied. Now – how's that list? Where should we be heading?'

'Marmalade. With J-cloths later. I've been to the Algarve,' said

Cally. 'I tried to learn a bit of Portuguese. Please and thank you, at the least.'

But Pauline didn't go on Thomson Holidays, she thought. I don't know what she did, or what that person she once was did, but it can't have been lying on the beach and looking for the right *taberna*. Not if licensed to kill. She stared at Pauline's back. Tweed-clad, somewhat bent, inscrutable.

Pauline stumped ahead, thinking again about faces. That gallery in the head. From a display of grapefruit, a particular mug-shot surged. Yes, yes, she said. I remember you. Without enthusiasm.

Training, of course. An essential technique. What you didn't know was that you would be stashing them away for ever.

A known face among the avocados, too – not unwelcome, but irrelevant, now. Get away with you, she told him. I'm through with all that, and so are you, wherever you are.

'Actually, we're the wrong way,' said Cally. 'We want to be over there.'

'Aim me at marmalade, then.'

Time was, one was pretty good at direction. Which came in handy, on occasion. Saved the situation, indeed, once. Peculiarly nasty area of Marrakesh.

She came to a stop. 'Thick-cut. Golden Shred. Lime, is that, for heaven's sake? Who needs all these? Where's plain Oxford? Right. What else?'

'I'll nip down there for the J-cloths,' said Cally. 'Then we're done.'

When she returned, Pauline was considering her purchases.

'There's an awful lot here. Are we going to be able to manage it?'

'Oh, yes. With your trolley thing. It holds ever so much.'

'Right. Let's get done with this, then.'

Queues at every checkout. 'Maybe here,' said Pauline. They lined up. Pauline noted that the woman ahead lived alone, had a cat, a weakness for milk chocolate, liked a glass of wine, planned to clean her oven and polish some silver. It dies hard, she thought, the instinct to observe, identify. Tiresome, rather, nowadays. I don't need to know about this lady's home life.

'Bear in mind,' she told Cally, 'that whatever you do choose as occupation, in due course, will form the habits of a lifetime.'

'You mean, Hospitality and Catering and I'll think canapés and cupcakes for ever?'

'It goes with the territory, I imagine. I am doomed to pry, and make informed guesses. But today I have made a bad choice. Wrong queue, we're in.'

Two customers ahead of them, trouble had brewed. A man had loudly pointed out that his egg carton included one that was broken. ('Should have checked, shouldn't he?' said Cally.) A replacement had been sent for but now he was in dispute with the cashier over whether or not the chicken korma was included in the mix and match offer.

'It said so. I saw quite clear.'

'You see, it means . . .'

'It's what was said. You telling me I can't read?'

The dispute smouldered. The queue grew restive. Pauline leaned against a display of fruit gums.

'Way back, in my training days,' she said, 'I went on that course where you learned how to strangle a person with the bare hands. I think I am about to exercise the skill for only the second time.'

Cally looked at her. Blinked. Looked away. Looked back, and Pauline was checking her purse for her debit card: dumpy, grey hair, that coat slightly worn at the cuffs. She did say that. Yes, she did.

Some accommodation had been reached, ahead. The man gathered his bags and departed.

'Just as well,' said Pauline. 'He was quite a big chap. Ah – here's my card. Now, are we really going to get all this in?'

The shopping was paid for, stowed away. They emerged into the street. Pauline paused to hitch her bag over her shoulder. 'There. Thank you, dear. Mission accomplished.'

Not that one ever said that. Merely – returned to the office and set about filing the report. Now, I file for my own satisfaction, and today is a reasonable day, with my knee not too bad, and those autumn leaves are as though never seen before and look, just look, at the berries on that sorbus.

Cally did not see leaves or berries. She saw street, cars, people, all much the same as half an hour ago but somehow vaguely unreliable. She felt, oddly, older. A slightly different person, who knew more. Who knew to make adjustments. Maybe not Catering and Hospitality, she thought. I may not be a Catering and Hospitality person. I don't know who I am yet, do I? Who I may be.

Mrs Bennet

In deepest Devon, in 1947, Mrs Bennet lived on. Not as such, you understand, fictional or otherwise, but in the person of a Mrs Landon, Frances Landon, who was married to a man of deficient means, and had three daughters, now of marriageable age.

The Landons had moved from Berkshire to Devon when the youngest daughter, Imogen, left school at sixteen. Pamela – now twenty – and Clare, eighteen, had also left at that age. They all had a taste for country life. Ted Landon's best attempts at successful work had been rural-based. Berkshire was edging towards suburbia, and, crucially, was without the sort of real country gentry that it would be promising for the girls to meet. You needed deep country, the shires. They would have to move.

A nice house was found, eventually, on the edge of a village in Devon, foothills of Exmoor. Pretty little nineteenth-century house with outbuildings, good garden, paddock, and an extension that could do for Ted's study or office.

Ted Landon drank a bit. Well, more than a bit. He had had a quiet war, tucked away in the War Office in some menial position, and had perhaps picked up the habit then, whiling away solitary evenings when his wife and the girls were safely away from the bombs.

He was supposed, now, in Devon, to be helping out a local land agent, but little helping got done. The land agent had picked up, early on, that Ted was not likely to be sparking on all cylinders after his lunchtime break in the Red Lion, and called on him less and less. Before the war, Ted had tried apple farming, and chickens, and cattle feed salesman, but none of these had seemed to be quite his *métier*.

He was fifteen years older than Frances. She had married him in a panic, when twenty-four, with no one else in sight and spinsterhood staring her in the face, she felt. Dread word, not yet at its last gasp, nowhere near, indeed, bouncing ominously back in the wake of the Great War. Men were at a premium; young, marriageable men were gold dust, sought after, fought over. The debutante dances of the early 1920s were red in tooth and claw, and Frances had not made a kill. She saw contemporaries succeed, and sail off into the sunset with a ring on their finger, or fail, and fade away to help Mummy in the garden, or do good works. In the circles in which Frances moved the Pankhursts had been referred to with shock and disapproval; a nice finishing school was all a girl needed – a course at a Constance Spry place. Which Frances had done; she could arrange flowers, bake a cake, whisk up a soufflé, cook sole meunière. She could smock a baby's dress, knit a sock, iron a shirt. Groomed for homemaking, she was. And then there were no men. Except for Ted Landon.

It had not been a bad marriage. Not too bad. The girls had been the great thing, arriving in quick succession, and Ted's inability to make a success of anything had become only gradually apparent. Apple farming was hard work; battery chickens brought in no money at all, by the time you'd paid the men and the overheads; cattle feed salesman was frankly demeaning.

What was in mind was unspoken, but they were all aware – Frances positively so, the girls nervously but dutifully. Ted perhaps not at all, comfortably inured with the *Sporting Times*, his pipe, and a brandy or two.

Once settled in the Devon house, everything nicely put to rights,

Frances looked about her. She soon saw that they did things differently here. Suburbia was far away. Here, the lanes rang to the sound of horses' hooves; daily, girls on nicely groomed ponies clattered past their door, done up in jodhpurs and hacking jackets. Young men, too. Periodically, the hunt poured past; hounds with waving sterns, the red-coated huntsmen, the whole field – an acreage of horseflesh, jodhpurs, hunting coats, bowlers. Girls, men.

They attended the Boxing Day meet at Churleston Manor, and stood on the fringes while the field milled about, reaching down from horseback to take a glass of sherry and a mince pie, shouting greetings: 'That the new mare, Jane? Super.' 'Good to see you out again, Oliver. Arm all mended, is it?' The four Landons looked and listened. Nothing was said, but everything was understood.

The girls were going to have to get into the hunting field.

'But, Mummy, we can't ride.'

That could be addressed. The local riding school was run by a Polish cavalry officer (or so he said). Colonel Kowalski was a part of the Second World War diaspora, washed up in Devon after heaven knows what wartime adventures, and nicely filling the slot left by the death of the ageing lady who had formerly been instructing the county's young. Colonel Kowalski had the indoor school re-floored, the outdoor manège re-turfed and re-fenced, and acquired a stable of ponies and horses of requisite size and temperament. The establishment was seen as vastly more professional.

The girls bumped round and round the indoor school and the manège, shouted at by the Colonel. 'Hup-hup-hup, Pamela. Clare – keep that pony's head up. Heels *down*, Imogen, *down*.'

After months, and considerable expenditure, the Colonel declared that Pamela at least could be considered a reasonably competent rider. Most work had been done on Pam, for obvious reasons. This was to be a carefully paced venture: Pam first, then the others in due course.

But there was more to come, much more. If you ride, you need a horse.

This was where Mrs Halliday came in. Marcia Halliday was the neighbour beyond the Landons' paddock, inhabiting a small thatched cottage that seemed inappropriate for its owner, a woman of patrician gentility, whose icy upper-class speech could freeze a room. She rode, she hunted. No, she lived for riding and hunting – out with the South Devon twice a week, the East Devon now and then, not forgetting the Devon and Somerset Staghounds. Her two horses occupied the field adjoining the Landons' paddock. Frances had struck up an acquaintance – passing, it seemed, Marcia Halliday's forensic social scrutiny, and when she confided that the girls were learning to ride and, well, Pam would love to have her own pony, Marcia had taken an interest. This was her territory entirely; possibly she sensed the general purpose, and saw the point. There was no Mr Halliday in sight, but presumably there had been one.

Marcia Halliday took the whole thing in hand. After a brisk sourcing operation she came up with Willow, a rather inaptly named grey cob, solidly built, fifteen hands, not much to look at, which was why he came relatively cheap, but sound in wind and limb. Marcia tried him out on a day with the South Devon, and said that for her he would be on the slow side but she thought he might do well for Pam: nice temperament, didn't shy or kick, not much good over fences but she had the impression Pam wasn't that keen on a jump anyway.

Pam was not. Jumps filled her with horror. Colonel Kowalski had forced her over the two-bar in the manège and then the three-bar, less than knee-high: 'Lift up into it, Pam, lift up. He can feel you holding back, so he does.' Pam clung to the horse's neck, heart thumping, stayed on, just about, came down on the other side. No, she was not keen on a jump.

Willow was installed in the paddock. One of the outbuildings became the harness room. Frances had had no idea a horse required so much equipment: the saddle, bridle, halter, blanket for winter. The brushes, the sponges, the buckets, the saddle soap. The bales of straw for the other outbuilding, converted to a stable. The oats. The expense.

And then there was Pam herself. Smarter jodhpurs than the

second-hand pair acquired for the lessons. Black hunting coat. Black dress boots. White stock. Bowler. And Marcia Halliday said she thought a veil: 'Not entirely appropriate if you're not riding side-saddle, but it does rather set a gel off.' Marcia herself did ride side-saddle, on occasion, and was definitely set off by the veil, haughtily handsome, like some Trollope heroine.

More expense. Alarming expense, but needs must. The season came. Pam was launched, shepherded by Marcia, instructed to the hilt: always keep your horse's heels away from the hounds, don't barge at gates – wait your turn, never get ahead of the huntsmen or the whippers-in, on a run . . . (as if that were likely).

In fact, as Pam soon discovered, a day out with the hounds was mainly spent standing around with fifty other riders at the side of some copse, while baying sounds came occasionally from within. Or proceeding slowly along a lane, jostled by fifty different riders. With any luck, you could avoid anything more alarming than a brief canter across a ploughed field. She never saw a fox. Marcia Halliday would sometimes disappear, and return exhilarated, having been in at a death: 'Never mind, Pam – I'm afraid you missed that run. Another time. Willow rather pulled up after that last sighting, didn't he?'

Willow was no more keen than Pam on a good gallop. By tea-time, he had his eye on home, his stable, and the cleaning-up process, no doubt pleasurable for him, hard work for Pam. The rubbing down of steaming flanks, the scrubbing of the tack, dunking of the bridle in a bucket of cold water, scrub and scrub, work with saddle soap on the saddle and all leather. It took ages. All to be done imme-diately, in the dark winter evening, with aching limbs, before you could collapse into a hot bath. Frances, Clare and Imogen would hover, help, anxious for a report.

Actually, it wasn't going too badly at all. Pam had been noticed. Quite right too – tallish, slim, good figure, she looked very well in the beautifully cut cream jodhpurs from Harry Hall (expensive trip to London), perfectly fitting black coat, crisp white stock, and the bowler and veil. On only her second day with the South Devon, hanging around a copse with a group of others, young James

Pinnock, son of a big local gentleman farmer, edged his horse along-side her. 'Haven't seen you out before. James – James Pinnock. New to the South Devon, are you?'

Pam introduced herself, shyly. She admitted herself new to hunting, indeed. That seemed to go down rather well. James Pin-nock became masterful, protective. He instructed her on hound lore – 'I'm not boring you, am I? Rotten scent today – we shan't get much of a run.' He produced a silver flask from his pocket, took a swig, wiped the mouth carefully with a remarkably clean handker-chief, offered it to Pam.

Pam took a sip of brandy, giggled, handed the flask back. The giggle gave her pink cheeks, behind the veil. James Pinnock gleamed at her, above his red coat – fresh-faced, confident, established, scion of Devon soil. 'Good show. See you out next week, I hope.'

And then there were others. The Master's son, who helped her to mount again after Willow had stumbled at a bank and unseated her. 'Clumsy fellow, he wasn't giving you a thought. Here, you need a knee up . . . I'm Tony Bateman. I don't think we've met?' And Adrian Slope, twenty-eight-year-old ex-Army, son of Sir John and Lady, who got chatting to her outside yet another copse. Quite a long chat.

The pinnacle of the season was of course the Hunt Ball. To which Frances had given much thought. She learned that you went to the Ball in a party, by convention, though once there things would become more of a free-for-all. The convening of the party was a major problem, and in the end she managed to do no better than herself and Ted, with the vet and his wife, Mr and Mrs Culver, and their seventeen-year-old son Gordon, mired in sullen adolescence, radiant with acne, but he would have to do as a partner for Pam. To start off with.

And, in the event, it was the Hunt Ball that did it. Pam danced the first dance with Gordon Culver (rigid, treading on her feet). Tony Bateman asked her for the next. And then James Pinnock demanded her. For the next, and the next. Gordon Culver spent the evening sitting at the side, staring at his shoes and wanting to go home. Pam danced and danced. With James Pinnock. Slow foxtrots, cheek to cheek, the lights down now.

The engagement was announced six weeks later. The Pinnocks were perhaps not too thrilled with the match – Devon nabobs farming five hundred acres – but declared gallantly that Pam was an awfully nice girl. Contemplation of the wedding was a matter of anguish for Frances. Expense, expense – how could it be done, on an appropriate scale? The Pinnocks, however, had summed up the situation: a financial imbalance, unfortunately, between the families, but they did not propose to lose face locally with a skimped affair. A tactful word was had with Frances: they would be chipping in, substantially.

The wedding was a delight. Mrs Bennet could relax, a little: one down, two to go.

Clare took over Willow. Married Pam had available any horse that she wished, and in any case she was rather phasing herself off the hunting field, to concentrate on life as landed gentry; she was to have her own bantam-rearing unit – so sweet, bantams. Absence from the hunting field would in the long run prove to be a bit of a mistake, leaving James a soft target for other men's bored and predatory wives, but that lay in the future.

Clare and Willow set to, next season. They both knew what to do: stick with the crowd, hang around copses, lanes, gates, and with careful management all but the briefest dash across a field could be avoided. Seize every opportunity to be noticed, to get chatting. Clare too looked well in the black hunting coat, altered to fit.

Off the hunting field, Clare had struck up an acquaintance with Jane, a girl her own age whose parents were both local schoolteachers. Jane did not hunt; she appeared surprised at the idea of hunting. Jane was going to Oxford. This, in turn, startled Frances. She couldn't see the point of Oxford, for a girl. Except, she remembered wistfully, for the men. There would be loads of men – you'd be spoiled for choice. In a wild moment she wondered if possibly Immy . . . No, no, that was outlandish.

The hunting season proceeded: mud, rain, frost, snow. The aching limbs, the harness-room housework. The gradual accretion of young men who greeted Clare, and with whom she exchanged pleasantries.

It has to be said that she did not do as well as Pam had done. David Hammond's father was the major estate agent in the area – well-regarded local figure, but perhaps not quite top-drawer. While Frances was just a touch disappointed, you do not disparage a bird in the hand, and the Hammonds had this lovely little manor house all lined up for the couple.

Another wedding.

Just sometimes, Frances felt an odd kind of unease, disquiet, as though there were some faint seismic shudder from her known world, known assumptions, known expectations. That Jane girl, with her Oxford. A cousin's daughter, Pam's age, who was working in the BBC. An old school friend of Pam's who was in Paris, doing a course at the university there.

And then there was Immy.

Immy had embarked on the hunting season, but with evident reluctance. Immy had become a bit – well, bolshy. She had lost the traditional compliance of the Landon girls, and argued about things. Had opinions. Refused to wear a nice skirt and twin-set all the time and acquired a pair of slacks. Insisted that they take a real newspaper, other than Daddy's *Sporting Times*. She read it. Wasn't interested in the royal family. Dragged her feet when asked to help Mummy with the flowers. Kept getting books from the local library. Said she wished she'd done Higher School Cert. Smoked.

And then, halfway through the season, she said she wasn't hunting any more. She hated hunting. I know what it's all about, Mummy, she said, and I'm sorry, but it isn't going to work, for me.

Frances remonstrated, sighed, admonished.

'But, Immy, darling, what will you *do*?'

Immy had that all arranged, it seemed. Sue Tallant who drove the Mobile Library was in desperate need of a voluntary helper (possibly paid a bit, in due course). 'So interesting,' said Immy. 'Helping people choose books. And we'll be going all over the place – up on the moor, everywhere.'

Frances had not, of course, meant 'What will you *do*?' in this narrow, practical sense. She had had the wider vision in mind: strategy, the essential goal. She sighed. 'Yes, dear,' she said. 'I see.' Sue Tallant was a nice enough woman. In her forties – competent, confident. Not married.

That seismic shift again. What was going on here? Why was Immy flouting the obvious procedure? The successful procedure – she had only to look at her sisters.

During the next months Immy and the Mobile Library trekked to and fro across the county – to villages and hamlets, up rutted tracks to isolated farms, to cottages where lived one old lady, up over the moor, down into the combes. The library always got through, rain or shine; books – the essential life-blood. Immy learned librarian skills; she learned also what in years to come would be called people skills – how to steer one client towards a good travel book, identify a thriller they had not read for another, coax the old boy who couldn't see a thing he fancied.

People abounded. Books are essentially a social medium. After a while, Immy had friends and acquaintances hither and thither – a range, a revelation of people, often quite unlike those among whom she had grown up. She felt interestingly untethered; she found that society is much more expansive, more flexible than she had ever realized.

She got to know Bruce Weatherspoon in the pub at Exford, where she and Sue would sometimes stop off for a lunch break. He was working behind the bar, an occasional day job that helped support his real work as a stonemason. Immy had felt awkward at first about going into a pub (I mean, women on their own don't, do they?), but Sue had no such inhibitions, and soon it became entirely normal – locals nodding a greeting. And Bruce Weatherspoon.

Bruce had been to art college in Bristol. His father was a blacksmith, so this was something of a departure, but welcomed by his parents. So Bruce too was Devon born and bred, but at the other end of the spectrum from James Pinnock.

As Immy was well aware. At first, their meetings were clandestine. Bruce had an old rattletrap of a car, and would pick Immy up at the edge of the village, well away from her home, and take her to his cottage, where he had his studio, and she would watch in fascination as he worked on a headstone, an inscription, a memorial.

By the time Immy took Bruce to meet her parents she and he had decided on the future. 'I can't tell them this time,' she said. 'Not right away. My mother may guess, anyway.'

Mrs Bennet did, but without the rejoicing that you would have expected (mission achieved . . .). Frances and Ted Landon received Bruce together, Ted so befuddled with brandy that he was vaguely under the impression that this was a chap about some plumbing problem, Frances speechless with surprise that morphed into dismay. Immy's face told her everything. That, and her ease with this person, this young man with beaming, ruddy face, work-calloused hands, and speech that . . . The West Country accent is charming, of course, but not . . . not on the lips of a potential son-in-law.

Immy and Bruce were married in Exford church, with a small gathering after in the village hall. Frances smiled and endured. Pam and Clare attended; and their husbands, visibly uncomfortable.

So that was that. In due course, Frances would enjoy her grandchildren; some more than others – Immy's children were, well, brought up rather differently. The 50s arrived, and the 60s; Devon still slumbered, perhaps, but elsewhere things were on the move. Girls were now women, and had their own ideas. Marriage held out, but as a choice, not a given. And so the century proceeded, to a time when the shade of Mrs Bennet would be laid to rest, except perhaps in some moribund enclave of the upper classes.

And from somewhere, many decades ahead, in a further century, a sensitive ear might have been able to pick up a clarion call, the emphatic tone of Immy's great-great-great-granddaughter, Britain's second woman prime minister.

Theory of Mind

Martin is a cognitive archaeologist. His professional interest is in how minds operated in the distant past. He is not the kind of archaeologist who gets his hands dirty, trowelling away somewhere. Martin mostly works in front of a screen, staring at images. His subject is Palaeolithic art; his thoughts, day after day, are far away with Aurignacian culture, with Magdalanian culture, as he considers the floating forms of horses and deer and bears and aurochs and bison, from Lascaux and Altamira and Chauvet. His head is in a cave, metaphorically speaking, though in fact it is in a three-bedroom semi in Walthamstow, where his partner Harriet is downstairs preparing supper and shouting at him that it is time to eat.

Harriet is a copy-editor. She too spends much of her time in front of a screen, putting to rights the raw version of someone's book, adjusting punctuation, correcting spelling, rescuing the author from semantic solecisms, reminding him or her that he or she has already said all this back on page 130, pointing out that he or she appears to have a kind of verbal hiccup when it comes to the overuse of certain words.

'Supper! Martin! Come on!'

Harriet met Martin because she copy-edited his first book. Author

270

and copy-editor do not normally meet; emails fly to and fro. But in this instance there was a little party for the publication, and Harriet was invited. She had found the book interesting and so was vaguely curious about the author. She noticed at once that Martin was not enjoying the party at all. He was embarrassed by it – not a party sort of man. He stood there, clutching a glass, receiving compliments on the book, and clearly wishing he were somewhere else. Harriet rather liked the look of him; not specially handsome, thin scholarly face (how can a face be scholarly? But they can, they can), thick hair flopping forward, spectacles, and, behind them, brown eyes that, she observed, had noticed her.

She introduced herself. The eyes widened.

'Oh! I'd somehow thought you'd be a much older person . . .' Confusion now. Awkward. Taking hasty reinforcing gulp from his glass. 'Well . . . Thank you so much for your work.'

'I enjoyed it,' she said. 'And I don't always.'

Harriet is not drop-dead gorgeous – dear me, no. But not bad, all the same. She is not the sort of girl who sends men weak at the knees, but there have been several who wobbled a bit. She has a good figure, she has been told. Pretty mouth, it seems. Her hair functions nicely – short, dark, glossy, neat. She is not too fat, except occasionally. She buffs up well, if she makes an effort.

Over the years, there have been long- and short-term arrangements with men. The short-term ones were – well, just that. The two long-term ones involved co-habitation with all the fall-out: rent, bills, shopping, washing-up, bathroom habits, television preferences, his friends and your friends. And, eventually, a terminal falling out. Harriet has no great regrets. She is quite good at being on her own, but, at the moment Martin hove on the scene, she was probably a soft touch – somewhat ready for someone new, perhaps the permanent someone new.

She left the party wondering. They had talked for quite a while, until interrupted. He had seemed to be possibly enjoying himself a bit more.

And, a few days later, there was an email. A faltering sort of email, proposing that maybe she might, just a thought that perhaps, conceivably, it could be an idea to meet up for a meal. On Friday.

So thus it began. Over Thai chicken green curry he started to talk about the Palaeolithic, about cave art, about the way in which the term art is itself an anachronism since those who created these images could not have been doing so with any understanding of the concept of art as we know it.

'The mind in the caves,' he said. 'Those minds . . .'

'Martin,' she said. 'I edited your book. I know about all that.'

He put down his knife and fork, looked at her. Shook his head. 'Of course you do. Sorry. I'm afraid I . . . Oh, dear. The trouble is I . . .'

'The trouble is that you're interested in what you do,' she said. 'Which is fine. Real trouble would be if you weren't.'

Indeed, indeed. Martin is interested in his work, in the attempt to penetrate the distant past. He is interested in the Palaeolithic, in the wild life of the Palaeolithic, in the nascent mind of Palaeolithic man. He is interested in all this sometimes to the exclusion of all else, as on this occasion when for a moment it slips his mind that the young woman with whom he is eating a meal is the same person who has been adjusting his colons and his semicolons and advising him not to use the expression 'I would argue that . . .' quite so often.

However, Martin is now interested also in Harriet, as she becomes interestedly aware.

He wonders if perhaps she would like to join him for a walk on Hampstead Heath. Next week. She does so. After that he suggests a day out on the South Downs. The day is had, and Harriet counters with the proposal of a film – fresh air is getting a bit monotonous. And so there is a film, and a supper at her place, and another; Martin's interest is made evident in all the expected ways and now here they are, much later, in the three-bedroom semi in Walthamstow.

Martin comes down, arrives in the kitchen. He has that abstracted, shuttered look that means, Harriet knows, that he is still locked away in some cave, studying the outline of a horse, or wrestling with the challenge of explaining his new theory.

She waves a hand in front of his face. 'Sit down. It's roast bison, with bone marrow for afters.'

Martin blinks, sits, smiles wryly, vaguely. 'Fish pie – great.'

So how has your day been, Harriet?

Martin does not say this, so Harriet thinks it, for him. Actually Martin has never said this, that she can recall. So she tells him anyway. She tells him that she has been to one of the publishers for whom she works – Harriet is freelance – to discuss a new undertaking. She tells him that the undertaking will be a challenge because it is a work on climate change, scientific, technical, but she welcomes it: 'At least I'll learn something.' She does not tell him that the commissioning editor, Jim Bowles, has become quite a friend. Martin is not really into her friends. That is to say, he is perfectly agreeable if he meets up with any of them, but he tends to forget who is who and what it is they do. For himself, he has colleagues rather than friends. Her initial observation that he was not a party sort of man was correct; Martin's attitude to social occasions is that if necessary he will oblige, but all things being equal he would prefer to opt out.

But that's fine, she has thought. I didn't set up with him for his carousing potential.

So she goes out on her own, quite a lot. And that is fine. Of course it is.

Harriet tells Martin about this new piece of work: 'But not for a couple of weeks or more – I'm still on the Ruskin book.'

Martin tells Harriet the fish pie is excellent. He adds, thoughtfully, that the Aurignacian fish-hook is proven to be perfectly viable. A colleague of his made a replica, out of bone, and tried it out in the Dordogne. He caught things. They ate them.

Harriet is intrigued by the thought of Martin hunter-gathering on the banks of the Dordogne. 'When was that? Who made the fish-hook?'

'Oh, ages ago. He was a German guy. Artefacts specialist.'

Harriet has had to piece together Martin's past. He does not seem to be all that interested in it, himself; he may be absorbed, Martin, but he is not self-absorbed. She has established his career path, just about, and she knows that he has had a couple of girlfriends – well, sort of girlfriends – but that she is his first abiding partner.

Abiding for a couple of years now. No – nearly three. Goodness, is it really?

Martin finishes off the fish pie, appreciatively. They clear up the kitchen, together. Harriet goes into the sitting-room, where she will read, or watch television. Martin returns to his study, and his screen. This is their evening, as are many others.

Sometimes Martin has evening commitments at his university. And sometimes Harriet will meet up with friends, or go to her book group. Harriet's friends are a mixed lot, but it is with other women that she is most intimate. The book group consists mainly of women, though this is fortuitous rather than deliberate. Perhaps women read more, perhaps men don't care to join book groups: discuss.

Plenty of discussion at the book group – about the book in question, about, often, much else. The book in question will have generated argument about why this character behaved thus, and whether that one was provoked by the behaviour of a third, and whether or not the narrative is credible. There will be conflicting theories. And a light supper with a glass or two of wine.

Harriet enjoys the book group. As much as anything, she enjoys the glimpses it affords of other people's minds – of how they are thinking, responding, as opposed to the way in which you yourself think, respond. A conflicting attitude can make you reconsider your own. Or you may think: Idiot! She just doesn't get it, does she? Either way, there has been a salutary shuffling together of individual minds.

Living with Martin, and with his work, has made Harriet think quite a bit about minds, about what they do or do not do. She has thought about the minds in the caves, those minds that so pre-occupy Martin, those unimaginably distant minds.

A mind rinsed clean of knowledge. A mind that knows nothing of time or space, that is rooted in its own here and now. A mind that has observed birth, and death, and is presumably impressed, in some way. But a mind that knows absolutely nothing about contraception or sanitation or immunization or the expanding universe or weapons of mass destruction or the law of gravity or economic determinism. Or, indeed, how to think about what this mind does not know.

I know, thinks Harriet, what I do not know. I know that I know very little, on the scale of what there is to be known. I am richly educated, in a twenty-first-century Western kind of way, so I have scratched at the foothills of knowledge. My head is stuffed, in fact, but an essential part of the stuffing is an awareness of my own ignorance. My limitations. The mind in the cave does not even know that it has limitations.

I know that I can find out. I can ask, I can listen, I can read, I can Google. I can be curious about the art of Michelangelo or the origin of species or how to set up my new Panasonic portable phone or cook Tuscan bean soup. My curiosity can be abstract, or practical.

Martin's interest in those cave minds includes speculation as to whether they were capable of something called theory of mind. He tried to explain this to Harriet once: 'It's the brain's ability to empathize – for a person to conceive of an alternative point of view, that someone else may be thinking or responding differently from oneself.'

'Oh, heavens,' she said. 'In that case I've known plenty of people without it.'

He frowned: this is a frivolous response to a technical term. 'If they were autistic, possibly. Otherwise, it doesn't apply.'

'So did the cave people have it?' she said humbly.

'We don't know. We may never know.'

In her early days with Martin, Harriet had been rather admiring of his capacity for detachment, and amused by that dismissal of bothersome things like bills that should be paid or bank statements that should be glanced at or his mother's birthday that should be remembered. Harriet found herself taking over these matters, and was aware that he was properly grateful. In those early days, the gratitude was often expressed – a quick hug, the book he was reading in bed discarded as she joined him.

Perhaps less often nowadays, but there you go. Nearly three years. A relationship sort of settles down, doesn't it?

Those other two longer-term relationships of hers had not so much settled as suffered internal combustion. So they were not comparable experiences.

Harriet had dealt with all there was to do with the acquisition of the semi in Walthamstow: the house search, the mortgage application, the removals from her flat and from his. Martin was comfortably impervious to his surroundings. So long as he had a room in which to work, anything would do. She would have liked to share the nesting process rather more, but learned that there was no point in trying to interest Martin in choice of curtains or the hanging of a picture.

Well, fine. That way, there are no disagreements.

In two years – no, nearly three – you do not so much get to know a person as discover them. You discover that weakness for *pain au chocolat*, the aversion to cats, the impressive mathematical ability, the inability to find the car keys, the preference for red wine, the horror of any formal occasion, the taste for old spaghetti westerns.

All of which adds up not to a person but to aspects of a person, and leaves out, of course, a vast amount – the seven-eighths of the iceberg, as it were, the more secretive aspects of the person that may never surface at all.

So which bits of Martin have not yet surfaced?

Harriet is copy-editing a book about John Ruskin right now. She has found this intriguing – the art, the writings, the Victorian mores. She has rather taken to Effie, Ruskin's wife – a marriage that ended in annulment. The marriage was unconsummated, and this writer, like so many others, speculates on the reason for this. It seems possible that Ruskin, who had never seen a naked girl before, had been aghast at the sight of Effie's pubic hair.

Poor Effie, thinks Harriet. For some reason, her thoughts turn to Martin at this moment. This is not a Ruskin situation; Martin has never been aghast at the sight of Harriet's pubic hair. He does not seem to have much noticed it. As indeed, she has come to realize, he fails to notice a good deal. But Martin is not Ruskin – oh, no. He has consummated. With enthusiasm, back in those early days. Off and on now. Perhaps more off than on. Well, nearly three years – obviously things would steady up, wouldn't they?

The Martin that Harriet now knows is not exactly the Martin with whom she had first embarked. That Martin was more indistinct; she had a good idea of him, but there was much infilling to be done. Today's Martin is more substantial – tastes, preferences, aversions and all, alongside, of course, the dominating tendency to be sitting at a screen considering aurochs and bison and the like and not to have noticed that it is time for supper, or way past time for bed.

A shortcoming that it is easy to live with, she thinks. My goodness – others have to endure infidelity, or alcoholism, or domestic violence. A degree of inattention is nothing to complain about. Some might appreciate it. You wouldn't want a man who was looking over your shoulder all the time, would you?

Harriet's friends sometimes ask after Martin, since they don't often come across him. As though to check up. And Harriet will establish him: he is working on such and such, he is off to a conference in Washington. She has outlined him, as it were, for Jim Bowles, this work acquaintance who seems to be becoming a friend. A new friend is always welcome. Harriet is reasonably well equipped, but can always find room. Essential ballast, friends, when you live with a person who doesn't care to socialize, and who doesn't much converse . . . No, that's not fair – Martin converses. But he converses rather on his own terms. If the matter in hand engages him, if he began the conversation.

Conversation, consummation, thinks Harriet. More off than on? Oh, stop this.

Sometimes, Harriet wonders about having a child. She is thirty-four. It is not yet a question of now or never. But getting that way. Once, she had wondered in the direction of Martin. Hinted. Floated the idea. Martin had not reacted. Harriet's wonder – her hint, her float – had not reached him, apparently.

So it would seem that he himself is not wondering.

And there is work, for both of them. And the daily, weekly, monthly, slippage of time. Harriet finishes copy-editing the Ruskin book, moves on to this new project, which is indeed quite demanding. Martin is . . . What is Martin doing? She asks him, over another kitchen supper.

He is assessing the incidence of portable art in eastern European cave sites, he tells her. The keynote talk for an impending conference.

Portable art? Oh yes, those deer and bears and things they carved on small pieces of bone. Nobody knows quite why. The minds in the caves at work.

When and where the conference?

Vienna, he says. In a couple of months' time.

Harriet has never accompanied Martin on any of these professional trips. He has not suggested it. Others, she has gathered, do sometimes take along wives and partners. Like footballers, she thinks – the glossy cohort of WAGs. Except that academic WAGs would not be like that at all, they would quite likely be academics themselves, and some of them would be men. Dowdy rather than glossy, and quite without any shopping inclinations.

Harriet would not want to go, in any case. She doesn't mind being on her own for a few days, or, indeed, for the occasional longer periods when Martin goes off for a serious encounter with some cave. She has occasionally taken the opportunity for a jaunt with friends.

But at the moment she is immersed in the complexities of climate change, with this new commission. Jim Bowles has been in touch, concerned that all goes well: the author in question is known to be tricky to work with. They have met up for a drink, with business not on the agenda.

If Harriet is late in, of an evening, Martin does not seem to notice. She may find that he has drifted down to the kitchen and is making himself an omelette. He neither complains nor enquires.

Over this time she is late in on several occasions.

She is late in, she is distracted, her mind is not on the things to which it is usually applied: work, remember to pay the council tax, remember to get stem ginger and kaffir lime leaves, phone Mum, get cash, go to the gym. It seems to her that this new, distracted mind must be visible, swirling above her head like a thought-bubble. Martin must surely see it. He has been talking and she has not heard a word he said; he has not noticed. She stares out of the window – and she is not a person who sits and stares; he comes into the room at that moment and she has gone on staring, but he just rummages around for the book he was after, and goes out again. Harriet's thought-bubble is invisible, it seems.

Theory of mind. So much for that, she thinks. My mind is churning away, it is loud, conspicuous, but Martin is quite unaware. My wildly unstable point of view is not apparent to him.

Which is, of course, just as well. She is going to be late home again tomorrow, and does not need to explain.

She feels guilty. Of course. She is taking advantage of . . . Of what? Of Martin's capacity for inattention. Of Martin's ability to be elsewhere. Her thought-bubble, in her mind's eye, has a sour yellow tinge of guilt.

But it is also a euphoric thought-bubble. It is full of surprise, of wonder. How can this have happened? Whatever it is that has happened.

And must not happen. Cannot happen.

How does someone morph from a man you have been talking to about a work commission to the person who fills your mind, the person you must see, the person you ache to see? How can a face that was neutral become the face that makes the blood run quicker, the face that lights up that pub, the sushi place, the Italian restaurant, the bar at St Pancras, that walk along the Embankment?

How can I, thinks Harriet, turn from a woman who was moving peaceably enough from day to day to one who can't sleep properly, who is forever in a state of anticipation or recollection? Who stares out of the window when working, doesn't listen to what people are saying, checks her phone every ten minutes?

Harriet knows that Jim Bowles is like this, too. Theory of mind is operative here. She knows what he is feeling, thinking; he doesn't have to tell her. She sees it in his eyes: at that pub, the sushi place, the Italian restaurant . . .

Jim Bowles is not a bit like Martin. He is expansive, he is talkative, he talks about books he is publishing, books he would like to publish, books that someone ought to be writing. He is convivial, gregarious, he likes to get out and about. He is prepared to get interested in anything. He is fervently interested in Harriet and is trying – pathetically – to play this down. He knows that Harriet lives with Martin. He knows that this is going nowhere, should go nowhere.

Jim Bowles is not with anyone. He once was married – he was until last year. He has a little girl of five, who stays with him every other weekend.

Harriet goes with Jim and the little girl to the zoo. It has come to this. Martin is at the university, where there is a weekend colloquium, so she has no need of explanation. Harriet is entranced with the little girl, Lucy. I want one, she thinks, I want one. Even, I want this one.

This may be going nowhere, but it goes on. Whatever it is has become inescapable now, a fact of life, a fact of Harriet's life, of Jim's. Harriet feels that she is two people: ordinary, workaday Harriet at home in Walthamstow, and the other Harriet, who is quite often not at home, and absent-minded when she is.

She came in quite lateish one evening, and found Martin in the sitting-room. Not up in his office.

He smiled at her. A smile that was reserved, friendly, almost complicit. 'Had a nice time?' he said.

She couldn't remember where she was supposed to have been. The book group? A film with Emma?

Yes. Thanks. A very nice time.

Harriet's thought-bubble filled the room, it seemed to her. The sour, yellow, guilty thought-bubble. They went upstairs to bed and it trailed up there with them. She prayed that Martin would not want to make love. He didn't.

The time came for that conference of Martin's. In Vienna. Where he would deliver his keynote talk on portable art in eastern European cave sites. He would be away for a week.

It was inevitable. Inevitable that Harriet should have told Jim Bowles this. Inevitable that when she did so they would have stared at each other in that pub, the sushi place, the Italian restaurant, wherever it was, and thought . . . thought the same thing.

They went to Lyme Regis. Chosen for no particular reason except that Jim had once published a book on Mary Anning, and had always thought he'd like to go there, and that a weekend of illicit love seems somehow to require the sea. They walked on Charmouth beach, they walked along the Undercliff. They ate fish and chips on the front.

They lay in a warmly friendly B & B that assumed them to be a couple, which was both disturbing and exciting. They lay in bed, sated, together, content. Harriet's thought-bubble was not around, whisked away by one of those crying seagulls beyond the window. Jim Bowles lay staring up at the ceiling, holding Harriet's hand. He spoke of Lucy. He said he had always hoped for another child.

That did it. That did it for Harriet, once and for all.

Back in London, in the sushi place, she said: 'I'm going to tell him next week. I tried last night, and then just couldn't. Next week, definitely.'

'I'll tell him tomorrow,' she said. In the Italian restaurant.

'I love you,' Jim said. In bed in his flat, early one evening. He has said this before, and will say it again. Harriet had not heard this for so long.

'At the weekend,' she said. On the Embankment. 'At the weekend I'll tell him. Oh God, I don't want to have to do this.'

'It's going to be such a shock to him,' she said. In the Starbucks round the corner from Jim's office.

'I feel so bloody awful about it,' said Jim Bowles. On the westbound Circle Line platform at King's Cross. 'Doing this to someone.'

And so, at last, Harriet forced herself to the point. Forced herself to honesty. Forced herself to say to Martin, as they sat at the kitchen table, supper eaten, an evening ahead: 'Martin, there's something I've got to tell you.'

A smile. That slightly odd smile she has seen once before. 'I know.'

'No,' she said. 'No, you don't . . .' He thinks I'll say I want to move house, that I want us to have a holiday, that, no, no . . . that I'm pregnant.

'You're going,' he said. Not smiling now. Just a level look across the table. Not questioning, either.

She could not speak.

'There's someone else,' said Martin. 'Has been for some time.'

No smile now. And a look she has never seen before. A different Martin.

She sat there. Wincing, cringing. How? But he never . . . Martin doesn't notice . . . 'I didn't think . . .' she said. 'I had no idea you . . .'

'No. I know you didn't.' A sort of sigh. And that look – a Martin she has not known who has surfaced and whose eyes meet hers. Eyes in which she sees – oh no, no – sorrow, regret. 'Of course I knew. You weren't the same. You became different.'

He is not accusing. He is not reproachful. He is just stating a fact. He is making a statement about . . . theory of mind.

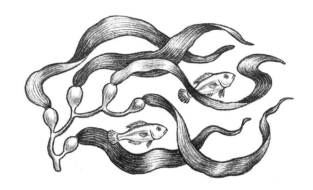

The Third Wife

They were viewing this house she fancied. He was quite happy with that. She would be paying for it anyway, and if she wanted to upgrade that was fine with him. Molly was his third wife, and had plenty of dosh – inherited from her parents, in her case. The other two had also been well bolstered – he'd always been careful to check that out. Sandra had had a business that was going great guns – designer children's clothes – and Louise had had a job in the City that paid a wad, annual bonuses and all that.

Molly had already had a look at this house – came back enthusing. It was substantial, Edwardian. Isolated, down its own drive, no near neighbours. Fine – one doesn't want rampaging children within earshot. Plenty of rooms. Secluded one at the end of a passage which would do nicely for his office.

Not that one was planning to be here for all that long. What Molly didn't know was that her days were numbered, as his wife. About a couple of months or so, when he'd sorted out some stuff with the bank accounts. Five years, she'd had, and that was just about his limit. Much the same with the others.

How do you dispose of a wife who is now surplus to requirements? Murder?

Oh, dear me, no. Far too untidy. Far too open to repercussions. Too banal, frankly. Only an idiot would take that risk. No, no.

Divorce?

Divorce is for the unimaginative. Divorce is for self-destructive fools who want to lose half their house and half their income and half their capital and prop up the legal profession. Divorce is for those who haven't a clue how to look after themselves. Divorce is for nerds.

Oh, no. The simple thing is just to leave. Creativity is what is required.

Molly, calling from some other part of the house. 'Here – come and see. The kitchen's fantastic.'

He had left Sandra on a beach in Australia. Quite literally. A rather remote and deserted beach, frequented only by penguins. She had been interested in these, was dying to see them. They had driven there from the hotel where they were staying on this Antipodean holiday he had proposed as a reward for all her hard work and to celebrate a particularly good year for her business. He had organized it all – the hotel, even this beach some way away and the interesting wildlife ('I say, darling, this is right up your street – we have to go there'). He booked them in under one of his other names; it was sometimes quite a job to keep all his names sorted, and the various bank accounts. So there was Sandra, happily stretched out on a towel, sunbathing (no penguins to be seen, so far), and he got up and said, 'I've left my book in the car – I'll just wander back and get it.' She had murmured something, half-asleep, and off he went, taking all his stuff, leaving her the sun cream and her dark glasses and her beach bag – no need to be malevolent. There had been a couple of other cars at the parking site, so somewhere on that beach there were others, and when eventually Sandra realized that she no longer had a husband to hand, someone would take her back to the hotel, where the staff would be confronted by a hysterical woman in a bikini, whose name was not on their screen, claiming that she was staying there.

Molly, outside now. 'Oh, you're going to love this garden.'

Sandra hadn't known, of course, that he had cleared out much of the business before they left for the holiday. Just a matter of some creative accounting. He had said right at the start, when they were first married, 'Look, let me deal with the paperwork for you. I can see to the financial stuff, all that nitty-gritty, and then you can get on with what you do so well. You shouldn't have to be bothered with the infrastructure.' So the money had gone into a special account, one of his accounts. Except of course that it would only be there until he needed it, by which time he wouldn't be there either.

Sandra had been his first. He was the marrying sort. He respected marriage; he approved of marriage. If you like a woman, can see yourself set up with her, then it's the proper thing to do. The decent thing. And there was the question of funding, too, always an issue for him.

The right woman can solve the funding problem. Call it venture capital.

Molly – going upstairs now. 'Four bedrooms, Stan. Two en suite.'

Louise he had left in Brent Cross shopping centre. In Swarovski, to be precise, where they'd been choosing his Christmas present for her, a rather pretty necklace. She was just checking a call on her mobile, and when she looked up he wasn't there any more. He hadn't yet paid for the necklace.

He had done some interesting things with their joint bank account the day before. Really quite inventive. For a woman who spent her days moving money around the world it was surprising how little attention Louise paid to her own. She had never noticed the steady seepage from the joint account, over time. The seepage was now a haemorrhage, though he had left her enough to get through until the next salary wad from her outfit. Again, no need to be malevolent.

Molly, down again, her footsteps now somewhere at the back of the house. 'Would you believe it, there's a walk-in safe! Come and see!'

There was still a bit of work to be done on the accounts, where Molly was concerned. She was no slouch, Molly – tended to be rather tiresomely attentive from time to time, wanting to take a look at the bank statements: 'You're so sweet to say you'll see to all that but you mustn't feel I'm leaving it to you entirely. Money's so boring.'

No, it isn't. Money is the one thing that is not boring. It is entrancing, invigorating. Motivating.

Molly was quite smart, really, though she had never had a job. Not a proper job. Well, she didn't need to, cushioned by that comfortable income from the parents who had died a while ago. She did various voluntary things now, and had a network of friends, was much on the phone. Even more so than usual, lately – he kept coming into a room where she was chatting away to someone, giggling from time to time, and would hang up as soon as he was there.

'Who was that, darling?'

'Just a girlfriend.'

Susie, or Janice, or someone. He couldn't keep track of her friends. They had stolid, tedious husbands who worked in local government and suchlike, middle-management figures who said breezily: 'And what's your line, Stan?' His reply was always the same: something vague about financial consultant. He had never been precise with his wives, either. They knew that he needed his home office, and had to spend a lot of time at the computer, and occasionally go away for a day or two.

'Stan, do come and see this safe.'

He was Stan now, and had been since he married Molly. Before that, he had been Peter, and Mark. You did get a bit confused occasionally. And the bank accounts of course had many names; they were legion, impersonal.

'Coming,' he said. 'Coming.'

He wasn't a big spender. Of course not. The point of money was accumulation, not disposition. The piling up of figures, that lovely intangible hoard. His wives did the spending, and that was fine because it meant you lived very well, and it was their money anyway, not that you wanted them to be getting rid of too much of it because there was a sense also in which it was yours, or would be in due course. No, you didn't spend the money, you tended it, shifted it, made it grow. Every day he was at the computer for hours; each wife had known not to disturb him. They tiptoed around his vaguely defined occupation. Financial analyst, they said to friends. It's something like that. He's terribly clever with money.

Too right, darling.

Molly was the only one who spent time on a computer herself. The other two never did. Louise said she had enough of it at the office. Molly would be checking out clothes and stuff, no doubt, consumer research. She was quite dressy, was Molly, and always looked good. She was fun, too. But he was getting itchy feet; it was time to move on. There was a woman he'd come across at an event in London, a presentation by some fund people, sounded as though she had a nice portfolio. He needed to get to know her better; Brian, he was, to her.

'Coming, coming. Where are you?'

He made his way to the rear of the house – warren of little rooms, back here. And there was Molly, in the passage, beside a hefty-looking steel door. She seemed to be on a high today, had done herself up in a red outfit he'd never seen before, and was waiting for him there – small, sparky, really pretty, that cap of dark hair, great legs. He'd miss her, no question, but there you go.

'Look,' she said, heaving open the door.

A small room, windowless, with shelves.

'What on earth's it for?'

'It's a strong-room,' she said. 'Sort of walk-in safe. For silver, probably. What fun! You can keep your gold ingots in here.' Laughing.

'You know perfectly well I haven't got any gold ingots.' He put his arm round her – quick hug. 'So are we buying this place?'

'Shall we? What do you think?' She peered forward into the room, switched on a light. 'What's that on the shelf at the back?'

He stepped down into the room, reached forward, and saw in his hand an envelope with his name on it, at the same moment as the steel door clanged behind him, and he heard the click of a lock.

Laughter again, barely audible. And he knew, began to know. Remembered that she'd been keen to drive, had the car keys: 'I know how to find it. I told the agent there was no need for him to come with us.'

He stood there for a moment. He opened the letter.

This is for Sandra, and for Louise, and for me. I can't tell you how long it's taken to find a house with a strong-room. They've been champing at the bit, Sandra and Louise, phoning and phoning. Incidentally, we're such good friends. I have that to thank you for – two really lovely friendships.

Elegant, isn't it? Like your own departures. That's the idea. Took us a while to come up with it. I wonder what you had in mind for me?

Don't worry – you're not there for ever. Depends when the estate agent turns up with another viewer. I did make a point of asking. This evening, I think he said. Or was it tomorrow? And you've maybe already found there's no mobile signal. I checked that out last week, when I had a first look. Bit of a worry, that had been.

I wonder what you'll say? Not – my wife slammed the door and did a runner. Oh, no. They might start asking questions, and you'll have thought of that. No, you'll bluff it out and be charming – that blasted door shut itself and apparently locked too, thank God you've come, if only my wife hadn't had to cry off because she had a dental crisis, and needed the car, and of course my minicab driver just dropped me off – I'd said don't wait I'll probably walk back to the bus stop when I'm through . . . You'll be out. In a while. You won't come home, of course.

Go wherever you like. They'll find you, sooner or later.

The police.

Songs of Praise (2021)

Songs of Praise

The Relfords are on display, lined up at the door, meeting and greet-ing: Colin, Tessa, Eleanor, Paul. They wear expressions of welcome tinged with sobriety, as is appropriate for this commemoration of the life of their wife, mother.

Two of those already met and greeted are now observers. They have struck up a conversation, though not previously known to one another.

'I'm Martha's cousin. Lucy Forbes. Don't know a soul here – friends, it seems, rather than relations. And you?'

Lucy is in her seventies. She is thin, brisk, grey-headed, sternly dressed in a navy trouser suit, and, it seems, judgemental.

'I'm a friend of Paul's. Jane Harrison. I don't really know people either. I met – Martha – a few times, and, well, she was lovely, wasn't she?'

Lucy Forbes makes no comment.

Jane continues, after a moment: 'I've never met Eleanor, and . . . Tessa, is it? Which is . . . ?'

'Tessa is the one in the pink jacket. Silk, by the look of it, and expensive, I'd say. Very Tessa. But do you wear such a bright colour to a memorial event?'

'Is there a dress code? And they don't seem to be memorial events now. The card called it a celebration.'

'Indeed. You're right. We are celebrating the life of Martha Relford.' Lucy is terse. She does not sound particularly celebratory.

'I liked her work,' ventures Jane. 'She did such a good portrait of Paul. He took me to her studio to see it. I believe she has work in the National Portrait Gallery?'

'I dare say she does.'

'Were you . . . Did you see a lot of her?'

Lucy shrugs. 'The occasional family wedding or funeral. She and my mother didn't get on particularly well. Martha was the glam older cousin when I was a child. Then . . . then Martha the artist.' A short laugh. 'And I was Lucy the boring librarian. I'd kill for a drink right now. Shall we . . . ?'

They move over to the side of the room where wine and canapés are on offer. Lucy takes a glass of white wine. Jane hesitates, settles for fruit juice.

Lucy contemplates the room. 'I do see another cousin. I am not alone. I suppose there will be . . . commentaries. People will say things.'

'Oh, is that usual? I've hardly ever been to one of these.'

'Absolutely normal. Obligatory. The songs of praise. A family chorus.' Lucy laughs again. It is never quite a laugh of merriment.

Jane is finding that she has not entirely taken to Lucy Forbes. She is wondering when she will get a chance to talk to Paul. Would it be rude to break away?

A few minutes later, she is able to do so, when Lucy is distracted, trying to identify some vaguely familiar face she has spotted.

Jane meets up with someone she knows. For half an hour or so there are conversations around the room. Then Colin Relford claps his hands, a hush descends, and it becomes apparent that Lucy Forbes is right. There are to be . . . commentaries.

Colin Relford's name resounds in the world of documentary film making. His company, Historyline Productions, has a backlist of highly regarded projects, specializing in forensic but eminently watchable examination of significant topics ranging from deep history – the Anglo-Saxon invasion of England, the seventeenth-century civil war – to more recent issues such as the suffragette movement, the Cold War, the miners' strike. Historyline's technique is the use of contemporary material in every form, backed up by informed comment from academics and, where feasible, those involved. Colin himself is now seventy-six, and has handed over much of the company's work to a swathe of hand-picked younger people, but he retains an extremely active interest – the productions continue to bear the hallmark of a Colin Relford enterprise.

And here he is today, a big man, not looking his age, wearing a dark suit in which he appears uncomfortable. With the meeting and greeting done, he has moved about the room, talking determinedly to this person and that, a dominant presence, the bereaved husband – but bereavement somehow does not fit him well. He is too positive, too clearly brimming still with purpose, with energy. And now he is requiring silence – politely, with a smile.

'First, thank you all so much for coming today. It means so much to the four of us to have you here to celebrate Martha's life. Thank you indeed. And since this is very much a celebration I thought it only right that we four, who have been closest to her, who owe her the most, who perhaps knew her best, each say something about her – how we saw her, what she meant to us, who she was, anything . . . Paul, why don't you get things going? As the youngest. We've never gone in for primogeniture, in this family.'

There is a little ripple of amusement. Paul steps forward to stand beside his father. He is a slight man, without Colin's height and bulk, and looks hesitant, embarrassed. But what has to be done will be done.

Paul is forty-three, which terrifies him from time to time. One was young, and now apparently is not. Things lay ahead; now too much lies behind. Paul is a poet, that is how he would describe himself. Effectively, he is a school teacher, because poets have to earn a living somehow. In poet circles, his name would be known to most; he has published two collections, had a poem or two in the *Times Literary Supplement*, when young he won a couple of awards. Beyond, no-one much has heard of him, but that's poetry for you.

He told his parents that he was gay when he was seventeen, which was fine as far as they were concerned. He has lived in reasonable accord with his partner Hugh Madden for the last ten years. They wondered, a while ago, about having a child, adopting a child, whatever it is you can do, and then abandoned the idea.

People gaze at Paul, expectant.

'Yes,' he says. 'Yes, absolutely – thank you all so much for being here.' He hesitates, looks round the room, clears his throat. 'Well . . . Martha. Mum. For me . . . she . . . well, she was always there for me. Best of times and worst of times. She . . . she'd bail you out, prop you up, and . . . oh, encourage and be reassuring. I can hear her now – Come on, Paul, it's not the end of the world. With a laugh, probably. Lots of us here will remember that laugh. And . . .' He breaks off, blinks, a pause . . . 'For me, she is wonderfully continuous. Young, youngish, old eventually, but always essentially the same. She'd let me be in her studio sometimes, when I was small, if I was quiet and didn't interrupt – not when she was painting someone, had someone sitting for her, but when she was touching up, that sort of thing, staring at a canvas with her eyes screwed up in that way, and then just flicking with the brush, standing back and looking intently again . . .'

Around the room, attention is paid. Or not.

Well, maybe, Eleanor is thinking. Maybe – for you. Her work always came first, when we were children. I'm not saying she was a bad mother, exactly, just that she was a much absent mother, absent in her studio. I hated that studio. I still dislike the smell of paint, turps, whatever it was that room smelt of. Not that we were allowed in there, but one peeked occasionally. Oh yes, Paul got in there – her favourite, of course. I think I can say with honesty that I've done things differently. I don't have a favourite. And the children always come first, for me, all of them. All right – I'm not an artist. I'm not anything in particular, but still.

When the three of them were children a heavy-handed grandmother called Eleanor the clever one, while Tessa was the pretty one – not that she was, particularly, but by comparison with Eleanor, which was what was meant, and which made it all the worse. Especially as Eleanor was not, in fact, a high performer academically, merely average when it came to exams, though good enough to get into one of the easier to get into universities. Tessa, of course, bypassed university, her sights set on RADA. Eleanor has never had a calling, a metier. This worried her terribly when she was young, surrounded as she was by people who very much had, and was probably why she jumped at the prospect of marriage, when Graham turned up. Marriage, and then three children, nicely spaced, meant that the necessity of some sort of career could be shelved for quite a while. Today, she works part-time at a Citizens Advice Bureau, which, while hardly a distinguished occupation, is patently useful and responsible, and gives her an answer when she is asked what she does. Actually, she rather enjoys it. And, on the brink of middle age, it is she who has weathered better than her sister. They are not at all alike; Tessa has her father's profuse gingery hair and fair complexion, which in her case have required much manipulation and titivation, resulting in today's rather overworked look, while Eleanor's minimal make-up and short-cropped dark hair make her look unassuming, neat, and perhaps younger than she is. They have always got on well enough, poles apart in outlook and aspiration.

'Consistent,' says Paul. 'I suppose that's what I'm trying to say. Firm about things – what she liked, didn't like. She liked order – people behaving as she felt they should, and if they weren't she'd . . . well, she let you know.' A pause. 'Not interfering, no way, she didn't do that, she gave everyone space. And not critical. Funny about people, she could be, lots of you will remember that – her wit, her humour. She could somehow sum a person up – I've often seen that as an offshoot of her gift as a portrait painter, the way she gets the essence of her subject.'

Firm about things? thinks Tessa. Oh, come on. You'd think an artist would be bohemian and let it all hang out, but I suppose she wasn't that kind of artist. I mean, she wouldn't let me wear lipstick until I was sixteen (I did, of course, slapped it on as soon as I was out of the house) and there was always a fuss about clothes – 'That skirt's much too short, Tess . . . that neckline's much too low . . . no, you can't have a bigger dress allowance, you're having more than Eleanor already.' Eleanor didn't care about clothes – I mean, look at her today even, bless her, that dreary outfit that screams M & S. Oh, she was lovely, Mum, I suppose we just weren't entirely on the same wavelength. I adored her, of course, but . . . well, she could be sort of irritating. Really intense about her work, and yes, she was good, I know that. I suppose it's just that art's not so much my thing. And she really didn't get it about acting, wasn't interested when I was at RADA, hasn't been much since, hardly ever watched anything I was in – 'Oh, you didn't remind me, darling – you know I never look at television.'

Tessa has acted, mainly in television roles, and rather more off than on, ever since she left RADA. She is useful rather than successful – one of a reservoir of reliable minor role players. Occasionally her face will give someone pause for thought, in the supermarket or on the Tube: haven't I seen her before somewhere . . . But when they approach her it is usually for her to confirm that she is a friend of their sister, or didn't we meet at that wedding last year? This is her career problem, perhaps – that she has a somewhat anonymous face. She is nice looking, but not especially so – not pretty enough, handsome enough, for those lead parts when she was younger, nor are her features quirky enough for a character actor. Within her trade, she is pond life – that orchestral players' term for the violins. Outside of it, she tends to milk actor status: statement outfits, self-conscious mannerisms. Her personal life has been somewhat dishevelled. An early marriage ended after a couple of years. Various liaisons followed, and eventually a second marriage in her late thirties to a television executive which rather staggers along but has produced a daughter, Chloe, who is here today, aged eight and guzzling canapés.

'But of course,' Paul is saying. 'Of course she was one thing for us, the children, and another, I suppose, for Dad, and I'm sure he's going to have something to say in a moment, but I would like . . . well, I've always felt they . . . that they gave marriage a good press, they never seemed to get in each other's way. But that's not for me to . . . Dad's turn in a minute.'

Good point, thinks Colin. Wife and mother. Two entirely different things, never mind that one leads to the other. So, Martha was two people, like many women, I suppose. Efficient enough at the mother part – coped well when they were kids, backed up by various au pairs and help of one kind and another. Well, she needed her own time, needed to work, I always understood that. But she took it seriously – mothering – dealt with Paul when he went off the rails, stood up to Tessa. Eleanor was always easy, of course, she didn't need much attention. And I was around a fair amount too, even in those heady early days of Historyline, I did my bit, the family wasn't just backdrop – always a central part of my life. Of course, I needed my space, like Martha, even more so, but there are ways of making that work, and I did. There was always a slap-up summer holiday for them – Majorca, Sardinia, that time in the Algarve, you name it. Christmas a big deal, birthdays. They had a solid family life. And it's gone on that way, I suppose you could say – all three off into their own lives but checking in, always in touch. The girls never close, but they get on. And here we all are today – minus, well, minus a crucial element.

Indeed. Martha is an absence, but she is also a presence. She is here now in many heads. Everyone here – nearly everyone – has her, they have the look of her, in some cases from long ago, in others from last year, last month – Martha in her seventies, before the sudden illness that struck her down. There are incarnations of Martha, invisible, all around the room: that quite tall woman, thin, with her long handsome face, the bush of wiry dark hair, elegant hands and feet if you happened to notice them. A memorable voice, deep, and a laugh you remembered too – loud, infectious. The incarnations are perhaps all similar – just as various portraits of a person by different hands will all offer a likeness. But, again like the differing portraits, for each person the further incarnation of Martha is different – it is accompanied by what they felt about her: like, dislike, indifference, love, envy, resentment, admiration . . .

So, the room is full of Martha. She is not here; she is very much here.

Paul has fallen silent. He glances at his father. Out of the corner of his eye, he notes his sisters, awaiting their turn. Two women he does not see much of these days, or, to be honest, think about all that much. But they are lodged there in his head, ineradicable – scroll back and he has them as girls, as children, an assortment of Tessas and of Eleanors that occasionally spring forward, random, now aged ten, now a twenty-something. They are embedded, memory slides that he will always have, he supposes. And today he adds some more. Tessa so emphatically clad – that pink; Eleanor looking round nervously all the time; she is not enjoying this. Nor is he.

A long time ago – in another life, it now seems – Paul took three pounds from Tessa's purse. The amount was careful – she had more than that there, but take too much and the loss would be more quickly noticed, three quid she possibly might not miss. Tessa was quite careless about many things.

He needed money. He was sixteen, and he seemed to need much. Sometimes he could not understand his own needs. Why had he picked up a steel tape measure in the kitchen of his friend Simon's house, put it in his pocket? He had no use for a steel tape measure. Well, because he could. No-one was looking, he could just take it. Later, he slipped it into the tool box at home; might come in handy for Mum or Dad sometime.

He took things in shops, mainly. It was so easy. Places like Woolworths, where everything was laid out in a casual, help yourself sort of way; they seemed to be asking for it. Sweets, it had begun with. Then he got bored with sweets – there's only so much Pick 'n' Mix you can get through. He had moved on to stationery – notebooks, pens – and tools – screwdrivers, pliers – then the occasional pair of socks, a scarf, even. It was a problem finding somewhere to put the stuff. Mum seldom went into his room – too much of a tip, she said – but that was still a bit risky. He had a box under his bed and he shoved things in there. If some acquisition posed a real problem, he would just get rid of it – chuck it under a hedge. Once he had the things they were superfluous, anyway. It was the taking that was the point – that quick lift, slipping it into his pocket, or his school satchel.

Money was best of all, of course. But that was more tricky – you didn't often get the chance. Hence Tessa's three pounds; her bag just sitting there on the hall table, no one about. Money was best not so much because you could spend it, but because it was apparently more desirable. Everyone wants money, don't they? Spending it was awkward, because he wasn't supposed to have money over and above his allowance – which had replaced pocket money last year. Allowance was seen as more grown-up. It was what Tessa and Eleanor had. So he couldn't spend money he nicked on anything conspicuous, and therefore he never nicked much. Just a bit, if it turned up: Tessa's purse, the cash his mum left out for the milkman, once – no, twice.

He relished doing it, and he hated himself. He hated the person who seemed driven to do this. There was something wrong with him, wasn't there? It was bad enough being sixteen, being on that interface between childhood and real, adult life, without having to go around doing something he didn't want to do but couldn't stop himself doing.

When he wasn't thinking about what he might nick next he was thinking about sex. Well, everyone was – everyone his age. Except that other boys were thinking about sex with girls and he was thinking about sex with other boys. Not that that meant there was anything wrong with him, not in this day and age. Gay was fine, or would be, in due course. His parents had gay friends right and left, and when eventually he got around to telling them about himself, he didn't think they would make a big deal of it. No, gay and all that that meant was alright – well, more or less. What wasn't alright was nicking stuff. Thinking about it, doing it.

Later, much later, he would wonder how long it would have gone on if she hadn't found out. His mother. And he would realize what a relief it had been.

The scarf gave him away. That first, then the rest. He had taken the scarf from Marks & Spencer, and actually he had rather liked it, so he took to wearing it . . .

'Where's that from?' she said.

In the hall one day, just as he had put it on, about to go out. And he had gone red, felt the betraying heat flood his face. Mumbled

301

something about buying it, and knew that she knew that buying a scarf – quite a pricey scarf – just wasn't something he would do. She had looked surprised – puzzled – said no more.

But the scarf must have alerted her. A couple of days later she said quietly, when they were alone in the kitchen: 'Paul.'

And he understood. The box. The box under his bed, pushed up against the wall, out of sight, full of . . . stuff. She had found it.

'How long, Paul? Since when?'

He wasn't sure. A year or so. About that.

A silence.

'Why?'

He had said that he didn't know. Which was the truth. He really didn't. Just because you could, it seemed.

She sighed. 'Well . . . What are we going to do? You'll have to stop, you know. Will you?'

He said that he would. And he realized that he could, now. Now that someone else knew. That she knew.

She nodded. 'Good.' A pause. 'Strictly speaking, we ought to give it all back. Everything.'

He noted the 'we'. He said that some things . . . some things he didn't even know where . . . And . . .

'Does everyone have to know?' he said. 'Does Dad have to know? The girls?' He thought of Tessa's three quid, and mentioned that.

She said, briskly, 'Dad has to know, but probably not just immediately. You can put Tessa's money back in her purse when you get the chance. She'll wonder why she suddenly got richer. As for the rest . . .'

They both thought of that box. Full of . . . screwdrivers and notebooks and pens and a pair of red socks and a hammer and a ruler and a penknife and goodness knows what else.

'The milk money, I suppose?' she said.

He said he'd pay her back. He wouldn't have any allowance this month.

She got brisk again. 'You'll pay me back by stopping this, once and for all. 'You can take that box to the Oxfam shop and say we've been having a house clear out. Right? And it stops. Now. Today.'

It did.

Years later, telling Hugh Madden about it, not long after they got together, he would say, like Martha: 'Why? Why on earth, do you suppose?'

Hugh had shrugged. 'You were adolescent. Plenty of adolescents are off their trolley. Count yourself lucky she didn't send you to a shrink. She didn't?'

'No way. It was end of. That was that. She never referred to it again.'

'Did she tell your father?'

'Apparently. But he never said anything.'

'Your sisters?'

Paul shook his head. 'I found a chance to put the money back in Tessa's purse. And I remember adding an extra fifty pence. As . . . either as an apology or as interest on the loan.'

Hugh had laughed.

Today, the whole of that episode flicks through Paul's mind as he stops speaking and stands aside, rather deliberately – there . . . I'm done – glances round the room, looking for Hugh, who is the only person he has ever talked to about that time. Ah, there he is, with Aunt Maisie – he's got stuck with her, I'm afraid.

This room seems to resonate with his past, for Paul. Here are his father, his sisters, relatives, friends, friends of his parents known since he was a child. Hugh, of course. Everyone here – pretty well everyone – knows something of him. And he of them. There is his friend Jane Harrison, an editor, of whom he sometimes thinks that if he were not gay she is the sort of woman he would have gone after. And there are others, who reflect one way or another some aspect of his former life – or indeed his life today. His editor at the poetry press who published his last collection, who has become something of a friend, and who had admired his mother's work.

Paul's poetry is mostly a response to and reflection about the physical world, strong in unexpected analogies and insights. He is an accessible, approachable poet, not that this has led to fame or fortune. He is not a confessional poet; reading his work, you would have little idea of him as a person, or of his life, which some readers might see as a count against him. He is reticent. Hugh often points this out: 'Come on, expand. Let it all hang out, for once in a while!' Laughing. But you can't hang out if it has never been a habit, and Hugh loves him as he is anyway. Others can find him hard to get to know, but worth it when you do: good at friendship, when he chooses, entertaining company, in the right mood, reliable, discreet.

He has taught English Literature, all his life since he left university. For over two decades now he has been trying to persuade mostly inattentive adolescents to respond to various Shakespeare plays, certain novels, a swathe of poetry – to respond, to enjoy as he does, and still does after all those years offering them up in sultry classrooms. He has taught across the social spectrum, from bog standard comprehensives where discipline was the main issue to private schools where the parents had deep pockets and the children were compliant and entitled. His working life is easier in the last case, but guilt has often driven him back into the state sector, feeling that it is here that you might more profitably be able to awaken some young mind, to prompt an imagination, to make a difference to someone's life. And sometimes he has been able to be aware that perhaps he has, and it has all seemed worthwhile.

He has explained this to Hugh, from time to time, after a battering day at the rockface, when Hugh has been urging a return to the sunny slopes of private education.

'The thing is, I had it so easy myself. Cushy schools, small classes, clever indulgent teachers – my parents did well by us all and . . .'

'And you feel guilty about it. It does you credit, by the way, but you don't have to pay penance for the rest of your life.'

Paul sighs. 'Not penance, exactly.'

'Compensation, then. And you're a closet Fabian, even though you claim to be apolitical.'

Hugh and Paul met when Paul was in his early thirties and Hugh somewhat older – a conversation at a publishing party that fired up mutual attraction, and, fairly soon, the relief for both of them of an attachment that felt permanent. They live now in a mews house in Camden that seems to Paul like paradise after his many solitary years in grotty flats.

Hugh is an editor at one of the big publishing houses, with a stable of well-known non-fiction writers. His field is travel, and the now fashionable trend of writing about the natural world. He is clever, positive in everything he does, and protective of Paul, who he knows to be less confident than himself. Standing in that room today, he has been feeling edgy while Paul spoke, knowing how much this is costing his partner. He has indeed been somewhat stuck with a Relford aunt – Paul was right – nice old lady but their small talk has been getting smaller and smaller, and in any case his thoughts have been drifting.

As is the case for many there, Martha has surfaced, in his mind. He remembered the first time he met her, taken by Paul to be introduced, when their relationship had prospered. He had been struck at once by her strong presence – this tall handsome woman opening the front door to them, eyeing him up, he at once feels, measuring him . . . finding him wanting? But no, it later appeared, after a kitchen lunch, because she turned to him when Paul had left the room for some reason.

'So . . . Are you a fixture? He needs that.'

Hugh was taken aback. 'Well, I . . . Yes, I . . .'

'Sorry. I tend to cut to the chase. He's my favourite. Mothers aren't supposed to have them, are they? My girls were more self-sufficient.'

Hugh had murmured something about he certainly hoped . . . he and Paul were . . . 'House,' he said. 'Rather looking round for somewhere to live at the moment.'

'Good,' she said. 'House hunting sounds good.' She paused, went on, thoughtfully. 'We nearly didn't have him. I hadn't really wanted another. Was all signed up for an abortion. And then on the way to the place I thought, no. So here he is.'

Taken aback yet further, Hugh was silent. Then he said, 'Does he know?'

'Of course not.' She laughed. 'And you're not going to be telling him, are you?'

And Hugh had not. Nor had Martha spoken to him with this candour ever again, over the years. He often wondered why she had done so then. And sometimes he would see Paul as only tenuously present, which also made him protective.

Paul, as his sister starts to speak, sees that his poetry editor is now standing alongside Jane Harrison, and thinks – yes, they know each other, I imagine. And remembers at the same moment the time he first met Simon, his editor, at the Society of Authors event when he was given a Cholmondeley Award, a considerable accolade for a young poet. And Simon had come up, had made the overture that would lead to their future association. But the memory of Simon is at once eclipsed by that of Martha, who he had brought to the event, and who had embarrassed him by a yelp of applause when his name was announced. She had already attracted attention – other prize-winners had brought girl friends, boy friends, partners, and here was this striking woman in a long red dress who did not look much like someone's mother in any case.

'Mum – honestly!' A few minutes later.

'Yet more polite clapping was out of the question. It was YOU.'

They had withdrawn to the side of the room, once the award announcements were concluded.

Paul said, 'I'm sorry I can't introduce you to more people. I hardly know anyone here.'

'I didn't come to meet people. I came to cheer my son the poet.'

'Part-time poet.'

'Are there any full-time ones?'

'Not many. Everyone has to teach, or something.'

'Much the same for artists, unless you get lucky. I was a barmaid. Dog walker. Cashier in Woolworths.'

He smiled. 'And then you got lucky.' He knew that Martha was expensive now, as a portrait painter.

'Not before your father had been paying all the bills for quite a while. Good thing I hadn't shacked up with some fellow artist.'

Paul considered this. 'Was there ever any danger of that?'

Martha took a swig from the glass of wine she was holding. 'Oh, yes. A couple, before Colin hove on the scene. One in particular.'

'What's his name?'

'You won't have heard of him. He hasn't flourished as an artist. Does commercial work now, I've heard. Adverts and stuff. Lovely guy, though.'

'So I might have had a completely different father. We might.'

She looked at him. Raised an eyebrow. Shrugged.

Paul said, thoughtfully. 'Of course, everything might always have been different. It's fortuitous that things are as they are. And I don't imagine you married Dad for his earning potential.'

'Oh, no. Though I will admit that came in handy later. No – quite another reason.'

'Really?'

'A girl I couldn't stand was after him and I decided to scupper her chances.'

Paul laughed. 'I see. So you married him out of malice.'

'Made the initial move out of malice, but then found that I rather went for him anyway. Does that cancel the malice?'

'Absolutely not. Our family life is rooted in malevolence. Was Dad clear about that?'

'Of course not. He was flattered by my interest. He probably hadn't noticed the other girl anyway.'

Paul had never taken Martha to any literary event again, not because he felt her to be an embarrassment but because he thought she would be bored – which she had been on that occasion once the opportunity to cheer him had passed. And in any case, he seldom went to such things – had only one foot, a toe, in the literary world, immersed as he was in the daily round of school life. And home life with Hugh, through whom there came rumours of the wider world of books, and those who wrote them.

Jane Harrison, who inhabited that world, had listened to Paul uneasily while he spoke. She knew that this must be an effort for him – knowing him well, liking him. And Martha surfaced for her too, as she had seen her in her studio that day, when Paul had taken her there to see his portrait.

She had not known what to say. What do you say to an artist? She was used to writers; she knew how to talk to writers about their work.

Eventually . . . 'It's . . . What's so interesting is that I can see a sort of different Paul there.' Oh dear, did that sound as though she didn't think it was good? 'Your Paul,' she went on, anxiously. 'The Paul you know best.'

It was the way Paul looked at you out of the portrait. He was looking at Martha, not at you.

Martha had smiled. 'Well, of course, I suppose. But you may have a point. Which Paul – what Paul – do you know?'

This was unanswerable. And yet Jane had found that she was warming to Martha. Positive, emphatic, even, but not off-putting. She felt herself to have been assessed, and to have passed muster. And Paul had come to her rescue.

'Jane knows various Pauls, some more likeable than others. She's my most tolerant friend.'

Jane smiled. 'Well, I don't seem to have been much aware of the unlikeable ones.' She looked around the studio. Stacked canvases. An easel. An armchair. A long table covered in paints and brushes. A sloping roof window through which light flooded; the room was the attic of the house.

'It's a lovely place to work,' she said.

'It is indeed. Except when I have perverse clients who insist on being painted in their own home, where of course the light will be all wrong.'

'And YOU can't insist.'

Martha pulled a face. 'In the last resort, they are paying.'

Jane found herself suddenly interested in the whole matter of portraiture. 'Are there . . . are there some faces you actually find you'd rather not be painting at all?'

A burst of laughter. 'I'll say! A face can be dead boring. But even then you can usually find some point you can make something of.'

'Is beautiful best?' said Paul.

'Not necessarily at all. Actually, can be dull. Old is often best. Old faces have character.'

Jane observed that Auden had said that his old face looked like a wedding cake left out in the rain.

'Ridiculous!' Martha snorted. 'He can't ever have seen such a thing, anyway. Who leaves wedding cakes out in the rain?'

'True,' said Paul. 'But one sort of sees what he meant. It was a pretty good face. An assemblage of wrinkles. You'd have loved it, Mum.'

Jane wondered if Martha ever did self-portraits?

Martha eyed her for a moment before replying – rather disconcertingly. 'I've tried once or twice, and failed. And don't remind me of Rembrandt.'

'She wasn't going to,' said Paul. 'But I'm interested now. Why couldn't you, Mum?'

Martha considered. 'It seemed like self-scrutiny. Introspection, even. And I'm not good at that. Know thyself.'

Jane remembers her saying that. Remembers quite clearly. And that Martha has gone on to show them some of her work in progress, at Paul's request.

And, looking at Paul in this room today, amid all these people, nearly all of them unknown to her, she thinks about introspection. Can you know yourself? Can you know anyone?

But it is Tessa who has the floor now. Without Paul's diffidence. Entirely without.

'Hi, everyone! And thanks a lot for coming. What a fantastic gathering! And how Mum would have loved it – the story of her life, all of you – well, up to a point . . .' – she laughs – '. . . I dare say bits of the story are missing, you don't know everything about anyone's life, do you, even your nearest and dearest? And Mum was that for me, very near and dear. Of course, we weren't really on the same page – Mum wasn't much interested in stage or screen, acting wasn't her thing, and I suppose art isn't really mine. Though I really appreciate her work – I mean, she was amazing, wasn't she? The people she painted somehow looked more like themselves than they really were – that politician she did for the National Portrait Gallery. The one of my brother, too – yes, you, Paul. Maybe she sort of saw into people – I certainly used to feel that when I was a kid. She always knew when I'd told a fib, or been playing up at school . . .' – more laughter – '. . . you could never get anything past Mum, oh no. She wasn't strict, exactly, but she ran a tight ship. No messing. And of course, I was always the one who messed, Eleanor and Paul were good as gold – no need to look like that, Paul, you were her favourite, anyway. But that didn't mean she couldn't be supportive if you'd run aground in some way, as I know all too well – not that I'm going to tell you about that . . .' – laughter.

Eleanor closes her eyes, takes a deep breath. For heaven's sake, Tess. Enough. Enough about you, anyway. And in fact you used to run rings round Mum when you wanted to. I know about the hidden lipsticks when you were about twelve, and the clubbing later with those girls she said you weren't to go with. You tried drugs with them, too, didn't you? I knew, and you're lucky I didn't tell on you.

In fact, Tessa seems to have sobered up, suddenly. She has paused for a moment after that last smothered laugh, as though distracted, and then pulls herself together and continues. 'Yes, supportive, absolutely – and a fantastic granny to Chloe, and to Eleanor's lot. What else? Mum, where are you? Style – yes, style. She had it, didn't she? Always looked – always had you looking at her. I know clothes aren't anything, really, but they sort of are, too, aren't they? Mum dressed – well, her own style. A long dress when you weren't expecting one, fabulous dresses. Lovely ethnic sort of things that so suited her. Those big stud earrings, and rings on almost every finger. Marvellous colours – that deep purple coat she had, lots of red – that shaggy red sweater she wore so much.'

Her audience, at this point, have become very aware of Tessa's own pink jacket. It is very pink. And it is either a stroke of genius with her ginger-red hair, or a strident mistake, according to taste.

Oh, come on, Tess, Paul is thinking, that'll do. That'll do nicely.

And perhaps there is some form of thought transference, because at that point Tess falls silent for a moment, blinks – as though she were surprised to find herself here – and concludes: 'Actually, I think that's enough from me. Thanks for coming again, everyone.'

She steps aside, backs off away from the others, abstracted, it seems, as Colin Relford suggests that Eleanor speak next.

In fact, Martha is suddenly very much present, for Tessa. Martha then, that day. That morning a long time ago when Tessa decided that if help was going to be had anywhere it could surely be had from Mum. Tessa was twenty-six, married for a year now, in determined pursuit of a career that had been elusive, hitherto, but now – now she had landed a part, in a popular television series. But there was this problem.

'Well, that's great,' says Martha. 'What's it called? I promise I'll watch this time.'

Tessa says that yes, it is great, it's fantastic, in fact, I mean it's not a huge part but I know I can make something of it, and it's a breakthrough, it'll lead to more. 'But the thing is . . .' She falters. Martha waits.

'The thing is, Mum, I'm pregnant.'

There is a silence. Martha says, 'And that's great too, Tess.'

'Well, it would be, I suppose, but actually, no – not now. I mean, absolutely not. They don't start shooting till October and I'd be six months gone then, I'd be showing. So I can't be pregnant now, right now. I just can't.'

Martha considers. 'Are you telling me you want to have an abortion?'

'Yes. I mean, I've got to, haven't I? And I don't know how you go about it. Do you just go to the doctor and say that's what you want?'

Martha enquires what Simon thinks about it. Simon was Tessa's husband at the time.

'Oh, he doesn't know. And that's not important. It's my problem, not his. Any doctor has to arrange an abortion for you now, don't they? You don't have to have – oh, health reasons or something?'

Martha gazes at Tessa. At last she says, 'Let's be quite clear about this. You are deciding between a part in a television series and the existence of a child, a person. A life.'

Tessa flails around. 'Oh, goodness, Mum, you can't put it like that. It's not even a . . . there's nothing there yet, it hasn't even begun. Not a person . . .'

'That's the way it is,' said Martha. 'There's no other way of putting it.'

'But you don't understand. This part . . . my agent says this is my first real opportunity. It's just an impossible time to be pregnant. I thought you'd see that at once. I thought you'd help.'

'Then I'm sorry to disappoint,' says Martha. 'And in my way, I am helping. I'm trying to make you see what you're doing – what you want to do.'

Tessa is routed. She is on the edge of tears, but is also impatient. Her mother is being so obtuse. Well, she'd just have to sort this out on her own, then, that's all there is to it.

'I wish you could understand, Mum, I really do. If you'd ever . . . well, ever known anything like this.'

They are in Martha's studio. Tessa had invaded, in her need. Martha gets up now and stands looking at work on her easel, her back to Tessa.

'Maybe,' she says. 'Maybe if I had. All I can say is . . . just think about what you're doing.'

But Tessa has done all the thinking she needed to do.

And now, today, all these years later, she hears Martha again. Eleanor has moved forward and is beginning to speak, but Tessa does not hear a word. Chloe – eight-year-old Chloe – has wriggled through the gathering and joined her mother. She clutches Tessa's hand, whispering.

'Ssh . . .' says Tessa.

Chloe is saying that she feels a bit sick. Tessa registers this, and hopes that Chloe will not get as far as throwing up. Maybe one should not have told her that she could go and help herself to the canapés.

Motherhood came late to Tessa, and has not entirely suited her. It is such a full-on business, being a mother, at least that is what it is expected to be, and this is a major challenge when you suddenly get offered a part, or need to go to an audition, or just want to get on with other aspects of your life. There have been sitters and au pairs galore, Tessa has rather run out of obliging friends and neighbours and has to rely on agencies with their inexhaustible supply of Italians and Czechs and Poles and Australians and Bulgarians and whatever; as a small child Chloe spoke a smattering of many languages. Sometimes one of these girls would become semi-permanent and stay for weeks or months, leaving eventually because they found Chloe too much of a handful. Tessa's husband Nick, rather older than she is, had not expected to be a father at all, and though devoted to Chloe, was inclined to stand aside. He was a busy television executive anyway, and safely out of the house most of the time.

For Tessa, though, work is intermittent. She is at the mercy of all those shadowy figures whose patronage can bestow a role as an accessory figure in some hospital series, police drama, or, with any luck, in a more significant one-off production, perhaps even a noticeable cameo part. She does her best to network, to be seen about. She chivvies her agent. And, occasionally, the lightning strikes and she is summoned. She made quite an impact as a flighty, chattering party guest in a dramatization of *Mrs Dalloway*. And again, as the chambermaid in a version of *Tristram Shandy*.

And there is always the chance, the hope, that something like this will happen again. At forty-eight Tessa has not relinquished the idea that some kind of late celebrity is just around the corner. Alright, she never achieved stardom in youth, wasn't pretty enough, wasn't charismatic, but she has a decent track record – reliable, versatile – and there are plenty of arresting roles around for older women. Sooner or later, one will come her way . . .

Chloe is still clutching her hand, and whispering now that she wants a drink of water. Tessa whispers back, 'In a minute,' and becomes aware of what Eleanor is saying.

Eleanor is not enjoying this, that is clear. She speaks with diffidence, is hesitant.

'The great thing about Mum,' she is saying, 'About Martha . . . Mum . . . Is that you always knew where you were with her. When we were children, and later, yes, later too you could always take your problems to her and she would try to sort things out, and she'd always be interested in what you were doing, well, mostly, unless it was something pointless, she wanted us to be doing positive things . . .'

Eleanor is on autopilot now, not really knowing what she is saying, saying whatever comes into her head. And Tessa hears her with a kind of sympathy – this isn't poor old Eleanor's scene, not at all – and also with dismissal. Oh no she didn't, oh no she wasn't.

Problems. If only. She let me down with a crash over the abortion, just when I needed someone to tell me I was doing the right thing, the only thing. Interested? Well, not when it came to something right off her radar, such as my career.

'RADA?' says Martha. 'What's that? Never heard of it.'

Tessa is eighteen, and single-minded. 'It's an acting school, Mum. I can't believe you haven't heard of it. It's – it's like university for people who want to be actors. Like art school,' she adds. 'Like you did, only for acting.'

'Really?' says Martha, reflective. 'I see.' They are in her studio. She is sorting through paints and brushes on her long work table, picks up an empty tube and throws it in the bin.

'So can I?'

'Can you what?'

'Go there, Mum. Apply. You have to apply. Not everyone gets in.'

'Talk to Dad, I suppose.'

'I'm going to. Of course I'm going to. You have to pay, I think – or there may be grants . . . But I want to be able to tell him you're keen.'

Martha is examining some brushes. 'Keen? I'm not sure how to be keen on something I don't know anything about. They teach you how to act . . . And are you a paid-up actor then? Actress. Employed? Earning a living?'

Tessa is angry now, and goes on the offensive. 'Well, the same as when you come out of art school. It depends on what happens.'

Martha looks at Tessa now. Touché, perhaps. She is silent for a moment. 'Well,' she says. 'This is what you are going to do, I can see. So good luck with it.'

And now, today, listening – half listening – to Eleanor, Tessa remembers that exchange and thinks: and she never did get interested. Not like she was with Paul and his poetry. Great to-do when he had his first collection published. But not when I got my first part, in that sitcom.

'. . . a wonderful granny, of course,' Eleanor is saying. 'Always available for them – for my lot – and they adored her. Letting them have a go with paints and paper, in her studio, not that any of them have turned out to have any talent in that direction, I'm afraid . . .' – a laugh – '. . . but they had such fun, they'll remember that . . .' – she glances round the room, where her grown-up children are somewhere, attentive perhaps, and the thought of this is making her even more diffident – '. . . won't you? Yes. And . . . and really, you know, I think that's all I've got to say. Just . . . well, she was a fantastic person. Artist, of course. Mother.'

She subsides. Steps back. There, that's done. Hopeless, of course. I can't do that sort of thing. And . . . and . . .

A kind of smokescreen, she thinks. Actually. Not quite how it was. All that's left out. I mean, she was all those things, sort of, but there was also – Well, much else.

'Another?' says Martha. 'Already?'

They are having lunch, in Martha's kitchen. The familiar old home kitchen. Eleanor has just announced that she is pregnant, with her third child. She is pleased, relieved. And shot down by her mother's response.

'Well, yes, Mum. Why not?'

Martha shrugs. 'Up to you, darling. If that's what you want.'

'You had three.'

'True, true.' Martha laughs, for some reason.

For Eleanor, this forthcoming baby is salvation – it means that for the next five years at least she is spared the requirement that she seek gainful employment, some occupation to define her. She is living in the age when that is expected; there are no longer housewives (her grandmother was that, she remembered, and it was perfectly acceptable). But this baby will protect her, at least for a while; with baby, toddler, and another at primary school she can justly claim that she is needed at home. Graham, her husband, is comfortable with that. He is a solicitor and has always found Eleanor's creatively achieving family a bit hard to take. He had thought a third child a perfectly good idea, to the extent that Eleanor has found herself wondering if she could push her luck and eventually go for four.

And now here is her mother displaying scepticism, instead of pleasure at the prospect of another grandchild.

Wonderful granny? thinks Eleanor, many years later, her smoke-screen speech done with, stepping aside with a sigh of relief. Well, yes, up to a point – it was true she used to let them mess about in her studio – for brief visits – but here she was not exactly welcoming this baby.

'We always meant to have three, Mum,' she had said. Four, possibly, but best not to mention that. 'We like children.'

'Of course,' Martha looks at Eleanor, contemplative. 'And you're quite happy – more than happy – to go on looking after them.'

Eleanor sees that she is rumbled. That her mother knows quite well why this baby is so needed. And she feels a wave of resentment. She wants to tell Martha that it is all very well for her – she always knew what she wanted to be, to do – Martha is an Artist, born as one, presumably. For her, children did indeed come along, and yes, she seemed glad enough to have them. But there were all those au pairs, thinks Eleanor, she was never hands-on, like I am. And some of the au pairs were a bit dodgy – that Italian girl who used to have her boyfriend in when Mum wasn't there, and bribed us with sweets not to tell, and the Australian who let Paul in his pushchair roll into the pond on the common – massive bribery needed that time. Tessa got a manicure set.

So all very well for her. And I am measured and found wanting because I am not like Paul, poet and teacher, or Tessa, who was dead set on acting ever since she was Mary in the school nativity play. I am not them. I am someone different, without any particular calling except for being quite happy with family life and what is wrong with that?

'Well, yes,' she says, with a note of defiance. 'I am. I mean, one day, later on, I expect I'll want . . .' Want what? Want a career? Want a job? '. . . maybe something different.' She trails to a stop, having betrayed herself, given in to the requirements of the day.

Martha smiles. 'Maybe. Maybe not. Whatever.'

And there the exchange fades away, in Eleanor's memory. And when the baby came – Luke, now a barrister – Martha was kindly enough, interested, up to a point.

But up to a point, thinks Eleanor, today. That was smokescreen too, more or less. You didn't go to Mum for sympathy about teething babies or recalcitrant two-year-olds, or advice about trouble with teenagers. Start talking about something like that, and she'd just turn away, or you'd see she simply wasn't listening. She must have dealt with all that, but didn't think it worth discussion.

And now Colin Relford is speaking. 'Thank you, Eleanor. And Tessa. And Paul. I do indeed have something to say myself but what I'm going to suggest is that we have a bit of a break first. Drinks and eats on offer and there are still some people I haven't had a chance to talk to. So – more in a while.'

The congregation – if that is what it is – relaxes and conversations start up once more. Some people take the opportunity to move away from someone they have spent too long with, others are looking around, or making for the table where drinks and canapés have been replenished.

All are conscious that the occasion, like all such, is something of an oddity. It has tension, an ambivalence. This is not a party, but yet it is a party, of a kind – a number of people are assembled and stand around talking to each other. There are refreshments on offer. But it is also a meeting, it has a purpose. It is about something – about somebody. Because of this everyone is faintly uncomfortable. You can't really relax when you are not quite sure what you are at, what might happen or not happen, whether laughter is acceptable, should you find cause to laugh.

Lucy Forbes has run out of people she knows – a couple of cousins and their offspring – and has found a chair, where she sits, glass of wine in hand, eyeing the room, curious, and also critical. That young chap might have thought to wear a suit – jeans really not appropriate. And that woman's dress is more suitable for the south of France than Wimbledon in May. Who is she with the daffy little hat – fascinators they call them, I think. Ridiculous, too. Martha's artistic crowd, I suppose. Eleanor's no public speaker – pathetic contribution.

A woman has just arrived to sit beside her. 'I must join you. Can't stand up any longer. Patricia Mellon. I work for Colin's company. I never knew Martha all that well but enjoyed seeing her. The children I've not met before.'

Lucy introduces herself.

'Ah, cousin. You'll know them all then. I've had a chat with Paul, but I haven't managed the girls – oh dear, women. Tessa's quite glam in her way, isn't she? Lovely jacket. I remember seeing her on telly once in some crime thing. She's very like Colin, isn't she. Whereas Eleanor . . .'

'Quite,' says Lucy crisply. 'You'd hardly think they were sisters.' A sniff, a swig of wine. 'So my mother always said.'

'Ah,' Patricia Mellon shoots a look at Lucy. 'Such a high achieving family, of course. Creatively achieving.'

Lucy inclines her head, noncommittal.

And now some colleague of Patricia's has come to greet her. Patricia rises, and they move away together. Lucy decides to allow herself one last glass of wine, and pushes past people to get to the refreshment table, where a man who is filling his own glass replenishes hers.

'Allow me. You have been pointed out to me as Martha's cousin. James Cadogan – I run the gallery that showed Martha's work and will continue to do so.'

'Thanks,' says Lucy. 'Yes, cousin.'

'Interesting mix, this gathering. Family. Martha's world. Colin's world. Others. People who wouldn't otherwise meet.' He smiles. 'Brought together by Martha.'

Lucy, who had been feeling a touch intimidated by someone very much not of her world, relaxes a bit.

'Yes, absolutely.'

'So you will have known her well,' says James Cadogan.

'Not really. We saw something of each other as children. But very little since.'

'And you didn't like her all that much.'

She is startled, taken aback. 'Well, I wouldn't say . . . not exactly didn't like.'

'And I can deduce that from you not seeing her since childhood. If you liked her – liked each other – you would have gone on seeing her.'

Lucy has to agree, not particularly embarrassed. She finds that she quite likes this man.

'Artists are famously difficult, at least from the point of view of people like me, who work with them on a daily basis. Martha was about average, I'd say. Perhaps a bit above.'

Lucy is intrigued. First time she has heard any remotely adverse comment about Martha. 'Really?'

'And I am being entirely indiscreet. But you don't seem to me the sort of person who would gossip.'

She likes him even more. 'Difficult in what way?'

'Oh, issues about the hang, when it came to an exhibition. Martha liked to dictate. Needed a party for the opening view – larger than our usual.' He laughs. 'Not a big deal. It could all be managed. But she made herself known, Martha.'

Lucy finds all this most interesting. 'I suppose she was very . . . Successful.'

'Indeed. Of course we didn't much handle her privately commissioned work – those portraits. Everything else. Over the last twenty years or so she was doing much more representational work – landscapes and so forth. She was hoping to be equally known for those.'

'And was she?'

He shakes his head. 'Not really, I'm afraid. They didn't have quite that spirit, that individual quality, that the portraits have. But I shouldn't be saying that. I rely on your discretion.' An enquiring smile.

An emphatic nod from Lucy. She is slightly ashamed of her satisfaction on hearing this.

But the conversation is to be cut short. Colin Relford has come forward once more, and taps a spoon on his glass to call for silence.

'Last words! And my turn, who had the privilege of spending more time with Martha than anyone, who knew her from young to old – fresh out of art school when she and I first met, the established artist we all remember at the end. And mother. And wife. Tessa, Eleanor and Paul have all spoken beautifully of her as mother. I saw her too as that but more still as partner, as life-long companion.'

His audience senses that they are perhaps in for the long haul. Several slide towards an available seat.

Colin speaks of his first acquaintance with Martha, of how she struck him – her looks, her vivacity – of his courtship. He is articulate, entertaining. There is some laughter – this long haul is perhaps not going to be too bad.

'. . . but would she have me, that was the question. There was this other chap, hanging around, first thing was to see him off.'

He is finding that he has an easy eloquence for this, he had not much thought what he might say, but there was no need, his natural persuasive authority steps forward, the memories and the words arrive in tandem, both as he speaks and in his head.

For there is a curious parallel. As he talks, images float in his mind – people, scenes, what was said or heard. That chap sniffing around Martha back then, his name is forgotten, but Martha speaks of him, laughing: 'Oh, you always had the advantage. He once took me to a cricket match.'

It is their wedding night, after a register office marriage and a somewhat raucous reception – her friends, his friends – at which parents and relations had seemed, and probably felt, sidelined. They were now in a hotel somewhere in northern France, embarked on a touring honeymoon. She would paint, sometimes, he would pick up material, sometimes, for an idea he had about a documentary on retribution in post-war France. Historyline was in embryonic form, already. They would eat, drink, make love a lot.

'. . . we were skint, back then, of course, and that was fine. Martha did skint with style, that warehouse down by the river that was Historyline's first office, with the flat above. Junk shop furniture, bean bags, chianti bottles, spag bol for a crowd. One or two of you were part of that crowd. Those were the days, weren't they?'

Well, maybe. But days, months, a year or so. That got shunted aside soon enough, let's not get nostalgic. Other moments float up for him – Martha saying 'I seem to be pregnant, time to get out of here.' And now they are in the Camden house, with Historyline's office elsewhere, and in it that flame-haired PA girl he had – he prefers that she does not float up, an aberration, that, stupid of him. Still, no great harm done – she is long since out of sight and out of mind – and Historyline on a roll now, a couple of award-winning programmes under the belt.

He does not talk much of Historyline, today – just the occasional oblique reference. Today is about Martha. And his audience knows well enough that Historyline is relevant, in any case. For him, its various projects, its successes, are continuously present, the substance of his life, with family, Martha, at a tangent – crucial, essential even – but apart. Even as he speaks of the move to Camden, of Martha's growing reputation, the way in which she blossomed as a portrait painter, the progress of Historyline is subliminally there – this was going on, that was when he was in Israel and Egypt for the Suez film.

'So you won't be here for my opening view?' Martha says. 'At the gallery.'

He agrees that he will not. It's a shame. He is devastated. But such is the filming schedule.

She shrugs. 'So it goes. We are diverging. Can't be helped.'

And so indeed it went, he now sees, but this is not something for his audience today. Instead, more about Martha's work.

'. . . commissions coming in now. You'll remember her stunning contribution to the National Portrait Gallery exhibition of new talent.'

He did get to that opening view . . . he remembers that he relished hearing complimentary remarks about Martha's work. And that he was annoyed when introduced to someone as 'Martha's husband'. Was there an ambiguity lurking? Quite possibly. Quite understandably.

'We are diverging,' she had said. He hears her still, had wondered at the time what she was talking about, but takes the point now. Had taken it, indeed, when Eleanor was born.

He had been blunt, only days after the birth, contemplating this baby.

'Is she mine?'

And Martha had considered. 'I don't think so,' she said at last. 'Do you? I mean, one can't be sure, under the circumstances, but she . . . not a bit like Tessa, is she?' And, after a moment, 'What do you want to do?'

The affair was over. Her affair. She had said so, and he believed her. 'A mistake,' she had said thoughtfully, looking at the baby, looking at Eleanor. A rather stupid mistake. But she isn't – a mistake. We were talking about having another, weren't we? So what do you want me to do? Go? With her?'

He had found that he did not want that.

Colin Relford is so arrested by that memory that he falters in his discourse today, distracted by the image of Eleanor back then, but he quickly pulls himself together and continues with what he was saying about the family's move to their current home.

'. . . plenty of room for Martha's new studio with skylight, and plenty of work for her now, more commissions than she could handle.'

And in any case Eleanor back then, that questionable baby, has morphed into Eleanor today, long familiar, just one out of his three children, never treated differently from the others, or, indeed, on the whole and by and large, never thought of differently. This made easier perhaps by the fact that she gave less trouble – Tessa always needy, demanding, Paul going off the rails in adolescence. Just occasionally, over the years, he will look at her and be aware of something alien, some discrepancy, and will dismiss the thought. Let's not go there, this was dealt with in the best possible way, the grown-up way. She must never know, the others must never know. This is between Martha and me, us alone.

And so it has remained, a never-mentioned item, amid the freight of their marriage. All marriages carry freight, some more perilous than others. The Relford marriage appears to have born up well, or so it seems, as Colin's audience hears him out, some people appreciative of his occasional dry humour, a few cynical or just bored. Lucy Forbes is thinking that he is a self-satisfied fellow and that when he greeted her it was clear he had no idea who she was and didn't care anyway. James Cadogan has heard enough about Martha, had mixed feelings about her anyway, and would like to get away now.

Colin has become conscious that he is saying one thing while at the same time quite other scenes are flashing up at the back of his mind. He is not particularly concerned about this – one could hardly stand here and give this audience an intimate account of one's family life. No, no – this occasion is a formality, and everyone understands that, don't they?

'Your lady friend phoned just now,' Martha says, bland – but then smiling at his ill-concealed expression of dismay. Laura is not supposed to use his home number, only the office, this is unacceptable, maybe time is up for Laura.

'I wonder why I've never painted you,' she says. Another time. A different time. And he had laughed, he remembers. Because they both know why. The scrutiny. The unflinching scrutiny. In both directions.

'It has sort of worked, hasn't it, you and me?' she says. Not long ago, this. Not long ago at all. Months. And this is hardest of all. If he remembers this he will not be able to carry on today. He must not remember. Not now, not right now. He talks and smiles, greets and smiles.

The event is coming to an end. Some people have already left.

Others are seeking out Tessa, or Eleanor, or Paul, or Colin, to say goodbye. The ritual is complete, the tributes paid, the ceremony done. The room is full of Martha. She is not here. She is very much here. She has gone where the dead go – into other people's heads. She is fragmented. There are now many versions of Martha, many truths, perhaps many untruths. Martha has become memory, but memory can conjure her up, so that for many here – saying their goodbyes, collecting their coats – there is a physical presence still, the shadowy presence of that tall, handsome, positive woman, who was one thing to this person and quite another to that. Gone, but never really gone.

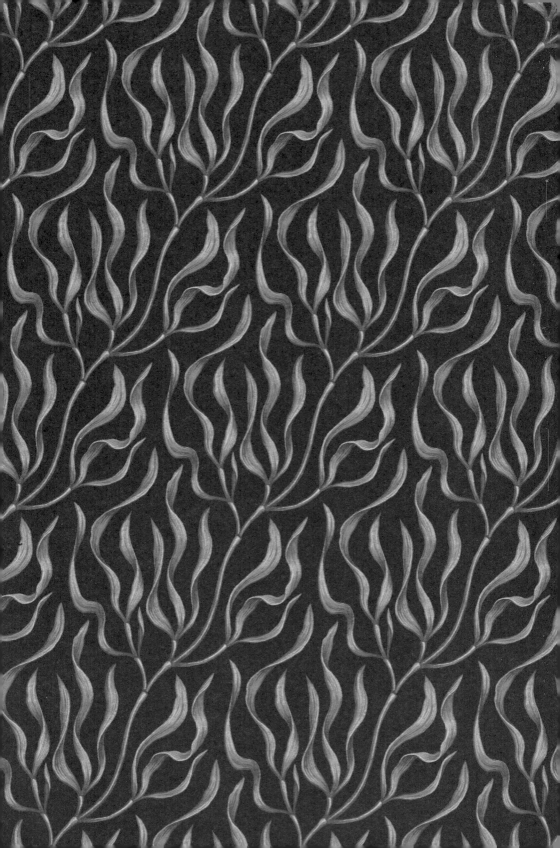